RESURRECTION

AVAILABLE NOW

RESURRECTION

RICHARD HATCH and STAN TIMMONS

BASED ON THE UNIVERSAL TELEVISION SERIES
CREATED BY GLEN A. LARSON

ibooks

new york
www.ibooks.com

DISTRIBUTED BY SIMON & SCHUSTER, INC

An Original Publication of ibooks, inc.

Copyright © 2001 Universal Studios Publishing Rights,
a Division of Universal Studios Licensing, Inc.

Battlestar Galactica is a trademark and copyright of Universal Studios.
All rights reserved.

An ibooks, inc. Book

Distributed by Simon & Schuster, Inc.
1230 Avenue of the Americas, New York, NY 10020

ibooks, inc.
24 West 25th Street
New York, NY 10010

The ibooks World Wide Web Site Address is:
http://www.ibooksinc.com

ISBN 0-7434-1326-1
First ibooks, inc. printing July 2001
10 9 8 7 6 5 4 3 2

Edited by Howard Zimmerman

Cover art by Matt Busch
Cover design by J. Vita

Interior design and typesetting
by Westchester Book Composition

Printed in the U.S.A.

There are those who believe that life began out there,
far across the universe, with tribes of humans who
may have been the forefathers
of the Egyptians, or the Toltecs, or the Mayans.

Some believe that there may yet be
brothers of man who, even now,
fight to survive, somewhere beyond the heavens. . . .

RESURRECTION

PROLOGUE

The void is full of death and dying.

A stinger from the great Chitain warship, easily twice the size of a battlestar, whips past Apollo's Viper, just missing him and destroying two other fighters. He prays to the spirit of his father and he prays to the Lords of Kobol—he prays to anyone who will listen—to just see them through this massacre, because he knows it's going to take a stack of miracles to survive this day, much less win it.

As he thinks that, the tip of the stinger glows ruby-red and discharges a deadly laser blast, vaporizing half a dozen Vipers; the brightness of the blast is imprinted on his retinas, even though his Warrior's helm automatically opaques when the flash of laser fire is too bright, and for a moment, Apollo is blind. In battle, a moment is all it takes to end up dead.

He knows his Viper is in the sighting hairs of a Chitain fighter, and his vision is coming back, but slowly. Too slowly. He's going to have to fire blind. Apollo remembers the position of each of the nearest fighters, Viper and Chitain alike, before the searing light from the laser temporarily stole his sight, and he trusts to his senses. He's a Warrior, after all, and he has been trained all his life for every eventuality. All of this races across his mind in a micron, and his thumb stabs the turbolaser.

In his shimmering, dancing vision, the Chitain craft erupts in a fire-flower, and Apollo offers a quiet prayer of thanks.

But this battle has been raging on and on for what feels like—may well be—centons, and there seems no end in sight. They've never faced anything quite like the Chitain before: a race so alien and war-like and fearsome as to make the Cylons seem civilized. Like the Cylons, the Chitain want to become the only sentient lifeform in their sector, even if that means eliminating everyone and everything else.

If not for the intercession of the colonials' valiant ally, the Sky, this story may end quite differently; even so, it still ends badly.

The Chitain dreadnought, itself almost indestructible, is surrounded by a nearly impenetrable forcefield. It is only by staying close to the ship's underbelly and harrying away at it, like skreeters on the back of a bova, that the Vipers have any hope at all, for the Chitain can't turn their weapons after the Warriors without destroying their own ship.

It is all chaos and confusion; red beams sizzle from a hundred different fighters, and the war-world's stinger tendrils answer with their own deadly voice. But the concentrated assault is working; the Chitain dreadnought is in trouble and the aliens know it. Like a mortally-wounded animal, the great mechanical beast is going to take down as many of its attackers as possible, and it looks like Apollo is going to be first.

Frak, he thinks, and grits his teeth, waiting for the inevitable blast from the onrushing Chitain fighter.

The blast comes not from the fighter, but is the fighter, vaporizing in a spray of brightly-burning fuel, then winking out. It's Starbuck, of course, there to save him as he's always been.

Apollo heaves a sigh of relief, more like a laugh, and he tells Starbuck he's going to buy him a tankard of grog in the aft ODOC. But Starbuck says, "Don't you remember? That's not the way it happened at all."

And he's right, it doesn't end like that, not even anything close to it; this is nothing more than wishful thinking and rewriting the ending to be more palatable than the truth was, because a moment later, Starbuck's Viper is caught in the rippling fireball of the warship, the size of a small planet, as it explodes. The shock waves spread out like circles in a pond, shattering everything they touch. The Sky don't even try to outrun the spreading death, but accept it as part of the endless cycle, the way of the universe.

Everything happens fast after that, but the image of Starbuck, slumped forward in his fire-blackened, shredded Viper, never seems to leave Apollo's vision, neither waking nor dreaming.

The colonial fleet has suffered devastating losses, more than half their force of Warriors and starfighters, and thirty-seven vessels, including the Agro-2. Devastating . . . but not nearly as devastating as seeing his oldest friend, closer than any brother, closer than his own brother, lying in his med-berth, kept alive only by machines. Starbuck's uniform is all but melted to his body, and his flesh is blackened, cracked, with crazy zigzags running off in every direction, as if his skin is a sun-blistered mudflat. There's been massive cranial trauma, and there's no way to know if Starbuck will ever awaken again. If not for the slow and labored rise and fall of his chest, anyone would think Starbuck a corpse.

Now Apollo is standing at another bedside, this time his father's, and he is saying his silent good-byes as Commander Adama slips away. And even through this, Apollo cannot express his feelings, except for perhaps an unsual brightness in his eyes, and the unusually-stern set of his jaw. There are so many things he wants to say, and yet, he says nothing. After all, he is like his father, and Adama knows the things Apollo feels, even if neither one can exactly say them. Knowing is not quite the same as being told, but it will just have to do.

So he watches him go, and a world ends for Apollo, the way a world always ends when a father dies. Athena, much closer to her emotions than her brother, buries her face in his chest and weeps openly. Apollo gives her his strength to draw from; he's good at that. He's just not so good at expressing his emotions.

They stand that way for a long time, neither speaking, Athena's sobbing is the only sound in the room. He doesn't hear Cassiopeia enter the room, but she must have, because she's asking him how he could let this happen.

Apollo shakes his head; he doesn't understand. "It was his time," *he answers.* "There was nothing I, or anyone else, could do."

"Liar!" *she shouts, and her vehemence rocks him back on his heels. For a moment, anger flares in him, one of the few emotions he can show, but that anger leaves him in a sudden wash, because when he looks past Athena, past Cassiopeia, he sees the funeral bier and the body resting in state upon it. He knows immediately it is not Adama because there are none of the ceremonial trappings as befits a man of the commander's station, and Apollo's heart breaks into a wild, galloping rhythm.*

Now that he thinks about it, it couldn't *be Adama, because their father died almost a yahren ago. Apollo is a strong man; he thinks he has enough strength within him that he can loan it out to anyone who needs it, and now, when he really* could *borrow some of that steel from Athena, she's not there. Neither, for that matter, is Cassiopeia. He's alone, and he has a bad feeling he's about to find out just how alone he really is, because the one he's always been able to draw strength from is Starbuck. They are always there for one another, and only a terrible catastrophe could prevent that. Apollo feels a catastrophe is imminent, the way bova and avions can predict an oncoming storm.*

Apollo takes a step closer, and then another; it doesn't seem that he's willing his feet to take him to the funeral bier so much as he's simply unable to stop their advance. He stands at the open casket for what seems like forever, but he knows it's not more than a few seconds, and at last he looks down.

His heart, racing out of control just a moment before, seems to stop beating altogether and he is hot and cold, all at once, because it's not Adama lying before him, but Starbuck, still clothed in his melted uniform, his flesh black and blistered.

Apollo hears a low, wretched moan from somewhere in the room but he ignores it and lightly touches Starbuck's lifeless cheek, causing a bit of his charred flesh to flake off. He's always been a strong man, but he can't prevent that low, anguished cry that escapes his throat or even the tear that falls.

The sound of his own misery woke him.

Apollo blinked, looked around his darkened chambers, caught somewhere in the borderless place between waking and dreaming, confused by the morbid keening sound that woke him. As in his dream, he realized that he was the source of that sound, giving time an odd sense of folding back upon itself. And then the entire dream came flooding back, too much like a premonition, and his heart smashed against the walls of his chest like an avion banging against the bars of its cage.

It only a dream, of course, but Apollo still caught himself glancing quickly around the darkened cabin, as if the funeral bier would somehow, illogically, materialize in the room with him.

"Commander?"

The door to Apollo's sleep-chambers whisked open and Gar'-Tokk bustled in, the muscles of his big frame coiled and ready for action. The Borellian Noman palmed the lights, filling the cabin with a cool, efficient, shadowless glow.

"Gar'Tokk?" Apollo murmured, his voice still thick with sleep, his eyes squinted against the light. "What—?"

"I heard you cry out," the Borellian explained, relaxing a bit, but his eyes still surveyed the room for signs of hidden treachery. "And, since you did not retire for the night with female companionship, I assumed your moan was not one of pleasure."

Apollo allowed himself a slight chuckle. "I'm fine," he told his bodyguard. Gar'Tokk's thick, beetled brow creased slightly. "Just a nightmare."

He threw his warmers back and swung his legs over the edge of his sleeping module to the floor.

The Noman frowned. "The last time I heard anyone moan like that," Gar'Tokk said, "was a human warden we tortured. *Nomen,*" he added pridefully, "suffer their pain with silent dignity."

Apollo smiled and said nothing. *If you only knew,* he thought. *If you only knew.*

1

THEY PRESSED on through the endless darkness, aiming toward the light of distant stars and the hope of better days. Hope was fading, and the stars whose light they followed doubtlessly long ago went nova. They were steering their lives by things that no longer existed, the light of forgotten days cast by stars that no longer gave light. No one dared think such things, of course; that would be too much like admitting defeat.

So, they pressed on, although there were fewer of them to do so, now.

The battle with the Chitain and the Cylons had cost the colonial fleet terribly, in terms of lives lost and lives ruined. There were very few whole family units aboard the rag-tag fleet; so many fathers died yahren ago, during the first Cylon raid, leaving behind women and children—children, grown now to young manhood and the age of their fathers when they perished, leaving behind their own women and children. Without fathers, or mothers, these children grew up wrong, and hard, and fast, and without much respect for anything or anyone. They were not much better than urchins, living in corridors and crawlspaces instead of streets and alleys, a whole subculture that existed, but no one looked at too closely. Some of these children, those old enough to be inducted, were given the choice by the council whether they would spend time in the brig for their crimes, ranging from theft to assault, or be conscripted into the military and became Warriors. Some disappeared, back into the hidden world of the poor and neglected; others chose prison, and still others chose the way of the Warrior.

Theirs was a terrible life; but, for some, it was the only life they had ever known. For some, it might be the only life they would ever know.

Still, there was some faint, small glimmer of hope—the chance that the planet Kirasolia might have once been visited by the Thirteenth Tribe, and it was toward this distant rumor of a world they journeyed.

They pressed on . . . but more of them began to wonder why.

It isn't fair, Apollo thought. He wasn't the first person to arrive at this conclusion, nor would he likely be the last. It was a destination everyone reached, sooner or later: it was simply through a path paved with a matter of differing events that made the journey short or long.

He looked again at the comatose figure of Starbuck, so still and so . . . *lifeless.* It was hardly a word anyone who knew him would have associated with Starbuck, but that was the word. His external injuries had healed, sped along their way by the med-berth in which he slept without waking these past weeks, but the most severe damage was internal.

Cranial pressure in Starbuck's skull had reached critical dimensions, necessitating a craniotomy to relieve the fluid build-up before the pressure squeezing his brain could render irreversible damage. The signs of the surgery had already healed, but nothing else had changed about Starbuck's condition. He slept on like a character from some long-ago children's fairy tale, neither dead nor alive in his glass coffin; but what would it take to wake him?

Apollo wished he knew.

Starbuck's was the only med-berth still occupied following the battle with the Chitain; all the rest who had been injured had either healed, or . . .

But there would not be an *or* for Starbuck. People like Starbuck did not die, not like this, anyway. He was always beating impossible odds, and what was more impossible than this?

"What did I get you into now?" Apollo said, softly. There was no answer, of course, except for the flat, idiot *ping* of the heart and brain monitors to which Starbuck was attached. They were impartial; they didn't care that they were recording the slow, winding down of a human life.

Apollo was unsure how long Cassiopea had been standing there, to his side and slightly behind, but he was glad she was. After a while, she placed her hand on his shoulder, and, after a while, Apollo placed his hand upon hers.

"I suppose it would be pointless to tell you to get some rest?" Cassie asked the commander. It was not so much a question as it was a statement of fact.

Apollo smiled crookedly. "I might ask you the same thing, Cass," he said. "How long have you been here, yourself?"

"Oh, no," she said. "That isn't a fair question. I'm here in the capacity of attending med, whereas you . . ."

Apollo glanced back at her over his shoulder. "We're both here for the same reason, Cass."

She let her hand fall away from his shoulder. There was nothing Cassie could do for Starbuck, but perhaps she could still do something for Apollo. Perhaps she could get him to live again before it was too late. She said, "I don't have an entire Fleet depending on me." Apollo opened his mouth to protest, but she pressed on. "There's nothing you can do for him that Dr. Wilker can't do better."

"I can be his friend," Apollo answered simply. "I can be here for him, like he was always there for me."

"Cut the felgercarb," she snapped. Apollo could only blink in dumb response to her outburst. "You're here for Apollo, not Starbuck. You're here because you feel guilty, you're here because you're the great Adama's son and you think that means you can fix everything. Well, I'm sorry, sweetheart, but there are some things you can't fix. There are some things you just have to accept."

"How do we know this is one of them until we've tried everything?" he countered. His eyes locked with hers, and it was she who looked away this time. Apollo stood quietly for several moments beside his oldest friend's med-berth, clearing his mind of clutter and anger. When he opened his eyes again, they were clear and focused. He placed his hands lightly against Starbuck's temples and let his consciousness expand in waves, as if his mind were being broadcast on a wideband frequency. And then, Apollo narrowed his thoughts to a wedge, like probing tendrils, and he felt his consciousness slipping into Starbuck's slumbering mind.

Apollo's consciousness skimmed like the shadow of a cloud passing over a lake, a dark and bottomless lake, tumbling down and down, into unrelieved, unbroken blackness and silence. Apollo probed deeper, but the jet blackness made it difficult to tell just how deep he had gone, and still there was no sign of Starbuck's own consciousness.

Deeper . . . *just a little farther,* Apollo promised himself; *just a little more, and then, if there's no sign of him, I'll turn back.*

And down his consciousness tumbled, pressing on until he began to feel the crushing, overwhelming weight of despair and hopelessness, the cold of the void, as if Starbuck's mind were at absolute zero. Nothing could exist here, no thought could resonate, no memory survive. It was the cold of the void, the cold of the waiting grave.

Are you there? Apollo's mind-thought called out, the sound of it tiny and swallowed by the greedy darkness. *Starbuck, can you hear me? Please, if you can hear me, just answer me, just give us something, some hope—*

And then he was racing toward a distant pinprick of light, far away, the light of other days, racing faster and harder, and for a wild, heady moment, Apollo thought he had found Starbuck, buried alive in a mental cave-in.

"Apollo?"

Starbuck—?

"*Apollo, can you hear me? Apollo—*"

Starbuck, where —

Suddenly, the light exploded all around him, momentarily blinding him, making him cry out in pain.

"—can you hear me?"

"Yes, of course I can hear you, but where—?"

The world swam back into a gauzy sort of focus, the light so bright after the long, deep darkness that it made Apollo's eyes tear and sting, but it was only the light of the med-bay, and the voice was only the voice of Cassiopeia. Her face, doubled and trebled by the prism of tears through which Apollo viewed it, was etched with concern. Apollo palmed his eyes dry, looked at Cassie, questioningly.

"Why did you make me break contact?" Apollo asked, anger alloyed with confusion. "I almost—"

"You almost got lost inside his mind," Cassie finished, forcefully. Apollo frowned because he knew she was right. He *did* almost get lost there, in the darkness, where Starbuck was also lost. Lost and alone and probably dying.

"I'm all right," Apollo argued. "I would have been fine."

"Who said anything about you?" Cassie asked. "Of course you would have been fine; you're always fine. But what about Starbuck? The man has a *brain* trauma! What do you think fracking around with his mind is going to do to him?"

Cassie stood over Starbuck and took his hand in hers, as she had done countless times since she first fell in love with him all those yahren ago, as she had done so many times recently as she kept watch beside his med-berth.

She realized she was angry with Apollo for getting Starbuck into the one bad scrape it didn't look as if he was going to escape; she was furious with the situation that had brought them to this. She cursed her helplessness and she cursed anyone who couldn't help Starbuck. She was a doctor who couldn't save the one she loved. What had she changed her entire life for, if she still had no control over it? And she was angry because blind, stumbling anger always attends loss, the unwanted guest that always arrives at the worst times.

"You're not the only one in pain, Cassiopeia," Apollo said, gently. After a moment, he circled her and Starbuck's hands with his, but neither seemed to notice. "Don't give up." Even Apollo wasn't sure to whom he was speaking. All of them, he supposed, himself included.

"I'm glad you're here for him, Cassie," Apollo said. "I know this has to be especially difficult for you, given your history with Starbuck."

"I used to think there was nothing harder than watching someone you love fall in love with someone else," she answered, ruefully. "But, what did I know?" Cassopeia glanced back at Apollo, a sad smile on her full, lovely face.

"You've suffered a lot of losses," she said. "I haven't had to deal with this before, on such a personal level. How do you get over it?"

That was a good question. It was not that he didn't have emotions, it was just that he was quite good at ignoring them. He had dealt with first Zac's death and his mother's, and then Serina's and Adama's by walling his emotions into a neat little pen. Occasionally one would escape, and he would regret that, of course, because they always got hurt whenever they did. Apollo would recapture his stray feelings, cage them, and keep a tighter guard over them. But what worked for him was not necessarily a good road for Cassie to embark upon. One look at her face, open and oddly hopeful and full of pain told him that.

"A day at a time," he said. "A tear at a time, but just know there will always be one more." Apollo looked at Starbuck, so still and too much like his dream, and said, "But, get over it? You never really get over it, you just . . . get by."

Cassie studied him for a moment, surprised to hear Apollo admit how deeply hurt he had been, and still was. He was like a thermos—you could never tell, just by looking, whether his contents were hot or cold. For the moment, she didn't see Apollo as the supreme commander of the fleet, or the indestructible man she had always thought he was. For the moment, he was human, and vulnerable, and she, as well as anyone, knew how hard it was to be that. But he had done it for her. "It never bothered you, did it? What I used to do."

"Socialator?" Apollo asked, and crinkled his nose. "It's not what you do that makes you who you are. I always thought you were a good person, Cassie, and I always will."

"I think you are, too, Apollo," she said, and smiled again, but this time it was not so sad, just wistful.

Apollo's commline, clipped to his belt, beeped with the same maddening calm as the monitors keeping track of Starbuck's vital signs, even though at this point they were somewhat less than vital. The commander unclipped the small, hand-held device and opened the frequency. "Commander Apollo," he said, tersely.

"Apollo," Athena's voice greeted him across the open link. "President Tigh and I would like to see you on the bridge."

He wanted to tell his sister to handle it, just handle whatever it was herself, but being commander was not about what Apollo wanted; it was about what had to be done, personal pain aside.

"On my way," he managed, and flipped the voice-pad closed with a flick of his wrist. Apollo clipped the communicator to his belt once more and turned to go. He paused a moment in the doorway to look back where Cassiopeia still stood, Starbuck's hand in hers.

"I'll let you know," Cassiopeia began, so softly at first that Apollo thought she was speaking to Starbuck; it was only when she looked up and met his eyes that he knew otherwise. "If there's any change, I'll let you know." Apollo managed a smile, but Cassie didn't see it; she had already turned back to Starbuck, studying the face she knew so well and feared she would soon never see again.

If watching a loved one die is one of the hardest things one can do, how much harder is it, then, when one has still not made peace with one's feelings for the dying?

Dalton sat alone in the hard, steel chair in the waiting hall just outside the med unit. She had been there since before Apollo arrived, and sat, unmoving, still. Hers was a complex relationship with her father, Starbuck, and now, faced with his imminent departure from this life, she felt . . . well, she was unsure of her feelings.

She loved him, of course; he was her father, and Dalton knew Starbuck loved her and her mother, Cassiopea, the best he could. Dalton was coming to understand these things about her father; it was her own unresolved feelings of love and resentment she was finding so difficult to understand.

And she wondered, not for the first time and not for the last, if Starbuck had marked her more than either of them could guess. Would she be as poor at giving and accepting love as her father? She loved Troy, she supposed, what was there *not* to love? Troy—*Boxey,* as he used to be called a long, long time ago—was her first great flame, the grace note that provided calm in the cacophony of her life, but just lately. . . .

Dalton glanced up, saw Apollo standing near her. She gave a start, fear scouring the inside of her brain, because the grim look on Apollo's face made her wonder if her father had slipped quietly away while she sat here, trying to unravel the scattered and tangled skein of her emotions.

"Don't give up," he offered. It was the same advice he had given Cassie, but it seemed the only reasonable thing to say at such a time.

It took a moment for the meaning of these words to penetrate Dalton's whirling thoughts, and she uttered a hitching, ragged, laughing sigh of relief.

"Everything all right?" Apollo asked, and stepped a little closer. He felt a knot in the pit of his stomach when he realized just how much of Starbuck he could see in Dalton's features, and he wondered why he never noticed that before.

"What a mess, huh?" she answered, but she wasn't sure if she meant Starbuck's condition, or her own. Both, probably.

"If you need to talk . . ." Apollo began.

She guessed she did, and if anyone knew Starbuck well, it was

Apollo. But before she could speak, Sheba and Boomer appeared in the doorway. It was one thing to unburden herself to Apollo; she might have been able to do that—*just*—but the moment had passed now, and Dalton stood quickly, unable to look at Apollo or the others. "Maybe later," she said, and walked briskly from the waiting hall.

I'll look after her, old friend, Apollo promised Starbuck in his thoughts, and knew when he did so that he had all but given up on Starbuck's recovering. Who was Apollo to tell Starbuck's family not to give up when he had already done so?

Grief came at him from a thousand different directions at once, like a rabid lupus, cutting and tearing at him with a whirlwind of fang and claw. It was impossible to defend himself from the savaging he was suffering; all he could do was bear it with quiet grace and wait for it to get tired of hurting him. The Lords of Kobol must have been cruel, indeed, he thought, to keep visiting such ruin and misery upon their race. How much longer would they all have to be tested before the gods decided they were, at last, worthy of their loving kindness?

"Apollo?" Sheba began.

The commander squared his shoulders and set his jaw, and managed to say, "I'm needed on the bridge," without his voice cracking too much. More than that would have been impossible. He turned and walked from the waiting hall before anyone could ask anything else, into the main corridor beyond, where Gar'Tokk was patiently waiting.

The Borellian Noman was perfect company for Apollo's present mood: Gar'Tokk would not ask the commander how he was, or if there was any sign of improvement in Starbuck. Gar'Tokk was simply present in Apollo's life in the capacity of bodyguard, but even the best protector couldn't defend Adama's son from the ache in his soul, or the sharp, wicked blade of his own thoughts.

The mood on the bridge was as somber as Apollo's own.

Athena glanced up at Apollo's entrance, a questioning look on her face; it was the same look she always had whenever he visited Starbuck, and, as always, his grim expression answered her quite well. Anyone watching might have thought it was the telepathic link the children of Adama, pure-blooded Kobollians, shared, but it was nothing more prosaic than the secret shorthand language of siblings who had grown up so close together.

"Glad you could take time away from your medical duties to join us, Commander," President Tigh said; it was Tigh's way of letting his old friend know he was displeased with Apollo's behavior. Apollo glanced from Athena to Tigh and back to Athena.

She said, "We're a little . . . *concerned* . . . about the time you spend away from your post, when there is so much to be discussed, and decided."

Apollo felt himself bristle at their rebukes, but maintained his calm. "I understand I've been a little distracted, lately," Apollo answered, spreading his hands expansively; "but I have full faith in your and President Tigh's abilities to lead in my times of absence from the bridge."

"But the people," Tigh said, pulling himself up, "don't seem to share that faith in *you,* Commander."

Apollo wiped his palm down his face; was this day really happening? He felt safer showing his pique than he did his pain, and felt his cheeks flushing red and hot. Athena interjected herself between the two men, and outlined the facts. It was nothing Apollo didn't already know, but it was a way of defusing a potentially volatile situation. No matter what, she would always rush to her brother's aid, even if she didn't always agree with him.

"The entire fleet is running out of energy stores and other vital resources," she said; before Apollo could interrupt, she pressed on. "Seditionist and other adversarial factions aboard the fleet—those who never looked with much favor upon you, *or* me—have become more vocally strident than ever in their opposition to us. There have already been several outbreaks of violence over dwindling food supplies, but nothing that we haven't been able to contain . . . *so far.*" She added this last with great emphasis.

"The violence can only get worse," Tigh added, grimly. "By traveling such a long distance to Kirasolia, we risk losing more people to starvation, more ships to energy depletion."

"I thought it was understood," Apollo responded. "We must buy ourselves more time. The Cylons know how badly damaged our fleet is. They'll expect us to find a planet on the holocube in closer proximity than Kirasolia. We cannot afford to make any more mistakes."

"Yes, Apollo," Athena responded with a curt nod. "We cannot afford to make any more mistakes. We're already so desperately low on fuel and resources that if anything more goes wrong, we will not make it to Kirasolia, or any other planet. Ask yourself this, Apollo: Are you sure you want to risk losing everything by trying to second-guess the enemy?"

"They're Cylons," Apollo answered. "They're predictable. 'Exterminate the humans.' There's not much margin for error in that edict, is there? They're hot on our trail and closing in on us." He looked from Tigh to Athena; he could tell, although they might not want to admit it, that they knew he was right. "We've seen firsthand the buildup of Cylon forces in these outlying quadrants. They shouldn't have much trouble finding us if we attempt to stay too long on any habitable planet. We'll be trapped then, no hope of defending ourselves or escape."

"And what happens when we deplete our fuel stores questing after this fabled planet?" Tigh snapped. "What happens when half our fleet is dead in space? It seems to me you're doing the enemy's work for them, Commander."

For a moment, Athena expected Apollo to boil over with anger, but he chuckled instead at the foolishness of the accusation. Tempers were short, he knew; it was not the time to engage in a shouting match, and besides, he knew Tigh's concerns about the welfare of the fleet were well-founded. He could hardly be angry with him for that, especially when Apollo, himself, had similar worries. The gods knew, it was indeed a possibility the fuel reserves would exhaust themselves before the wanderers reached Kirasolia. That was logic talking, but Apollo's focus was on something that had little to do with that concrete mindset: he had faith, and his faith told him his way was the correct path. Logic was hard to refute, but faith was harder still to argue with.

"And let us suppose we do reach Kirasolia," Tigh allowed. "Won't the Cylons simply find us there? How will Kirasolia be any more defensible than the nearest habitable planet?"

Apollo smiled crookedly; he didn't realize it, but it was the same rogue's smile he'd seen Starbuck flash countless times before. They were more alike than he knew. "We will be on Kirasolia only long enough to take on fresh supplies and building materials to repair the damage to our ships," he said.

Tigh looked astonished. Apollo's plan seemed madder by the moment. "We'll have to remain in deep space while we refurbish our fleet," Apollo said. "That will make us more difficult to locate, buy us more time to make our repairs and augment our fighter fleet and weapons."

Before Tigh could respond, the communications screen linking the bridges of the battlestars came to life, and, a moment later, the stern, no-nonsense face of Commander Cain filled the screen. The man was intimidating enough at normal size; seeing his grim features magnified was ten times more imposing.

Gar'Tokk, who had entered the bridge with Apollo but had remained a discreet distance from the proceedings, folded his sinewy arms across his massive chest. Humans had no idea how entertaining they were to the Borellian Nomen.

Cain did not waste time on small-talk or pleasantries, but cut straight to the heart of the issue. "Our initial estimate of the damage we suffered from the Chitain was optimistic," he said. *Optimistic* was not a word Apollo would have associated with Commander Cain. "Recent analyses indicate the damage done to the *Pegasus, Daedelus,* and several other fleet ships, was much more extensive. Many of our ships are operating on half- or emergency-power reserves. Much of that power is being diverted to keep the life support systems functioning. Without the Agro ship and additional medical facilities, we will not be able to continue feeding and tending to the needs of such a large number of wounded civilian and military personnel."

Apollo stepped forward to address Cain's concerns, but it felt to him as if he had simply opened himself to the commander's critical scrutiny. "You will have to tend to these matters as best you can, Commander Cain," he said. "We are hopeful that Kirasolia will fulfill many, if not all, of our needs, but the fleet will have to return to deep space, even if the planet turns out to be habitable."

Cain said nothing for a long time. He was trying to unnerve Apollo with his glowering silence, but Apollo met his unwavering gaze with one of his own.

"The strategies you follow are deeply flawed, Apollo," Cain said at last. Apollo noticed Cain did not do him the courtesy of addressing him as *Commander* Apollo, as if the older man did not feel Apollo was worthy of that post. Worse, Cain sometimes made Apollo feel as if he were not worthy of that title. "You will soon have a mutiny on your hands if you do not start listening to my counsel. If we'd had a few more centons before we left Poseidon, we could have taken on food and fuel reserves, tended to our wounded and repaired our ships. This would have provided the opportunity for the fleet to travel a longer distance through space and explore planets not on the holocube, so the Cylons would have an almost impossible task of finding us. You have no foresight, boy.

"You ignored my advice then and insisted we leave for Kirasolia immediately. And now look at the hell we're in because of that. Because of *you*."

Gar'Tokk, his back to the great screen holding Cain's image, pulled a sour face that only Apollo could see.

"Now who's ignoring facts, Commander?" Apollo responded. "You seem to have conveniently forgotten the food on Poseidon was creating genetic mutations. That is not a risk I was willing to allow my fleet to take. And with the Cylons knowing our whereabouts, we could not afford to chance them mounting a major attack against us while our fleet was so vulnerable."

Apollo did not need the giant screen to magnify the contempt Cain felt for him; it was big enough already. "I'm beginning to wonder if you're a coward, Apollo," he said, and for the first time since this heated discussion began, Cain actually smiled. "With the *Galactica, Pegasus, Daedelus,* and Poseidon's newly built warships, we could have easily fought off any Cylon challenge until we were sufficiently prepared to leave, instead of slinking away like whipped curs." He almost spat this last word. "You're very good at running from fights, Apollo, but are you any good at making the hard choices? Can you face the hard truths? Sometimes, people have to die. You can't save everyone. There are going to be losses; you have to decide if they are losses you can live with."

Apollo's hands fisted at his sides.

"Your strategies may differ," Athena said, stepping closer to the screen, "but Commander Apollo is not a coward."

Cain chuckled, his smile becoming a smirk. "Allowing a woman to fight your battles, Apollo? That only proves my point."

"No one fights my battles, Commander," Apollo said, forcing himself to remain calm, although he was seriously beginning to wonder why he was making the effort. "Athena, stay out of this."

"It would have taken significant time for the Cylons to arrive in sufficient strength to be a real threat to us on Poseidon," Cain continued, his voice growing more agitated. "And I believe your arrival on Poseidon may well have been the very thing that alerted the Cylons to our whereabouts and robbed us of the opportunity to go on the defensive for the first time in twenty yahren."

"The Cylons already knew about you," Apollo said, his own voice becoming more strident. "It would only have been a matter of time before they attacked you in force and annihilated your entire fleet."

Cain started to respond, but Apollo would not allow him the opportunity. "I am supreme commander of this fleet, and under military law, my orders will be followed implicitly."

A deadly quiet settled over the bridge, and Cain, when he spoke again, did so with great effort to contain the rage within him. "We shall see about that, Apollo. As senior commander and—pardon my bluntness—a more skilled battlefield tactician, I believe the council will find me a more reliable and competent choice for supreme commander of the fleet." It was out in the open, now. It was what Cain had intended to say, all along. "You're a good man, Apollo, and I believe you have in you the makings of a great Warrior, but experience must lead. I tell you this to your face, Apollo: I will place my case before the council, as soon as possible."

The screen went blank. A good strategist knew when to fight his battles and when to make his retreat, and Cain was a good tactician.

Tigh patted his old friend on the shoulder, and, although it pained him to say it, warned Apollo, "The council will definitely have leanings in Cain's direction. He's quite a lot like your father, and the people had great faith in him. Just so you know what to expect."

Of course they would; of course. Still, to hear it so flatly put. . . .

Apollo turned away from the blank, gray screen in whose glass he saw his own image reflected, and looked to Athena, wondering just how bad it really was. She didn't look away; at least she could still stand to meet his gaze, but Apollo could not read much meaning into it. In the past, they'd had many disagreements, and they held different opinions on just about everything, but they were blood; they were Adama's children, after all, and their hearts held a deep and profound love for the other. But more than that, they shared a unique spiritual bond that kept growing and evolving, one which Apollo felt sure must hold a key to unfolding revelations about the history—and the future—of their people. It had to mean something. Either all of it mattered or none of it did, and Apollo refused to believe that.

"He may be right, you know," Athena finally offered, and hugged herself. "Many more people may die, and many more ships may be lost if we don't soon find a habitable planet capable of sustaining us. But, whether he's right or you are—" She shook her head, and added, "I just don't trust Cain's intentions."

"Neither course is without risk," Apollo admitted. "But I believe Cain's path leads to suicide." Still, on what did he base this pronouncement? Just because Cain was less about faith than blood and thunder did not in itself make him wrong. It was a fine line to walk, faith, knowing when the voice that told you things was the voice of divine intervention, and when it was your own wishful thinking.

"Nevertheless, Apollo, he will make a powerful case before the council," Tigh warned him. "You will not have an easy time of it, swaying them over to your side, when most of them already believe as Cain does. And, to be frank, Commander Cain's record—"

"Cain's record, Cain's record," Apollo growled, and threw his hands up in the air. "Gods! Does everyone here let the past blind them?" He turned to Athena, and the anger was already gone, and in its place was the look of a man skirting the edge of some great and grand disaster. "I'm asking you for your support, Athena, Tigh—I'm going to need it, if I'm going to have any hope of blocking Cain's appointment."

"And you shall have it, Apollo," Athena promised.

"Of course," Tigh agreed. "But even with our support—" It wasn't spoken, but Apollo thought what Tigh was really saying was, *Why would we* want *to block Cain's appointment?*

Apollo nodded. "I understand," he said. "And thank you, both of you, for your support. I'll do my best to justify it."

He turned and walked from the bridge, followed by Gar'Tokk. Apollo had built up his defenses to guard his heart against the hard world in which he had to live, to ward off the blows of fate thrown at him by a sometimes seemingly indifferent universe, but there was no defense for this. How does one guard against simple kindness?

2

THE HEART of the ship—the *true* heart—was not the bridge or the mighty engines that propelled it through the void, but its sanctuary.

Once, it had been Adama's, his place of quiet, the refuge he sought when the weight of all the worlds threatened to crush his spirit and break his heart. Apollo had known of its existence for several yahren, but until this moment, he had perhaps never understood completely the need for such a place.

The room itself was just a room, not blessed with any magical properties, except that it was where Apollo felt closest to his father, and there was magic in that. Star charts, drawn from legend, and etchings of galaxies that unwound like clocksprings, filled the otherwise cold and gleaming, featureless walls. Occupying the center of the room stood a tall, high-backed chair of ancient wood, one of the few such pieces still in existence among the entire fleet.

Directly opposite this antique seat was a computer that was even older, perhaps by as much as five centuries, and still it was more advanced than the rest of the electronic intelligence aboard the *Galactica* or any of the other ships in the fleet. Its one red eye light stared back at Apollo, comforting and disquieting all at once.

The computer was almost organic in its design, with sides that curved with a graceful flow, upward and outward. It always made Apollo think of an old friend waiting with opened arms to receive the careworn traveller. After all, the computer did convey Adama's final holographic recording to Apollo after the old man's death, like some kind of binary seance.

Apollo hoped, foolishly, he knew, there might be another message from his father hidden away in cold logic chips, waiting for the right moment to play. Well, if that were true, this would be that moment; he could use his father's level-headed wisdom now.

He held the Star of Kobol in his hands, tracing his thumbs over its frictionless surface, thinking nothing as best he could, losing himself, his individuality, in the whorls of light that raced and eddied across the stone, like strange, deep-sea marine life.

Apollo slowed his breathing, and his heart rate dropped correspondingly.

He could feel himself slipping away, his mind slipping free of its moorings, no longer part of anything and thus, becoming a part of everything.

For a moment, the commander allowed his consciousness to brush once more Starbuck's slumbering mind, to see if there had been any change, any response to his earlier efforts to jumpstart his old friend's neural activity, but there was nothing. In this state of elevated consciousness, Apollo's emotions were left behind like so much detritus, and yet he felt a momentary, impossible stab of disappointment.

Apollo moved on.

Dreamwalking, as Apollo sometimes called this expansion of consciousness, was not just a variant of the Kobollians' telepathic abilities, but part of the meditation stage that allowed the mind to address matters of great importance without the body's wasteful clutter of emotion and worry and illness to act as an impediment while seeking a solution. It was a way of seeing things whole, and fresh.

One step removed from the immediacy of his own personal

involvement, Apollo could grasp the entire situation, rather than grappling with it a piece at a time, as they had all been doing. The threat from Commander Cain to have Apollo replaced as supreme commander of the fleet was not the whole of the dilemma, although it was a big enough part of it to cause Apollo to block out the rest of the picture.

Until now.

Now, his subconscious mind could speak directly to his consciousness and show him the concerns that hadn't quite found their way to the surface, like artifacts buried in the ground. Trying to haul these objects to the surface had only resulted in broken corners; but now, his subconscious allowed them to float, complete and unbroken, into the light of analytical clarity, and Apollo wasn't sure he liked what he saw. Not a bit.

It was not enough to assume the Cylons were simply following the fleet; a more immediate concern was, how could the Cylons be following them in such great numbers? Their increasing presence, coupled with their recent astonishing, fluidly evolving technological advancements, was the real enigma. Even allowing for Cylon outposts in other quadrants, it would still take time for warships dispatched from these planets or basestars to join the armada trailing the fleet. And yet, for all the Cylon Raiders the colonial Warriors dispatched, their numbers did not seem to remain diminished for long. It was as if the Cylons had found some way of circumventing space traveland simply teleporting any number of replacement Raiders into the vicinity.

Nor could the Chitain alliance with the Cylons be so easily dismissed. Their defeat at the hands of the humans and their growing hatred for them would surely cause them to seek revenge. Apollo could understand the Cylons' temporary relationship with the Chitain, but it was unlike the xenophobic Cylons to allow another race to operate on an equal basis with them. From what Apollo could discern, the Chitain would never allow themselves to be subservient to the Cylons; therefore, the alliance was one of equals, not commanders and troops.

If this were true, and Apollo could sense it was, would the Cylons share whatever seeming teleportation technology they possessed with the Chitain?

There was something there, something vast and terrible that, even in his holistic state, Apollo could not quite completely grasp.

Something vast . . .

Vast—

Apollo blinked, allowing the image to come; it all but clawed its way into his brain, and he could not have resisted it for long.

A vast Cylon armada filled his vision, countless warships, endless and numberless as grains of sand, swooped and dived, firing their deadly lasers, filling the darkness with lightning.

Aboard one of the colonial ships, the blasts from the Cylon Raiders took their toll and the hull's integrity failed. Civilians were killed in the fiery blast; danger lights flashed; the living and the dead were sucked into the cold vacuum of space by explosive decompression. And all without a sound.

Apollo wasn't sure if it was a blessing or a curse that his vision was silent. He couldn't hear the screaming, but then, to watch people die so horribly and in such eerie quiet—

"Oh, Gods of Kobol," he whispered, and turned his head away. As if that could shut out the frightening images inside his own mind.

The void was littered with debris from destroyed Vipers and Raiders, bodies of those who had been torn out of the fleet ships by the powerful Cylon weaponry, and still the Raiders came.

But beyond them—

Looming like a planet of cold steel, the biggest Cylon basestar Apollo had ever seen.

And then, thankfully, mercifully, it was over, and Apollo was staring at the face of Baltar in place of the horrifying vision.

It took Apollo a long and confused moment to realize it was not Baltar standing before him, but his holographic image, projected by the red eye of the computer station opposite Apollo's chair.

"—require a moment of your time, Commander," the holographic Baltar was saying, in oozing, unctuous tones. "I wouldn't dream of imposing, Commander Apollo, only I believe I have some information that may prove vital to our continued survival in light of our less-than-envious predicament—"

"Where are you?" Apollo interrupted, curtly. He was really not in the mood for this.

"Yes, of course," Baltar answered, contritely. "At the moment, I'm in the science labs with Dr. Salik."

"Apollo, out," he said, and ended the holographic transmission. He sat with his palms on the heavy wooden arms of the great, wooden chair, and glanced idly down; his fingers gripped the ends of the arm rests and his knuckles were white and bloodless, as if this was all that kept him from being hurled into the void. The commander forced his hands to slowly unclench, and as he did, he noticed something he hadn't before: there were countless little scratches in the surface of the wood, crossing and crisscrossing, all of them about the size of, say, a man's thumbnail.

"Father," he whispered, tracing one of the tiny nicks with the ball of his finger.

It was easy to imagine Adama retreating here to contemplate some great quandry that needed clear-headed solution, and, as he allowed his mind to empty of clutter, perhaps he absently raked the horn of his thumbnail back and forth along the groove of the wood, over time wearing away the dark luster of the varnish, leaving his own mark in its place.

Apollo didn't know why, but this remnant of Adama, this emotional hieroglyph, only made his father seem more real to him, more human.

As he left the sanctuary, Apollo was smiling.

Outside Apollo's chambers, Gar'Tokk stood silent guard duty, and whatever thoughts he thought were his alone. He was not one to shed light on his own inner landscape for benefit of anyone else; it was dark, but he knew his way around.

Apollo often thought the Borellian Noman was more like Apollo, himself, than Gar'Tokk realized. As the commander left his chambers, Gar'Tokk fell into step beside him, asking no questions. It was not his place to ask, only obey.

At first, Gar'Tokk's constant presence had disconcerted Apollo, but he had grown, not just accustomed to it, but to almost enjoy it. He wanted to think Gar'Tokk considered him a friend now, as well, but wondered if the Noman's sense of duty permitted him to think in such terms.

"Don't you wonder where we're going?" Apollo asked, glancing sidelong at his grim bodyguard. "I mean, *ever?*"

Gar'Tokk shrugged with a downturn tug of the corners of his mouth. "It matters not," he said. "Wherever you go is where I follow."

"Even if you know I'm heading into a suicidal situation?" the Commander asked. This was something he and Gar'Tokk had not discussed before, and he was genuinely curious as to how far the Noman's debt of honor extended. "If you knew that, by following me, you'd surely die, too?"

Gar'Tokk arched a thick eyebrow, clearly puzzled by the question. "Of course," he said, simply. "It is my duty." After a pause, the Noman asked, "Is that where we're headed now?"

Apollo laughed, the sound of it catching them both by surprise. "Whoever would have known Gar'Tokk had a sense of humor?" Apollo said, catching his breath. "I was just wondering where your debt to me ended, that's all," he explained.

"Until my shame has been erased, I will always be in debt to you," Gar'Tokk answered, his thick neck lowering his broad head until his chin almost—but not quite—touched his chest. "Until then, my life is yours."

Apollo had to look away; it was difficult enough to look upon another man's pain, but almost impossible to endure that sight, knowing that he, himself, was the cause of it. He had only meant to defeat the leader of the Nomen to ensure their loyalty to Apollo; he had not meant to publicly humiliate Gar'Tokk or win his servitude. As Apollo was learning from his dreamwalks, events over-lapped and interlocked so many other events, like stones in an ancient wall, that it was impossible to remove one and not cause the whole thing to collapse into rubble. Endings overlapped beginnings. He was also learning things happened for a reason, even if that reason was not always readily apparent, so he accepted that Gar'Tokk's presence in his life had a purpose, but still. . . . It was a coldhearted fate that furthered its own blind end at the cost of a decent man's pride.

Doctor Salik usually had a dozen or more experiments running at once, all of them totally unrelated and each of them requiring his full attention, but as Apollo entered the science lab, he was surprised to see Salik, standing still at a work bench, chatting with Baltar.

No; that wasn't quite true, Apollo saw as he came a little nearer. Salik was busily scribbling down notes on a pad, long strands or theoretical equations, the way some people scratched meaningless shapes and symbols as a distraction. Baltar sat facing the door and saw Apollo and Gar'Tokk enter over Salik's shoulder. He raised his eyebrows by way of greeting.

"Ahh, Commander, prompt as ever," Baltar said, smiling expansively. Salik turned and greeted Apollo warmly.

"What's so important, Baltar?" Apollo asked.

At Apollo's side, Gar'Tokk let his gaze roam around the science lab, taking no particular notice of any one thing, missing nothing.

"And, ever to the point," Baltar muttered. He stood, stepped forward, a smile stitched to his face. "It, therefore, behooves me to respond in kind."

Apollo glanced at Salik; the scientist nodded, said, "You might want to hear him out, Commander. What he has to say . . . I think it could be very important." He held Apollo's gaze a moment, then looked at the reason they were all gathered here. Apollo's eyes followed Salik's, fixed on the seemingly imperterbable traitor to the entire human race.

"You've got my attention," Apollo informed Baltar. "How long you keep it is up to you."

"Commander, you are making a grave error in proceeding to Kirasolia," Baltar said. "An error fraught with almost certainly fatal consequences."

Apollo sighed impatiently, his hands resting on his hips. "And you're going to enlighten me as to the nature of my failings, I suppose?" *You, and everyone else.*

Baltar inclined his head to indicate he would. "Whatever merits your plan to stop at Kirasolia may—or may not—have, is not the issue," Baltar said.

"It isn't?" Apollo asked. It was more a declaration than a question.

Baltar shook his head. He was serious now; Apollo thought he might also have been a little frightened. "No," he said. "Think, Commander. The Cylons had the holocube before you. They know of Kirasolia, they knew of it before you did. They will be waiting for us. Think about it, Apollo: the Cylon fleet behind us, somewhere . . . herding us straight into the trap they set."

And there it was. That was exactly the thought that tickled the back of Apollo's mind, the one that refused to coalesce entirely. Still . . . this was Baltar, the man who betrayed the entire human race to the Cylons, who lived among their human enemies for several yahren until a reversal of fortune forced him back into the society of other colonials. He might be telling the truth . . . but then again, he might be in league with the Cylons or the demonic Count Iblis, trying once more to curry their favor. Endings and beginnings, like a daggit chasing its own tail.

"I see," Apollo said. "And, I take it you've got the solution to this little quandry we find ourselves in?"

"I'm not at all sure I care for your tone, Commander," Baltar said, stiffly; "but, given our past history, I suppose it's understandable, if unfortunate. And in answer to your question, yes, I believe I do have an alternative proposal. I have the coordinates of another, supposedly habitable planet—"

"Supposedly," Apollo repeated.

"—a planet the holocube has no record of," Baltar pressed on. "The Cylons won't think of looking for us there."

"How did you learn of this planet?"

Baltar swallowed, said, "Its knowledge came into my possession during one of my missions with the Cylons. They don't realize I know of it; I'd stake my life on that."

"You are, Baltar," Apollo said. He spoke softly, without emotion. "Believe me, you are."

"Oh, spare me, Commander," Baltar said, leaking the words through gritted teeth. "Do you think I want to die any more than the rest of you? Whatever else you think of me, you insult me if you believe I'm such a fool as not to realize my continued well being is wrapped up with yours. I know my only future lies in redeeming myself with the colonials, and I am trying to do that . . . if you will allow me."

Apollo shook his head, threw up his hands, and started to turn away. Perhaps Baltar was telling the truth; perhaps he was even right, but there was nothing Apollo could do about it. Cain was already gunning for the supreme commander's chair; to inform the council that the fleet was changing course on Baltar's recommendation would only do Cain's job for him. The only thing more sure to do the job was for Apollo to head back to his chambers, pull his sidearm, place the barrel to his temple, and squeeze the trigger. Either way was suicide; one was just a little messier than the other.

There was a sudden and brief scuffle just behind Apollo. He sidestepped and looked back to find Gar'Tokk holding Baltar several feet off the floor by the scruff of his collar, as if the traitor were a condemned man hanging from the arm of a gallows.

"Put me down, you ignorant creature!" Baltar cried, indignantly, puffing and panting.

"Gar'Tokk, what are you doing?"

The Noman held Baltar at the end of his arm, suspended above the floor, kicking and thrashing. He turned to Apollo, ignoring the traitor's weight and struggles, as if they were inconsequential and not worth mentioning.

"He tried to grab you, Commander," Gar'Tokk reported.

"I only wanted to stop you leaving!" Baltar gasped, his face reddening. The viselike grip on his collar was cutting off the flow of air.

Apollo nodded for Gar'Tokk to set him down. He did, and Baltar raked great gasps of air back into his chest, his hand tenderly massaging at his throat. Baltar tried to speak, coughed, and tried again, with better luck this time. "Are you so certain I'm lying, Commander, that you are willing to put up the life of everyone in the fleet against those odds? Are you really that certain?"

"Such disrespect," Gar'Tokk clucked disapprovingly. "Say the word, Commander," He held his massive fist above the crown of Baltar's head, as if he were nothing more than an anchor spike to be driven into the deckplate. Baltar flinched and stepped out from the shadow of Gar'Tokk's fist.

"All right," Apollo said. "Baltar, I mean, not you, Gar'Tokk," he quickly amended. "Let's say, for the sake of argument, I believe you. What proof do you have? What are the coordinates for this planet?"

Baltar swallowed, twice. "They're in a code...one I don't understand and have not been able to break, thus far, unfortunately, but the quantum shift effect technology might be able to unravel it."

"The QSE?"

"It's more than you think," Baltar continued. "The Cylons didn't invent it, they plundered it from an alien civilization they had conquered."

That made sense, Apollo thought; more sense than thinking the nearly-mindless Cylons could ever have developed such advanced technology themselves. "The QSE has more applications than you've seen. Not only does the quantuum shift generator break codes and shift objects into alternate space, but it also creates rifts in space."

Salik had been working on just such a diagram to better explain and understand Baltar's assertions: he had drawn an image, which he handed Apollo, one in which space was best depicted as a U-shaped piece of parchment. Normally, a ship would have to travel from one end of space—or, in this instance, the parchment—to the other, but if the QSE could open a rift in space, it would be like punching a tunnel through one side of the parchment to the other, forming a bridge between the two legs of the "U"; the ship would enter on one side and emerge on the other almost instantaneously.

The implications were staggering. The fleet would be able to travel untold distances—thousands of parsecs in the blink of an eye—and explore territories never before reachable. And was it possible the Thirteenth Tribe had this technology? Was that how they were able to reach such far-flung corners of the galaxy? It would explain a lot.

It would explain how the Cylons had been able to build up their fleets such a vast distance from their homeworld, and it made Baltar's assertion that the Cylons would be waiting for them on Kirasolia that much more frightening. Apollo was beginning to wonder if, perhaps this once, Baltar was telling the truth. Inner vision and logic were at snarling, fang-toothed odds with one another over this one.

Salik's notes, in his careful, cribbed handwriting, postulated "Time does not move forward smoothly, in an analog fashion, but in a series of little 'jumps' or 'ticks.' There are so many jumps in one centon—trillions and trillions—that it goes unnoticed by living beings. But if we could push someone forward just one 'tick' in time, they would be in the same place spatially, but temporally out of phase with our existence . . ." The notes, from here, collapsed into an inescapable black hole of lengthy equations, and Apollo knew better than to enter their gravitic pull. He set the notes aside, and looked at Salik's anxious, eager face.

"Doctor Salik," he said. "I want you to research the QSE technology, ascertain if our friend's claims are correct."

"Does this mean you believe him?" Gar'Tokk asked, clearly surprised.

"It means . . . it means I don't know what to believe," Apollo admitted, and he didn't know if that was good, or bad. Everything was changing around him, and he had the sense they would change more before it was finished.

As he thought that, a flushed and breathless Cassiopeia appeared in the lab doorway, leaning against the wall for support.

"Cassie. . . ?" Apollo said; it was the moment he had been preparing for these past few weeks, but the moment he also thought would never come.

"It's Starbuck," she managed to gasp. "He's awake!"

3

STARBUCK IS *awake.*

As Apollo and his bodyguard raced down endless steel corridors toward the med-unit, he kept replaying those words over and over in his head, like the tolling of a cloister bell: *Starbuck is awake. Starbuck is awake. Starbuck is awake* . . . He had to keep examining the words to make sure they carried no hidden loophole or subtext he was missing. But they seemed clean, not fraught with buried meaning which would later explode like a time-bomb in Apollo's heart.

Athena, Dalton, Sheba and Boomer were already seated in the waiting hall outside the med-unit, and they all looked up as Apollo and Gar'Tokk entered. They all had, to greater or lesser degree, tears welling in their eyes; everyone except Gar'Tokk and Apollo.

Athena stood and hugged her brother and, in a moment of unself-consciousness, Apollo returned the hug. "How is he?" he asked, stepping out of Athena's embrace. "Has anyone talked to him yet?"

He looked from face to face and, one by one, they each looked away.

"What is it?" Apollo asked, and he felt as if a cold, skeletal fist were squeezing his heart. "What's the matter? What aren't you telling me?" Somehow, it seemed, the words that had scanned and declared harmless just moments ago were laden with slow-acting poison, and Apollo was beginning to have a bad idea what was wrong.

Apollo frowned and started past them, for the med bay, only to be met by Dr. Wilker on his way out. He had just come from Starbuck's med-berth, and his face was unreadable, neither happy or pained; simply neutral.

"Doctor Wilker?"

"I guess that's everyone," Wilker said, glancing around. "I've already hinted to them what I'm going to tell you now, Commander. Your friend has had a massive cranial trauma . . . he was also deprived of oxygen for quite a while before you could rescue him from his Viper."

Apollo held up his hand. "I already know all of this, Dr. Wilker," he said. "Just get to the point . . . please." The longer it took to get to the point, the easier it was to allow one's imagination to gallop out of control, opening a whole encylopedia of potential tragedies. Better just to get to it.

"I just want to caution you—all of you—not to expect too much. Your friend may not be the same man you remember."

"What are you—"

"It's too early to tell, yet," Wilker said, and shrugged. "He may not remember you. He may not even recognize you. Just . . . try not to let it alarm you. It's a miracle he's alive at all."

Apollo shook his head. He felt as if he were riding the emotional equivalent of a Viper flight simulator, and all its ups and downs and gut-wrenching loops and dives. The only thing missing was the holo-images of Cylon Raiders trying to destroy him.

"I'm going to have to ask you all to keep your visit brief," Wilker said, ushering the little group into the med unit. "He's still very weak and too much excitement could set his recovery back."

Apollo turned to Dalton. "Do you—?"

She shook her head. "Not just yet," she said. "I will . . . soon . . . but not right now."

Apollo and Athena stepped closer to Starbuck's med-berth, and the Commander noticed there was some hesitation in their approach. It was as if they were coming upon the wreckage of some horrible disaster, and neither wanted to be the first to iden- tify the mortal remains.

As they neared the med-berth, the rest of the group bringing up the rear, Starbuck slowly turned his head toward the sound of their shuffling footsteps. Apollo noted with a start that Starbuck's eyes were glassy and unfixed, as if he weren't seeing them, but seeing through them.

It was a miracle he was even alive, but was it a blessing? Based on this, Apollo didn't think so. He was learning each day the world was full of cruel miracles. Apollo felt hot and cold all at once; he wanted to close his eyes and make this nightmare end. He wanted to be somewhere—anywhere—other than here. But most of all, he just wanted his friend back.

"Hey, buddy," Apollo said, softly. He sat beside the med-berth, his face inches from Starbuck's. Still no sign of recognition, just one of puzzlement, as if Starbuck were one of those who had taken a few too many brain crystals. Behind him, Apollo thought he heard Dalton catch herself—just—before she could cry. Starbuck didn't seem to notice. "Look at you . . . always have to be the cen- ter of attention. Couldn't you think of some better way than all this to get noticed?"

Starbuck's eyes turned toward the sound of Apollo's voice, and for just a moment, he seemed to finally fix on his oldest friend of all, but then he was cast adrift once more, buffetted about by whatever forces were at play in his wounded brain.

Gods, Apollo thought; *oh, gods, if I'd known . . . if I'd sus- pected . . . I never would have prayed . . . not for his awakening, anyway, but that he wouldn't . . . gods, this is no life for him.*

"Starbuck, it's Athena. Do you know me? Do you recognize Apollo?"

Apollo closed his eyes; he couldn't watch this. He couldn't do this. He would remain a few moments longer, out of respect, and then he would have to go. This was too much like visiting an open grave, except the corpse in it didn't realize it was dead just yet—

"Apollo—" Athena gasped, and squeezed her brother's shoulder.

He opened his eyes, saw what had caused Athena to react: Starbuck was smiling, or trying to. A faint, familiar ghost of a smile, weak but still the rogue's smile they had all come to be so familiar with, was creasing the corners of Starbuck's mouth. "You should see the look on your faces," Starbuck croaked, his voice hoarse, his throat as dry as baked enamel.

"Like you've seen a ghost."

"Don't be silly," Athena managed to say before she collapsed into tears. "Everyone knows there's no such thing as ghosts."

They all laughed, an odd amalgam of laughter and tears, but that was all right. Everything was all right.

"How long do you plan on lying there, you old slagger?" Apollo asked.

Starbuck shrugged, folded his hands together across his chest; that gave Apollo a momentary chill, because it reminded him too much of his dream, but he pushed that thought aside. Not all dreams were premonitions.

"Long as I can," Starbuck answered. He tilted his head toward Apollo, as if really seeing him for the first time since he regained consciousness. "Listen, if you guys don't mind, I could really use a good fumarello and maybe a glass of aged ambrosa. Even that swill they call grog would do nicely."

"I'll see what I can do," Apollo promised, blinking back tears.

"How long have I been here, anyway?" Starbuck asked, his face lining with confusion. There were some huge gaps in his memory, and everything following the explosion of the Chitain warship was a bad, hazy blur. "Why am I here? I can't seem to remember."

"A little over three weeks," Athena answered. She knew Starbuck well enough to know he would want the truth, and she respected him enough to tell it.

Starbuck looked surprised, then smiled. "No, really," he said.

"Really," Apollo said.

Starbuck studied Apollo and Athena's faces, looking for any sign that they were playing with him, but he could see they were not. He let his head fall back softly on his pillow, staring up at the ceiling. "Three weeks," he muttered to himself. "As long as that."

He was quiet for a while, as if he were trying to make peace with so many days vanished from his life without the involvement of ambrosa or socialators in their disappearance. Before he could— if he ever really could—another thought slammed into his consciousness. "What about the fleet?" he asked, suddenly.

Apollo took Starbuck's hand in his, noticing as he did how weak the other man's grip was. He felt as breakable as glass, as fragile as hope. "Athena can fill you in on that later," he said. "But right now, you just rest and work on getting better. We need you back." As fragile as hope . . . and as tenacious.

He smiled, a look of profound relief in his eyes. There was more he might have said, but words were small things, and all of them together could not carry the weight of what Apollo felt at this moment.

"This man needs his rest now," Dr. Wilker announced, stepping closer to Starbuck's med-berth. Cassiopeia ran a green-glowing hand-scanner over Starbuck's head.

"I thought there was no rest for the wicked," Starbuck complained, but Apollo could tell from the sound of his voice that he was already exhausted. This little bit had worn him out.

"Don't fool yourself," Apollo said. "The wicked sleep just as well as the good. Which would explain why you were able to nap for three weeks."

Doctor Wilker walked the little group of visitors from the room, while Athena remained behind with Starbuck. There was something she still had to tell him, something she didn't feel she could say in front of the others.

Outside the med unit, Dr. Wilker asked Apollo for just a moment more of his time. Apollo looked at the others, feeling a growing sense of unease, then joined Wilker just out of earshot. "Starbuck's revival is nothing short of a medical miracle," Wilker admitted, "but his condition is still very unstable. It's remarkable he's retained his memory and cognition, although further tests will have to be run before we can tell how extensive the damage is, if any, if his motor skills are at all impaired."

"We'll keep a close eye on him," Wilker concluded. "There could still be some serious repercussions. But for the moment, I have something else I'd like to show you."

"Of course," Apollo said again.

"I believe you're going to find this quite interesting," Wilker said, placing his hand on the broad of Apollo's back and giving him a gentle nudge in the direction of the science labs. "Doctor Salik and I have been dissecting the remains of one of the destroyed Cylons we've had in storage for a few yahren."

"Oh?" Wilker was right; Apollo did find this turn of events quite interesting, and he had the sense it was going to become a lot more interesting very soon.

"I almost lost you," Athena said, her lips mere inches from Starbuck's ear. She held his hand in both of hers and ran her fingers over his palm, and the back of his hand, and his knuckles, as if she were some bold new explorer charting foreign lands. In some ways, that was true. This was a foreign land to her, and equally alien to Starbuck. Athena was not one to be the first to let a man know she was interested in him, but then, Starbuck was not really just another man. He was . . . well, he was Starbuck.

Nearby, Cassiopeia went about her duties, pretending not to notice. It's the hardest thing in the world to watch someone you love fall in love with someone else. Hadn't she, herself, said that to Apollo not long ago? Her words flew back at her like homing avions. Athena tried not to call attention to how jubilant she was at Starbuck's miraculous recovery, but it was impossible. And, really, would it be so wrong if she were happy?

"I missed you so much," she continued, kissing the knuckles of Starbuck's hand. Athena rubbed the back of his hand against her cheek, brushed her hair with his limp fingers.

Starbuck blinked groggily; the pain-meds and tranks were acting like a rheostat on his consciousness, dimming it down to almost full-dark, but this much was getting through to him. He was just having a little trouble making sense of it.

"I came too close to never seeing you again," she said, a tear welling in her eye and spilling down her cheek, tracing the soft, round contours of her face. "It made me realize how much I really care for you."

They were interrupted by the harsh sound of a trayful of medical equipment clattering on the floor. Cassie bent to retrieve it, hurriedly placing the tools and equipment back on her tray. She looked up and saw Starbuck and Athena looking at her. Cassiopeia smiled and turned away and went on about her business, the smile fading the moment her back was turned.

Athena's declaration had caught them all by surprise, even Athena. But it was out now, for good or ill. Starbuck just looked at her, and perhaps it was only the wits-dulling effect of the meds, but for once in his life, he could think of nothing to say.

"I'd better let you get your rest," Athena said, her cheeks red and hectic. She rose and hurried from the room, past the ward of empty med-berths and past Cassiopeia, who was filling out her duty log at the desk.

Cassie didn't bother to look up. She was quite used to seeing women leave a room in tears when Starbuck was involved. She had done that more than once herself. He was a rogue, impossible not to love, but impossible to stay in love with for any great length of time. She had always known that Starbuck was not the kind of man to ever love one woman, but still, there was always the hope that he would, if she were the *right* woman. And Cassie had tried to be that woman, leaving her socializing behind like a change of old clothes, and throwing herself into her med studies, but she was coming to face some hard and unpleasant truths.

As much as he might be the man she loved, she was not the woman he loved. Not enough, anyway.

She looked up from her duty log and watched Starbuck lying in his med-berth. His eyes were still open, despite the tranks coursing through his system.

Starbuck could still feel the tingle of Athena's cheek on his knuckles, and he wonderingly rubbed the tips of his fingers over the back of his other hand. He looked over at Cassie, who sat with her head bowed over her notations, studiously avoiding making eye contact with him.

"Cassie," he said, softly, little more than an exhalation of breath that formed her name. He loved her, gods knew he did, but he'd hurt her so many times before without meaning to. It was as if some part of him refused to allow anyone to get close enough to hurt him, as if breaking their heart was little more than a pre-emptive emotional strike. He didn't mean it that way, but he was beginning to wonder what this said about him.

He couldn't hurt Cassie again, not after all he'd put her through already, and in his heart, he had already begun to say good-bye to her. If he were honest, he had begun to say good-bye to her after she had first declared her love for him, as if he collected hearts the way some savage tribes collected fleshy mementos of their conquests.

Still, he couldn't deny the idea of a serious relationship, after playing the field for so many yahren, was appealing to him, and Athena, hard-headed, two-fisted Athena, might be woman enough to go the long distance with someone like him. Maybe it was time for just one woman . . . but he didn't want to hurt the sister of his best friend. Adama had taken Starbuck in when his own family was killed, raised him as if he were his own son; how could he repay that kindness with his usual coin of hurt and disappointment? Apollo, as understanding as he was, would not understand if Starbuck hurt Athena. Was it worth the risk of destroying his friendship with Apollo?

The idea intrigued him, and frightened him, as well—more than facing a Chitain warship.

Cassie's replacement had arrived and began making her rounds, stopping at Starbuck's med-berth to check his monitor readings.

He felt the old rogue's smile coming to his lips, an involuntary reflex, the way a man's leg will spasm when a doctor taps it with his rubber hammer. Starbuck just couldn't help it.

The attendant—Tamara, according to her ID badge—paused a moment, long enough to return his smile with one of her own. Their eyes met and held for a moment too long, and Starbuck could feel the old dance of seduction beginning yet again.

Maybe it was time for a serious relationship . . . and, then again, maybe not.

"Hey!" he called out, "where's that fumarello and ambrosa I asked for?"

Ahhhh, frack! he thought. *That coma's looking better all the time.*

Apollo had seen more of the science lab in the last hour than he had in the past three weeks, but he had to admit, it had been an eye-opener, both times.

Doctor Wilker called up two images from the computer and projected them on the monitor. Apollo looked at them, unable to determine any great difference between the two. "What am I looking at?" he asked.

"Human DNA, and Cylon DNA," Wilker answered. "Notice anything?"

Apollo looked closer; apart from a few very minor differences in the cellular structure, he had to admit he did not notice anything.

"They're almost identical," Apollo said. "What does this mean?"

But he thought he already knew.

"The DNA sample on the left is human, taken from Doctor Salik," Wilker explained. Salik held up his palm, to indicate a small bio-plasteen patch where the sample had been recently taken. "The sample on the right is taken from the biological brain of the destroyed Cylon we've had in storage all these yahren."

"I think you can guess the implications," Salik added.

"I can guess," Apollo muttered, "but I'd rather have no room for error. What does this mean, exactly?"

Wilker thumbed a button on the computer key-pad and the two slides converged in the center of the screen. Apart from a mismatched strand or two, the DNA samples lined up almost exactly. "It means this," Wilker said, turning to look over his shoulder at Apollo. "They're using human DNA to upgrade and stabilize their own reptilian DNA. We know the Cylons are ever-evolving—or, perhaps more accurately, ever-adapting—their race, whether it's scientifically or, in this case, through genetic enhancements. They're obviously looking for ways to improve their stock and evolve a race genetically superior to humans. I'm afraid, Commander, based on the sample taken from our frozen friend—and remember, he joined us on our trip many yahren ago—they may be very close to doing just that."

Outside the science lab, Gar'Tokk waited.

His thoughts, like Apollo's, were his own, but he would be surprised to learn they were not so different in the long run. Gar'Tokk thought of family, and friends, and a home he would never again know, and he missed all of them. He had loved someone, once, long before Apollo bested him in combat and earned his servitude. Now, of course, the one Gar'Tokk had loved was gone, dead, as all the Borellian women were. Perhaps that was just as well: she would be too shamed by his fealty to a mere human to love him in return. He could expect no less, and who was he to win the heart of his woman, when he could not even win his own freedom?

He watched silently as two of his people passed him in the corridor and disappeared at the juncture farther on. They had seen Gar'Tokk, but had chosen to ignore him; he was dead to them, after all, no longer fit to wear the crown of leader of the Borellian Nomen. If, on those rare occasions, he ever wanted to return to his people, something like this would quickly remind him it was best not to. He was dead to their world, and the dead cannot care. At best, they can only be missed.

Missed . . . and then, forgotten.

4

THE OFF-DUTY officers club—the ODOC—was a dark room filled with a scattering of tables and a long, wide bar made of rare katsaguri wood. This, like Adama's chair in what was now Apollo's sanctuary, was one of the very few items made of wood in the entire fleet.

The Viper pilots who came here did not come for the ambiance; they came to get drunk. They came to brag; they came to meet socialators; sometimes, they came to fight; but sometimes they came because love was where you found it.

It was no different for the female pilots who came here; they had their own cliques, their own friends, their own stories to tell, their own drinks and their own fumarellos, their own hearts to break or have broken. It was a Warriors' bar—genderless, simple, and functional, with male and female pilots and cut-throat games of pyramids—where mostly they commiserated with one another over the circumstances in which they found themselves. They were men and women of action, all of them; the inaction was making them edgy and quick-tempered. It was ironic—peace was what they fought for, what some of them died for, and peace seemed to be the hardest battle they would have to survive. Even the young ones, who had never fought a battle, were edgy, trained to be weapons and having no enemy at which to point themselves. Sooner or later, those weapons would turn upon one another, the only release they knew for their frustrations and tensions.

Jolly was trying very hard to live up to his name.

Flanked by Omega and Rigel, Jolly had spent the last half centon telling the story of how he had been out on routine patrol when he spotted a contingent of Cylon Raiders hiding behind an asteroid, waiting to ambush the Warriors. It had taken so long to get to this point in the story because Jolly kept remembering details he had previously omitted and felt necessary to backtrack and factor in. During his numerous trips back to the starting point, the size of the Cylon ambush squadron grew large enough to almost encompass the entire Cylon empire.

He was making it up as he went, of course, the few grogs he'd already quaffed making it difficult to maintain the narrative thread of his story, but that was all right. Everyone knew he was felgercarbing, but no one minded. The pretend battles were the best, because they always ended heroically, with as few tears and heartaches as possible. No one badly injured, no one dead. It was all anyone could ask from a story.

Jolly looked up, saw Troy, and waved at him. Troy nodded and kept looking for Dalton.

"Where was I?" Jolly asked the little group. They had imbibed almost as much ambrosa as he had, and couldn't recall. Magnanimously, Jolly said he would just start at the beginning.

Troy was learning that, although love may be where you find it, it may not always stay where you last left it. He had not seen much of Dalton lately; with the fleet diminished as it was, they were all required to assume extra duties, and Dalton had spent most of her free time in the med-unit, waiting for word on her father. Understandable, of course, but frustrating for a young man in love.

He regretted he had not been able to be with her as she passed the long and lonely hours in the med-unit, but he had managed to arrange the duty roster so that he had a little free time when Dalton had hers. It would be good to see her, spend time together again, and as he thought that, he realized how much he truly missed her, how deeply he cared. It is usually during such moments of romantic self-realization that the world explodes; there is nothing the universe loves so much as bitter irony.

As he entered the ODOC, Troy spotted a group of young cadets and Warriors gathered around a small table, like the spokes of a wheel, and something in his heart told him only Dalton could command such intense interest in so many men. As Troy made his way through the crowded bar, weaving between tables and chairs and a tangle of legs and feet, he could see the face that was becoming daily more dear to him, just above the shoulder of a cadet who sat with his back to Troy. Dalton was smiling and laughing and she seemed radiant . . . more radiant, in fact, than she had seemed in quite some time, and Troy felt a wild slurry of emotions washing through him. Somehow, he knew, her happiness did not extend to him, had nothing at all to do with him, in fact.

Dalton felt his eyes upon her and she looked his way and nodded, then returned her attentions to her original focus. Annoyed, Troy walked closer, seeing now the object of Dalton's interest. As Troy feared, it was another man. He was blonde-haired and possessed of handsome, chiseled features, blue, piercing eyes and a sly, winning smile. And he was sitting beside Dalton, his arm around the back of her chair, her body language open and inviting. There was the crackle of electricity in the small space of air between them, the sound of a close connection being made.

The other cadets and Warriors greeted him warmly, offered Troy a chair around the table, as if nothing were wrong, as if this were the most normal thing in all the world, and a feeling, like drowning, told him perhaps it was. Perhaps this had been going on all along.

"What's going on here?" Troy asked, trying to keep something like calm in his voice.

The interloper glanced at Troy, a casual thing, but Troy felt he was sizing him up with that glance. Taking the measure of him . . .

and then, dismissing him, just as casually. The interloper turned back to Dalton, Troy already forgotten.

Troy slipped in on the other side of Dalton, taking her firmly by the arm. "I'm talking to you," he said, his lips pressed close to her ear.

"Boxey, what are you doing?" she snapped.

Boxey? She only called him that as an endearment ... or an embarrassment. Troy could see the smirk spreading on the interloper's face, and understood at once which of the two it was.

"Boxey," the new man repeated, and laughed.

"Come with me."

Troy stood up, almost jerking Dalton to her feet. She bumped the table with her hip, rattling the load of drinks, making the glasses chatter amongst themselves, as if in admonishment, spilling the more precariously balanced glasses.

"Are you crazy?!" she shouted. "Troy, stop it! You're hurting me!"

Hurting you? he thought; *gods, you have no idea what real hurt is.*

"She's doing fine right where she is," the interloper said.

"This is none of your business," Troy snapped, rounding on the man. He pulled Dalton closer to him, his hands gripping her shoulders. "You and I—we have to talk."

Dalton raised her arms, bringing them up between Troy's, and levered his hands away from her shoulders. "I'm not in the mood to talk about anything serious," she informed him. "But if you want to act like an adult, sit here and have a drink with the rest of us. You're more than welcome to stay."

"Act like an adult?" he parroted. Her words, on top of her inexplicable actions, nettled and stung him. "I'm not the one sitting here, making time with a Starbuck-simulacrum."

Dalton's mouth worked without forming words; her expression was as if Troy had slapped her. Before either could say anything else, the new man was there, grabbing Troy by the shoulder and spinning him around.

Trays, Troy remembered, a sudden burst of useless illumination. *His name is Trays, and he's from Commander Cain's group of pilots. Grew up on Poseidon.*

"All right, Boxey," Trays said, a sneer curling his lip. "She asked you politely to leave her alone. If I have to ask you, it won't be so nice."

"I'm so glad you said that." Troy balled his fist and brought it up in a powerful uppercut, corkscrewing his wrist as he struck, the extra torque splitting open Trays' lip. Trays staggered back, clapping his hand to his spurting wound.

The sounds of the bar stopped all at once as all heads turned toward the fight.

"That your best . . . Boxey?" Trays asked, spitting a mouthful of blood onto the floor. "Maybe I should be babysitting you instead of beating you."

That was enough for Troy; he flung himself headlong at Trays, taking as many serious blows as he landed, feeling the dull impact of the other man's fist thudding off his ribs, his chin, his belly. But it was only pain; he'd lived through painful times before, and he'd survive this.

Trays fought wild, and that made him dangerous. He had his own style, which he had learned growing up on Poseidon, and Troy was having a hard time finding a pattern, some little bit of body language that Trays had that telegraphed the blow. Troy thought he spotted an opening, and swung, realizing a micron too late that he had only set himself up. Trays sidestepped the punch easily, and brought his outside leg up in a snap-kick, catching Troy full in the stomach.

The air *whooooshed!* out of Troy's lungs in an explosive exhalation, but he refused to go down. Instead, he lurched forward and grabbed Trays, pinning his arms and standing too close for him to use his legs again. That made no difference to Trays; he simply snapped his head forward, bashing Troy's nose with his forehead. What kind of scraps did Trays get into on Poseidon, where he learned to fight like this?

Dalton, watching this display of territory and testosterone, let fly an inarticulate cry of anger, turned on her heel, and ran from the lounge.

By this time, the other pilots had pulled Troy and Trays apart, although they were finding it somewhat more difficult to keep them that way. Each combatant surged forward against the hands that gripped him, wanting only to finish decisively the battle they had begun. Troy, jostled around by the Warriors holding him back, saw Dalton just as she left the ODOC.

"Just calm down," Jolly said, gripping Troy's shoulders. "She's gone, you don't have to prove anything to anyone now."

This gave Troy's struggles to break free a renewed strength, and he shook himself loose. He pelted after Dalton, pushing past the curious bystanders who blocked his way, and caught up with her out in the main concourse, in front of the restaurant.

"Didn't you hear me calling you?" he asked, touching her on the inside of her elbow.

"Just who the frack do you think you are?" she spat, rounding on him so viciously that Troy found himself taking an involuntary step backward. "You don't own me! Nobody owns me! So you can just take your jealousy and stuff it up your exhaust baffle!"

Troy blinked, found his own anger rising. "Well, forgive me if I misunderstood," he said, "but for some reason, I had the impression you were interested in me. After all, you were the one to come onto me, remember, so what was I supposed to think?" A fine, crimson spume of blood flew from his lips as he spoke.

"That doesn't mean we're sealed," Dalton said, folding her arms across her chest. "I'll live my own life, without your approval, and right now, I have a father who's dying and I don't need you interfering with who I hang out with and how I deal with my grief!"

"How long has this . . . have you two. . . ?" Troy stammered. He wasn't sure he really wanted to know.

"Does it matter? Either one?" she asked, her head bowed, her chin touching her collar bone, her hair framing her face.

She blinked back a tear, and for a moment, all Troy could think about was Dalton, and how much pain she was in, and how much he wished he could take some of it for her. He reached to touch her face, and she slapped his hand away.

"Just—stay away from me," she said, and stalked off, leaving Troy to wonder just when his life had slipped so far out of control.

Starbuck slept; it seemed funny to think a man who had been in a coma for more than three weeks would want to sleep, but he was ravenous for it and wouldn't have needed the tranks at all if Dr. Wilker had just waited a few more microns.

Cassiopeia stood watch beside Starbuck's med-berth.

"They always look so cute when they're sleeping," Athena said from behind Cassie.

"Yeah, but then they wake up and ruin it all," Cassie answered without turning.

Athena stepped closer to the med-berth, standing almost shoulder-to-shoulder with Cassiopeia. They pretended to watch Starbuck for a length of time, neither wanting to be the first to speak what was really on her mind. "A micron of your time, Cassiopeia?" Athena asked at last.

Cassie nodded. "Of course," she said. *I've been expecting this, anyway.*

She led Athena out of the med unit and into the small waiting hall, empty now, and dimly lighted. Cassie dropped some cubits into a beverage dispensing unit, pressed a button. A cup dropped and a pre-measured amount of some unidentifiable manner of liquid poured itself into the cup. Cassie removed the first one, handed it to Athena, fed another round of cubits into the unit, took a second cup for herself. They drank their beverages quietly, the silence becoming a weight neither would be able to grapple with much longer.

Athena had wanted to speak with Cassie, get certain subjects out into the open, and now, she wasn't sure how to begin. The two women had always had a caustic, adversarial relationship from the time they met and began to compete for Starbuck's attentions.

"I know we rarely speak to each other," Athena began; she still wasn't sure what, exactly, she wanted to say, but hoped she might be able to define their perimeter and then work her way inward, toward the heart of the thing. "Then, when Starbuck was injured . . . I thought this conversation would be a moot point, at best, but obviously, things have changed now . . . again," she added, and laughed a little.

"Yes, that's Starbuck," Cassie agreed. "Unpredictable, even when he's comatose." She did not want to be the first to say what they both knew Athena was angling toward.

She finished her drink and pitched her cup into the recycling bin. "You've never shared anything with me before," Cassie pointed out. "Never tried to reach out as long as we've known each other. So—pardon my directness—why start now?"

Athena stared into her half-empty cup, as if the answer might be found floating there, but all she saw was her own small reflection looking back at her, and neither of them seemed to have an answer.

"When I first met you," Athena began, surprised to hear the sound of her own voice; she hadn't really known what she was going to say. "I thought you were a cheap. . ." She caught herself before she could finish, but it didn't matter. They both knew what she meant: *Being a socialator and all.*

"Well, anyway, what I mean is," Athena continued, face lowered, hoping it hid her ruddy cheeks, "you've worked really hard, and look what all you've accomplished. You're almost a doctor now. A *doctor,*" she repeated, almost in awe. Cassiopeia was becoming so much more than Athena could ever have envisioned for her, becoming invaluable to the *Galactica.*

It surprised Athena to hear herself admit it, but she was actually coming to admire Cassie. What an uncertain world they lived in. If ever Athena needed a reminder of that, this was it.

"I've had to study and work hard all my life," Athena confessed. "Gods know, Adama was a great man, but he expected his children to surpass him. How do you surpass a legend? And I don't know if I've ever completely proved how capable I really am. So I guess it was really hard to see Starbuck falling for, well, for . . ."

"For someone like me?" Cassie finished, a smile of bemusement on her face.

Athena laughed, despite herself. "You're not going to make this easy, are you? Yes, for someone like you. I felt like I had to work hard for everything I accomplished, for every bit of recognition I got, and then, you just breeze in and make Starbuck fall for you."

It was Cassiopeia's turn to laugh now. "It's one thing to make Starbuck fall for you," she said; "it's something else trying to keep him."

"Well, be that as it may," Athena said, setting her cup aside on the small table top beside the beverage unit, "I was unfair to you. I made it my personal mission to undermine you and your integrity and . . . I'm sorry. I had no idea who you really were and I'm sorry.

"I hope we can be friends," Athena continued. "I really don't have any close friends, you know. Everybody's afraid to get too close to Adama's daughter."

Whatever it was Cassiopeia might have been expecting Athena to say, this was not it. For a moment, she had no idea how to respond. Her thoughts were tripping all over themselves, so she pushed reason aside and let her emotions take the stage. She was genuinely touched by Athena's honesty and the fact that she had taken that first, difficult step toward reconciliation.

Before she knew she was going to do it, Cassie placed her hand on the back of Athena's, resting lightly against the edge of the small table. The gesture surprised Athena, but she made no effort to pull away.

"Thank you," Cassie said, and broke into a warm smile. "And, I'd like to be friends, too."

Athena squeezed Cassiopeia's hand in hers, quick and brief. She was learned in many things, but simple human friendships were new territory to Athena, and she was unsure how to proceed from this point. She did not make it easy to get to know her, but then, she really didn't know how. The map of the human heart is not charted on any holocube; in that territory, we're all just blind explorers.

"It's all right," Cassie continued, sensing what this talk was really about, or at least, what it started out being about. "I know how you feel about Starbuck. I will always love him, and I will always lust after him, but I cannot allow myself to go through all that again. It isn't healthy for me."

She took Athena's hands in hers, as if she were passing on some torch, and said, "Go to him. Go, with my blessings. I only hope you have better luck than I did." And, since they were being honest, she added, "Thank you . . . for coming to me first. That shows you respect me . . . even if you don't like me very much."

Athena said, "You need to understand how I was raised. Who my father was—"

"Doesn't work," Cassie told her. "Adama never looked down on me. Apollo never has."

Athena nodded. "That wasn't really quite what I meant. Adama raised us both to be our best, and Apollo *is*, whether he realizes it or not. But to be the best means you get what you go after, and I went after Starbuck and you got him." She sighed, and drained her drink. Being honest was thirsty work. "It all seemed so easy for you. All the men, all the attention, all the friends—"

"You've had men. You have friends."

"I have acquaintances," Athena corrected her. "Gods, how I wish I could just, I don't know, free myself from Adama's upbringing just long enough to . . . I don't know . . . dance on the table-tops, or drink until I pass out. . . ."

Cassie laughed at the idea of Athena doing either one of these things. "There, you see?" Athena said, jabbing her with her finger. "That's my point. Even the idea of Adama's daughter doing something like that is just ridiculous, isn't it? But you—"

"Hold up there," Cassie said, putting up her hand, palm to Athena. "Little Cassiopeia hasn't danced on tables in a long, long time."

"But you *did,*" Athena said. "You weren't afraid to do that. You weren't afraid what anyone thought of you."

"Of course I worried what people thought of me," she said, softly. "That's why I did it. They might not have liked me, otherwise. And then, I realized they liked me all right, but for all the wrong reasons. That's when I decided to start pulling my life together."

"You've done well," Athena told her. "I just wish . . . I could be a little more like you."

"So, what's stopping you?" Cassie shrugged.

"My father —"

"Your father, sweetheart, is dead," Cassie said, a touch sternly. She was trying to get Athena to cut through some felgercarb. "Sorry to be so blunt, but . . . frack! Get over it! Start doing what makes you *happy.* Adama wouldn't begrudge you that, I'm sure of it."

Athena hugged herself, head lowered. "It isn't that easy."

"What is? Hell, even I'm not, any more," Athena looked at her, and Cassie had to laugh at the expression on her face. "It's a joke . . . it's okay to laugh."

Athena did, a trifle hesitantly, but it was a start.

"Well, whoever would have thought this day would come?" Cassie commented. "Commander's Adama's snooty daughter and the ex-socialator, sharing a drink and a laugh."

Athena checked her cup, found it empty, but upended it anyway, taking what little bit of liquid still clung to the bottom and sides, and wiped the corner of her mouth with the backs of her knuckles. "I appreciate the frank talk," she said, "but if you ever call me snooty again, I'll kick your frackin' ass."

Cassie looked at her, mouth agape, afraid she had, perhaps, been a little too honest and frank for her own good. And then, Athena laughed and placed her hand on Cassie's shoulder. "It's a joke . . . it's okay to laugh," she assured her.

Cassie laughed and hugged Athena. They made a little more small-talk, and then, Cassie said she had to get back to the med-unit. Athena nodded, said she understood and promised they'd talk again, real soon. Cassie watched her go, and wondered how long it would be before Athena was back, crying for a different reason.

"You're going to need all the luck you can get," she said softly, and returned to work.

5

KIRASOLIA.

It had taken weeks of traveling, weeks filled with bickering and dissension, but at last, the northern hemisphere of the mythical planet loomed into view. Athena and Tigh stood on the bridge of the *Galactica,* watching silently as the planet filled the great forward flatscreen. There was cloud cover; somewhere over Kirasolia's equator, an ocean storm was battering the injured coastline. Flashes of lightning stutter-pulsed at the membranous edges black-gray clouds, and gale-force winds blew great troughs in the face of the sea.

"Gods of Kobol be praised," Apollo said softly. Tigh and Athena had been so intent upon their planetary approach they had not noticed Apollo as he joined them on the bridge.

He stepped nearer the flatscreen, approaching the projected image of the giant planet with awe and reverence. The holocube had been right; Kirasolia existed. There was, at last, proof of the Thirteenth Tribe. Apollo placed his palm against the screen, and tropical lightning on the surface of Kirasolia seemed to leap and dance beneath his hand, as if he controlled the very elements.

"Send a scout team, scan for minerals, life forms; confirm a breathable atmosphere." Apollo said, unable to take his eyes away from their possible salvation. He also knew it was the source of his possible downfall, for soon he and Cain would present their vastly differing ideologies to the Quorum. But for the moment, he could only smile, and offer a silent prayer of thanks to the Lords of Kobol and his father's spirit for bringing them to this place.

Word was instantly relayed from Omega through Rigel to Dalton, Boomer, Jolly, and Troy, to prepare for immediate launch.

Troy scrambled for his Viper, but he couldn't help but notice Dalton, standing near Trays' ship, talking with him.

He couldn't hear what was being said, but from the look on their faces, it wouldn't take much imagination to guess. Dalton slipped her arms around his neck, standing on the ball of one foot to reach his mouth, her other leg canted at a ninety-degree angle, and kissed Trays.

That used to be me, Troy thought, feeling his face burn.

"Suck face later," he yelled at Dalton, purposely spoiling her moment. But what was one moment when she clearly had countless others with this new man? "We have an order, let's do it."

Trays said something that made Dalton laugh, and gave her another quick kiss on the cheek. She was running across the great, open floor, heading for her Viper as Troy climbed into the cockpit of his own. They had flown a Viper Duet before, had surrendered to one another's rhythms and become one, now that seemed a lifetime ago. It was almost inconceivable to him they had ever been that close, when now the sight of her was a brutal dagger stab to his heart. He couldn't imagine ever being that close to her again, and he felt *lost.*

Still, he watched her safely into her own ship before he sealed the hatch of his own.

"Now who's holding up the show?" Dalton's voice sounded tinny in Troy's helmet's comm-unit. "Shake your pogees and let's go."

Troy fitted his Warrior's helm into place and sealed it. A helm was open at the face until it was donned, at which time a barely visible energy shield would activate, sealing the face and neck breach. The sealed helm also housed a rebreather/filter function, allowing its wearer to breathe normally in any environment containing at least a trace of oxygen.

Forward, the launch aperture had irised open and Vipers were already hurtling down the long, lighted launch tube. Troy loved the building g-forces that pressed him back into his seat, because they meant flight, and freedom, and infinite possibilites.

Troy's Viper blasted from the *Galactica's* launch bay and began its descent toward Kirasolia. The other ships followed, in formation.

A constant stream of data, or info-scroll, flooded across Troy's helm, but he ignored most of it. It was important to know what to ignore and what to pay attention to: paying attention to all of that data could make a pilot lose concentration on the immediate matters.

He looked, instead, at the shimmering holomap of Kirasolia, then up through the thermal ranges; the surface of the planet was incredibly hot, and seemed to be a constant roil of electrical storms. On the holo-map, a small, clear opening appeared in the planet's bristling atmosphere.

Troy set his Viper's coordinates and made his way toward the eye of the storm.

The atmospheric turbulence was terrible, and Troy had to grip the navi-helm with both hands to keep the shimmying Viper from losing control. "Brace yourselves for a rough ride," he warned the other pilots trailing him.

He might have said more, but the Viper had suddenly taken on all the aerodynamic qualities of a flung stone, and he fought hard against the navi-helm, feeling himself being thrown from side to side in the cramped little cockpit, his head banging sharply against the canopy. He yiped his pain, and hoped the others hadn't heard his outcry. "Everybody all right?" he asked over his comm-link. A volley of grunted affirmatives followed, and he immediately refocused on cutting his way through the turbulent atmosphere. The muscles in his arms were as hard and stiff as marble, and he gripped the stick as if a galvanizing current of electricity kept him frozen there.

And then, his Viper was below the worst of the buffeting winds and Troy almost over-compensated as control returned to him. The other ships blasted through the eye of the storm and beneath the slate-gray clouds. Below the storm, the cyclonic winds were powerful, but the little Vipers had been built to withstand explosive stresses.

"Can we send a narrow-beam transmission back to the *Galactica?*" Troy asked Boomer over his comm-link. "Let them know we've made planetfall?"

Boomer's voice crackled in Troy's helm, shredded by the high concentration of ions in the atmosphere. "Not through this weather," Troy managed to make out. "They'll just have to wait for it. Nobody fan out too far," Boomer cautioned. "If we lose you in this, I can't guarantee we'll be able to find your homing signal."

Troy checked his external sensors. Temperature on the planet seemed to be hovering around one hundred degrees Celsius. This explained the terrible storms—the heat would only agitate the atmosphere, forcing it to erupt in violent electrical storms. Troy had a feeling there hadn't been an actual rainfall on Kirasolia in quite some time; if any moisture ever fell, it would quickly evaporate before it ever struck the ground, boiled away by the stiflingly hot air.

Off to his starboard side, Troy saw a great bolt of lightning spike downward from the heavens, just missing Dalton's Viper. The backwash of the charged atmosphere made her ship shudder spastically, and Troy cursed loudly. "Save your concern," Dalton answered across the staticky comm-link. "I'm good."

"Forgive me for caring," Troy muttered in hurt and disgust.

The landscape of Kirasolia was rough and craggy, heat-blasted earth and jagged rock. The bits of flora that survived the brutal temperatures were as harsh as the planet that had spawned it. Great, twisted plants, brown as mud, thrust their way up from the ground; they were covered with spikes and veiny growths, as if there were some predator this natural defense kept at bay. If that were true, Troy decided right then he didn't want to see the fauna that fed upon the plant life.

The horizon rolled on into darkness; lightning struck at the rim of the world and illuminated the distance in fitful, angry bursts. But even from here, the Warriors could see the unrelieved, blighted landscape, just rocks and dirt, an endless carpeting of ruin.

"One pass to get our readings," Boomer's voice crackled, fading with a pulse of white noise, then roaring back stronger and louder. "And then, we head back. Understood?"

No one argued.

"How is this possible?"

Apollo looked at the report the survey team had filed just moments ago, bewilderment etched on his features. If there had ever been life on Kirasolia, it either did not survive or it had moved on to a less-hostile world. There were no Tylium deposits; even the atmosphere was unbreathable. He shook his head. The long-range scanners had given them cause for hope, but the survey team's report would thoroughly dash it.

He tugged at his lower lip, pinching it between his thumb and forefinger.

The report was suddenly slapped from Apollo's hand, the papers fluttering and see-sawing to the floor. Apollo looked up, staring into Cain's nearly-apoplectic face.

"Are you happy now?" he thundered. "Now that you've gambled everything on a fairy-story and doomed the fleet?"

"Commander, this is not the time—" Apollo began, stiffly.

"You are correct, Apollo," Cain agreed. "The time was earlier, when we might at least have stocked up on reserves of Tylium from one of Xeric's many moons. It was a terrible error to travel such a great distance without taking on stores of fuel."

Apollo sighed wearily. This argument again? "Weren't you there?" he asked. "Perhaps I saw something you didn't, such as the arrival of three Cylon basestars."

Cain nodded, his lips slicked back in a feral snarl. "I saw them, and instead of fighting them off until we could take on supplies, you turned tail and ran. *That,* I wish I hadn't seen."

"Our fleet would have been annihilated!" Apollo argued. "We were already suffering heavy damages; to take on three basestars would have been suicidal!"

The older man turned toward the flatscreen, still projecting the image of Kirasolia. Apollo followed his gaze; the planet didn't seem as much like salvation as it did just a few centons earlier. It seemed like a bad dream. It seemed like someone's really bad idea of an ancient Kobollian joke. If this planet was inhospitable, were any of the planets on the holocube habitable?

"There would have been casualties," Cain agreed. "But you have to learn the difference between suicide and acceptable losses, boy, or you'll never be a good commander. The risk was worth taking, because now we are left here without resources and not enough fuel to reach another planet.

"You've brought us a long way, just to die," Cain concluded, his words like a punch to the gut.

Apollo gritted his teeth, biting back the caustic reply that wanted to fly from his tongue, and looked from Athena to Tigh. They said nothing, but their expressions seemed to indicate they were in agreement with Cain. There was no point in arguing his case now; there would be a more formal time and place for that, and soon, he knew.

"This fleet cannot afford to make any further mistakes," Cain warned, as if he were some one-time, wild-eyed prophet shouting down fire and judgement from some mountaintop. "This fleet needs a strong leader, capable of making hard decisions, more experienced decisions. You mark my words, Apollo: I will do everything in my power to see you removed as supreme commander of the fleet, do you hear me?"

Apollo waved a hand as if to dismiss this argument, and walked from the bridge. He squared his shoulders and set his jaw; he didn't want this to be viewed as a retreat, merely a timely withdrawal. Any good commander knew the difference.

"I will have you removed!" Cain shouted after him.

The old man turned to face Athena and Tigh, his eyes bright and twinkling. It was the light of victory, and Tigh and Athena were beginning to wonder if, despite their love and support for Apollo, perhaps Commander Cain had been right, all along.

In his quarters, Apollo closed the door behind him, Gar'Tokk standing faithful vigil on the other side. The Noman had seen Apollo's confrontation with Cain on the bridge, but said nothing. It was not his place; but Apollo supposed Gar'Tokk had his opinions about how to handle this. Presumably, all of those solutions entailed eviscerating Cain, or casting him adrift in shoreless space in a Viper with no guidance system or navi-hilt.

Apollo studied the holocube he kept in his chambers, unable to understand how things had gone so wrong. If the Thirteenth Tribe had ever stopped at Kirasolia, what had they found? Surely not this. Over time, the planet's temperature must have risen, for whatever reason. If that much had changed on this planet, would the others be similarly transformed? There was no way to know, that was the hell of it. Perhaps it was time to put aside the myths of the past and move on, before Cain could take it away from him. That was what logic told him, anyway, but he still heard another voice, the inner voice that said *Don't give up*. But how much of that was real, and how much of that was his own battered and dented pride, not wanting to accept defeat? He had always felt he had much to live up to, being Adama's son, and he was right about that; Adama was a hard man to replace. Apollo's mistake was in trying to *be* his father, instead of his own man. He was at war with everyone around him, but more than that, he was at war with himself.

The commander activated his S-cube, linking his quarters with the science lab. A holographic projection of Dr. Salik appeared before him.

"Commander," Salik said, pleasantly surprised. He had been

sequestered away in his lab, immersed in his work, and had not heard the bad news from the survey team, but Apollo knew it would not be long before the entire fleet knew of his failure. Cain would see to that. It was the first step in undermining Apollo's command. It was a classic battle strategy: divide and conquer. If he did not want to lose his command and bring shame to Adama's memory he would have to act soon, and decisively. He could afford to *re*act no longer.

"Doctor Salik," Apollo greeted him, no trace of the anxiety he felt in his voice. "Have you been able to determine anything about the QSE?"

Salik nodded, smiling at the S-cube. "The device seems to have a limited capacity to bend space, with some modifications," he said. "I'm ready to proceed, pending your orders."

"What about the coordinates Baltar gave us?" Apollo asked, his eyes straying to the holocube. The nearest habitable planet was far behind them; after Kirasolia, what next?

"I've tried inputting the coordinates and it seems that the device registers a positive response to them," Salik reported. "But what that means, I have no way of knowing, as yet."

It meant they weren't dead yet, Apollo supposed. It meant things were so desperate, he was considering trusting the worst traitor the human race had ever known. But was he doing it to save the fleet or to preserve his own position as its supreme commander? Both logic *and* inner vision told him not to trust Baltar, but there was a *third* voice, it seemed, that superseded both of these and told him to see it through. He closed his eyes and the world seemed to move around him, and he intuited that this was the true nature of events at the moment.

After a long moment of contemplation, Apollo opened his eyes, and Salik could see the steely resolve in them. "Finish the modifications," he ordered. "I'll contact all the ship crews and have them input the modifications on all the fleet.

I want us to be prepared to use it, if necessary."

Boomer had trained them all.

Starbuck, Apollo, Athena, Jolly, Sheba, those who had distinguished themselves in the first wave of cadets; Dalton and Troy in the last batch of sky-jockeys. And now, Boomer, along with Sheba and Jolly, were training the newest wave of cadets. He would always say they all had the potential for greatness within them, and that was true enough. They all did. The problem was, not all of them would reach deep down inside him- or herself to find that core of burning gold. But those who could, and did, well, they did great things, indeed.

The last clash with the Cylons and Chitain had diminished the ranks of the Warriors greatly, and Boomer felt the pressure to raise them back up to fighting strength as quickly as possible. He walked through the rows of cadets, shaking his head. Some were really too old and past their prime to be pilots; others were little more than children, so young, so small, that their feet barely reached the floor of the Viper when they sat in the pilot's seat, but what choice did Boomer have? He had always trained his cadets hard; now, he pushed these new cadets to the breaking point, and past it.

Still, it was Sheba who effortlessly earned the respect of the new recruits; the females all respected her, while the males were all a little intimidated by her piloting skills and her ability to outdrink most men. She was showing them a maneuver on the flight sim, but their attentions were torn between Sheba, and Starbuck, who was also practicing on one of the sims. He knew he was being watched, and decided to put on a good show for the cadets. He didn't have to try hard; his easy grace at the navi-hilt, his coolness under fire, the way he treated his Viper as an extension of himself, and the fact that he was a legend among pilots, second only to Apollo, didn't hurt. He was a man who had nearly died and come back, good as ever. He was laughing, he was joking. He was Starbuck.

Sheba cleared her throat, a little loudly, and even Starbuck looked up at her. She stood with her hands on her hips, expecting their full attention. "You'd better pay attention to what Sheba has to tell you," Starbuck warned them. "You really don't want to get on her bad side."

"Neither do you," Sheba told Starbuck. He grinned and went back to his training. Even so, the cadets' eyes drifted his way, occasionally.

Nearby, Dalton was talking with Trays, while Troy could only stand apart and watch. He shook his head, not able to understand her recent attitude change; or had this always been Dalton? Had he just been in love with a facade? He didn't want to think that was so, but he was no longer certain. It was one thing for her to fall in love with someone else; but to treat Troy so shabbily as a result of that, to make him miserable, was, he felt, inexcusable.

Dalton laughed, and snapped Troy out of his reverie. She touched Trays' handsome face, and Troy thought again how much like Starbuck this new, arrogant pilot was. Was Dalton trying to work through her ambivalent feelings for her father by dating a younger version of him? Troy supposed it was possible; no one goes through life without acquiring some scars, and he was beginning to wonder just how badly scarred Dalton was, and if she were subconsciously looking for someone who would win her heart and then break it. How better to prove to herself she was unworthy of being loved than by loving a man who would, in time, reject her?

She laughed again, and glanced over Troy's way to see if he was watching, but he had already turned away. It was a cry for help, a plea to be loved anyway, but Troy was blinded by the pain his own wounded pride. *Fine,* he thought, *I've been thrown out of better lives than yours.*

"Everything all right?"

Troy looked up; he had almost bumped into Apollo.

"What do you know about women?" Troy asked.

Apollo turned to look for Dalton and found her, still talking with Trays. "Oh," he said. Hadn't he been here himself?

He thought so. The territory looked pretty familiar.

"Yeah," Troy agreed. "Oh."

"She's going through a hard time now, Troy," Apollo said. "And it's probably going to get harder for her before it gets better."

"Then why doesn't she let me in instead of shutting me out?"

"Some people aren't very good at accepting love," he answered. "You'd think there's nothing to it, giving love and taking love, but some people just . . . *can't*."

"What do you do with people like that?"

Apollo shrugged. "Love 'em anyway."

After a moment, Tray laughed, and Apollo clapped him on the shoulder. "If you need to talk," he said, "I'll be in my quarters later . . . come on by."

"I'll do that," the boy promised, and left the training area with a backward glance in Dalton's direction. She didn't notice he had gone, or at least, pretended not to. Either way, Troy's pain was the same.

"Apollo!" Boomer called, hand raised in greeting. The commander smiled warmly and joined Boomer and Sheba while the cadets took a welcome break from their rigorous training.

"How do the new recruits look?" Apollo asked, scanning the motley assemblage of faces and bodies.

"Any Starbucks, you mean?" Boomer joked. He shook his head. "I'd even settle for an Apollo."

"Oh, you would, would you?" the commander laughed easily. It was good-natured ribbing between two old friends who deeply respected one another. It had been a while since Apollo had been able to laugh. "I hope you didn't call me down here just to insult me."

"I could insult you anywhere," Boomer said, dismissively. "But we have a surprise for you."

Apollo couldn't read anything in Boomer's face, so he looked to Sheba. She betrayed the surprise with an involuntary flicker of her eyes in the direction of a Viper, and Apollo turned to look. As he did, a grubby, bearded old tech stepped out of his place of concealment behind the fighter. Before he could react, the older man closed the distance between himself and Apollo and grabbed the commander in a bear hug, lifting him up off the ground and spinning him around.

"Do you remember me, Apollo?" the big man asked, laughing.

He set Apollo down once more, but seemed ready to scoop him up in powerful arms at the moment of recognition. Apollo stared at him for a moment, studying his face, subtracting years and grime, and his eyes widened with the shock of realization. "Bo jay?" he asked, incredulously. "Is that really you?"

The other man laughed, rich and deep, and slapped the Commander on the shoulder. "That's *me,* you old war daggit!" he said.

Apollo could scarcely credit it. He said, "I haven't seen you since you were lost on that reconnaissance mission with Jinx. Where have you been hiding all this time?"

"Well, that's a good question," Bo jay allowed. "I survived, but I lost my memory from a head injury and was lost on some god-forsaken planet, until I was found by a patrol sent out by my old Commander, Cain."

"You've been with Cain all this time?" Apollo asked.

"Just like the old days," Bo jay said. "But I sure did miss flying your ass off."

Apollo laughed. "Not on your best day," he said, amiably.

Bo jay pulled a pained face. "Now who's lost his memory?" the old tech asked.

The dead are coming back with alarming regularity, Apollo thought, and shook his head. "Didn't anyone recognize you?"

"Can't say as they did," Bo jay replied. "I looked different by then. Even you didn't recognize me, right off, did you?"

That was true enough; Apollo didn't recognize him because, as far as Apollo knew, Bo jay was dead. Being presumed dead was a very good disguise.

"They put me to work in the mines and, believe it or not, another accident to my head from a cave-in helped me regain my identity just as you were all getting ready to leave," Bo jay continued. "So, here I am, in all my glory." He stood with his arms spread at his sides, revealing his shabby glory. His coveralls were streaked with grime and grease, and they ill-fitted a man of Bo jay's size, but there *was* a glory to this man, all the same.

"Why are you working as a tech?"

Bo jay's face soured and he dismissed it with a wave of his oil-smeared hand. "They don't think I can still fly. But let me tell ya, Apollo, I can fly with the best of them." He folded his arms across his chest, stood closer to the commander and nodded in the direction of the new cadets. "These young recruits—so arrogant," he said, and curled his lip, as if even speaking of them left a bitter taste. "They think they're Warriors, but they don't know what that word means. Not really. You put me back in the cockpit and I'll show these buggers a thing or two."

Apollo put his hand on the old man's shoulder and squeezed. "I wouldn't worry about it, Bo jay. The way things are going, you may well get your chance before long."

"Ahh, that's music to an old man's ears, Apollo," Bo jay said. "By the way, how's Starbuck doing?"

Apollo thought about that for a moment, and realized he didn't know what to say. He needn't have worried, for Bo jay was called back to work to finish repairing a Viper before Apollo could answer. "My adoring public," Bo jay joked.

"I'll meet you later and we can catch up."

He hurried across the bay and climbed back up onto the Viper's wing, where he had left open an access panel to check a faulty relay circuit.

Trays and a group of his friends stood around, watching Bo jay scramble. The idea of an elder being subservient to them was enormously amusing, and they laughed as he fussed over the circuit boards. "Hurry it up, old timer," Trays commanded, imperiously. "I have to fly patrol, and I can't do it with you on my wing."

Apollo had moved closer to the group during all this and grabbed Trays' flight suit. He bunched it up in his fist and hauled the boy closer, until he was mere centimetrons from his face. "The old man could make you eat his vapor trail," Apollo said, and turned to face the others who stood watching. "I want you all to listen to me. Boomer and Sheba can teach you to be pilots, but they can't teach you respect. You think being a Warrior makes you special, and it does, but only if you learn to respect and honor each other, regardless of your age and ability.

"Our best pilots have given their lives so that you might be here today, and believe me when I tell you that, at this juncture, you don't hold a candle to those pilots or my good friend, Bo jay."

Bo jay stood on the wing of the Viper, embarrassed to be the center of attention . . . *this* sort of attention, anyway, said, "Commander, it's all right, I'm sure they didn't mean—"

"I know what they meant, Bo jay," Apollo told his friend without looking back. "You should all feel privileged to fly with him or any of the other experienced pilots who have survived this long only because of their incredible skill and courage. If I catch any of you disrespecting your fellow Warriors again, I will personally kick your ass."

"Better hurry," Trays said, pulling free of Apollo's grip; it was only because Apollo allowed him to. "Way I hear it, you'll be out of a job soon."

Dalton scowled at Trays, and whispered loud enough that everyone could hear, "You should listen to him. Apollo is still one of the best pilots in the fleet, along with Starbuck, Sheba and Boomer."

Trays dismissed her with a sneer. "And I'm telling you, the older pilots can't fly worth beans any more, and with the loss of so many Warriors, we'll finally get our chance to see some action and show everyone how good we are. It's our time."

Troy had returned to the bay to suit up for his patrol and had overheard most of the exchange. "You'd better watch your step, hotshot," Troy warned. "The only thing you'll get your chance at is time in the brig, for insubordination."

Dalton pressed her fingertips to her temples and squeezed her eyes shut. "Not this again," she muttered. "I can't stand this."

You never know what you can stand until you have to, Troy thought, and slung himself into the small cockpit. Trays and Dalton moved off to their respective Vipers, but Trays took time enough to cast a smirk back over his shoulder at Apollo before he climbed into his own Viper.

Boomer shook his head and looked apologetically at Apollo. "Many of the younger pilots are hard to control, due to having lost their parents at a young age. They never had any discipline or a proper upbringing."

"They won't find a better father figure than you," Apollo told Boomer, and he meant it.

Sheba agreed. "They've also had to replace their more experienced counterparts due to injuries and attrition before they're properly trained," she added.

"That may be," Apollo said, and sighed. "Unfortunately, we don't have any other options I'm aware of. All we can do is push them to their limits during their training, and hope for the best."

"You hope, and I'll push," Boomer offered, and gave his former cadet a thumbs-up sign. Apollo smiled wanly; they both knew they were going to have to carry a heavy load and set an example for this next generation of pilots and Warriors if the fleet were to have any hope of survival.

"It's a deal," Apollo said.

He glanced over at Starbuck, still seated in one of the flight sims. He had watched Apollo's confrontation with the the new cadets, ready to jump in, if it looked necessary, but his old buddy had handled it, and so he went back to his retraining.

"How's he doing?" Apollo asked Boomer. "Seriously."

"Seriously? He's doing amazingly well," Boomer said. "He doesn't seem to have lost a step and he's biting at the bit to fly again."

They watched Starbuck for a while; the fluidity of movement was still there. When he was in the cockpit, Starbuck was like some weird hybrid of man and Viper, but the concentration on his face . . . that was something different, wasn't it? Apollo worried it wasn't quite as easy for Starbuck as he tried to make it seem, at least when he knew they were watching him. Unaware of their scrutiny, Starbuck had let the mask slip a little, and Apollo wasn't sure he liked what he saw beneath the disguise.

"What does his doctor say?"

"The same thing you're thinking," Boomer said. Apollo looked surprised, but supposed Boomer knew him as well as almost anyone. "He's concerned, and thinks it may be premature, and that Starbuck needs more time to heal. Well, that *is* what you were thinking, isn't it?" Apollo smiled crookedly. "Can you guess my weight, too?" he joked.

Boomer shrugged and nodded toward Sheba. "I can't, but she probably could," he said. "Why, Commander, are you blushing?"

"I have a pocketful of cubits," Apollo told Starbuck, leaning against the flight sim. "So you can ride this thing all day, if you want."

Starbuck hadn't heard him approach, and his face was still etched with the same serious concentration Apollo had seen moments earlier from across the bay. He looked up, focused, and favored Apollo with a big smile as if the grim determination his friend had seen had never been there at all. He could almost believe it . . . *almost.*

"How are you doing?" Apollo asked. "No felgercarb."

"No felgercarb, I'm doing great," Starbuck anwered. His face was still a little flushed, and rivulets of perspiration ran down his brow, but otherwise, he looked as well as he claimed. Perhaps they were all being overly-cautious, Apollo thought. Or perhaps Starbuck just wasn't being cautious enough. "I'm ready if you need me," he said. "And with the loss of so many pilots, you're going to need all the help you can get."

"You're right about that, Starbuck," Apollo agreed. "But you just take it easy for now. I don't want to lose you again."

You're my closest ally and my dearest friend, Apollo thought. He would very shortly regret not having said this to Starbuck. But they were close friends, closer than some brothers, and even if Apollo didn't say these words, he knew Starbuck sensed them.

"You can't blame yourself for what happened," Starbuck told him. "With me and the explosion. And whatever else may happen . . . you understand me?"

Apollo didn't. Not at all. But he was a little frightened, at that moment, for his friend.

"Things happen. Things *have* to happen in certain ways, even if we don't know why." Starbuck finished, seemed a little shaken by the things he had just said, as if he were merely the medium, not the message. And then, because he *was* Starbuck, talk quickly turned to women. "I'm at a crossroads," he said. "There's someone who would like to get serious with me—"

"Gods help her," Apollo answered automatically. He didn't know the special someone was his own sister. "Gods help anyone who wants to get serious with you."

"You don't think I can do it? Settle down with just one woman?" Starbuck asked, a little crestfallen by Apollo's blunt appraisal.

Apollo chuckled, gave Starbuck a playful pop on the shoulder. "You're a great guy, a great friend, and there's no one I'd want more than you covering my ass in a fight, but, let's be honest—I wouldn't want you dating *my* sister."

"No," Starbuck agreed, softly. "Certainly wouldn't want that." He forced a smile to his face, and he was Starbuck once more, the rogue whom no one could hurt because no one ever got close enough. "I don't know what I was thinking, getting serious with one woman . . . must have been the head injury and near-death experience talking."

"Must have been," Apollo agreed, and confessed, "I felt so help-less, just watching you. Not being able to help when you were comatose."

Starbuck glanced up from the flight sim. "You helped," he said. "I knew you were there."

"You did?"

"Of course. You've always been there for me. And I'm here for you, Apollo," Starbuck said, with great gravity. "You know that, right?"

"Of course I know—"

"Even the Lords of Kobol can't take me away." They gripped one another in a Warrior's handshake, and in that moment, Apollo felt a terrible chill slither up his spine and perch at the crown of his skull, as if icy fingers had traced their way up his vertebrae.

Apollo studied his friend's face; this was an odd talk, as if he were saying good-bye and didn't realize it. Before Apollo could pursue it Starbuck's attention was drawn back to the flight sim and the battle with Cylon Raiders he was fighting there.

Apollo backed away, watching Starbuck for a moment or two, then turned away, almost bumping into Sheba. "I just wanted to tell you," she began without preamble, "I'm here for you, too. I know things haven't worked out for us, Apollo, but at the end of the day, I'm still your friend and I always will be."

On an impulse, she kissed him, and hurried away. It was a chaste kiss, so chaste it might not have been there at all. The boom of thrusters broke through Apollo's musings, and he watched Troy's Viper streak down the long launch pad and disappear into the aperture. A moment later, Trays' Viper, followed by Dalton's, sped after him.

Starbuck, hidden inside the flight sim, felt his hands tremble and jitter, unable to grip the navi-hilt. He grabbed one hand with the other, and wrestled them down into his lap, forcing them to quiet. He squeezed his eyes closed, biting his tongue against the cry of pain that kept laddering up and up, until he felt certain his head would simply explode. And, as quickly as it had begun, the attack was over. He sat back in the cockpit mock-up, letting his tense muscles uncoil. A sound of alarm on the sim's audio told him his Viper had just been fragged by a Cylon Raider.

Game over. No problem. He could just re-set the controls and start over. In here, anyway. Out there, he wasn't going to be so fortunate.

He opened his eyes, wincing at the pain, and, with hands that barely shook at all, started the sim once more.

6

WHOEVER SAID *Love is blind* just missed it. In truth, *Love makes us blind* might have been a little closer to it.

Bad enough, Troy thought, to have to fly patrol over a dead planet, but it was worse to have to fly patrol over a dead planet with Trays and Dalton. Their antics together made Troy's stomach clench like a fist ready to strike a solid blow. He supposed others might have felt the same way when it was himself and Dalton, but *this* was just obnoxious.

"You're getting off formation," Troy warned the hotshot new pilot over their helm-link. "Trays—"

"Cool your thrusters," the voice Troy hated crackled back. "You sound just like Apalling."

Troy's face flushed red. "That's Commander Apollo, Trays," he said, through gritted teeth. "Show the man the respect he deserves."

"Lighten up, Boxey," Dalton interjected. *Fine,* Troy thought, *it's going to be like that, is it?*

"I'll show him some respect when he respects my abilities," Trays answered, and let fly a wild, giddy *Whoop!*

He jammed his Viper's navi-hilt forward and his little fighter went into a power-dive toward the face of the storm-wracked planet far below them. Before the Viper could disappear into Kirasolia's roiling atmosphere, Trays put it into a long, graceful backward loop. Troy remembered something Commander Apollo had said to him long ago, when the whole horrible nightmare was just beginning, and Troy was just a kid they all called Boxey: *Fighter ships are no place for boys*. The admonition was right, it was just wasted on the wrong little boy.

"Very impressive," Troy said, peevishly. "Now, cut the felgercarb and get back into formation before– "

And then, Dalton's Viper was tumbling out of formation and bulleting after Trays' ship. The two errant Vipers zig-zagged around one another, like children playing tag. The planet wheeled along beneath the ships, as they wove in and out in opposing arcs, their vapor trails leaving long, fiery streaks in their wake, like the tails of shooting stars.

"Think you're pretty good, don't you?" Dalton asked Trays.

"You think I am, too," he answered smugly.

Troy bit his lower lip; it was like eavesdropping on lovers, and he supposed that's just what he was doing. And then, she was laughing, free and alive, and Troy wondered if he had ever made her laugh like that, and if he would ever again have the chance. He watched them go, playful as daggits, and would have palmed the tear from his eye if it weren't for the shimmering energy screen that enclosed his Warrior's helm.

Troy pushed his Viper to chase after them; they had already disappeared over the slow, graceful curve of the planet's horizon, and he had to thumb the apex pulsar for a little more speed. He felt the hum of the thrusters behind and beneath him, and took some comfort from that. It was like a mindwipe as Troy felt the reassuring vibrations of the powerful engines *thrumm* through his nerves and muscles. At least he could count on his ship.

His Viper was still far above theirs, skimming along the very top of Kirasolia's stratosphere, and so his monitor could see farther over the horizon.

Blip.

Troy glanced down at his scanner, puzzled. What was there to go *blip?*

The starfield consisted of only what a pilot could see through the canopy of his or her Viper, but the laser readout on Troy's helm's face shield gave him a detailed map of the planet and its moons. Whatever his scanner reacted to, it was not there when the survey team had mapped Kirasolia and its satellites just a few cycles earlier.

But coming up over the rise of the planet, Troy could swear he saw a moon—*two* moons, in fact. Only, as he got a little closer and the shadow of the planet no longer obscured the moons, Troy realized just what he was looking at.

"Gods," he whispered.

It was two Cylon warships, shaped like basestars but larger, more heavily armed, and those two idiots were piloting their Vipers straight for them. Did love really make them that blind? Did love make them stupid? But then, he already knew, first hand, the answer to that one.

"Get out of there!" Troy shouted into his comm-link, but he was already too late. He watched as a cluster of Cylon Raiders birthed from the launch bay of the first basestar. They hadn't seen Troy's Viper yet; they were intent on Trays and Dalton.

Troy's heart thudded against his chest like a first beating on a closed door as he watched the first Cylon Raider target Dalton's Viper, and she was still unaware of its presence. Troy locked his firing screen on the Raider and thumbed the turbolaser on his navi-hilt. He watched anxiously as the beams sizzled across the distance and struck the Raider; a moment later, a fiery new star blazed just above the planet, and winked out. He'd saved Dalton; he just wondered if he'd have made such an effort for Trays, and of course knew he would. The question was, would Trays do as much in return?

"Dalton!" he was almost screaming in the comm-link. "You've got Raiders on your tail!"

"Troy, what are y—?"

Troy watched as Dalton's Viper took a tangential hit from Raider lasers, but she was able to slam her navi-hilt hard to the left and avoid the next barrage. The lasers just missed her, but he knew the Raider was already targeting her for another pass, and this time she wouldn't be so lucky.

Trays was arcing his Viper back around, headed straight for the onrushing Raiders that were close to Dalton's ship. He was a lot of things, but Trays was not a coward. Either that, or he was just completely insane. Troy hadn't quite decided which. Troy broadcast a narrow-beam emergency signal back to the *Galactica*, then dropped his fighter into formation above and behind the Cylon Raiders. Between Trays's head-on suicidal rush and Troy's somewhat more classical maneuver, the two Warriors had this phalanx of Raiders locked in a deadly crossfire.

And then, another wave of Raiders blasted from the launch bay of the basestar.

"Prepare to pull out!"

Commander Cain could not credit his ears with the news they brought him. "Pull out?" he repeated Apollo's orders to the fleet. "Did I hear you right? You want us to pull out?"

"This isn't the time for debate, Commander," Apollo reminded him; the sound of klaxons resounded throughout every ship in the fleet.

"There are only two basestars!" Cain roared, incredulously. "We have to stand and fight them! We haven't got the fuel to outrun them! We—"

Apollo silenced the flatscreen, but the giant image of Cain continued to thunder on, without sound. It trans-vid to the rest of the fleet and ordered them to prepare to escape into space.

She's going to make it, she's not going to make it, she's going to make it . . .

These thoughts chased after one another, like a daggit following its own tail, through Troy's mind as he watched Dalton's Viper speed back toward the fleet. The void above Kirasolia was filled with Cylon Raiders, and only the Warriors' superior flight training had kept them alive this long. Trays threaded his Viper in and out between the laser blasts from the attacking ships, running interference for Dalton. Her Viper had been more badly damaged than they had first believed, and her little fighter limped its way along.

The fleet seemed impossibly distant.

All he could think of was Zac.

Apollo watched Dalton's wounded Viper as it fought its way back to the *Galactica's* landing bay, but his mind was twenty yahren in the past, when his brother Zak was in a similar impossible race against Cylon Raiders. History had an awful way of repeating itself, like some old man with a faulty memory, telling the same story, over and over; Apollo prayed the ending this time was happier than the one about Zac.

Suddenly, a fourth, then a fifth, Viper rocketed into view on the monitor, seemingly appearing from out of nowhere.

"Who the frack is that?" Apollo asked of no one in particular.

Tigh shook his head.

Athena gasped but said nothing. She had an idea who it was, but prayed she was wrong.

The fourth Viper strafed the nearest Raider, its resultant fiery blast enveloping the two nearest Cylon fighters. Apollo was on the comm-link already, speaking with the launch bay, but the fighting style had already told him the pilot's identity. "Who's in that ship?" Apollo asked. "I didn't give any orders for Warriors to engage the enemy!"

"Uh, Commander, it appears Captain Starbuck has confiscated a Viper and taken off with Boomer," the communications officer hesitantly replied.

"Damn it," Apollo muttered, and ended the connection.

He glanced at Athena, who was intently watching the scanner. They both knew there was no way Starbuck was going to sit this dance out, no matter what his specific orders might have been, if Dalton's safety was involved. "You aren't ready for this," Athena whispered. "I'm not ready to lose you."

"Commander?" Tigh said, staring at the screen. Apollo had already seen what Tigh was reacting to: rising above the rim of Kirasolia, like twin moons, appeared the huge Cylon basestars.

Fight those? Apollo's astonished mind asked. *Stay and fight those? Is Cain insane?*

"What—" Athena gasped. "What are they?"

"Cylons," Apollo answered. "And I don't think they're here to welcome us to the neighborhood." He opened the S-cube to the science lab, and Salik's image appeared before them. "Are the devices installed yet?" Apollo shouted.

"We need just a few more microns," the holograph replied.

"That's about all I can promise," Apollo said.

As it turned out, he couldn't promise even that, for the monstrous basestars began firing at the fleet. The first blast struck the *Galactica* and shook her violently. Alarms sounded at once, and everyone scrambled for his or her battle station. Klaxons shrieked like souls in torment.

"Damage reports!" Apollo ordered.

The basestar and its Raiders unleashed a powerful salvo at the fleet, and Apollo, Athena, and President Tigh could only watch in horrified silence as the blasts struck other, less heavily defended ships, punching holes through their hulls. Inside the ships, visible through the breach, the flash of explosions could be seen as the ship plunged into darkness as its power cores suddenly failed. With the power went the life-support. It was a horrible thing to die; worse to die in the dark. Another explosion, somewhere deep within, and the hull blew outward, and bodies were flung into the airless void. They struggled for a few brief seconds, then were still.

Gods, he thought, *this is just like my dream.* . . .

"Salik, we have to have those devices operational, now!" Apollo shouted.

Salik's holographic image said something Apollo couldn't make out as the image wavered and shredded apart.

"Do you really think the QSE will work?" Athena asked her

brother. "What if Baltar has betrayed us again? Do you really want to trust our survival to a traitor?"

Apollo turned on her, his eyes almost wild. "Do you really think we can fight *that?*" he answered her question with one of his own. He jabbed a finger at the scanner and the massive basestar that filled it. "Look at it, Athena! It's as big as any moon!" Basestars were massive ships that tapered to a point, and had been described by many who saw them as resembling a child's top. They bristled with row upon row of plasma cannons and deck upon deck of Raider launch bays. Each class-four ship carried enough firepower to shatter a world from pole to pole.

The view on the scanner shifted to show Starbuck's Viper, followed closely by Boomer, roaring back into the fray, turbolasers blasting. Energy blasts scored the side of a Raider, ripping it open just before it could lock on target Trays' and Dalton's Vipers. The out-of-control fighter spiraled in a trail of burning fuel into the side of the *Galactica*. A moment later, the resulting explosion shook the bridge. Athena bit her tongue to keep from crying out.

She had to look away from the screen; Athena could no longer stand to watch the battle. It was hard enough, watching someone you knew racing into a skirmish, but it became almost unbearable when it was someone you loved, someone who was just barely recovered from his last near-death brush, heading out to war.

It was just as well Athena didn't watch. Starbuck's reactions seemed slower, somehow hesitant, as if there were some great gap between the impulse firing in his brain and the action of his hands. Too many times he just narrowly avoided Raider fire, and would have been destroyed several times over, had Boomer not been watching his back.

She looked at Apollo; he was not one to wear his feelings where anyone else might see them, but she knew him well enough to know something was tearing him up inside, some hard decision he was on the verge of making.

And then, of course, she looked once more at the monitor. It was hard to watch, but harder still to not know.

Trays and Dalton punched their turbos, extracting the last extra amount of thrust from their Vipers as the big ships moved into attack position.

Starbuck watched as the reason he was out here streaked back toward the relative safety of the *Galactica*. He could feel a tree of sweat forming on his back, and a trough dripping from his brow into his eyes. He blinked it away, but within microns his eyes were stinging again. He *was* having difficulty making his hands listen to his mental commands, as if there were some frizzort in his brain that sputtered and shorted out before the message could be translated into a language his body could understand.

It wasn't just fear causing this hesitancy, although he certainly was frightened; he had very nearly died, three weeks carved out of his life and removed like a block of stone, but he was also afraid he would freeze at the wrong moment and get those who relied upon him killed.

"We need to head back," Starbuck muttered over his comm-link, but his voice was small, his throat dry and pinched. He felt a tight band around his chest, constricting his lungs, making his heart thud like a bad engine bearing. *Gods,* he thought, *so this is what a panic attack feels like.* He decided immediately he didn't care for it.

Not that he could do anything about it except ride it out. For a few moments, Starbuck pushed it aside, thought he might be all right, and then the chest-crushing terror would come roaring back and bury itself more deeply in his heart.

"Apollo, sensors indicate the basestar is targeting us with its lasers," Tigh reported, studying the read out that scrolled past him on the screen.

The S-cube shimmered into life and Salik's holographic image appeared before Apollo. "Commander, the QSE is ready, awaiting your command."

Apollo looked at the scanner, saw the Vipers were still impossibly distant. One look at the anguish on her brother's handsome face told Athena what he was thinking. He knew what Cain said about acceptable losses, and knew what the old man would say about this, and, he would be right. But being right didn't make it any easier.

"Apollo, no!" she cried. "You can't!"

He looked at her, his face set. "I don't have any other choice," he said. "We lose a few pilots, or we lose the Fleet.

Which would you choose?"

Raider after Raider filled the screen, as plentiful as the stars, taking their positions, ready to attack the stranded fleet. Apollo understood at once this was why the Cylons hadn't made much of an effort to destroy the Vipers; what did a handful of fighters matter when the entire fleet was laid out before them?

Even though the basestars were still far away, still just rising over the rim of Kirasolia, their powerful plasma cannons could be seen to flash, like the strokes of lightning that scoured the surface of the dead world so far below. The pulse that would tear the *Galactica* in half would strike within microns. The pulse would not stop there, but keep ripping through any other ship unfortunate enough to be near the *Galactica,* and any ships near *that.*

"Forgive me," Apollo whispered to the Warriors who piloted their Vipers back to safety. "Salik, activate the QSE," he commanded. "Now."

The scanner showed the plasma bursts drawing closer, locked into a certain, fatal trajectory with the *Galactica.* Apollo took Athena in his arms and tried to shield her eyes from the impending doom as it filled the scanner, but she refused. She would not be spared this. She would be Adama's child to the end.

The glowing pulses streaked closer, until their intense brightness filled the screen, and even Athena, in her stoicism, had to look away or risk burning out her retinas. Apollo threw an arm across his eyes, and for a wild moment, he was sure he could see the bones in his forearm silhouetted through his flesh against the terrible light.

"Lords of Kobol, take us into your merciful arms," Apollo whispered an ancient prayer for the dead.

The scanner went blank.

7

"I S IT just me, or is reality getting a little . . . *fuzzy* . . . around the edges?" Starbuck asked. He wasn't being facetious; his fractalated vision made him question what he saw, but he was, in this instance, correct.

"Oh, frack," Troy's voice came back to Starbuck on his Warrior's helm. He saw it, too. They all did. The entire colonial fleet began to shimmer and ripple, as if it were something viewed through a distorting wall of heat. "They've activated the QSE!"

"Don't stop!" Starbuck shouted.

Dalton's Viper was the nearest to the warbling wall of energy and she unhesitatingly piloted her ship straight into the unsettling shift phase. To those watching from their respective vantage points, Dalton's Viper also began to ripple and distort. Inside the shift field, however, to Dalton's perspective, everything remained the same solid matter.

Cylon laser fire splashed off Trays' port wing, threatening to send his Viper spinning out of control. Inside the cockpit, sparks leaped and danced along the control console. Trays' face shield instantly and automatically dimmed to prevent the stuttershot of glaring light from momentarily blinding him and rendering him helpless in battle. Trays had been trying, rather unsuccessfully, to target the attacking Raider in his turbolaser sights, but the sudden, erratic flight path of his Viper made that even more difficult.

Starbuck's hands were jittering too badly to risk a shot at the Raider, and the ringing in his ears was rising to a high-pitched scream that, soon, only daggits and the certifiably insane would be able to hear. His vision began to blur, to double and treble. It was just a *fit,* he'd pull out of it momentarily, but his hesitation was going to get Trays killed.

"Troy . . ." he managed to gasp across his commline.

"I'm on it," Troy said, and thumbed his own turbolaser.

The Cylon Raider that had been harrying Trays disappeared in a wild, flaming spray of shrapnel, and Trays could hear the wreckage clanging and echoing off his main shield, even as he fought to keep his Viper under control.

"Nice shooting, Tr—"

A moment later, he was within the quantum shift effect himself, speeding toward the fleet. His comm-link vanished as soon as he entered the field. It was a very odd sight: the Viper just seemed to stop cold where it was, as if it were stuck between the tick of microns, and then, it slowly faded from view.

Two Cylon Raiders were bulleting for the shimmering wall of the QSE, speeding past Troy, Boomer, and Starbuck's Vipers. The Raiders could still do an incredible amount of damage to the fleet if they were in the same shift phase with it. Time only appeared to halt within the shift to those viewing it from without.

"Sorry, no free rides," Starbuck informed the Raiders, and locked the farther of the two into his sights. His vision was beginning to strobe with wild, purple splashes. Whatever was going to happen, he would have to finish his business here as quickly as possible. He had flown enough missions with Troy that they each knew the other's skills and battle tactics, and there was never a doubt as to which of the Raiders they would each attack. Starbuck had a long pursuit vector on his quarry, and he thumbed his turbolaser three times in rapid succession. If that didn't do it, he wasn't sure he could focus long enough again to try another time.

He was getting ready to alert Boomer to the situation when he saw his lasers slam home.

The Raiders had powerful shields, and anything but a direct hit would simply slough off them like rainwater. The third turbolaser scorched through the shields and struck the Raider, shredding it into flaming confetti.

In the distance, the powerful plasma cannons of the basestar targeted the *Galactica,* and a massive charge of energy built and danced, eddied and flowed, awaiting the moment of release.

Troy's quarry presented less of a target, as Troy was directly behind the Raider. He sighted the Cylon fighter's thruster and pressed the turbolaser on his navi-hilt. The burst went straight up the Raider's unshielded exhaust and ruptured the pulsar engines. The explosion of runaway energy instantly vaporized the Raider and its occupants.

"Troy!" Starbuck shouted into the comm-link.

Despite the opaquing effect of his Warrior's helm, the dazzling light from the vaporized Raider still burned an afterimage through Troy's closed lids, and he had to blink the world back into view before he could see what Starbuck was so excited about. There wasn't much doubt, because the entire fleet was . . . *gone.*

"Keep going!" Boomer ordered him. "There may still be a chance—"

The Vipers entered the space where, mircrons earlier, the fleet had been, and were instantly funneled down the same maze of spiraling tunnels of light.

The plasma bursts from the basestar burned through now-empty space, just missing the vanished, intangible fleet and ripping through a phalanx of circling Raiders. The fighters seemed to come unglued, molecule by molecule, evaporating under the deadly scythe of energy.

On the bridge of the *Galactica,* Apollo looked up from where he stood with his arms around Athena and at the scanner, which had flashed a brilliant, blinding white. He had assumed it was the fatal impact of the plasma burst the scanner was showing them, but now he saw the shifting lights of the tunnel through space and dimensions that the adjusted QSE had opened.

He felt a smile flow across his face, and he broke into laughter. Athena, puzzled, looked from her brother to the screen.

"We made it!" he said, and hugged her. "We're in quantum space!"

She watched the scanner and their journey down the hyperspace highway. Lights, the color of which she never dreamed, strobed intensely, stitched through with shorter, then longer, bursts of colored light, as if the universe were sending out a secret code. The lights resolved themselves into whorls that seemed to support the walls of the incredible tunnel through which the entire fleet now traveled.

"It's . . ." Athena began. Beautiful didn't come close. No simple, mortal word did.

"I know," Apollo agreed softly.

The pulsing lights and tunnel seemed to stretch on and on, and they all began to fear Baltar had betrayed them one final time, that the fleet would simply travel for all eternity down this endless, mad highway, with no hope of escape. Apollo had used the QSE technology before, but it was nothing like this. Before, he had felt like a phantom haunting the world of the living; but now . . .

He had to look away from the scanner. They all did. The things the universe had to show them, the secrets it was trying to tell them, to whisper in their eyes and ears and brains, would turn them all into gibbering, slobbering mindwipes if they looked at it for long.

"Where are we going?" Athena asked him. "Do you know?"

He stood with his back to the screen, and he had to fight the urge to turn and look. He didn't dare, and yet he had never wanted anything more. "I don't know," he admitted. "We're following coordinates given to us by Baltar, but I never imagined . . ."

Tigh looked alarmed, and there was something else there on his face, something Apollo couldn't recall seeing before, but there it was: terror.

"Baltar?" Tigh repeated. "You're using untested technology and unverified coordinates given to you by *Baltar*?"

"Doctor Salik has tested the adapted technology to the best of his abilities and determined both it and the coordinates to be reliable," Apollo offered in his defense.

Suddenly, the entire bridge was flooded with a brilliant light that erupted from the scanner, so bright that all shadows were washed from the room; so bright that, even through closed eyelids, they could all see the details of the bridge quite clearly. And then, the tunnel end frayed apart like old flexi-weave and the fleet appeared once more in normal space. There was no sense of deceleration because the ships had not actually moved under their own power; rather, the space around them had moved and shunted them down the long hyperspace corridor.

On the scanner, in the distance, a planet and its satellites wavered and warped into sight.

As Salik had observed, time and space were both dramatically distorted near an intense source of gravity such as a black hole. Space, he said, could literally be folded back upon itself, but, due to temporal inertia, time tended to flow in one direction. The quantum shift effect, however, was powerful enough to fold time, to push the fleet out of phase, if only for a very brief period. With a technology that could fold time, Salik reasoned, the fleet simultaneously possessed an ever-greater ability to fold space. And the proof of that lay before them, in the new constellations that wheeled about them, the foreign alignment of planets, and suns.

When they all dared to look again at the scanners, the images had resolved themselves into solid shapes once more. "We made it," Tigh announced unnecessarily. "But . . . *where* did we make it to?"

Apollo studied the screen, his face puzzled. "It's familiar," he muttered. "That planet . . .those stars. They all look familiar."

Athena was studying the scanner, too, but it wasn't the planet she was looking at. Rather, it was the absence of the Warriors that concerned her.

"Where are they?" she asked. She turned to Apollo, and repeated her question, more stridently this time. "The Vipers," she insisted. "Where are they? Did they make it, or did we leave them back there, with the Cylons..."

Before Apollo could respond, four ragged Vipers, all heavily damaged, exploded out of the shimmering curtain of quantum space. They had entered hyperspace with their thrusters burning, and the trip had done nothing to subtract from their momentum. The Vipers rocketed toward the landing bay of the *Galactica,* their destination before the phase shift phase, and that trajectory had not altered.

Apollo realized at once what was about to happen and opened the comm-link to the launch bay. "Lock onto those Vipers," he ordered Jolly. "Override their manual controls!"

Jolly studied the starfield from his point in the launch bay and saw the Vipers bulleting toward the ship. He keyed in the override command on the computer console and switched the Vipers to automatic pilot. The nearest fighter—Dalton's—responded to the dedicated slave-link that the launch bay's SYSOP established with its own navigational computer and fired its retro-thrusts; it began slowing down. The other three Vipers, also slaved to the SYSOP, began decreasing their terminal velocity as well.

Athena had been watching it all on the bridge scanner, and although she was relieved the others were safe, her heart felt as if it were about to burst in her chest. "Where's Starbuck?" she uttered. "Where's *his* Viper?"

Apollo had been wondered the same thing. He felt as if he were being buried alive in shifting, freezing sand; every decision he made was cursed with consequences out of all proportion, making it harder and harder to get back to solid ground. But he was still the commander and could not let personal pain interfere with his ability to lead. And most of all, he could not doubt his decisions—nor did he. Apollo ordered an emergency rescue team to deploy at once, to retrieve the Warriors and their Vipers.

But once that was done, Athena turned to Apollo, tears standing in her eyes, and said, "If anything happened to Starbuck, I will hold you personally responsible."

He looked at her, and made a sudden connection to something Starbuck had recently revealed and his own flippant response: *I wouldn't want you dating* my *sister*. Even words spoken in jest came winging back at him like shrapnel now. "Forgive me," he said. "I, I had no idea . . ." Still, there was nothing he could have done differently. Nor could he have stopped Starbuck from charging headlong into battle once more.

Athena said something, but he didn't hear her. He was too busy studying the scanner, and the planet that seemed improbably familiar.

The med and support teams launched from the bay less than a minute after the order was given.

Their ship was a shuttle designed for short-haul journeys, and was equipped with everything necessary to free and resuscitate a trapped or unconscious pilot from his fighter, but the Warriors were neither trapped nor unconscious . . . just dazed and confused by their unimaginable trip through quantum space.

Reaching the stranded fighters, the shuttle airlock cycled open and the rescue team spacewalked out, using controlled streams of compressed air to jet closer to their targets.

The first med on the spot, Nagi, reached Dalton's Viper, which had sustained some heavy damage from Cylon turbolasers, but was nonetheless intact. Her canopy was cracked, no doubt from the stresses of traveling through quantum space, but as Nagi rapped his gloved hand on the side of the little ship, the sound made Dalton stir and look his way in dreamy disorientation. If any oxygen had escaped through her breached canopy, her Warrior's helm still held enough to keep her alive.

Nagi called the support team over, and within moments they had attached a great length of fiberline to one of the Viper's landing gear. The other end of the line stretched all the way back into the *Galactica's* launch bay, and the signal was given to begin reeling her in. The Viper moved forward smoothly.

Trays was quite awake and animated, cursing them all for seizing remote control of his Viper when he had been perfectly capable of bringing it in for a landing under his own abilities. Nagi shut off his comm-line; he didn't need to listen to this.

As they were securing the fiberlines to the other Vipers, the fifth fighter, Starbuck's, suddenly burst through the still-fading rift in space, trailing fire and spiraling helplessly, unable to control its unchecked flight. One wing had been ripped away, either by Raider fire or the forces inside the hyperspace tunnel, and the fighter's hull had been punched through by laserfire in a dozen places. It had lost much of its momentum because its pulsar engine had been destroyed, and its wild trajectory kept it from slamming broadside into the battlestar. It glanced instead off the *Galactica*'s bristling array of sensors and communications antennae. The deflecting force managed to slow Starbuck's Viper enough for the rescue team to jet alongside it.

Nagi could not see in through the canopy; it was cauterized, like the cataracts in an old man's eye, and his rapping on the hull went unanswered.

He didn't have a good feeling about this one. Not at all.

Trays couldn't wait for his Viper to come to a stop and be locked down before he flung open his canopy and scampered out onto the wing. He hopped down and ran in great, scissoring strides across the bay toward Dalton's Viper.

She was shaken and dazed, being helped out of the cockpit by meds, but Trays elbowed his way through them to the girl's side.

"Are you all right?" Trays asked her, his hands under her arms. He lifted her down from the fighter's wing and tried to help steady her on her feet. "If anything had happened to you—"

"If anything had happened to her, it would have been all your fault," Troy said. He clapped his hand on Trays' shoulder and squeezed hard, spinning the other man around into a looping roundhouse right. Troy's fist connected hard with the Warrior's chin, driving him back against the side of Dalton's Viper.

"That is the last time you ever disobey an order and put the lives of your teammates and the safety of the fleet in jeopardy, or you will be grounded, do you understand me?" Troy grabbed Trays' flight suit collar and banged him back against the hull of the fighter to punctuate every word. Trays was still too stunned by the surprise punch to gather enough wits to defend himself.

Boomer had managed to extricate himself from his Viper and hurried to Troy's side and, with Jolly's help, pulled Troy away from Trays. There was a wild moment there when Boomer thought Troy would lose control and throttle the brash upstart, possibly even kill him. Not that he could blame Troy for the impulse, but it wasn't worth seeing the boy throw away his career.

"That's enough, son," Boomer said; it took everything he and Jolly had to keep Troy from breaking loose and going after Trays again. "He gets the message . . . don't you, Trays?"

Trays, without Troy's hands around his throat, slid down the side of Dalton's Viper, coughing and wheezing for air. He loosened the collar of his tunic, massaged his throat, which still held the purple imprints of Troy's fingers, and said, "That's the last time you ever lay a hand on me." He broke into a jagged coughing fit, regained his composure. "Next time you touch me, you're a dead man."

Dalton, ever the nurturer, knelt beside Trays and helped him to his feet, but he shucked off her hands and her concern, seeing it only as one more humiliation—a Warrior being helped up by a girl.

"I'm only trying to help," Dalton snapped, stung by Trays' rebuke.

"That goes for you, too," Trays warned her. "Don't ever touch me again."

Dalton's mouth opened, then snapped shut as she set her jaw in hard resolve. She wasn't going to let him know how much that hurt. No one would ever know how much anything hurt her.

"That's enough out of you, Trays," Boomer warned him. "That's enough out of all of you. Gods, when I think of all the good Warriors who died to keep snot-faced mugjapes like you safe . . ."

"Oh my god," Dalton gasped, her hands clapped over her face.

Troy snapped his head around, thinking Boomer's words had upset her, but she wasn't part of this conversation any longer. She was peering off in the opposite direction, back toward the launch aperture, watching Starbuck's badly damaged Viper being towed in, surrounded by swarming meds and carts full of equipment. His fighter's canopy was heat-welded shut, and the techs had to blast it off with a small wad of shaped explosive jelly. The hatch fell away in shattered, ragged pieces, and even from here, Dalton could see Starbuck was lying slumped back against his seat, unmoving.

"Not again," she whispered. She sounded like a lost child, one who lived in a world built on a foundation of shifting sand and peopled with uncertain relationships.

Dalton pushed aside the last of the crawlon webs from her thoughts and forced herself, on legs that felt too long for her body, to cross the landing bay to her father's blasted and scored Viper. The med crew was lifting Starbuck's limp body from the cockpit as Dalton reached his side. Nagi held her back as the meds placed Starbuck on the crash cart. One of the meds deactivated Starbuck's helm and removed it. Another ran the green-glowing hand-held scanner over his body, and as it passed over his head, it flashed a serious red.

"Get this man to the med-bay—*now*," Nagi ordered.

"What is it?" Dalton asked, her voice rising in panicky steps. "What's the matter with him? Is he going to be all right?"

But the meds were already bustling the cart bearing the unconscious Starbuck through the cavernous landing bay; any questions Dalton had would just have to wait.

"He'll be okay," Troy said, regretting it at once, hearing how foolish it sounded. But what else could he tell her? She was tough, but she wasn't indestructible.

"What do you base that on?" she asked, shrugging his hand off her shoulder.

Because he's Starbuck, he wanted to say. *Because people like Starbuck and Apollo don't die.* But although he may have believed that when he was just some kid named Boxey, Troy knew differently now

"That's what I thought," Dalton said, her lip curled in a sneer. "I can't waste any more time here." She didn't bother to look back, but ran away from Troy, from Trays, from the landing bay and after her father.

Troy was heartsick at his impotence in comforting Dalton, and heartsick, too, that whatever fragile thread had once brought them together seemed irrevocably sundered. But that was life. All that you love will be carried away. It seemed to be full of more good-byes than beginnings, and sometimes even the wisest men couldn't tell them apart.

"You asked to see me, Apollo?"

The security man escorted Baltar onto the bridge, where Apollo, Athena, and Tigh stood looking at the scanner and the planet that was so impossibly familiar. Apollo glanced sidelong at Baltar, and gripped his hands together behind his back. He wore an expression of tight, barely constrained rage.

"Is something wrong?" Baltar asked.

"That's what you're going to tell us," Apollo said.

Baltar studied Apollo a moment longer, then turned to face the scanner. Apollo watched him from the corner of his eye, and if he was pretending to be surprised, Baltar put on a good show of it.

"How is that possible?" the traitor asked, and shook his head.

"That can't possibly be . . . these aren't the coordinates I gave you. What are you playing at?"

One of the bridge crew, seated at his work station, finished studying the scroll of numbers and matching star-charts on his computer. "Coordinates match . . . and confirmed," he announced, and removed his headset, placing it down gently on the console before him.

Baltar shook his head. All of a sudden, he didn't like where this was headed, didn't like it any more than the rest of them.

The tech exhaled, a slow breath trickling from his nostrils, and pinched the bridge of his nose. He turned in his chair to face the quartet, and stood.

"Welcome to Kobol," he said.

8

I T'S A trick," Baltar said. "I don't understand why, but you're trying to trick me into believing we've come back to Kobol—"

Apollo moved with surpising speed, grabbing the traitor and flinging him back against the wall, at the same time pulling his sidearm from its holster. He shoved the laser's business end into the hollow under Baltar's chin, and pressed his face close to the traitor. "This is the last time you're going to trick us," he promised the frightened man, and felt his finger tightening on the trigger.

His anger and frustration taking over, Apollo prepared to blow Baltar's brain out of his skull, feeling as though he were watching the action like some disinterested third party. Well, gods knew, a small voice in his head rang out, *maybe it's time.* Adama would never have allowed himself to be made a fool of by this miscreant the way Apollo had.

"Please, I swear," Baltar gasped. Fat beads of sweat rolled lazily down his forehead and stung his eyes. He blinked, but couldn't seem to clear his vision. "I swear to you, Apollo, I didn't *know,* I *didn't* know—"

"Didn't know what, traitor?" Apollo asked. His voice was little more than a whisper. "Didn't know I'd finally grow the pogees to do what I should have done a long time ago?"

Baltar squeezed his eyes shut, his mouth open in a silent cry of terror. He wouldn't feel the laser blast that ripped through his skull, and death would be instantaneous, but that was of little comfort to him.

"Please—"

Athena had motioned for a support crew to surround Apollo, and now, she stepped closer to try to dissuade Apollo from making a mistake he would forever regret. "He may well die, Apollo," Athena said, reasonably; "but you don't want his blood on your hands. If it's going to happen, it needs to be carried out by a military court . . . not here, and not by you."

Apollo forced himself to regain control, and it was like the dream of falling where one awakens with a jolt and a racing heart. But he didn't feel yet as if he had completely awakened; in fact, Apollo was sure he was still falling. He slipped his sidearm back into its holster and snapped the safety strap closed.

Athena's body seemed to unwind like a taut spring that had been suddenly released. "Guards! Take Baltar back to his quarters and stand watch outside his door," she ordered.

Apollo, jaws set, eyes glaring, slowly nodded his assent.

Doctor Wilker had been trying, unsuccessfully, to make contact with the bridge. Now the tech who had delivered the devastating news confirming that the planet around which the fleet orbited was Kobol, saw the flashing light on his console and ordered the computer to open the frequency.

"Commander," Wilker said, his face as grim as his voice. "We need you in med-unit, right away. It's Starbuck . . . it isn't good."

Apollo turned to Baltar, who was being escorted from the room by the Black Shirts, and thundered, "If Starbuck dies, I swear by the Lords of Kobol you won't outlive him by long!"

Baltar's mouth opened, perhaps to plead for his life, perhaps to swear once again he knew nothing about this, but he said nothing.

The fire in Apollo's eyes made him rethink whatever it was he was going to say.

"If you say one word, Baltar, one little word, I swear I'll kill you now," the commander warned him.

"Go ahead," the captain of the security guards whispered in Baltar's ear. "Say something. It'd save us the bother of keeping an eye on you."

"I'm on my way," Apollo told Wilker. When he looked again, Baltar had been led from the bridge.

"This could be a trap, you know," Athena told her brother, nodding her head slightly to indicate the impossible planet on the scanner.

Apollo nodded. "I know," he said. Gods, what had he gotten them into now?

The great minds were wrong when they proclaimed nothing travels faster than light. They had failed to take into consideration bad news, and the speed at which it travels. If starships could be made to travel at the speed of bad news, the longest journey would be over almost before it had begun.

Aboard the bridge of the *Pegasus,* Commander Cain had already heard the news, and was livid with rage and confusion.

"We're in contact with the *Galactica,* Sir," the communications officer told Commander Cain.

"Put them on screen," Cain ordered, his hands grappling with one another. His normally gaunt features, wrinkled as an origami sculpture, seemed ageless now, as if he had sloughed off all his many yahren by sheer force of will.

Apollo's features filled the flatscreen; he was not happy, but Cain didn't seem to notice. "What is it, Cain?" he asked, curtly.

"What have you done?" Cain asked, his outrage barely in check. "How did we get back here? Of all places, Apollo, why Kobol?"

Apollo and Tigh glanced sidelong at one another, and although their eye contact was brief, everything that needed to be said passed between them in that moment.

Their understanding had been forged by yahren of friendship, and in many ways, Apollo considered Tigh a mentor and second father. They had, over time, developed a deep love an abiding respect for each other's wisdom and abilities. No one else would even have noticed the look that passed between the two men, but volumes had been spoken in that look, and all without a single word.

"I appreciate and share your misgivings, Commander," Apollo began, treading lightly. He did not need to alienate Cain now, of all times. "For the moment, we're away from the Cylon armada, a breathing space that gives us the chance to study our options at greater detail."

"Options?" Cain thundered. "We're right back at the beginning of our journey, like a bad children's game! I'd be very interested in hearing what you believe these options you mentioned are."

Apollo did not get the chance to respond to Cain and, considering the reason, his words would not have mattered, anyway, for in the next moment all the ships in the fleet were simultaneously contacted through their communications channels. A holographic image of a hooded woman, smiling beatifically and seeming to radiate light, appeared on the bridge of every ship.

"I bid you peace, travelers," she said, her voice as mellow as temple bells, "and welcome to Kobol."

They all stared at her, every ship's captain in the fleet, because she was *human*. There hadn't been a human on Kobol for many eons. Even Cain, for once, was speechless.

In the exact center of the basestar, the Cylon equivalent of a battlestar, sat the Imperious Leader. His chambers were a dark room located at the end of a dark corridor, and in the center of the room, which was the exact center of the basestar, there was a platform that stood nine steps high, and in the center of this platform was the seat of power from which the Imperious Leader oversaw all things.

The sides of the pedestal on which he sat were marked and studded with hundreds of sharp points that seemed to cut the very light they reflected. In the corners of the room, torches burned, throwing off fitful light and dancing shadow.

The double doors to the chamber opened and the cogitator called Lucifer entered. The Imperious Leader's chair was turned away from the door, and he slowly swiveled around to face his visitor.

Each Imperious Leader had a specific reign, a length of time equivalent in human terms to three-quarters of a century. But Cylons did not recognize the passage of time in such linear terms, and each Imperious Leader chose his own succcessor. This was only logical, for Imperious Leaders were the only Cylons with a third brain.

Lucifer had ambitions; he hoped he would be chosen one day to replace the current Imperious Leader. He did not have a third brain; these were awarded, implanted, and along with them, according to Cylon belief, the capacity for limitless knowledge. The first brain was little more than the body's guidance system, the bit of matter that assured efficiency of task, while the second brain contained such necessary skills for Cylon officers as analyzing and interpreting facts. Acting in tandem with the first brain, the second brain ensured its host would rise easily to the level of executive officer. But the third brain allowed the Imperious Leader to elevate above such mundane and prosaic matters as facts, and deal in abstracts. Cylons were not great thinkers, and the second brain was always hungry to join with a third, as Lucifer so well knew. With the gifting of the second brain, true hunger began.

The Imperious Leader knew this as well; Lucifer's transparent skull atop his cyborg head flashed with the sparking of his thoughts, and so many flashes meant many, many thoughts. A cogitator with so many thoughts was one who saw himself in higher places, and who schemed to get there.

Lucifer stopped before the towering throne and formally petitioned the Imperious Leader, a tradition as old as the Cylon race itself.

"By your command," he said.

"Speak."

"The humans have evaded us," Lucifer reported, "and are now on an unknown course."

The Imperious Leader, far from being wrathful, steepled his fingers together and nodded. "All is well," he said. "All goes according to plan."

And then the Imperious Leader made a sound Lucifer did not recognize, but it was no wonder, for it was a sound never heard among the cold-blooded Cylon race.

It was the sound of laughter.

About that time, Apollo could have gladly used a third brain to help him make sense of all the contradictory facts with which he had been presented.

Segis, as the robed woman identified herself, was infuriatingly calm and evasive, vowing that "All will be revealed in its time." But was that because the fleet was safe here, and had all the time in creation, or because the jaws of the trap into which Baltar had led them were not quite ready to snap shut? Apollo wished he knew.

"You must understand our caution," Apollo tried again. "If you could only give us some . . . token of faith . . . a gesture of trust between us. . . ."

But Segis just smiled her maddening smile, and said, "To pick something up, Commander, you must first place something down."

Apollo sighed, rubbed his tired eyes. About the only thing he had to put down was his own neck on the butcher's block. Unfortunately, it was ultimately not only his head that would roll, if he was wrong. A commander had to be quick and decisive, but too many things were being hurled at him at once.

"All things in due time," Segis vowed again.

"First, I must see to the safety of my fleet," Apollo said.

He ordered the ships to take stationary orbital position on the far side of Kobol, in case the Cylon armada followed them through the hyperspace shortcut. At least the fleet would be in something resembling a defensible position, rather than waiting like a flock of bovas for the pack of lupuses to bring them down. Plus, despite their hostess's graciousness and warmth, something about Segis did not sit well with Apollo, and he could not shake the feeling this was a disaster waiting to occur.

Apollo again turned his attention to Segis, who stood waiting patiently, her smile undimmed.

"Where will we find you?" the commander asked.

Segis laughed, softly. It was a laugh Apollo knew, somewhere, somehow, a laugh that set off tripwires and alarms.

"The coordinates have already been forwarded to your bridge's computers, to be input to your docking shuttles," Segis explained. She raised her arms from her sides, her robes unfolding, spreading, and, for a moment, Apollo was reminded of angel wings . . . or the wings of some noble hunting avion. She gestured warmly, and said, "If you please. I know you have many, many questions, and I shall endeavor to answer them all, once you join us on the surface."

"Us?"

"Of course, Commander Apollo," Segis answered, coyly. "Did you think I was alone?"

For the travelers, returning to Kobol was a bittersweet experience.

As the shuttle descended through the cloud cover shrouding the planet, they felt a sense of connection, of belonging to a place once again after so many yahren of living a forced, nomadic existence. But as they drew closer, and the irregular shapes of color resolved themselves into the ruins of a once-proud civilization, that sense of home became a sense of loss, a reminder of how much had been taken away. If they feared that they had doubled back through time as well as space, one look at the ruined surface of the planet quickly disabused them of that fanciful belief.

The rusted wreckage of long-ago downed Viper fighters lay scattered around and through the cracked and broken city streets; great weeds and vegetation thrust their way up, nature's reclamation of a planet mankind arrogantly believed it possessed.

The canopy of one of the fighters had been shorn away, and the pilot's skeleton still sat at the controls, fleshless fingers locked about the navi-hilt, faithful to his duty unto death, and beyond. The cage of his ribs provided a home to a murder of small avions. Nothing was wasted in nature; from endings grew new beginnings.

Shattered buildings canted against those still upright, leaning like a drinking buddy who needed a little help. In the doorways of the buildings, Apollo imagined the bodies of those who had huddled there in a foolish, desperate attempt to avoid Cylon laser fire or falling debris. It was there they had huddled, and there they had died.

The great presidium, buckled and tossed in crazy, ragged angles, still bore a faint message someone had painted there: "PEACE!" It had been an entreaty to the Cylon juggernaut, and Apollo recalled a similar presidium on Caprica, bearing the same hopeful message. Serina had been broadcasting live from the Caprican presidium, where the peace ceremonies with the Cylons were to have begun; instead, she had broadcast betrayal and the death of hope.

Another message, written over the single word, was equally chilling: GODS HAVE MERCY ON US. As if the Lords of Kobol could see that message when the prayers of countless dying could not be heard.

How could the gods not have heard those last, weeping prayers? Apollo could hear them, still.

Apollo looked away from the shuttle's flatscreen to observe Cain's stern profile. The old man stood with his hands behind his back, one hand tightly gripping the other. To the casual observer, he looked unmoved and impassive, but Apollo saw, on closer examination, the slight quiver in Cain's lower lip. He felt it, too.

This was a hallowed place, and haunted, if there was any such thing.

And then the ruins fell away, slipping into the distance behind them, and the ancient pyramids grew up out of the wilderness. The vegetation dropped away, leaving only rock and stone and sand.

Even the pyramids had not escaped the relentless brunt of the Cylon attack; great, broken stones lay thrown about everywhere, like playthings that had fallen out of favor with some monstrous, angry child.

Their destination seemed to be a large pyramid, ringed by several smaller ones, all of them heavily damaged and jutting up like rotten teeth, and the shuttlecraft began a long, easy descent toward this site. It felt funny, to think of this landscape as a limitless vista, when the travelers roamed all of space, but there, it was as little more than prisoners inside flying metal boxes. Here, with the land rolling away in all directions, beneath a cloud-filled sky of blue that snuggled the world in its embrace, in this place that was ancient beyond imagining, this place that was the cradle of life, they felt small, and humble.

"I've been here before," Apollo reminisced, softly. "With Father."

"What's that?" Cain asked.

Apollo shook his head. "Nothing."

The shuttle gently touched down, its cushion of air kicking up a spume of dirt and dust. The hatch irised open and Cain swung down out of the ship, his sharp eyes surveying their surroundings for potential danger or hidden traps. Seeing nothing, he drew a deep breath, filling his lungs with the air of a dead world. It was heady and intoxicating; it was pure and unspoiled, and had been so for a thousand yahren. Gar'Tokk followed Cain, and also sniffed the air, but not for the simple pleasure of breathing unrecycled oxygen for a change; he was sniffing for danger.

Apollo swung out next, helping Athena down. All around them, stones as big as the shuttle that had brought them here lay scattered, and a vagrant wind wandered aimlessly through the debris and between the stones like an unquiet spirit. Athena looked up at the towering pyramids, feeling the enormous weight of their antiquity pressing down upon them. Even Gar'Tokk, who guarded his thoughts like a treasure, and who cared not a whit for humans or their history, was visibly awed.

"It's . . ." Athena began, and stopped. It was many things, and all of them too large for simple words to contain.

"Yes," Apollo agreed. Once again he knew what she meant. "It is."

"We're about to meet our hosts," Gar'Tokk observed, pointing through the field of stones. He had caught glimpses of them as they wove their way through the labyrinth of stone blocks, but had not caught scent of them. His eyes narrowed; something was wrong, but he couldn't say just what. Cain stood with his hand resting casually on his hip, but it was anything but casual: from his hip, it was a quick, fluid motion to draw his laser, if circumstance demanded.

Apollo and Athena looked to where the Noman had pointed, and the robed figures, led by a woman, emerged from the stone passageway. They all wore the same humble clothes, for they were all equal, their faces concealed by the shadows cast by their cowls. And yet, her cowl did nothing to conceal the eyes of radiant green that stared at Apollo, and he felt his breath catch. There was something about her that put him at ease, something as familiar as home.

"My name is Talen," she said, and smiled, and her voice was like a snatch of song Apollo had once heard, long ago, and could not quite place. "Welcome, all."

Commander Cain surprised them all, taking Talen's hand gently in his and kissing the back of it—he was as much schooled to be a gentleman as he was a commander. "On behalf of my fellow officers and the entire colonial fleet, we are grateful for your hospitality," he said.

"So charming," Talen said, and laughed delicately. Cain was a decorated hero, but he was also prey to the same feminine flattery all men, great or humble, find irresistable.

"We were under the impression Kobol had not been home to humans for millennia," Athena said bluntly.

Talen nodded. "Not home as you may know it," she answered; Talen was already proving to be as enigmatic as Segis.

Gar'Tokk stood quietly, nostrils widened as he again tried to catch some manner of identifying scent from the robed figures and the one who called herself Talen, but the only trace aroma he could detect was like burning ozone. He frowned and grunted. It was not danger, not precisely, but neither was it particularly reassuring. This would bear watching.

"Is Segis with you?" Apollo asked.

Talen turned again to look at Apollo and favored him with a smile. It was a smile that seemed as familiar to him as Segis's laugh had. But this sense of deja vu, at least, did not alarm him. Rather, it made him feel . . . *whole.* "Segis awaits," she said, and placed her palm flat against one of the featureless stones that formed the base of the largest pyramid.

The entire stone recessed quietly into the ziggurat, but all the travelers could see of the pyramid's interior was darkness, as if these ancient cairns were built as nothing more than a place to store shadows. Without waiting to see if the travelers would follow, Talen entered the tomb and, after a moment, as she knew they would, the travelers followed.

Eerie light flooded up from the floor of the pyamid, and as their eyes adjusted to the change in brightness, the colonial party could see a stone staircase that wound down and down into the earth, seeming to spiral tighter and tighter in upon itself as it descended, reminding Apollo of a conch shell, or the whorls of human DNA he had seen in the science lab. There were patterns everywhere, echoes within other echoes. It was the universe speaking in subtext, trying to assure her children that nothing is ever gone, nothing ever dies. It all goes on, somewhere, in some fashion.

They followed Talen as she descended the stone stairs, worn by millennia of use. Her tread was silent, while the footfalls of the others echoed and re-echoed off the narrow walls. The stairs continued to circle downward, as if they were following the teeth of some giant auger, screwing itself into the heart of the world.

Gar'Tokk, more attuned to these things than his companions, could feel the air becoming heavier, and he knew they were deep beneath the surface of Kobol. He hated the feeling of claustrophobia this elicited in him, and would have gladly left this place never to return, but Apollo was here, and his duty was to Apollo.

"Is this what you meant before, when you asked me if I'd follow you into a suicidal situation?" Gar'Tokk muttered to Apollo.

Even in the diffuse light that spilled up from somewhere below, Apollo could tell Gar'Tokk was in great discomfit and realized this was especially difficult for someone who lived so close to his animal instincts. "Do you want to return to the surface?"

Gar'Tokk scowled, as if the suggestion were the worst insult Apollo could fling at him, and the commander again felt guilt at stealing away the noble creature's pride, and knew he had to restore it, somehow.

The stairs finally came to a halt in a cave that opened out into a larger cavern, and as they approached this larger chamber the light grew brighter, and there was a low, almost sub-aural sigh, like the sound of some restless, mighty sea. The susurrus grew louder as they walked down the low, arched corridor, like a million voices all talking at once, finally becoming a roar as they stepped through the arched doorway of the passageway and into the gigantic chamber.

Whatever the travelers were expecting, it could certainly not have been this: they emerged into the main cavern and were instantly awed by what they beheld. A city, a smaller, mirror image of the one that once stood above them over a thousand yahren ago, spread and sprawled outward and spiraled upward, with soaring towers and crenellated structures. The roof of the cavern itself was almost lost in the distance, and the walls and ceiling glowed with an eerie phosphorescence, as if some mineral or naturally-occurring moss gave out a vaguely-green, diffuse light.

"This is what Kobol must have looked like, before . . ." Athena said, her voice breaking with emotion. She wanted to run through the city streets and see the places she had only heard about in stories passed down generationally, this place she knew so well already and yet had never seen.

Cain nodded, although he barely registered what Athena had said. His mind was already thinking ahead, wondering how well this city could be defended against attack, whether Cylon or Chitain.

"It is exactly what Kobol looked like," Talen confirmed Athena's observation. "The old city plans were followed precisely."

"Followed by whom? No on survived," Apollo said. "Not on Kobol, anyway. The Cylons saw to that."

Talen raised an eyebrow and her eyes locked with Apollo's. He couldn't explain it, but he felt something powerful passing between them, an ember, a current, a raging flame. Who *was* she, to hold so much power over him? It was as if he had known her all his life, and in a lifetime before that. "Then, how do you explain *this,* Commander Apollo?" she chided, gently. "Are we ghosts?"

"I can't explain it," he said. "I'm hoping you will." *And I'm also hoping you'll explain why I feel this way about you,* he thought.

Talen smiled, a trifle coyly, Apollo thought, and continued leading the little group through the mirror city. If there were any answers to be had here, they would not come from Talen. And yet, Apollo felt as if the answers would only raise even more questions. Into the heart of the city they walked, the buildings seeming to grow taller around them, and then they were standing in the recessed well of the presidium. Arborial growths flourished in stone pots and in terraced steps in a graceful hemisphere embracing the presidium.

In this clearing stood Segis, one hand behind her back, the other lightly holding the stem of a blossoming flower, inhaling its intoxicating fragrance. She heard the echo of the group's footfalls but pretended not to until they were mere feet from her. Then she appeared to notice, and turned to face them, greeting them with a slight and dignified bow, so slight as to almost not be there.

"Greetings, children of Kobol," she said, her tones mellifluous and purring. "Welcome home."

Segis studied the travelers with dark, penetrating eyes, stopping momentarily on Apollo, then slipping away to settle on Commander Cain. Apollo didn't know why, but he felt this was more than a simple slight; there was something else at work here. "Your returning has been prophesied, in the ancient writings in the temple above us. The way has been prepared. Once you determined to take the journey through quantum space, we were able to remotely input the coordinates that brought you here, rather than your originally-intended destination."

"*You* brought us here?" Apollo asked. Far from putting him at ease, this new information only troubled him more. Collusion between Baltar and Segis had yet to be proven, but then, it wasn't as if either of them would admit to it, if it were there.

"Of course, Commander," Segis answered. "The timing seemed quite expeditious, as you would have found your original destination a rather inhospitable place, overrun by Cylons."

"Thank you," Cain said, stepping forward and bowing with a military stiffness and precision. "We are honored to be here."

"It is you who honor us, Commander," Segis said, humbly, and then smiled disarmingly. "I am sure you have many questions, and I shall endeavor to answer them. We," she said, and spread her robed arms expansively, and again Apollo thought of wings, "are the caretakers of this city. We and our offspring have been living here for succeeding generations since the last humans left for the stars, many millennia ago.

"We know of the Cylons, of course," she continued ruefully; "but the Cylons have no way of detecting our presence here due to the unique protective shield that surrounds us."

"But our ships—" Apollo interjected.

Segis smiled and shook her head. "Screened from detection by the same protective energy that surrounds us," she explained.

She began walking, Talen falling into step two paces behind her, as if she were not of an equal station, but rather Segis's servant. Cain and Tigh walked next to Segis, while Apollo found himself walking beside Talen, Athena on his other side. Apollo caught himself stealing surreptitious glances at Talen, as if he were some infatuated adolescent smitten with the prettiest female in his class. It was foolish, he knew it, and yet that was exactly how he felt.

Several times she glanced his way, too, but whether that was because she felt his eyes upon her or because she felt as he did, Apollo could not guess.

"You say this was all prophesied," Cain began, breaking the silence.

"Many millennia ago," Segis nodded, "yes."

"Then you won't mind, showing us these ancient writings?" Apollo asked what he was sure was on Cain's mind; the same thing that was on his. "We mean you no offense, but this is all a little hard to take in—"

"Not at all," Segis agreed, and Talen, Apollo thought, smiled a little more brightly at him.

"The ancient writings also prophesied a great commander would lead the humans into final battle with the Cylons, and reclaim the colonies."

This time, Apollo saw Talen look down, averting her eyes from his, but he thought, just before she did, the smile on her face vanished.

The city was as ancient as the great one that lay in ruins, but was nevertheless extremely sophisticated; safely away from the elements, this mirror city showed none of the signs of antiquity. The buildings, Apollo realized, were also made of the same light-emitting stone as the cavern walls, as were the stones that paved the streets. Gleaming white obelisks jutted up at the four corners of the tallest buildings, as straight as soldiers on review.

Trees and close-cropped shrubbery lined the sides of the long, shallow reflecting pool of clear water that shimmered in the refracted light of the mirror city.

Everything is a reflection, Apollo mused. Avions, nestled in the trees and perching on window sills and rooftops, sang to one another, and Apollo wondered how long it had been since he had heard such music, such unfettered, unconditional happiness. But that wasn't entirely accurate and he knew it. It had always been there; he had just not paid it much attention since Serina had left this life. She had taken with her much of the light from his world.

"You still haven't said who built this city," Apollo reminded Segis.

Segis glanced back over her shoulder, and offered the commander a warm smile. "Your ancestors did, Apollo," she said. "The ancient Kobollians built this city to house the last generation of its people and preserve their sacred records. All of the information and wisdom of the ancients is to be found here."

"What manner of information?" Cain asked.

Segis made a small, shrugging gesture with her hands. "I could not say, Commander Cain. It is not our place to examine these ancient texts. We are merely the caretakers."

"Are you Kobollian?" Tigh asked the question they were all thinking.

"All humanoid races come from Kobollian blood," Segis answered. "The Kobollians long ago seeded the stars. We are merely a . . . shall we say, distant *branch* of your race."

Apollo let his mind open, like the petals of a flower unfolding, and tried to slip into Segis's subconscious; if the caretaker really was of Kobollian stock, Apollo reasoned he should be able to pick up her thoughts, or at least her emotional state and whether she was what she claimed to be.

His consciousness brushed Segis's, and for a moment he thought he might actually be able to make not just contact, but to enter and explore, but then it was as if some massive gate slammed closed, shutting Apollo out before he could fully enter. Whether it was because Apollo's own nascent psychic abilities had chosen that particular moment to falter, as they sometimes did, waxing and waning, or because Segis had sensed his psyhcic intrusion and set up mental safeguards and barriers to keep him out, Apollo couldn't say. There was something oddly familiar about the brief contact he had been able to establish, but the feeling was fading . . . gone.

Apollo heard Cain whispering something to Tigh; he didn't catch it all, but he heard enough to know his world was spinning on an uncertain axis: " . . . incredible. Everything we need to survive and rebuild is available to us here. Of course, we need to verify these 'ancient writings' with one of the scholars from the *Cerberus* . . . scout the planet, make sure this is not a trap . . . ."

Tigh nodded. "Of course."

Cain was growing more animated, more excited by their prospects, and gestured around them at the city and the walls of stone that had kept it safe and untouched during the worst of the Cylon Wars. "We couldn't have found a more ideal location from which to reclaim our homeland."

Segis, of course, had heard Cain's dialogue with Tigh, but then, it was not Segis whom Cain was trying to keep from overhearing his plans. "You and your people are all most welcome to stay as long as you desire," Segis informed Cain.

"This city is yours, as the children of Kobol. You are safe here. And we—" she turned and gestured at the faceless, robed acolytes which followed many paces behind them "—are here to serve and assist you in anything you ask."

Apollo looked in alarm at Athena, but she would not meet his gaze. Instead, he tried to probe her mind, but he found himself blocked from this as surely as he was barred from Segis's thoughts. She could not look at him, not yet, because she knew he would ask her for her support in influencing the council against Cain's obvious plan to stay on Kobol indefinitely.

But she couldn't do that, because, she realized with some surprise, she found herself siding more and more with Cain than with her own brother.

The return to the *Galactica* was brief but, for Apollo, it seemed interminable. With the assistance of Uriah, from the *Cerberus*, the fleet's archives ship, the ancient texts of which Segis spoke were translated, and Uriah confirmed them as having been inscribed in stone long millennia ago, in the same hand that had inscribed other texts about the ancient temple. The writings were genuine; the prophecy, it seemed, fulfilled. Even Commander Cain, who decried all such prophetic writings as fairy tale thinking and felgercarb in its most unrefined, unappealing form, could barely contain his growing enthusiasm over having found a safe haven, at last, and President Tigh, for all his friendship and loyalty to Apollo, seemed to be similarly swept along by the same tide.

Athena spent the journey back not speaking to Apollo, or, at least, not speaking of things that mattered. She talked around the issue, choosing instead to concentrate on how terrible the destruction on Kobol was, and said she was eager to see how Starbuck was doing. Apollo agreed that, yes, the damage was, indeed, awful, and said that he didn't know if it could be ever fully rebuilt.

She couldn't look at him after that, not for a while, anyway, because she knew what damage he was referring to, but she couldn't help how she felt any more than Apollo could.

He allowed himself to wonder if Cain was right, after all, and perhaps his resistance to the idea of reclaiming Kobol grew out of his increasing conflicts with Cain: Anything Cain was *for,* he must therefore be *against.*

But the fact was, he just didn't trust anything that came about because of Baltar, no matter how often or how loudly everyone else proclaimed the hand of Providence at work. There was *something* at work here, Apollo was certain; the temple writings supported that much, at least, but he didn't know what, exactly. Whatever it was, he had the feeling it was not benevolent.

Apollo looked out the viewing port of the shuttle and watched Kobol slip farther away.

As soon as he arrived back aboard the battlestar, Apollo headed for the med-unit, where he found Dr. Wilker in the waiting hall and took him aside. The prognosis, Wilker told him gravely, was not promising.

"His brain has hemorrhaged," he said. "His condition is critical. Frankly, I don't know how he's lasted this long."

Apollo felt as if someone had sucker-punched him; he had expected the worst, of course, had tried to prepare himself for it, but the fact was, when it happened, the worst was still the worst. He nodded, and walked away on legs that felt too weak to support him.

Inside the med-unit, Apollo found Dalton keeping vigil at her father's death-berth. She did not look up at Apollo's approach, but that was just as well; she might have seen the tears welling in his eyes, and he already felt vulnerable enough.

He stood beside Dalton, and finally placed a hand on her back. *It's the end of an era,* he thought. Starbuck would really die this time; he would be forever gone from Apollo's life, from all of their lives. Apollo felt a tear tracking slowly down his cheek and he palmed it away. It was just the one; he would not indulge himself in more than this. Not here, anyway; not yet. He would not be there to see the new world. He would not be there to offer his counsel to Apollo. He would not be there, period.

He studied Starbuck's face and the rogue's smile that was still there, but it wasn't really a smile; it was just the crippling, twisting after-effects of the brain hemorrhage. There was nothing to smile about here.

Apollo felt Dalton's shoulders shudder beneath his hand, knew she was fighting the tears even as he was, and promised Starbuck, silently, *I'll look after her. You just . . . you just do what you have to do. I'll take care of things here.*

"This is because of me . . . isn't it?" Dalton asked, snuffling back the tears.

"You? How do you figure that?"

"Because he came after me, to help me," she said, her voice thick with emotion. "He pushed himself too hard and he wouldn't have had to do that if I hadn't been fracking off with Trays . . . "

"No," he said. "It wouldn't have mattered who was out there. He would have gone to help them. That's just the way he was."

Apollo realized with some horror he was already speaking of Starbuck in the past tense. "Did you ever hear the story about how your dad and I met?" he asked, wanting desperately to turn away from these dark thoughts, as much for his own sake as Dalton's.

"He only told that one about a million times," Dalton answered, and smiled a little. It was weak, barely there, but at least it was better than tears. "But I wouldn't mind hearing it again."

But before he could speak, Apollo was interrupted by a young, dark-haired female aide. She stood just inside the door, trying to be respectful of the raw emotions the commander and Dalton were grappling with, but feeling a sense of pressing urgency, as well. "Commander," Lyrra said. Apollo turned to look at her. Now that he did, she felt like an intruder. "I'm sorry to do this, Sir, but they want you in the council chamber, *now*."

"What do they want?" he asked.

"I think they're about to vote on something."

9

T HE COUNCIL had already started hearing arguments over who should be the fleet's supreme commander without Apollo's presence; that did not bode well for him.

As he hurried down the corridors for the council chambers, Apollo's mind was more on Starbuck than his own future as supreme commander. He felt as if he were abandoning his friend when Starbuck most needed him, but intellectually, Apollo knew there was nothing he could do for him. He could not even offer words of comfort; the part of Starbuck that would understand him was trapped somewhere deep inside a dark and silent place.

The chamber door opened with a sigh, and Apollo was inside the room before the door had cleared the frame. President Tigh was arbitrating a heated debate between Athena and other council members, and Apollo had the sense it was not going well, for his old friend and mentor was rubbing his left temple with the tips of his fingers, as Tigh always did when the stresses brought on a skull-popper. The council members were not brilliant leaders, they were not possessors of courageous hearts; they were a group of twelve men and women banded together by a deep and abiding mistrust of change.

Change had to be forced upon them, by circumstances beyond

their control. Then, they voted almost unanimously to accept events over which they could not exert influence. It would have been laughable—if these men and women did not decide the fates of so many.

Not that long ago, Apollo had faced a similar battle after Adama died, and the Quorum had to elect a new fleet commander; now, Apollo felt as if time had cunningly doubled back upon itself and he was yet again arguing his worthiness to hold that post.

But it was a little more than that, this time.

"I agree that there are many advantages to reclaiming Kobol," Athena said, barely aware of her brother's presence. "We're all tired of running and fighting."

"Are we all so tired that we're willing to accept these caretakers at their word?" Apollo interjected, stepping before the Quorum, next to Commander Cain. The room was white and featurelessly austere, with only pictographs representing the star system from which each council member had once departed, harried along by the Cylon war machine. "We have only spoken with them once, and, while the texts seems to bear out their assertions, we have not had time to consider their offer and its ramifications completely—"

"There is nothing to consider," Sire Belloch of Gemon said. He was a tall and thin man, as gaunt as death. "They are offering us a safe planet from which to rebuild, no matter that this world is not homeworld to any of the rest of the Quorum members."

"It is the last place the Cylons would think to look for us," Cain added, as if that were enough to decide the matter.

Apollo felt his own skull-popper coming on. "You're forgetting, the Cylons have the same QSE technology as we do. The coordinates Baltar gave us are those he stole from the Cylons. Council members, I assure you the Cylons *will* find us; it remains only to be seen how long it will take."

"The fleet is safely concealed," Sire Belloch intoned. "The city is hidden below the surface of a planet the Cylons have already decimated. Even if they did follow us here, the Cylons would find a dead world, exactly as they left it a thousand yahren ago."

The Quorum murmured assent amongst themselves, and even Athena was nodding in agreement.

"Your concerns are noted, Commander Apollo," Sire Belloch stated coldly, "but, unless you can present a more persuasive argument as to why we should not accept the caretakers' offer, this council has enough information before it to take a vote."

Apollo's mind raced at near-escape velocity, looking for some solid reason to stay on Kobol no longer than it took to replenish and refuel, and realized he had none. All he had was a very unsettling feeling that this was a colossally elaborate trap, but that was hardly a rational argument, and it certainly would not sway the Quorum. It was the prelude to a raging paranoia, but that was all he had to argue with, the only point from which he could argue, so he pressed on: "Members of the council, you know as well as I that the Cylons will not rest until the last of the human race are all captured and enslaved, or annihilated, and with their technology, assimilated from planets they've conquered, they will certainly locate us before we've had the time to fully implement Commander Cain's plan.

"Rebuild a *world?* Build our armada and take the battle to the Cylons? Reclaim the colonies from them?" Apollo shook his head; it was not for effect. Hearing it spoken aloud made him see just how monumentally large and far-ranging Cain's plans were.

"These things will take time, much time, and while we rest, the Cylons will not. They will not stop until they have found us."

He paced, drawing their attention toward himself and away from Cain; it was a trick he had seen his father use successfully in his dealings with the Quorum. "What I propose is this: I beseech the council to allow the *Galactica* and those who choose to join us to leave Kobol for the haven of deep space as soon as we are able."

Cain had been quietly fuming the entire time Apollo was making his impassioned plea, and now erupted defiantly.

"If we are to succeed in our mission, we will need every ship and every man available to us. We cannot allow Apollo to further divide our diminished forces! The Lords of Kobol have at last answered our prayer and blessed us with an incredible opportunity to finally avenge the deaths of millions of our countrymen."

He drew himself up to his full height, seeming to swell with the passion of his words. "We will be looked upon by history as cowards if we run yet again and shirk our duty as Warriors, and men and women of honor and integrity. Future generations will remember us and thank us for the sacrifices we are about to make. If we continue to run, we will be running forever, looking back over our shoulder in fear. I say if we are to die, then let it be in a blaze of glory. Let our deaths be deaths that matter!"

Apollo had been watching the council members during Cain's spittle-lipped call to glory, and, to a man, they had all been clearly and visibly moved. Even Athena. It was a lost cause, and his heart was not into fighting any more battles he knew he could not win, but he was Adama's son, the supreme commander of the fleet, and he had to try. Perhaps logic would yet prevail over Cain's jingoistic entreaties. And perhaps Starbuck would walk through the council chamber door. Anything was possible; just how *probable* remained to be seen.

"My father, and your great leader for nearly twenty yahren, led our people to safety and maintained peace among many different races and ideologies aboard this ragtag fleet," Apollo began, speaking from his heart. It made only slightly more sense than speaking from his intuition. "He believed, as I do, in a great vision, one which would carry us across the heavens to a new homeland. One where we could truly start anew and begin the rebuilding of our society in peace and harmony.

"This," he continued, speaking more softly, forcing them to truly listen to what he was telling them, "is a natural progression. Over the aeons, our race has evolved and migrated from first Parnassus to Kobol to the Twelve Colonies. It has always been our destiny, to continue expanding out into the universe, and the ancient Kobollian writings have spoken of a great journey to a faraway star system, where our race would one day finally understand its origins, and complete the circle of life.

"I, and those who have not forgotten our proud heritage, believe that the Thirteenth Tribe, our Kobollian forefathers, are our guide, and that they have left us a map that beckons us to follow them to our new home among distant stars. We must go on or we will surely die!"

Cain stood smirking, and moved into position before the Quorum once more, like a lupus angling in for the kill, ready to bring down the lone bova. "The writings are fairy tales," he said, softly, like a gentle deathblow, a silencer on a gun barrel. "Ripping good bedtime stories for children, but that is all they are. No one has believed in them for aeons. You and your father are embarrassing throwbacks to an age of superstition and belief in magic . . . omens and augurs . . . mystic portents. Your father was a great man, Apollo, I have always said this, but he was misguided."

"Your words, Commander," Apollo answered. "Why are you so willing to risk the safety of the fleet upon these ancient texts that you claim are fairy tales? Are we to pick and choose the writings we believe and those we don't?"

"Of course," Cain answered, simply. "To not do so would make one a fool."

Apollo's hands fisted at his sides, and his jaw muscles worked as he tried to maintain his calm. It was one thing to attack him; it was another to speak ill of his father, in whatever terms Cain chose to couch it. He looked to Athena, who seemed torn by what she knew and what she felt, the heart ever at war with the brain.

"But it is time our race followed a path of our own making," Cain said flatly. "I am sorry, Apollo, but history will belong to me and those who have the courage to take back our birthright from the invaders."

It was Apollo's turn once again. He had spoken from intuition, addressed the assemblage from his heart. Now, he had only ragged emotion and faint hope left in his arsenal. "Our forefathers, the Thirteenth Tribe, evolved a technology many aeons ago that our race has never equaled. Are we so arrogant, so debased, to believe that we are so much wiser and sophisticated than they were?

"Had we not forgotten our roots and ancient ways, perhaps we would not be standing where we are today, on the brink of the precipice of total annihilation. History will belong to those who have the vision to see the truth and the courage to follow it."

That was enough for Cain. He turned defiantly toward the council, eyeing them with steely determination, knowing Belloch was his, and Tigh and Athena, for that matter. He thought if they voted for him, the rest of the Quorum, followers that they were, would not want to buck the trend. His sense of battle strategy told him when to strike, when to divide and when to unify, and that same sense told him it was time now to force the council to decide. It was a challenge, and most of these council members would back down from a real challenge.

"It is time to decide between myself and Apollo," he said, throwing down the gauntlet. Apollo looked startled; he had known this was coming, he had to. Perhaps he thought he would have longer to argue his case, and perhaps he could even have persuaded the council to his point of view. That was why Cain decided to press the issue, force them to decide now, while their blood was still hot from his oration, before Apollo could force his own seductive reasoning upon them.

"You all know me, and you know Apollo. Who would you want to save our worlds and lead the fleet into battle, if the situation demands? Apollo . . . who has fled from battle when possible, rather than engage the enemy and defeat them, soundly and decisively . . . or me?"

The council members stood, one after the other, each of them voicing his or her vote for Commander Cain. After the majority of the Quorum had voted for Cain as new supreme commander of the fleet, what was painful for Apollo simply became a cold-blooded beating he had to endure. But the worst of it for him was when both Tigh and Athena, albeit reluctantly, added their voices in support of Cain. What did it matter if the blow was delivered slowly or swiftly? The thrust was just as fatal.

The Quorum cheered Cain's appointment, and Apollo could

only stand silently and accept it. The cheering seemed to last much longer than it actually did, but at last the applause died down and the members each returned to their seat, and all eyes turned toward Apollo. All, that is, save Tigh and Athena, who could not quite bring themselves to meet his pained gaze. It's no easy thing to betray a man, and harder still to face him.

Through gritted teeth, Apollo said, "I accept your decision, but in protest. But I demand that Commander Cain and I have the opportunity to present our arguments to the people and then let the entire fleet decide."

Tigh massaged his temple; he hadn't stopped for more than a few seconds during the whole duration of the gathering, and Apollo thought the man would simply wear away the hair and flesh covering his skull. "Commander Apollo has a very good point," Tigh addressed the council. "On such an important matter, and under such unique and difficult circumstances, we will allow the people to vote on this matter."

He declared the Quorum adjourned, but Apollo had already started for the door. Athena jumped up from her seat and hurried after her brother, hoping to explain, perhaps even console him, but he was beyond consolation. What could she say, anyway, that would repair the damage? Apollo was a proud man, and they had stolen that away from him.

Sometimes one just had to stand and fight, whether the battle could be won or not. And sometimes, it was easier just to walk away.

10

THE FIRST wave of colonials was shuttled down to the hidden city after the Warriors, upon Apollo's insistence, spent two days on a reconnaissance mission determining the city and surrounding caverns were not concealing any hidden dangers. The caretakers had harvested enough food to provide ample sustenance for the first arrivals, and continued to gather food for the greater immigration still to come. Everything seemed perfect. Everything *was* perfect. And yet—

Apollo could not dismiss the feeling there was more here than they could see, but that was surely just paranoid thinking . . . wasn't it? And still, there was something about Segis, for all her grace and charm, Apollo did not trust, something deep within his gut that not all the logic he could throw at it could quiet.

But to not think like that was equally dangerous, even though Apollo remained the lone voice in the wilderness. When it was clear the Cylons were not following the fleet, and the colonials felt somewhat more secure in their sudden return to their journey's beginning, Segis offered the ships safe harbor. Circling the planet, in geosynchronous orbit, was a massive asteroid, the size of a small, bone-shaped moon. It was several kilometrons long, its black face pocked from countless astralon strikes. The asteroid reminded Apollo of a giant cinder, black, and lifeless, like some-thing coughed up from a giant volcano . . . or from hell.

"You may dock safely here," Segis informed them.

Apollo started to protest such an unlikely landing site, when three straight-edges of light appeared on the nearest side of the asteroid. The top edge of light was perhaps half as long as the asteroid itself, while the other two, forming perfect ninety-degree angles with their longer complement, were almost as tall as the giant rock.

"It's a door," Tigh said, his voice hushed with awe. "But, the size of it . . . the sheer scope . . . "

Apollo, mistrustful of this entire situation, ordered the gunners to stand by. He was certain at any moment a vast armada of hos-tile starfighters would swarm out of the hollow asteroid, or a bar-rage of plasma cannons would begin blasting away at the idled fleet, but no such thing occurred. And, he reminded himself, hadn't he not long ago accused Cain of picking and choosing which texts he believed? Wasn't he, himself, guilty of the same thing, if he chose to ignore the prophesied writings Segis had shown them?

As they all watched, the straight edges of light within the face of the asteroid grew larger, and lost their sharp definition. Now, light spilled out in crazy shapes, and, through the glare, painfully bright against the blackness, those watching from their bridges began to make out shapes and depth inside the huge rock. Here were the great, giant gears that opened the door, and there were the massive engines that powered the gears. Recessed lights, in the walls, in the ceilings, even in flush strips set into the steel-plated floor, illuminated every centimetron of the cavernous interior. The walls were an odd amalgam of steel and rock, with great beams and girders ribbed in the stone and veined with thick power cables.

Athena shuddered; she felt as if she were looking into the belly of some monstrous, space-sailing beast that waited patiently to devour the colonial ships.

As the *Galactica* neared the open hangar door, the scanner revealed something Apollo had not noticed before: although many of the cavities that adorned the planetoid's rugged face were from astralon strikes, many more were roundels of cold, gleaming steel, and Apollo understood at once these were concealed thrusters. The asteroid's course could be corrected, should the need arise. It was a ship of rock and metal.

"Take us in," Apollo commanded the bridge officer, and, to himself he murmured, "This is incredible."

"Honestly," Athena chided, gently, "you boys and your toys."

The asteroid contained its own artificial atmosphere and gravity, but it contained a great deal more than that as the commanders discovered once they stepped off their docked ships. At the far end of the cavern, Apollo spotted ancient mining equipment: picks, laser-borers, uniforms, hardhats, landrams to ferry the gathered ore to shuttles that waited to carry it down to the Kobol for refining. Everything necessary to run a full-scale mining operation, and it was evident this had been underway for a long, long while. Cain, standing beside Apollo, nevertheless had to shout to be heard over the low, bass throbbing of the planetoid's mighty engines. "It's a Tylium mine!" Cain said. The giant cavern swallowed the sound of his voice, making it seem flat and small.

He clapped both hands on Apollo's shoulders and squeezed them, his face breaking into a wide, toothy grin. "It looks like we may have all the Tylium we need!"

The living legend turned and looked at the raw mineral that marbled the dark cavern walls; the deposits stretched back and back, away into the depths of the asteroid's interior. The glow of the Tylium lit the way as far back as the eye could see. The Tylium was everywhere, glittering in the darkness like stars in the heavens.

Branching away from the main cavern were many more side corridors and galleys, and these tunnels honeycombed the asteroid as if they were the warrens of underground-dwelling animals.

"Look at those deposits, boy! There's enough in here to fuel the entire fleet—twice!" Cain said, and slung his arm around Apollo's shoulders. He pulled the younger man closer in an almost fatherly, one-armed hug. For a moment, Apollo allowed himself to believe everything was going to be all right. Maybe it *would* be all right. He couldn't help but think he was on the verge of some grand awakening, some epiphany that would make sense of everything he had recently been through. There was a sense of destiny charging the air, humming just beneath consciousness the way the mighty engines of the asteroid rumbled beneath their feet

As it was aboard the ragtag fleet, so it was in the city, races settling into parts of the city apart from other races, like calling to like. Just because they were no longer trapped aboard a flying iron box did not mean they were any less prisoners; trading their cages of iron for cages of glass and brick. Things changed, but people did not.

Trays and his group of fellow Warriors from the ODOC wandered the ordered, sensible streets of the hidden city, as young men have always done. They were the next wave of Warriors, the defenders of this place, this world, and everyone knew it.

"We'll see some real action," Trays promised his friends, "now that Cain's in charge of things."

And they slapped each other on the back and laughed. They were young and felt indestructible. As if battle were something to be wished for, hoped for. They did not understand, as those Warriors who came before them knew, that peace was the goal toward which they struggled, for which they laid down their life. Peace to the young Warriors was merely an absence of conflict, a lull between battles.

They were young, and they were foolish.

When Apollo was not aboard the *Galactica,* at Starbuck's bedside, he, also, wandered the streets, but not those of the underground city; he preferred, instead, to explore the wreckage of the ancient buildings. It was easier to imagine life once existing up here, easier to feel some closeness and kinship.

Today, Apollo chose to explore the pyramids, following his feet to the same site he and Adama had visited nearly twenty yahren earlier. He found the temple easily, and located the sigils that were carved into the base of stone. They were actually a code that would open the secret door. Apollo cleared his mind, and allowed his hand to sequence the runes in the proper order.

A moment later, the slab of limestone concealing the entrance rumbled open, and Apollo entered the long narrow passageway that led into the pyramid's deepest chambers. Still hanging on the wall was a pitch-soaked torch, which Apollo scraped into life, and by the fretful light of this small fire he made his way unerringly toward the heart of the pyramid, recalling his previous journey with Adama.

The past was never dead, never gone. It was like quantum space, existing side-by-side, but just out of synch with this world.

He found the temple, and ignited the four braziers that hung in each corner of the small chamber. Apollo laid the torch aside, and stood with his hands on his hips, studying the little temple. He could still recall every word Adama had said to him here, as if those words still echoed in this room as well as in his heart.

He needed a sanctuary, and this place, with the ghosts it held, was better suited to his needs than anything in the mirror city beneath him. Apollo needed to commune with the spirit of Adama and the Lords of Kobol, to make sense of what had happened lately, to understand his fate, and to pray for the destiny of the fleet, and his part in that.

Apollo sat on the low, flat marble slab in the center of the chamber, clasped his hands together, between his legs, below his knees, and closed his eyes. Was it possible his role was already over and that, all along, Cain was meant to shepherd the flock? If that was so, if the Lords of Kobol so decreed, then Apollo would accept it, but he didn't think it was. Things didn't feel complete; they felt . . . asymmetrical, and he was beginning to understand more and more clearly that the universe, life, death, love, was all one great circle, always returning to where things began. And Apollo's journey felt unfinished, as if it were a seventh note introduced into a passage of music to let the listener know things were not yet resolved.

As he sat with his eyes closed, praying for clarity and understanding, a black, particulated mist, perhaps no more than the soot from the burning torches, seemed to drift through the chamber and hover near Apollo, like a cloud of despair.

"Apollo?" Athena's voice seemed to be nearby and far away at once, made so by the distorting qualities of the long winding stone passageway through which she approached.

The darkness that had nearly touched Apollo rose like frightened avions, as if driven away by the sound of Athena's voice, or perhaps shredded apart by the vagaries of shifting wind currents through the ancient corridors, to hide among the gloom of the shadow-clotted ceiling.

"I've been looking everywhere for you," Athena scolded her brother from the doorway.

He finished his prayers and opened his eyes. Oddly, he felt more confused than ever, and he couldn't say why.

"What are you doing in here, anyway?" she asked, looking around the temple. Apollo stood, dusted down his trousers. He couldn't bring himself to look at her. He was more hurt than he wanted to admit, or to let her see.

"Praying," he said, simply. "For myself, for the fleet—" And now he did look at her, and he said, pointedly, "for *you.*"

Athena bit her lip. She supposed she deserved that. But then, as much as she hated to let herself think this, Apollo had deserved his comeuppance before the Quorum. Now he had a little taste of how it felt to be second best. It was well deserved and overdue. Still, he was her brother. She wished she could feel one way or the other about things, but she was split and torn and tugged straight down the center.

"Look," Athena began; she had to say this all at once or not at all. "I'm sorry about what happened, but I truly believe Commander Cain is the only one who can lead us at this time. He's had some experience with colonization, on Poseidon, and—"

Apollo cut her off. "The food on Poseidon was *mutating* the people," he reminded her. "Cain won't even acknowledge that. You've always underestimated me because you underestimate yourself. We both know it's no easy thing to be the children of Adama, but I've had it luckier than you, because I've had the opportunity to explore my limits."

As he spoke, Apollo went around the room, capping the braziers and snuffing their fires. He picked up the torch he had earlier set aside and turned once more to Athena.

"I guess . . . I've always been a little jealous of you, because of that," she admitted. *Jealous, angry, resentful* . . . she thought. Until this moment, until she opened that particular locked door, she hadn't really known just how jealous she was.

"I guess there's nothing to be jealous of now, is there?" he asked. "You humiliated me, but worse than that, you betrayed me." His anger was spilling out now, but it was anger at more than just Athena's actions. He was also confused by his own spiritual awakenings, finding it harder and harder to reconcile his Warrior's nature with this other side of himself he was still discovering. "Couldn't you trust me with this, Athena? Couldn't you have given me the benefit of the doubt?"

"Like you have me?" she shot back.

"What are you talking about?"

"You've never been able to completely trust my decisions," she said, pacing the small chamber like a caged animal. That was how she felt, too. "You've never completely been able to let me make any decisions of any consequence. I just want to know, Apollo— how does it feel? Now that you've found yourself in my place . . . how do you like it?"

Apollo looked at her as if he couldn't believe what he was hearing, and, in a way, he couldn't. "Is that what this is really about?" he asked.

Athena had to look away. "I didn't think so," she said, softly. "I didn't want it to be, but . . . "

"I can't believe this," he said. "I've done everything I can to help you . . . "

"That's just it!" she snapped, rounding on him with such fury that he took an involuntary step away from her. "You do every-thing to help me, but you never let me help myself!" She forced herself to remain calm, or at least as calm as she could. They were each saying things that probably should have been addressed long before this, and if anger and resentment intervened, these things might not be said at all. "I know you feel an enormous amount of pressure, trying to live up to Father, and I think, sometimes, you feel like you have to shoulder the burden alone, that any idea that doesn't agree completely with yours is going to undermine your abilities as a leader and a decision-maker. Actually, I just want you to see the other perspectives and consider the possibilities."

"Off of the bridge, I know all that," he said.

"We need to get you off the bridge more often."

"You try so hard to prove yourself," Apollo continued, "and I don't know who you're trying to impress. Me? There's no need. Father?" He shrugged. "He knew you had in you the makings of a great leader, but he drove you even harder, I think, because he knew you'd have to be tougher."

"Did he tell you this?"

"Yes," he said. Adama had not told Apollo this, not in so many words, but had, at least, spoken of it in his own oblique way. And it was what Apollo had intuited, right from the start, when they were children and he watched Adama reprimand Athena perhaps a little more harshly on her mistakes than Adama did Apollo. Not that he didn't correct Apollo, but Adama had doubtless known Athena would face opposition from so many males in the fleet, males whose culture did not allow for a woman in a position of authority, let alone one who may one day command, and so he had driven her a little harder, as if her womanhood were just one more mistake she could correct.

But instead, this treatment had only made Athena more methodical, alienating those around her with her obsessive drive for perfection, both in herself and in them. She had become harsh, and critical, and judgmental, undercutting herself by her very need to be respected. She had tried hard to earn Adama's love, never quite believing she already had it, mistakenly assuming because he pushed her a little harder that he loved her a little less than he did Apollo. She was wrong, but she would never believe it. She would spend the next several yahren trying to cope with it. Apollo understood her pain, her confusion and her resentment, but his own pain was too fresh, his emotions still too raw by what she had done to try to convince her Adama's love was equal and impartial. She still heard only his words of reproach, and not the countless little kindnesses he spoke to her.

"Cain may be a highly skilled battle tactician," Apollo admitted, "but no one could be better at commanding a fleet than the two of us, if we can only learn to work together as we have begun to do these past few yahren. Our individual strengths complement each other, when we allow them to." As Adama had, no doubt, intended, nurturing each of his children's natural gifts and abilities, surely knowing that, as good as they may be separately, together, they could be the best leaders the fleet might ever know. Apollo was more and more coming to believe this; he just had to make Athena start believing, but first, he had to make her believe in herself.

He ushered her from the temple, back up the winding passageway, the torch held above their heads. Their shadows pooled like spilled ink at their feet. "You've just begun to explore your Kobllian abilities, and one day you'll realize that your logical and left brain thinking does not hold all the answers and solutions to life."

He was learning this himself, more and more, as he bounced back and forth between the two, like the ball in a game of triad.

His voice and their footfalls echoed and re-echoed off the narrow hallway walls, until it seemed as if all the voices of those who had walked this sacred place were speaking at once. And perhaps they were, if one but had the ear to hear them.

"Sometimes, you have to move from a narrow and logical point of view to a more expansive viewpoint to really understand the dynamics of what is truly going on, and the only way you'll do that is to learn to tap into your deeper vision."

Athena stopped. "If we could see what was on the other side, we'd never want to climb a mountain," she said.

He smiled and told her, "It's not that we want to climb the mountain, it's that we *need* to, for a better perspective."

Apollo patted one of the stone slabs behind him. "What's this?"

Athena looked at him as if she expected him to make light of her, but she saw Apollo was quite serious. "It's a stone," she answered.

"Is that all it is?"

She looked at it, or pretended to, more as a courtesy to her brother. "What is it, then?" she asked, at length.

Apollo took her arm in his hand and they stepped back a few paces, their shadows dancing and capering by the fitful light of the torch. "Now what do you see?" he asked.

"It's still a stone—" she began, feeling annoyance. But then she realized what he was trying to show her: it was a stone, viewed up close, but a few paces removed, and it was just a brick in the wall, of no greater or lesser importance than those stones which butted up against it.

"That's what your *eyes* tell you, but take another step back, with your *mind*, and see the whole pyramid," he instructed, and, like mentioning a purple bova and then telling someone *not* to think of purple bovas, Athena could imagine the pyramid, stone upon stone. The image crowded its way into her mind's eye.

"And that's the whole pictograph," he said, sensing that she understood now. "That's what inner vision is. Someday, you'll understand how the left and right brains have to work together to successfully determine the best course of action."

They began walking again, and Athena walked beside him in

silence. She had always been strong willed and opinionated, and she knew, in her secret heart, that Apollo may well have been right, but she was not about to admit that, not when she still felt more at ease with her logic than her unpredictable intuition. Logic was the one commodity that had never failed her. Intuition had told her to go after Starbuck, and that had not come to much, except a budding friendship with Cassiopeia.

Their shadows fell behind them, like children racing to catch up.

Starbuck was slipping away a piece at a time.

His escape was cunning, so subtle that not much of Starbuck remained in his prison of flesh and bone, and it was beside the prisoner Dalton sat, speaking softly to him, then lapsing into lengthy silences. The only sound in the otherwise empty room was the flat, stupid *ping!* of the vital-signs monitors, and the papery *whuppp!* of the ventilator that breathed for him.

Troy stood watching Dalton from the doorway of the med-unit, feeling like a terrible voyeur but unable to look away. He waited until Dalton had fallen silent once again, then made his way to where she sat. Troy knelt beside her seat, and put his arm around her shoulder, his other hand resting on hers, where it lay on her leg.

"I'm here," he said, softly.

"I see you are, but why?" Dalton answered. "I don't need you here."

Troy felt his frustration rising, but asked instead, "Is there anything I can do?"

Dalton laughed, a ltitle shrilly, and turned to face him, her eyes red from crying. "Not unless you can raise the dead, Boxey. Think you can do that? Because if you can't, just leave me the frack alone."

She turned away from him, her eyes focused once more on her father, as if she needed to burn his image into her brain now, or risk losing the memory of him forever. Troy sighed explosively and stood; he knew she was in pain, that was clear to anyone, but she wore it like a badge that allowed her to lash out without consequence to those nearest to her.

"If you don't feel comfortable opening up to me any more, that's fine," he told her. "I'll leave you alone from here on."

"Good, thanks, you do that," she muttered, dismissing him with a shooing motion.

He stood a moment longer, biting back words that he wanted to fling at her; but what would that accomplish? He'd feel better for a moment, then regret them for the rest of his life. Troy backed out of the room, perhaps a part of him still believing she would reconsider and call him back, but that wasn't going to happen.

Troy thought of trying, one more time, to get through to her, to comfort her, but she had made it painfully clear comfort, at least not from him, was not what she wanted.

He turned on his heel and walked straight into Apollo, who was about to enter the med-unit.

"Troy?" Apollo began. "Everything okay?"

Troy nodded. It wasn't, but feelings were easy enough to deny. "We haven't had the chance to talk much lately," Troy said, "but I want you to know . . . I still have faith in you, no matter what the council does."

Apollo surprised them both and took the boy in a tight embrace. He couldn't remember the last time he had done this; perhaps not since Troy had gone by the nickname of Boxey and ran with the company of a daggit named Muffy.

"Thank you," he said.

Troy could see, over his father's shoulder, Dalton, still seated with her back to the entrance, still holding Starbuck's limp hand.

"It'll be all right," Apollo said, as if he could sense Troy's agony. "You'll see."

"What will?" Troy asked, stepping away from Apollo's embrace, his eyes never leaving Dalton. Why was it so easy for some people to receive comfort, and impossible for others? Why did it even matter?

"*Something* will," he said. "It *has* to."

Troy chuckled, and left his father with a smile and a thumbs-up gesture.

Apollo peered into the med-unit, spotted Cassiopeia seated, as ever, at her station. She motioned him over, meeting him halfway. She hugged him, perfunctorily, and said, "It's only a matter of centons now before he passes."

He nodded. He had known those words were inevitable, but he supposed he had hoped, since they seemed to be handing out an inexhaustible supply of miracles down on Kobol, there might be one last bit of magic that would correct this injustice, but he saw now there was not.

Apollo hugged her again, this time holding her closer, longer, and neither seemed to be in a hurry to end the embrace. "How are you holding up?" he asked her. It was one thing to watch someone you cared about die, but quite another to be the attending med as it happened, and he wondered why he had never considered that before.

She shrugged, buried her face a little deeper against his chest. Her hands, fisted behind his back, relaxed, and she rested her palms against his shoulder blades. "You know me," she said, "I'm always all right."

Before he knew he would do it, Apollo kissed her softly on the top of her head. "I know you are," he said. "But, just in case you're not, well, I'm here for you."

"You're more like him than you know," she mumbled into his chest. "No wonder he considered you his brother."

"He thought the world of you," Apollo said, his words overlapping hers. "He loved you as much as he ever loved anyone."

"As much, or as often?" she joked, and felt her eyes prick with tears.

Apollo laughed softly, and hugged her a little tighter. "You go say your good-byes," Cassie told him. "We'll talk later."

He nodded. Apollo could see why Starbuck had fallen for Cassiopeia; she had a rare quality that one didn't find often in this hardscrabble life—it was kindness.

Dalton glanced over at Apollo as he stepped quietly next to her. She held Starbuck's nerveless hand in hers and, after a moment, took Apollo's hand, as well, joining all three of them together in a clasp. But Starbuck's hand was cold, and stiff. Apollo realized with growing horror there was not enough magic left in all of Kobol to bring Starbuck back from this. There was no bargain Apollo could make, no deal he could strike. There was no last-minute reprieve. There was only the sharp, antiseptic smell of the med-unit and the machines that went *ping*. Human life and misery seemed out of place here, in this place of cold indifference.

Athena, Sheba, Boomer, and Tigh had entered the room and stood on deathwatch, each of them holding his or her memories of Starbuck closely, as if death would steal these as easily as it was robbing them of the man himself. They spoke softly, recalling his or her favorite story about Starbuck, but there were many, too many to tell. But the heart of each story was the same: *he was my friend, and I loved him.* When you got down to it, there really were no new stories, just variations on all the others that had gone before. Before it was Starbuck lying here, wheezing out his last, few ragged breaths, it was someone else's dearest friend, someone else's great love of her life, some mother's adored son. Who were they to think pain made them unique?

Apollo slowly became aware the med-scans were no longer making their infuriatingly calm pinging sound, but were a low, strident wail.

Cassiopeia moved with fluid efficiency, shutting down the monitoring equipment, hushing their cries the way a mother calms a child who awakens in tears from a bad dream. Unfortunately, bad as this was, it was not a dream that could be soothed with just a few soft words. These tears would not dry with a kiss, nor this pain be turned away by a gentle song. This was real. This was forever.

Dalton hugged her father and christened his face with bitter tears. Starbuck's only family offered and received comfort from one another, but Apollo had already turned and left the room, wondering why he was still alive and not his closest friend, out-ward bound now on a journey with no ending. In his chambers, Apollo took down the bottle of ambrosa from which he and Star-buck had sometimes drunk on special occasions, and each drink brought the tears a little closer, and every moment took him a little farther away from someone he already missed with all his heart.

Even as he cursed the drink that gave him hope, he poured himself another.

11

T HE MOURNERS for Starbuck's funeral began to gather as the hour of his service crept closer.

Apollo couldn't say why, precisely, but he felt the ceremony should be held in the temple inside the ancient pyramid; it was just something his intuition told him should be so, and even if he didn't always understand the reasons, he had at least learned to trust his feelings, and he felt this one quite strongly.

Starbuck's funeral bier rested atop the marble dais where, the day before, Apollo sat praying for guidance. It was a small chamber, but then, Starbuck had few close friends and even less family. Everyone admired him, but only a small handful really *knew* him. Apollo stood in the back, away from everyone else, his hands clasped together in front of him, watching the mourners. Dalton sat near the bier, and Troy sat as far away from her as he could, present as a show of respect for Starbuck, whom he considered a great man and a great friend, more than out of concern for Dalton's feelings. Trays was there, as well, seated beside Dalton, and Boomer, Sheba, Athena and Cassiopeia, suffering their loss together, having come together at last as friends.

Tigh was officiating, as he had done at Commander Adama's ceremony, and he stepped forward to the little rostrum and began to speak. He had prepared notes, and they were laid out before him on the stand, but he ignored them and spoke from his heart. What he thought was unimportant; what he felt was all that mattered. "Another great man, Commander Adama, once said, 'A Warrior has nothing to fight for, if he does not allow himself to love, and be loved in return.' Well, Captain Starbuck was a man who loved many, and was loved by many more," Tigh said, well aware of the irony. Tigh glanced at Cassie and Athena, but they had taken his comment with the same good grace in which it was delivered. "That made him a great Warrior. But he was also a great man, and a great friend to many of us."

Tigh swallowed, his voice beginning to crack. It was impossible to not be affected by the moment, and to help him recover, the Leonid thought of Starbuck, sitting and listening and laughing at this incredible outpouring of affection and sentiment on his behalf. He would have been amazed, and probably a little embarrassed, but that was Starbuck, and thinking such things helped Tigh get through the rest of his speech.

He kept it short, not because there wasn't much to say about Starbuck— *"Some are good stories, and some are the truth,"* Starbuck used to say—but because there wasn't much he *could* say about Starbuck without the sting of tears, and sadness and sorrow were not the way Starbuck would want to be remembered.

From the back of the room, Apollo watched the others in the temple grapple with the weight of their grief, joining them all together like some enormous black yoke.

Cassiopeia wept openly, and bitterly, and Athena held her and cried as well. Apollo never thought he'd live to see this day, but then, he also never thought he'd live to see the day Starbuck was no longer here. Dalton's head was bowed, and Trays' hand rested on her back.

And Troy . . . well, Troy was like his father, in some ways. His face betrayed little, but the unnatural brightness of welling tears in his eyes gave him away. He had never really gotten to know Starbuck in quite the same way Apollo had, but that kind of camaraderie was lucky to happen once. It could never happen a second time because there would never be another like Starbuck.

"Starbuck was an example of courage, and cooperation—" Tigh continued, casting a meaningful look toward Trays as he did, but it was a wasted effort "—and, above all, humor. I think above all the things about Starbuck I'll miss, it's his humor I'll miss most. The sly grin on his face, a tankard of grog before him, one of his horrible fumarellos clenched between his teeth, possessing a losing hand of pyramids but trying to bluff everyone into believing otherwise."

The room fell quiet. It was easy to picture that.

"And I think that's where I'll leave him," Tigh said. "He'll always be there, when I think of him, which will be often, just another night in the ODOC, with just another bad hand, and just about to tell another bad joke." He swallowed, hard, and twice, and his Adam's apple bobbed up and down as he fought to keep the tears he felt from his eyes. "He will be missed," Tigh managed, and then he had to nod that the service was over.

As the ceremony concluded, an eerie light, seemingly from nowhere and everywhere at once, filled the chamber. It was a light Apollo had seen before, many yahren earlier, in this same chamber, with Adama. No one else seemed to see it, but Apollo watched as the beam bounced in geometric shapes off the symbols and sigils on the walls, at last striking Starbuck's head, suffusing his peaceful, slumbering face with a brilliant glow that lingered, then winked out.

No one reacted; no one else had seen it and Apollo might have doubted the proof of his own senses, if he hadn't seen the same thing before. But he had to wonder if perhaps Starbuck *was* Kobollian, after all.

Apollo watched them all slowly file past the casket and out of the temple. When he was alone, he crossed to Starbuck's coffin and stood looking at his oldest friend's peaceful face. There was a slight smile on it, but then, there usually was. Even death was not serious enough to change that.

"You're already missed," Apollo said. "But your journey's not over yet. It's just beginning."

Centons later, after the last goodbyes had been spoken, the final farewells whispered, the coffin bearing Starbuck's body was placed into his favorite Scarlet Viper. Bo jay had spent the time during Starbuck's ceremony readying the Viper, removing the seat and navi-hilt, making sure there would be enough room in the cockpit to fit the coffin. After the service, Apollo had tucked a deck of pyramids, a pack of fumarellos, and a gold cubit into Starbuck's pockets. Beside him, in the coffin, he laid with reverence a bottle of Starbuck's favorite ambrosa. Bad enough his friend had to take this trip alone, but Apollo couldn't allow him to make it unprepared.

Apollo stood with his hands on the ledge of the cockpit, looking down at the coffin. The lid had been closed and sealed, and all that remained was for Apollo to lower the canopy into place, but he found he wasn't ready to do that. Not quite yet. For when that happened, Starbuck would really be gone.

"Somethin' wrong, Apollo?" Bo jay asked, wiping his greasy hands on his jumpsuit.

Apollo looked up and forced a counterfeit smile. "Everything's fine," he said, and closed the canopy. The hull damage, suffered during Starbuck's last battle was left untouched by Bo jay, a testament to Starbuck's courage under enemy fire. Bo jay watched as Apollo's fighter sped down the launch tube, followed by Starbuck's Viper, slaved to the lead fighter's controls until this last task was completed.

The launch aperture irised open and the two fighters boomed out of the man-made asteroid and into the vacuum of space, leaving the tug of gravity farther behind with each moment. *At least this time you're not following me into trouble,* Apollo thought, and smiled sadly.

Not that there'd been a shortage of those times, Apollo recalled; he'd always been the gung-ho one, first to charge into trouble, while his old friend was content to drink, gamble, and womanize.

Sure, Starbuck was a hero countless times over, but that was because Apollo would get them both into situations against overwhelming odds, and then he and Starbuck together would have to battle their way back out.

"Who's going to watch my back now?" Apollo asked.

From the start, they had watched out for one another—on the ore planet Carillon, and the insectoid Ovions and their grisly casino; their search-and-destroy mission on the ice world; and Starbuck had been there for him after Serina had died.

It was funny how they had both had one great love, and had dealt so differently with the loss: Starbuck, by avoiding a serious, committed relationship, and Apollo, withholding love, as if he were still inextricably bound to Serina, as if to love anyone else was a betrayal, an infidelity. It had been almost twenty yahren, but the hands that held Serina close in the night had never really let go.

Apollo sighed and dragged himself out of his musings, studying the scroll of information flashed on the screen of his helm, but it only confirmed what he already knew—it was time to let go.

He thumbed off the slave unit, freeing Starbuck's ship from its lock-step course with Apollo's own fighter, and made a slow, graceful arc out of the Scarlet Viper's path. Apollo watched the fighter drifting into deeper space, receding from sight; soon, it would be gone from his instrument panel as well. "Well, old buddy, I guess this is it," Apollo said. Although no one would hear him, he refused to let his voice quaver with emotion. He was a leader; that may be taken from him by Cain and the will of the people, but for now, he was still commander, and would comport himself as such. "Maybe you'll find one of those light ships out there and they'll take you home. If there's any justice in the universe, they'll make you an honorary Kobollian. Frack!" he said, and slammed his palm against his thigh. "We're all descended from the Kobollians anyway, so what the frack difference does it make if you're from the same House as my family or not?

"Maybe one day those light beings, or whatever they are, will explain it all to me," Apollo continued; it was not so much a statement as it was a prayer toward understanding a cold and sometimes wicked universe.

The light of distant days, traveling all this time through endless space just to heliograph on the scored metal hull of Starbuck's Viper, twinkled, and then Apollo lost sight of the funeral ship. "For all our great dreams and great sorrows," he said, as softly as farewell whispered over the coffin, "we all return home again."

Apollo sat quietly for a long while. At last, he turned his Viper and started toward back toward the asteroid.

But one man's ceiling is another man's floor, and while Apollo was saying goodbye to his friend, and mourning, the mirror city was echoing with the sound of merriment, and laughter, and music. The colonials were celebrating the colonization of their newfound homeworld. Reassured by Uriah's validation of the ancient texts prophesying the fleet's return to Kobol, Cain had pushed for—and gotten—the council to allow the colonization of Kobol.

Mead and ambrosa, grog and ale, flowed in golden rivers, free and easy. The first toast that night was drunk to the memory of Adama, and to the far-seeing vision of Commander Cain, who had led them here. Already the truth was being rewritten. That's not the way it was, at all, but if that was how they chose to remember it, then that was how it happened.

The caretakers and several citizens had spent the better part of two days in the mealprep getting ready for this moment; but everyone agreed, the end result was well worth the effort. Trestle tables groaned under the weight of food, heaped high with fresh game, roasted avion and the tenderest bova the colonials had tasted since . . . well, it seemed like *forever.* Livestock was something of a rarity among the fleet, reserved for the more special occasions, but here, all manner of wild game walked and prowled and flew, and succulent fruit and vegetables grew fat and fell from trees everywhere.

Lashings of coneth stew laden with mushies, bowls of tulupian buds and trays of oglivs and the best kirasolis the little travellers had ever tasted. The children ran and played and laughed and shrieked their joy, and hid beneath tables and finally grew bored, and tired, and fell asleep at their parents' feet or in their laps.

Life had a way of adapting to almost anything, and going on.

The Warriors had their own tables; like calls to like, after all. Troy, one of the few pilots at the table old enough to know Starbuck and have the honor of flying with him, stood, and raised his mug of ale. "To Captain Starbuck," he said.

The cadets raised their mugs and drank to his memory, without knowing why. One couldn't remember a man one didn't know. Dalton knew that as well as anyone.

She sat at another table, with Trays and his group of cadets, drinking more ambrosa than was good for her, then pouring herself another. Trays barely noticed her; he was too busy laughing with his friends, being the center of attention, reliving the battle with the Cylons above the storm-wracked planet of Kirasolia. He was the hero, this time; Starbuck was merely a postscript to the story, barely a footnote, and Dalton was too deep in her grief to protest.

Troy had left his group and wandered past Dalton's table, pausing a moment to overhear the conversation.

"You owe your life to Captain Starbuck, Trays," he said. The conversation and laughter stopped, for a moment, and all eyes turned to Troy. All, that is, except Dalton. She had gotten good at avoiding him. "We all do. You can lie about anything else you want to, but you'd better always tell the truth about Starbuck."

He gave Trays a meaningful look, and moved away from the table, heading to the bar for another drink. He had barely turned his back on the group before the jokes and laughter began again. Jokes were fine; laughter was good; they were here to celebrate, after all, and Starbuck, more than anyone else, would have understood that, but it felt *sacrilegious* to Troy to be having a good time when his uncle was not here to lend his laugh to the chorus. How dare life go on?

"Ambrosa," he told the servitor at the counter. "Something to alter my mood."

She smiled, a trifle coyly, batted her blue eyes, and said, "I could alter your mood, and it wouldn't take ambrosa."

Troy glanced over at Dalton; she didn't even seem to know he was still alive, and the servitor *was* lovely, but . . . life was a circle, and right now, Dalton was in her opposing apogee, but he thought she might be around again, sooner or later. He wanted to make sure he had both hands free to grab her when she did.

"Thanks," he said, turning back to Jasmine. "But, I'm waiting for a friend."

"Did you ever think you'd live long enough to see *that?*"

Boomer looked at what Bo jay had pointed at with his flagon of grog. It was Baltar, released from lockdown in his quarters on a reprieve from Commander Apollo, walking and smiling among the celebrants. Baltar could not be allowed to wander amidst the general populace without an armed escort; this was not so much to keep him under observation, although that was a side benefit, as it was to keep him safe. Not many among the citizens or Warriors would pass up the chance to take the life of Baltar for his past crimes against humankind.

"When Baltar, the greatest traitor in human history, would be allowed to walk freely among his former enemies," Bo jay finished, and shook his head.

Boomer turned away from the sight of Baltar and drew himself around his drink. "Times change," he said.

"Yeah, maybe," Bo jay grudgingly allowed, "but I'm not so sure people ever do."

Sheba and Jolly barely noticed Baltar's presence; they were heavily involved in a serious drinking competition, and so far, it was neck and neck. But Sheba drained her mug of grog, banged it down on the tabletop, and snatched up the next flagon and drained it in three huge gulps. She smeared the foam away from her lips with the back of her hand and, smiling to the cheers of all the pilots, young and old at her table, belched in a most satisfying, unladlylike manner.

"You're perfect," one of the younger pilots blurted out, smiling foolishly at Sheba.

She laughed heartily. "And you're drunk."

"I'll be sober tomorrow, but you'll still be perfect."

But she hadn't heard him; her eyes were scanning the crowd for Apollo. It was a faraway look, one Boomer knew quite well, and he felt sorry for the pilot who fell into those sultry eyes, because there was no escaping them once you did. If it hadn't been for his love for Phaedra, he might have been tempted a time or two himself.

And speaking of Phaedra, he thought, it was time to find her, and take her in his arms, and whisper in her ear the things he hadn't told her in too long. He was soon to be a father, after all, and it was time to start acting like it. Boomer excused himself and stood up, patting Bo jay on the shoulder. "Keep an eye on things for me, old man," he said.

"I will, youngster," Bo jay answered with a grin.

Boomer pulled a pained face, to everyone's amusement, and left the table. Sheba held out her hand to Jolly. "Pay up," she said.

"Best two out of three?" he suggested, and filled the mugs to the brim once more.

She shrugged, and smiled, her eyes as clear as this moment. "Sure," she said. "I'm still a little thirsty."

Baltar smiled and nodded at the citizens as he made his way through them, flanked on either side by heavily armed security agents, their hands never moving far from the butts of their unsecured sidearms. Gods, they thought, the nerve of the man! To move amongst the Citizenry took pogees enough, but to *wave* at them as if he were some kind of hero to be adored—

"Traitor!" Trays yelled. "Do the new world a favor and quit fouling its air!"

"And who do you suppose *led* you all to this new world, boy?" Baltar snapped back. "Someday, I will be looked upon as the savior of our race. Greatness is always conferred after one's passing."

"Then by all means, let's honor your greatness," one of Trays' cohorts said, and flung his mug at Baltar. He pushed away from the table and lurched to his feet, staggering over to Baltar, but in that moment of hurling the flagon, the security detail had drawn their weapons.

"Frack, what do we do now?" the first guard asked his compatriot. "We can't shoot a *kid*. These people'd have our pogees in the grinder!"

"In case you haven't noticed . . . they already are," his partner answered.

The citizens who had been near enough to witness the men draw their weapons now rose to their feet and surged forward, while Trays' group of cadets swarmed the guards and their hated charge. Baltar's hand clasped his temple, where the mug had struck him a solid blow, and a slow, fat drop of blood oozed from between his fingers and dropped to the ground.

"What're you gonna do, *shoot* us?" Trays hectored the Blackshirts. "Shoot a bunch of unarmed *kids? For him?*"

The security men stood in front and behind Baltar, weapons still drawn. "We have orders," the first guard warned in a loud, unwavering voice, "and, like them or not, we *will* execute those orders."

"No one wants this," the second guard said sensibly. The events of the next few moments were balanced precariously on a fulcrum, ready to teeter or totter in either direction; it just depended on which side had more weight of conviction.

"Let's all just go back to our friends and family and finish this celebration quietly."

Baltar started to speak; whether it was to excoriate the citizens for their barbarous bloodlust, or to plead for his life, the words never left his lips. The first guard glanced at Baltar over his shoulder, and growled from the corner of his mouth,

"Not a word, not a frakkin' word from you. I'm on duty now, and I'm sworn to protect you, but if you say anything to incite these people to riot, if I have to shoot any of these citizens because of you, I promise you, the moment my cycle is over, I'll come for you and blast your traitorous brains out of your skull."

Baltar shut his mouth with an audible *Click!* of his teeth.

And then, while no one was really watching, the moment regained its center of balance, and the chance of violence passed. Citizens and cadets turned grudgingly away, one after the other, grumbling amongst themselves, complaining of the way Baltar hid behind the guards, and there was some talk, mostly for show, to assuage dented pride, of finding Baltar later, when he was alone. But it was just talk.

The guards waited until the citizens had returned to their tables or their places on the dance floor before they holstered their lasers once again. Even so, they kept them unsecured, ready to be drawn at a moment's notice. "Had enough fun for one day?" the second guard asked Baltar.

"We'd better get him back to his quarters," the first guard said, and gripped Baltar unpleasantly tight by the arm, herding him along through the gathering, giving the citizens as wide a berth as possible

"But, I *saved* you," Baltar whined, blood dripping down his cheek; "I really have changed . . ." He was genuinely confused and didn't understand why they all reacted to him so angrily. In his mind he was a hero, even if it was only the hero of his own life.

He was going to feel this in the morning, but, for now, he would settle for not feeling much of anything at all.

Apollo had never been much of a drinker because he didn't care for the way it dulled his senses and made him less than totally in control of his own body, but just lately he had come to realize there was an upside to deadening his mind—it shut up that pesky, nagging voice that reminded him he was alive, and Starbuck was not. He knew that voice very well, although he hadn't heard from it in several yahren. Apollo had gotten well acquainted with it shortly after Zac was killed, and, just in case he thought he'd lost touch with it, the voice came roaring back, strong as ever, after Serina died. Same voice, same message: there was no need to listen to it again. At the bar, he ordered an ambrosa and stood alone, drinking it. Apollo glanced toward the presidium, where the council and Commander Cain sat in the place of honor. The seat beside Cain was empty, and why not? It was intened for Apollo, but he didn't feel like being a part of anything: he just felt like being *apart*.

"You know what they say about a man who drinks alone, don't you?" Bo jay began, ambling over to the bar to get another round of drinks for his table. Apollo looked over at him but said nothing. "He's too cheap to buy a round for his friends."

Apollo laughed softly, reached into his pocket and drew out a couple of cubits, plunked them down on the bar. "On me," he announced, and looked over at Bo jay's table, where Sheba and Jolly were between rounds. Apollo caught Sheba's eye, but she looked away, suddenly fascinated by the empty mug sitting on the table between her resting hands.

Bo jay caught Apollo studying her, and said, "She's easy on the eye, for sure." Apollo turned away from his star-gazing and looked at Bo jay, who laughed and slammed his palm down on the bar top. "Don't even try to pretend you'd rather be lookin' at me, Apollo! I'd worry about you if you did."

Apollo smiled and looked into his mug, took another draught of ambrosa.

"You're welcome to join us," Bo jay told him.

"Maybe later," Apollo said.

Bo jay wrapped his arms around the commander and lifted him up off his feet in an embrace that seemed a lot like a wrestling hold to Apollo, and shook him, playfully and affectionately. "*You're* still alive, Apollo," Bo jay said. "You remember that." He put him back down, Apollo's ribs still aching from the hug.

"I have a voice that reminds me of that," Apollo assured him. The older man thought it was a joke, and laughed. He picked up his tray, filled with fresh mugs of grog, and told Apollo he'd see him.

Apollo raised his almost-drained flagon and winked at him,

then turned back toward the servitor and indicated he wanted a refill. During that time, Bo jay took the cue and made his way back to his own table, and, with no longer any need to pretend, Apollo's face sagged once more into the map of unhappines he had so lately been charting, going deeper into unexplored regions by the moment.

How could these people go on as if everything was all right, when such a terrible thing had happened to Apollo?

Didn't they realize?

"Are you sure about that?" someone asked Apollo. He turned, expecting to see Troy or Boomer, perhaps, or even Tigh, but it was one of Segis's hooded minions. "You never could hold your ambrosa," the figure reminded him. Before Apollo could say anything, the figure tossed a gold cubit on the counter to pay for Apollo's drink. Apollo picked it up and studied it, and when he turned back to ask the man where he had gotten this particular cubit, the hooded figure was gone.

"Did you see—?" Apollo began, hoping the servitor had seen it as well, or had seen how the figure disappeared so quickly, but she was busy chatting with one of the Warriors who had come by for a refill.

Apollo turned the cubit over and over and over between his fingers, watching the light race along its smooth, curved edges.

Sheba thought that if anyone ever needed a friend, it was Apollo, and she promised herself, after this next round of drinks Bo jay so generously bought for them, using Apollo's cubits, she would go talk to Apollo and, well, who knew where that talk would lead? She made a mental note to herself to get over there before Apollo had had too many ambrosas, although she was reasonably confident she had the wiles and the ways to counteract any adverse effects the drink may have.

It was funny how the world could change in the time it took to finish a drink. As Sheba sat listening to one of Bo jay's horrible jokes, Cassiopeia spotted Apollo, sitting off at a side table by himself, and took the opportunity to join him. Sheba was laughing one moment, and when she looked toward Apollo once more, she no longer felt like laughing. Her cheeks flushed and she looked down at her drink, letting her hair curtain her face and the look of hurt she wore.

She supposed it was inevitable; Apollo and Cassie had both suffered a devastating loss with Starbuck's death, and it was only natural they would spend so much time in commiseration. From grief comes bonding, and from their bonding came grief for Sheba. She suspected there was more to it than just the sharing of memories and tears, even if neither of them quite realized it themselves. And maybe, Sheba told herself, that was for the best. Maybe it was time she moved on, because the woman Apollo really loved was perfect. Frozen in time and in his heart, Serina was the ideal woman because she could never change, could never hurt him, she could never disappoint him. And he, for his part, was faithful to her because he had never fully allowed himself to love anyone since her death.

Until he laid that ghost to rest, he would not be able to move on, but would remain forever in place, like a heart frozen between beats.

Sheba drew in a deep breath and let it trickle out in a long, slow sigh. She forced a smile onto her lovely face and turned to Jolly. "Buy me a drink?" she asked.

But before Jolly could respond, one of the young Warriors who had been smitten with Sheba since he first beheld her during his cadet training, had finally managed to drink the exact amount of grog necessary to give him just the right amount of courage and invulnerability to potential rejection, to sidle over to her at the crowded table and sit next to her in the place vacated by Boomer. She looked over at him, a trifle surprised, but maybe a little shake-up was just what she needed.

"I was wondering," he started, his throat suddenly dry, despite all the grog he'd drunk. "That is . . . would you . . ." Sheba was quickly losing interest in this conversation, and the Warriors knew he'd have to spit it out now or forget it. "Would you like to dance with me?" he blurted.

She looked at Bo jay, then back at her suitor. "Ah, what the frack?" She nodded and stood. The Warrior, as if unable to believe his luck, remained seated for a moment, then realized she was waiting for him. Taking her by the hand, he led her to the middle of the dance floor where dozens of other couples already swayed to the music.

Her chin resting on his shoulder, Sheba closed her eyes and they danced, slowly; he, to the music the band played, she, to a song that was playing in her head, and if she happened to think of a certain, dark-haired, handsome commander, well, blame it on the drink, or the music, or an unquiet ghost of her own.

"I have something for you," Cassiopeia told Apollo.

He smiled, a little drunkenly. "I'll bet you do," he said.

She laughed, and said, "You're kind of cute when you relax, you know that?" Cassie reached into the small pack she wore at her hip, rummaged through the items it contained, and found what she was looking for. "Anyway, that's not what I was talking about. Here," she said, and handed Apollo the small, framed object. He took it, blinked it into focus. It was an old pictograph of Starbuck and Apollo, taken yahren ago when they were both just out of the academy.

"Where'd you find this?" he asked, unable to look away from those young faces gazing back at him through the yahren, a little piece of frozen time in his hands.

"It was in Starbuck's things," she answered. "I framed it. He would never have done it himself."

Apollo laughed at that thought. "No, you're right, he wouldn't have."

"Anyway, I saw it when I was. . . clearing out his chambers. . . thought you might like to have a little keepsake of him."

They were both silent for several centari, neither knowing quite what to say. Apollo was still looking at the pictograph, remembering the day it had been taken. They had both just earned their wings, and Starbuck could barely wait to hit the OCDC, now that he was a real Warrior. They had both drunk too much that day, and

Starbuck had suggested they have a pictograph taken of the occasion. Apollo had never known what happened to it after that; he could barely recall what happened to himself that day, after the pictograph was taken, except it involved a lot of grog and even more socialators.

Even in death, Starbuck was full of surprises.

"He loved you, you know," Cassie said quietly.

Apollo nodded, and tucked the pictograph away in his pocket before he could be overcome with grief. "I know," he said, and, after a moment, asked, "Did he—"

She nodded. "Of course he knew. You always know when someone loves you," she said, and brushed her finger lightly beneath Apollo's downturned chin, lifting his face so their eyes met. "Don't you think?"

His eyes shifted toward where Sheba sat, or had been sitting; he found her out on the dance floor with one of the young cadets, holding one another as close as praying hands, her head resting on his shoulder. "I thought so," he muttered, and forced himself to look away.

"Do you want to get out of here?" Cassie asked him.

He nodded. More than anything, he wanted that. Apollo tried to stand and stumbled, sat down hard in his seat. "How many ambrosas did you have?" Cassie asked, laughing, but she wasn't laughing *at* him. He shrugged, admitted he had no idea, but thought it might be only one, just spread out over several flagons.

Gar'Tokk, who had been standing back at a respectful distance to allow Apollo room to grieve his friend, now stepped forward and helped him to his feet, Cassie holding him steady as Gar'Tokk lifted. It was not as if Gar'Tokk couldn't have managed the commander's weight on his own; it was just an excuse for closeness and simple human contact.

"I'll get him home," Gar'Tokk promised.

"Actually," Cassie said, and gave the Noman a sly smile, "my compartment's closer."

Living quarters in the mirror city were small but efficient, with the larger compartments going to families, and those of a more distinguished stature, such as Commander Cain, Apollo, Athena, and the rest of the Quorum. Cassie fell somewhere between the extremes, since her status as a med practitioner elevated her to a somewhat loftier position than simple citizen. Even so, small as it was, her compartment also felt, at times, at night especially, much too large for her, and she was grateful to have Apollo there to make it more intimate.

Her quarters were still in a state of flux, as were those of everyone else throughout the underground city, as she unpacked and stored her belongings and tried to find a way to make her cell, practically identical to all the others in the city, uniquely her own. Med texts sat on shelves, and charts hung on the otherwise featureless walls.

Gar'Tokk took his surroundings in at a glance, grunted something that may have been approval, or could just as easily have been distaste, and tumbled the commander into Cassi's narrow berth. "This where you want him?" Gar'Tokk asked, and favored her with one of his few smiles.

"That'll do nicely," she said.

The Borellian Noman grunted again, and this time she was sure it was the sound of laughter, and said he'd leave them alone. He stopped at the door long enough to inspect Cassie's still-shapely body, and shrugged; he really didn't understand what humans found so attractive about each other's almost-hairless bodies, but then, he really didn't understand much that humans did. He just worked here.

Cassie closed the door and turned back to Apollo, who was sitting on the edge of the berth, gripping the edge of the mattress with both hands as the room began to swim around him. "You all right?" she asked, sitting carefully beside him, near enough he could feel the heat rising off her body. He nodded that he was, then wished he hadn't as the room took that as a cue to start pinwheeling in the opposite direction. Apollo was afraid to let go of the berth for fear he would fall up to the ceiling. "You miss him, don't you?" she asked, softly. "It's all right, you don't have to say anything; I miss him, too."

She leaned closer, somehow slipping her right arm around his back, and cupping his face with her left. Cassiopeia's breast pressed into Apollo's side, and he made no effort to move away. She kissed him gently on the temple, and at the corner of his eye.

"It sounds trite, but, you know, he'll always be alive for us," she continued, interspersing her words with soft kisses; the space between them grew smaller, the kisses more plentiful. "In our hearts, in our minds." He nodded; it did sound trite, but it was something to hold onto, and that was better than nothing. The silence that followed Starbuck's passing was like the silence that follows a storm or a battle.

He lifted his face toward hers, and her kiss, meant for his cheek, found his mouth instead. Apollo was reasonably sure it was safe to let go of the bed now, and slowly put his arms around Cassie, pulling her nearer. Their mouths found one another once more, this time more squarely on, and she slipped her tongue between his lips and teeth. Cassie stroked his tongue and the roof of his mouth with her own, and, as she pulled slowly away from the kiss, nibbled lightly on his lower lip and let it go with a little pop.

"You taste like ambrosa," she joked. Her fingers began unbuttoning his uniform, opening it, slipping it away from his chest and off his shoulders, exposing his chest and flat belly. She kissed between his pectorals and licked and kissed her way down his abdomen to his navel, where she swirled her tongue playfully.

"Starbuck used to say I was like ambrosa," she told him, a wicked smile on her lips. "He said I used to go straight to his head."

Apollo giggled, and Cassie laughed, too. "You're drunk, aren't you?" she asked. Apollo placed a finger to his lips and made a *shushhhh*-ing sound, as if that were some carefully guarded secret that absolutely must not fall into enemy hands. Cassie laid him down slant-wise on her berth, pulled off his boots and stood them side by side, like an honor guard, and unbuckled his pants. She slid them down and off, and before she could fold them and drape them over the back of her chair, she heard Apollo murmur something and begin to make sounds like a daggit being choked.

"Oh, you aren't going to get sick now, are you?" she asked in horror.

He didn't answer; just made another one of those choking-daggit noises, and she realized he had passed out the moment his head touched the pillow.

"Oh, *frack!*" she hissed under her breath.

Cassie sat beside him on the edge of the berth, looking at his peaceful face, his mouth open, and for a moment, she considered trying to rouse him, then wondered if perhaps this was better. She asked herself if this made any sense, and she couldn't honestly answer. This may have been nothing more than one of those chance encounters that come about from opportunity, and the false sense of closeness.

Then again, she thought, it also made perfect sense, didn't it? She and Apollo had known one another for yahren, and liked one another as people, and friends. The best romances began as friendships . . . and, then again, the best friendships have been ruined by romances.

Frack! Even when he was unconscious, the man was infuriatingly complex!

Well, she supposed; it anything was meant to be between them, it would happen. And, if not . . . well, if not, it was nice to not have to sleep alone for once.

Cassie lifted Apollo's legs and swung them around so he was length-wise in her berth, and took down a warmer from the closet, shook it loose, and covered him with it. She undressed herself and slid into bed beside him, giving herself a treat for being good. Cassie rested her head against Apollo's chest and shoulder, and snuggled closer to him beneath the warmer. She studied his face by the ambient light in the room, and, when she thought she had it memorized, closed her eyes and fell into a warm and comfortable sleep, untroubled by bad dreams.

The celebration was breaking up, fragments spinning away from the mass, joining with other fragments. Troy watched as Dalton left the dance floor with Trays, where they had been dancing as closely as if they were cojoined, and then Troy could watch no more. They were leaving the fete together, and Troy decided he had enjoyed just about as much of this celebration as he could stand. "She's all yours," he muttered under his breath, and made his way to the bar, to see if Jasmine's offer was still good, but she had already hooked up with another cadet. She saw the look of disappointment on Troy's face and shrugged as if to say, *You had your chance. This could have been you. Better luck next time.*

Troy watched them leave together, and, before any other heartache could find him, he decided he'd better head for his own compartment. He walked down the still-crowded street, the sound of music and laughter nipping at his heels and making him walk a little faster.

The young Warrior found his building and made his way up the ascensior to his floor, and down the corridor toward his compartment. All the Warriors were bivouacked in the same building, and he heard the sound of female laughter coming from just around the right angle of the hallway ahead. He knew that laughter, and had a good idea who was causing it, but Troy's compartment was at the far end of the next corridor, and there was no way to avoid what he knew he would see. Taking a deep breath, Troy rounded the corner.

He stopped when he saw what was occurring: Dalton was backed against the wall, her head turned demurely away from Trays' face. He stood with both hands braced against the wall, his arms on either side of her head, his knee bent just enough to rest against the outside of her thigh. He was whispering something to her, and she was blushing and shaking her head. Trays bent his arms at the elbows and pressed in closer, giving Dalton little pecks on her cheek. She turned toward him, and he kissed her mouth. Momentarily, she returned the kiss, but then she pulled away.

Trays stepped back, and took her hand firmly in his. "My compartment is right there," he said, nodding toward one of the many identical doors. "This is what we both want, isn't it?"

Dalton shook her head, uncertain. She really didn't know what she wanted. "I don't know, "she protested weakly. Trays took advantage of her indecision and pulled her a few steps closer to his compartment door. "Trays," she said, "I really like you, a lot, but this is . . ."

"Don't give me that virgin stuff," he said, angrily. "Everybody knows better. C'mon, I mean, Starbuck's daughter? Like father, like daughter—"

Her mouth fell open and for once in her life, Dalton was speechless. But she wasn't helpless. She snapped her knee up hard into Trays' groin, and, as he started to fold up, gasping in pain, Dalton finished the job with a solid right cross to his lantern chin.

"Nobody knows *anything* about me but me, got that?" she shouted.

Ohh, that's gotta hurt, Troy thought, almost giddy with delight. But his delight turned to horror as, the next moment, Trays shook off the pain in his swollen pogees and split lip and lunged at Dalton, throwing her back against the wall. Her head struck the doorframe, stunning her.

He pressed his mouth to hers, smearing her lips with his blood, even as her nails raked at his face, laying it open in red, weeping furroughs. But this only seemed to arouse Trays more, and he began to grind against her, his hand covering her mouth so she could only manage helpless mewling noises.

Troy had been too stunned to act before this, but he regained his wits enough to run to Dalton's side in three great strides, and grip Trays by the collar. He jerked him away from Dalton, Trays' face a stew of anger and surprise. "That's *it!*" Troy shouted, his lips slicked back in a snarl, flecks of spittle flying. "You've crossed every line there is this time!"

Trays started laughing. "Why don't you go play with your little daggit, Boxey, and leave the grown-ups alone?" He shot a wild, drunken, looping swing at Troy, who threw up his left arm and blocked the punch, tangling Trays' arm up within his own. Troy jerked the other pilot forward with his left arm, and brought his right elbow up hard into Trays' nose. He felt it flatten against Trays' face, and a jet of dark blood spurted from his nostril.

Troy still had Trays' right arm tangled in his left, and he delivered two quick body blows to Trays' unprotected gut, and a final, powerful uppercut to the hotshot's chin, making his jaws click shut together on the tip of his tongue. He groaned and staggered backward, and Troy let go of his arm, letting Trays stumble, his arms whipping like rotors as he tried to regain his balance.

His feet tangled and he went down, the breath leaving him in a grunt. Trays' hand fumbled for his broken nose, touched it gingerly and he winced in pain. He groaned and let his hand fall limply to his side.

Troy's rage was not spent yet, and he started forward to beat Trays into a med-unit berth, but Dalton shouted her anger and frustration and weariness. "Just stop it, both of you! I'm sick of this! I'm sick of all of you! I'm—" Her mouth snapped shut, and, with tears in her eyes, she clapped a hand over her mouth and turned and ran down the corridor. Troy stood over Trays a micron longer, then chased after Dalton. Trays was not going to cause them any further problems; not any time soon, and maybe never again, if he had any sense. The real problem now seemed to be about to explode within Dalton, and Troy hoped he would be able to fit all the pieces back together again.

Dalton banged her palm futilely, impatiently, on the ascensior button, but it crawled slowly up the building's cables, and she wanted out of here, now. She cursed and ran for the steps and took them, two at a time, barely seeing where she was going.

"Dalton!" Troy called after her, his voice echoing in the stairwell. But she didn't stop. Far away, at the bottom of the spiraling staircase, Troy heard a door latch open, then bang shut once more. "Ahhhh, frack," he said, and chased after her. All things being equal, he thought this was a hell of a way to get over a pleasant grog altering.

At last he found Dalton, in a cavern on the outskirts of the city, where the buildings gave way to natural rock formations. She was drawn up into a small ball, knees against her chest, arms hugging her legs, head resting against her knees. Dalton didn't seem to notice Troy approaching, but she said, without looking up, "Thanks for back there."

"No problem," Troy said, feeling like an intruder. Dalton rubber her eyes against her sleeve and looked up, a forced composure on her face. "You okay?" She was clearly not comfortable expressing her vulnerability around anyone, even someone she had known as long as Troy.

"What do you think, Bo—Troy," she caught, and corrected, herself. Maybe later she would be tough as anchor spikes again, and maybe she would go back to calling him Boxey, but for now, he didn't deserve that kind of treatment. "Of course I'm okay."

"Really?" he said, walking closer. He stood beside her, then knelt, so his face was even with hers. "Because it'd be okay if you weren't."

"I'm *all right!*" she shouted, and shoved Troy backward. He fell, caught himself on his elbow, tearing the sleeve of his shirt on the rocky ground. He bit back an angry response, and sat down in front of her.

"You're not going to drive me away, all right?" he told her. "So just settle down and talk to me."

Instead of soothing her, Troy's concilliatory tone only seemed to enrage Dalton, and she landed a solid blow on his chest, and another. He threw his arms up across his face in an X, but didn't try to stop her. This was something she had to release, if she could, at least enough to slow the poison that was spreading through her system. She rained blow after blow on his arms, his chest, his knees, drawn up to protect his belly, and, all at once, she simply stopped.

Troy lowered his guard enough to look at her, half-expecting her to deck him with a solid jab, but she was sitting once more in her balled-up position, looking more lost and hurt than ever. He risked another beating by gently stroking her hair.

Dalton looked up, this time making no attempt to disguise the tears that fell from her eyes, and asked, pitifully, "What am I going to do?"

Troy smiled and kissed her eyelids. Dalton did not fight him.

They walked slowly back through the ancient city, talking a little, lapsing into long, companionable silences. Troy felt comfortable with the quiet; at least it wasn't directed *at* him, for a change. By this time, the celebration was winding down, and only a few serious revelers were left at their tables, drinking, talking, laughing, bargaining with the few socilators who hadn't already been purchased. But they all ignored Troy and Dalton, and that was fine.

She hesitated, just for the space of a heartbeat, at the entrance to their building, but she said something to herself that Troy couldn't quite catch, and then she was all right. She pushed open the door, and they entered the foyer. They rode the ascensior up to her floor in silence, and stepped quietly out when the computer announced this was their floor. Troy looked up and down the hallway for Trays, but there was no sign of him, as he was sure there would not be. It was too soon. He would want to gather friends behind him before he came after Troy. Well, that was fine. Let them come.

Dalton's door opened at the touch of her palm on the identi-pad, and Troy helped her inside and into her sleeping module. As exhausted as she was, she would be glad to sleep in her clothes. "You going to be—" Troy started to ask, then thought better of it. He was going to have bruises as spectacular as one of Caprica's sunsets by the morning as it was. "Well," he said, and, not sure what else to say, he wished her good night, and started to leave.

"Wait," she said, and gripped his hand between hers. It was a strong grip, but it was a strength born out of the fear of being alone and dreaming lonely. "Please, don't go."

Troy sat on the edge of her sleep module, each of them looking at the other, neither sure what to say. Dalton drew her long, shapely legs up, and for a moment, Troy thought she was going to curl up into a ball once more, but she was just giving him room. "I'm sorry," she said at length, "I'm not very good at opening up."

He laughed gently; for a moment, she thought he was making fun of her, but his expression was without guile. He reminded her, "Yeah, you forgetting who my dad is?"

"I'm serious, Troy. I've had to be tough all my life, trying to live up to being Starbuck's daughter, so it isn't easy for me to let anyone see how I really feel."

Troy took her gently in his arms, slowly and tenderly, as if he feared he might frighten her off, like some skittish avion, but she flowed into his arms like quicksilver. After a quiet while, he laid down behind her, with her back against his chest, snuggling like spoons in a drawer. Her hair tickled his nose and cheek, but he wouldn't brush it away for all the world. He inhaled softly, catching her scent, intoxicated by it. He wanted to kiss her ear, and jaw, and nuzzle her shoulder, but at the moment, she needed a friend who would listen, and he loved her enough that he could be that for her.

"I guess I've always felt, I don't know, abandoned by him— always going away and leaving me alone," she continued; it was easier for her to speak her feelings this way, without looking Troy in the eyes. If she disappointed him, at least this way she wouldn't have to see it. "All my life, I've blocked my feelings for him out of fear of being hurt again, and now I'll never have a chance to tell him how much I *love* him and respect him, no matter what kind of father he may have been."

The tears burned a slow track from the corner of her eye and over the bridge of her nose and down her cheek to fall upon her hair and pillow. "I know I'm going to miss him for the rest of my life, and I'll always regret not being able to say the things I really wanted to say," she managed. Troy held her a little tighter, a little closer. "But I'm also truly afraid of loving anyone because I don't know if I know how, and my feelings for you are so confusing. That's why I've been ... that's why I pushed you away. I knew

Trays was no good for me, knew he'd reject me or I'd reject him, and that was easier than facing my feelings for you."

"Your feelings for me?"

She shifted in his arms, turned to lie facing him, and even though her eyes were red and puffy from crying and her hair was a mess, she was still the most beautiful woman Troy had ever seen.

"I think I'm in love with you, Boxey," she said.

"We have to work on that Boxey thing," he told her, and they both laughed. He kissed her, and kissed her again, and they came together as close as praying hands, and out in the streets far below Dalton's window, the last of the party goers finally left for home, but in her room, the real celebration was just beginning.

Cassiopeia awakened to the feeling she was not alone; that was true, since Apollo slept like one drugged beside her, but she felt another *presence* here in the room with them. She gasped when she saw the hooded figure standing at the foot of the bed, its eyes glowing red.

Before she could speak, or scream, or rouse Apollo, she felt her will being deadened, as if she were some insectoid trapped in a crawlon's web, injected with numbing toxins. The robed figure stepped closer, and its eyes seemed to glow brighter still, boring through her skull and into her brain, and deep into the core of her being. There was something unspeakably evil about it, something unutterably corrupt, but she could not look away. If it cost Cassiopeia her soul, she could not look away.

She threw back the warmers and let loose her hold on Apollo. Perhaps if she had not done that . . . but then that slow, clanging alarm was silenced. Cassiopeia belonged to this thing now, heart and soul, but it cared not a whit for her heart.

Cassie nodded, and, smiling, she stood and spread her arms to take this nocturnal lover to her bosom. "Darling," it said.

At about the same time the celebration in the hidden city was beginning, the Scarlet Viper bearing Starbuck's body continued on its lonely, endless journey, already far away from Kobol, moving into deeper space. Odd pulses of light filled the cockpit of the funeral ship, then, darkness, as if the ship were signaling to something or someone.

Out past the farthest moons of Kobol and the next planet in the Kobollian solar system, and out beyond that, and still the little ship sailed on.

Another burst of light from the cockpit, this time brighter, and sustained, and the entire ship seemed to glow now, as if it were made of solid light.

In its path, far away but growing nearer, larger, came a beacon of light, its ray shining through the cold gulf to play upon the Viper's hull. The funeral ship grew brighter still, until it was almost translucent, little more than a carving of light, every nut and bolt and plated seam clearly delineated. It was not just following the path of light now, it was *becoming* the light, and its speed increased as it drew nearer the source of the radiant beam.

The light and its source were almost too brilliant, too beautiful to gaze at, but it was equally impossible not to look, even if it meant being struck blind. And then, as the Viper rode the ribbon of light up into the source, for just a moment, just before it vanished, the radiance revealed itself to be a Kobollian Light Ship.

And then, the Light Ship and the Viper vanished, and the darkness crowded in once again.

12

C YLON RAIDERS *stipple the sky, as plentiful as the fluff of weeds, blotting out the sun.*

Vipers scramble to meet the attack, but there are so many Raiders, and they seem to have come from nowhere, just appearing over the planet, that many Warriors and their fighters are destroyed before they can even leave the ground. A few Vipers get airborne and instantly engage the Cylon invaders, but it doesn't matter, because for all the Raiders that are destroyed, the base-stars, each as big as a small moon, disgorge a dozen more to replace each one that's fallen. The basestars themselves are bristling with armaments, and enough raw firepower to rip Kobol apart down to its molten core.

And now the plasma cannons power up, and the first blast is loosed, tearing through the tallest building in the city, where the civilians are housed. It is just meant to be an opening salvo, a shot across the stern, with no purpose other than to show the colonials just what kind of power they are up against, and that resistance is futile.

Another plasma pulse rips through the base of another building, triggering a series of explosions that grow exponentially larger. The building stands upright a moment on support columns that no longer exist, and then topples with an exaggerated, comic grace into the building next to it. Windows shatter, followed a micron later by walls, and countless bodies, many of them still alive, tumble one after another to a horrible death.

Apollo stands in the center of all this, watching, not understanding why he isn't already scrambling for his Viper, why he's letting everyone else face the juggernaut and die in his place.

The toppling buildings strike the ground hard enough to shatter it, and wild zigzags race across the earth in all directions, past Apollo, and directly beneath his feet. He hears the ground sigh, as if it halfway expected something like this to happen, all along and it's been proven right, and a micron later, the ground vanishes beneath his feet and he is dropping into the caverns below this city.

Impossibly, he is not hurt, but is standing on his feet, even though great slabs of the world above litter the cavern on all sides of him. He looks up, but there is nothing to see. The roof of the cavern is miraculously healed, as if by faith. The sounds of battle filter down through the blanket of stone, and puffs of dust and small rocks tumble from the roof, shaken loose by unimaginably powerful explosions, but it is all distant, and far away, part of another world, not his, like hearing voices and laughter coming from the living compartment next door. Whatever is happening above, Apollo senses his business is down here, among the ancients.

Circles of light appear on the path before Apollo, and he follows them the way a man will use stepping stones to cross a stream. Somehow, the lights lead him to the temple, and the indecipherable writings and runes and sigils and mimms and japps on the wall are glowing like witchfire. He squints because their light is so intense, and even through slitted eyes he can feel the light burning itself on his retinas, bouncing off his optic nerves and racing up into his brain, where the symbols brand themselves indelibly.

Now he closes his eyes, but the symbols are there, like the information scroll on his Warrior's helm, and the symbols are racing faster and faster, spinning and whirling, fusing into new words *that he thinks he might be able to understand, if they'd only slow down for just a moment.*

There's music now, and he doesn't know how long it's been playing; it's like the sounds of battle filtering down from above, through countless tons of earth and stone, distant and vague and just . . . there. But now that Apollo is aware of the music he can hear it more clearly, and he realizes it's a verse of some kind, being sung over and over. With that snatch of tune in his head, the symbols suddenly seem to make sense, and he's about to decipher their meaning when he feels a touch on his shoulder.

He turns and finds himself looking at the serene face of Talen, standing there in her white robes. She smiles and her hands reach up and shake loose the cowl that half-hides her face, and Apollo wonders how he could have been so blind, how he could have not recognized her. And he begins to speak her name, with the prickling of tears in his eyes . . . as he wakes up.

"Are you all right?" a woman's voice asked him. He blinked, confused by his darkened surroundings, in that half-world between waking and dreaming, at the borderland of fact and fancy. "Apollo, are you all right?" the voice repeated, and he finally recognized it as belonging to Cassiopeia, although that only created more confusion: How the frack did he get here? He touched his hand to his temple, throbbing from too much ambrosa not that long ago. A black wrecking ball of pain had set up inside his skull and begun demolition.

He nodded, wished he hadn't, and said softly, "I'm all right." His tongue felt as fat as Gar-Tokk's thumb, too big for his mouth, his eyes too small for their sockets. *Gods, how did Starbuck do this night after night?* Apollo swung his legs over the edge of the sleep module, realized he was naked, and looked with some alarm at Cassiopeia

"On the back of the chair," she said, pointing. She drew her legs up to her chest, and wrapped the warmer around her naked body. Apollo pulled on his trousers and punched his arms into the sleeves of his shirt, feeling the blood drums pounding in his head with every movement he made. "Where are you going?" she asked.

He considered for a moment. "I don't know," he admitted, "I just have to go."

Apollo pulled on his boots and stood; the room swirled around him and he had to sit down on the edge of the berth until it stopped. "You're in no condition to leave here," Cassie warned him, placing a gentle hand on his shoulder. He shook it off and stood up, and this time the room decided to cooperate and obey the rules of gravity.

He didn't know what else to say, so he repeated himself, "I have to go." As if that would make it all clear to Cassiopeia, when it wasn't clear even to him. Apollo reached the door and stepped out into the corridor, where Gar'Tokk sat on his haunches, back against the wall, eyes closed in a light doze.

At the end of the hallway, Apollo saw Talen standing there, smiling, as she had been in his dream. He opened his mouth to ask her about the dreams he had been having, but she motioned with her hand for him to follow her, and then, as if it were assumed he would, she turned and walked down the corridor.

"Wait!" Apollo called after her. Gar'Tokk's eyes opened and he was on his feet at once.

Apollo hurried after Talen, but even though he ran and she walked, she remained too far ahead for him to do much more than narrow the gap, as if this were still somehow a dream of running and staying in one place. Gar'Tokk was at Apollo's side, his long, muscled legs keeping pace easily. "Two women in one night?" he asked the commander, something like a smile on his broad face.

"Just keep running," Apollo told him.

The entire chase took on a dreamlike quality, as Talen led them down winding side-streets of the mirror city, passing through alcoves whose walls dripped with water from the underground river that passed just above their heads, then on street level once more, but the maze was no less twisting and labyrinthine for all that. Talen, herself, appeared only as a furtive figure, a glimpse of white through dark, shadowed alleyways, just enough to convince Apollo they were still on the right trail, but never long enough to catch up with her or for her to answer any of their shouted questions or demands to stop. With every step he took, Apollo could feel the physical exertion burning off the dulling effects of the ambrosa, but the whole, surreal quality of the night journey remained.

Gar'Tokk noticed what Apollo was beginning to suspect, that their pursuit formed an inward spiral toward the very heart of the underground city.

As they wound their way ever inward to the ancient city's core, the buildings themselves seemed to become more ancient, as if the city had not been built, but had grown organically from these primitive structures.

Even Gar'Tokk became confused in this winding maze, and took a frustrating turn down a wrong avenue, leaving Apollo to run on ahead. By the time the Noman retraced his steps and made his way back to where he had lost Apollo, the commander was gone. Gar'Tokk's nostrils flared as he sniffed the air, but Apollo and his scent had both mysteriously vanished.

In point of fact, Apollo had not gone that far; a simple stone facade was all that separated the two men—the width of a wall. Apollo had followed Talen into the open doorway of a tumbledown kiosk, and then lost sight of her. As his eyes adjusted to the darkness, he realized there was a staircase leading down beneath the underground city, and, after only a moment's hesitation, Apollo began his descent into the underworld.

The steps also spiraled, as if everything turned inward upon itself in this city, on this planet, and even in the murky darkness, Apollo saw the narrow staircase was carved from one colossal pillar of stone that stretched from the obscure depths below, up to the roof of the cavern. One stumble would end in a broken leg . . . or neck. Apollo's hand felt the main support column from which the steps had been hewn as he wound his way down and around.

At last he reached the bottom of the staircase and stepped off onto solid ground once more, but the room into which the steps delivered him was not much larger than his sanctuary aboard the *Galactica*, and the walls were without doors on all four sides of him. Of Talen, there was no sign, but then, he really wasn't expecting there to be. Of course, he was familiar with this particular bit of camouflage from his own chambers and the sanctuary Adama had kept hidden for so many yahren; there was a concealed door, obviously. It was just a matter of finding it and determining how it opened.

Apollo ran his hands over the smooth stone, surprisingly warm to the touch, almost as if it were alive . . . or else hell was just on the other side of that wall. At this point, Apollo didn't think either revelation would particularly surprise him.

As he brushed the wall, more ancient symbols appeared, glowing from within, as if awakened by his touch, and from everywhere and nowhere at once, he heard the song of the bells that he had heard, or dreamed he heard, in the temple. His instinct, or his inner vision, told him what to do: listening to the music of the bells, he vocalized the same few notes he heard in his head. It was a simple passage, but achingly beautiful for all its simplicity. The wall before him began to shimmer and warble, and phased out of the three dimensions it had occupied. Behind it, a sudden wash of light flooded out of the now-revealed chamber, but as bright as it was, Apollo found he did not have to blink. The light was gentle, comforting, and Apollo stepped into the hidden chamber and into another, impossible world.

Delicate crystalline towers soared so high that Apollo had to crane his neck back to see their uppermost spires. Glass walkways connected the topmost floors of the structures, radiating outward from one central spire, joining with others, and, from there, leaping outward to still another ring of towers, like strands of a crawlon's web. Overhead, a great crystalline ball hung from the ceiling of the cavern, catching the diffuse light and shining it back upon the city; the buildings themselves reflected the light in prismatic hues and chromatic values. Apollo followed the graceful, fluted curves of the buildings from the topmost tower down, down, into the abyss from which the glass city grew.

And now he realized he could see through the buildings, see their inner floors and the walls that made up the separate rooms, as if he'd been suddenly given the ability of X-ray vision. It was disconcerting, an information overload with too much to take in, and he had to look away or lose himself in the details. Before he did, however, Apollo absently wondered what it must be like to live in a building of crystal, to walk on floors that were essentially invisible, walls that were little more than windows, ceilings that were skylights. For a private person such as himself, he thought this would be the worst hell imaginable.

A circular glass platform hovered at the abyss's edge near Apollo's feet, and only the helioscoping of the light on its crystalline surface made the commander aware of its presence. He took a tentative step forward, gingerly placing one foot on its surface; it seemed capable of supporting his weight, and, trusting that Talen had led him here for a greater purpose than falling off a glass disc to his death, he stepped off the stone ledge and onto the platform.

The disc dipped slightly beneath his weight, and Apollo had a heady, frightful moment when he thought perhaps Talen had gone to such complex lengths to assure he *would* plummet to his death, but then the platform was moving effortlessly through the underground sky, winding its way down toward the base of the glass city, weaving in and out between the buildings, and even if he had died there, Apollo would have left this life with a look of pure marvel on his face, because this was as close to unaided flight as any human could dream of having, and the rainbow of lights that skated along the edges of the buildings was haunting, dazzling and hypnotic.

He vaguely understood the disc was winding its way down in ever-decreasing loops and arcs, as if that was the only way to reach any other point in this city—by traveling in spirals.

The disc reached the crystalline streets of the city and skated along just centimetrons above the surface. Apollo watched the ground slip past beneath his feet, as if he were still altered from all the ambrosa, and somehow, that was a comforting thought; perhaps this was all just a dream, but if it was, he felt as if it were telling him something he needed to know. Dream or not, he was determined to see this through.

Closer to the buildings, nearer the ground, Apollo could see something else: they were crystalline, yes, but they were an odd suffusion of technology and organics, a techno-organic hybrid. He wondered momentarily if the city were one massive computer chip, and then, the platform set him down in the central area of the subterranean metropolis.

He stepped off the disc, hearing his footfalls echo hollowly around him, and made his way toward the aperture in the primary control area that opened before him. The glass here was opaqued, and he could only see his own reflection staring back as he stepped nearer the doorway that stood open like a dare.

It never occurred to him not to enter the darkling edifice, and he wasn't sure the city would have allowed him any other choice.

Apollo paused only a moment at the open doorway, feeling an odd undercurrent of raw energy skittering across his brain and through its crevices as soon as he drew near. Still, he didn't think it meant him any harm; the city had already had several opportunities to slay him, if that was what it wished. Taking a deep breath, he entered the building, and another pool of lights came up, showing him the path. He followed them deeper into the heart of the humming building, feeling the fluid behind his eyes start to tingle.

The last spotlight brought him to a place before a computer that echoed the ancient Kobollian work station that occupied one wall of his sanctuary aboard the ship, but this one was unimaginably vast. The one aboard the ship had graceful wings that seemed to want to encircle him, and that was true of this one; it was just that the wings, the computer, were the entire edifice in which he now found himself. A heartbeat later, this impression was confirmed as the structure began to make a high, frail whirling sound, like a struck tuning fork, resonating in his ears and bones and brain and every atom of his being.

Lights winked at him like a socialator, and he could only watch them with a dreamy detachment. Around him, holographic images appeared, like specters in some high-tech haunting.

"Hello, Son," a rich, deep voice addressed him, warmly. It was a voice Apollo thought he would never hear again, for the speaker was long dead.

Apollo turned slowly, not afraid of what he would see, but afraid of what he might not see, because he desperately wanted to see the owner of that voice one more time. "Hello, Father," he said, and swallowed.

It *was* Adama, of that there was no doubt. Holographic image or not, it was bliss to see his father again.

"Your brain is being rewired," Adama told him calmly, gesturing at the computer all around them, "so you can understand the ancient Kobollian texts."

Gods, how he had missed that warm and reassuring voice, and being able to come to Adama with anything, at any time. He was a man who missed his father, because in all the endless worlds out there, Apollo knew there would never be another person who would understand and love him quite like his father had. There were so many things Apollo wanted to ask him, but Apollo understood he was not here as Adama's son, but as the supreme commander of the fleet. It was hard, but that was the way it was. Apollo nodded, and Adama continued. "You, and I, and the colonials, are not here upon Kobol by chance, but by design."

"Whose design?"

Was it possible, what Segis had claimed? That she and her acolytes had shifted the coordinates through the spirit masters, to the Cylons, to Baltar, and, finally, to Apollo? It seemed so; Adama himself was bearing this out, and yet . . . Apollo still did not quite trust Segis. It struck him as just a little too convenient that the ancient texts that supported Segis's tale, that the fleet's return had been prophesied, was also incomplete.

Sometimes, he thought, the words that aren't there can tell you as much as the ones that are.

Adama went on, as if Apollo had not spoken, and Apollo knew their time was short. His questions and their answers would have to sort themselves out later. "It has always been foretold the colonials must one day return to Kobol to complete unfinished business." Apollo again felt the question rise to his lips, but this time did not voice it. He wasn't sure he liked being a pawn in a game of the gods. The gods had a nasty way of discarding their plaything, once they were finished with them. "What transpires now will determine if the fleet will be allowed to venture with new technology across many universes, to far distant galaxies that will eventually lead you to the planet Earth, and beyond, to your new homeland."

"It exists . . ." Apollo muttered. Earth was not a fable, then. He had always believed it was true.

The whirring sound cycled up another octave, up and up, until it passed beyond the range of the keenest human hearing; Apollo suspected Gar'Tokk might have been able to hear it, but then, Gar'-Tokk had been left somewhere along the way. He didn't think now that was by accident.

Adama nodded, once, efficient as ever. "Your race is facing extermination and it is imperative that you understand that the decisions and choices you and your people make now will seal your futures forever. The Lords of Light have led you back here, but that does not mean you are guaranteed victory. The Lords give us free will because they aren't here to guide us. We must clean up our own mistakes—the House of Kobol must be put in order once more. Choose wisely!"

"What decisions?" he asked, even though he knew he would receive no answer. "The visions I've been having of the Cylon armada attacking Kobol . . . are they real, or just nightmares stirred up by this place?"

Adama's eyes twinkled with something that was more than the light of holographics, and he nodded, almost imperceptibly. There were only so many things, it seemed, he could tell Apollo, directly or indirectly. But the one last thing he told him was, coincidentally, the thing Apollo most needed to hear. "I'm very proud of you, Apollo," he said. "Remember I will love you always; be sure to trust your inner vision, no matter what appears to you. There is so much more at stake than you imagine, or can imagine."

Certain words did not come easily to Apollo, and even though he knew he might never have this opportunity again, he had to force himself to say to Adama, "I love you, Father. I miss you so much." Adama smiled, and Apollo recalled something Cassie had told him earlier that same evening: You always know when someone loves you. The simplest words are often the hardest to speak.

A light began to swell and fill the chamber, its brightness causing Adama's image to dissipate, and Apollo felt as if he had somehow lost his father a second time, but in his heart, he knew he would never lose Adama. The light bounced off the crystalline walls of the room, crossing and re-crossing its own path, weaving a complex geometric shape that surrounded Apollo; then, the light ricocheted off the floor and slammed into Apollo's forehead, and even though there was no weight to it, the impact made the commander's head jerk back, as if he had been struck a mighty blow.

For a micron, he saw the entire journey of the Thirteenth Tribe laid out before him in his mind, stars and nebulae and suns and constellations; all of these things appeared and fell away, replaced by another universe, faster and faster, images overlaying images. Along the way, Apollo could see the numerous planets the Thirteenth Tribe had colonized or populated, scattering the seeds of humankind everywhere. Some would take, some would not. He saw, also, the colonies as they were today, overrun by the Cylons, the worlds stripped and plundered and gouged out, turned into little more than husks, a mirror image of Cylon, endless vistas of technology that had been plundered from other worlds, other civilizations, and thrown together into a mad quilt of circuitry and steel, and he knew, without question, even if these worlds could be re-taken by humans, they would never be fit for colonization, not for many, many generations. They were a lost cause, the cost of reclaiming them too great for the infinitesimal dividends they would return. Better just to move on, forget them. Whatever purpose the fleet's return to Kobol served, Cain was wrong if he thought it was to re-take these worlds. They were, now and forever, part of the Cylon empire.

Apollo's eyes were wide and fixed on something beyond himself, beyond this room, and his mind continued to expand with the rippling universe and the journey of the ancients, and he had to shut down then, had to pull his mind back before it widened like the concentric rings on a lake after a stone is dropped. As he closed his awareness, he pulled over himself a warm blanket of darkness, and he fell into a deep and dreamless sleep.

For the second time that night, Apollo woke to confusion, in an unfamiliar room, in an unfamiliar sleeping module, next to Cassiopeia, and the memories of that evening flooded back to him, like air rushing to fill a vacuum. He wiped his hand down his face, his body sore and tired. Apollo grimaced at the stiffness in his limbs, and as his eyes became adjusted to the darkness, he became aware of someone standing next to the sleeping module. He turned with a start, and saw Talen standing beside the berth, looking down at him, a smile on her face.

13

APOLLO FELT as if time had doubled back upon itself, spiraling back around like everything else in this city did, because here was Talen once more, standing before him, telling him he must follow her.

"I am sorry to disturb you," she said, with just the slightest hint of amusement in her voice, "but your communications device must be defective. They've been trying to reach you. Your Quorum and the citizens are all gathered in the great hall now, to debate and vote on who will be the new supreme commander of the fleet."

Apollo blinked the world back into some kind of muzzy focus. "So soon?" he muttered, his tongue all but spot-welded to the roof of his mouth. "The celebration just ended . . . didn't it?"

Talen smiled the way Apollo remembered his mother smiling when he didn't want to go to instructional period. "that was last night," she said. "You've slept the day away."

Had he? Apollo certainly didn't feel very refreshed, for all of that extra sleep. He felt as if he'd been chasing phantoms all night long, instead. He studied her, a look of puzzlement shadowing his features, wondering if the whole thing had been a dream.

Apollo slipped quietly out of bed, without disturbing Cassiopeia, and replaced the warmers around her. Cassie made a morning sound, almost awake but still not aware, and Apollo whispered that he had to go and kissed her temple softly. Talen watched him, as if she were fascinated by his thoughtfulness, and looked away before he could catch her staring. Apollo realized he was wearing his uniform from the night before, although he thought Cassie had . . . but then, perhaps that was all part of the dream. It was all starting to lose the hardline focus he held between reality and fantasy. Most of what had happened—or not happened—between himself and Cassiopeia was a blur.

"I guess I'm ready," he announced to Talen. Now it was his turn to stare once more, because he had a strong sense of deja vu. He was not an ambrosa drinker (and hadn't one of Segis's hooded acolytes warned him about that very thing, last night at the bar? He thought so, but, then again . . .) and perhaps this feeling of recursion was just his brain trying to compensate for the lag-time between sensory input and the processing of his thoughts. Apollo realized he was not sure of anything, anymore, where Talen was concerned.

The door to Cassie's compartment whooshed open and Apollo stepped into the hallway with Talen, where faithful Gar'Tokk still sat, ever vigilant. The Noman seemed surprised to see Talen emerging from the compartment, as if, however she had entered, it had not been past his post.

Apollo stared directly into her glowing eyes, and finally said the things that were on his mind. "I don't know how to explain this to you, but . . . do you have the feeling that we know each other? You seem so familiar to me and I keep seeing you in my mind and—" He stopped, almost embarrassed by this next sentence, but he had to get it all out in the open or it would continue to fester, like some small piece of shrapnel embedded just beneath his skin, or, in this case, his consciousness "—and in my *dreams*. Why is that?"

She continued to meet his gaze, saying nothing, neither smiling nor frowning, giving no hint of anything she might have been thinking or feeling, until, at last, Apollo had to avert his eyes, feeling embarrassed and uncomfortable. "Excuse me," he said, trying to recover from his error in confessional judgment. "We really should go."

Gar'Tokk turned to leave with Apollo; this wasn't the Noman's mystery, and it held interest for him only insofar as a potential threat to his master. But he could sense, even if Apollo could not, that there was no threat in Talen.

"Choose wisely," Talen called after the departing commander. Those words froze him in his tracks; Adama had said the very same thing to him.

"What did you say?" Apollo asked as he turned back, but Talen was gone, and he really hadn't expected an answer, anyway.

Apollo sighed his frustration and raked his hand through his hair. He shook his head, then continued on toward the ascensiors. "You have very interesting friends," Gar'Tokk pointed out.

No one noticed the robed and hooded man who moved behind the scenes of the last minute preparations for the vote and installment of the supreme commander. He was just one more of Segis's acolytes, and everyone had gotten quite used to the comings and goings of these silent, hooded caretakers. No one knew, precisely, where the caretakers lived within the ancient city, but then, no one really gave much thought to the robed figures, once they were out of sight.

Within the great hall, multitudes of citizens, Warriors, and techs had gathered, awaiting the appearance of President Tigh, Athena, and Commanders Cain and Apollo. Giant flatscreens flanked either side of the presidium, and another flatscreen hung above the seating area. The hall was filled, from front to back and wall to wall, ground floor and balcony. As much as possible, the different groups sat with their own kind; Warriors sat with Warriors, techs sat with techs. But even so, there was quite a lot of division from one individual to the next as to who would best serve their needs as supereme commander. An undercurrent of tension ran through the hall, as if some low charge of static electricity informed the air. Security men stood on guard at various points throughout the assembly, but anyone who glanced their way could see they were nervous, even frightened. There was the potential for violence here, a continuation of the narrowly averted riot from the night before, and this time, it might not be so easily turned away. The lupus at the door tended to get a little bolder when it knew the weapons were no real threat.

The robed man stood near the presidium, watching from the wings, looking out at the sea of faces, knowing that for all of those who sat inside the auditorium, that many more had been lost in futile battle with the Chitain and the most recent attack by the Cylons. Once, the fleet's populous could not have been contained within these walls. Now, this was all that was left. Still, it was a miracle this many had survived so much over so many yahren.

Approaching from behind, the hooded man could hear the sound of footsteps and voices, and he stepped back into the shadows that haunted the proscenium. It would not do for him to be found out just yet. He watched silently as Athena, Tigh, Cain, and Segis passed by without noticing him, making their way to the platform.

The giant flatscreens suddenly filled with the images of the quartet as they walked onto the stage. It was President Tigh who stepped forward to the rostrum, and stood looking out at the gathering. He raised his hands to either side, even with his shoulders, and such was his presence that the crowd fell silent, as if it were some great machine that had suddenly been switched off.

"Welcome, everyone. These are very rare and unusual circumstances that draw us all together today," Tigh began.

In the audience, Bo jay sighed and turned to Boomer, and whispered, "He should always open with a joke."

"Not one of yours," Boomer answered. "Not unless you want to clear this hall."

"You all no doubt realize we are at a crossroads in our journey," Tigh continued, "and we are at a crossroads as regards our leadership. This is a momentous thing, too great for the Quorum alone to decide. This affects all of you, so you will all be allowed your say.

We will listen carefully to each side's arguments, both Commander Cain and Commander Apollo, before we place it in your hands for a vote." Tigh looked to his side and behind, where Segis stood patiently and quietly.

"But first, I think it would be appropriate and right that we give thanks to our benefactor, and listen to what she has to say," Tigh finished, and stepped away from the rostrum.

Segis approached, her smile growing wider with every step she took toward the rostrum. As she stood there, hands resting lightly on the rostrum, she seemed to radiate peace, and contentment. Even the tense guards could feel it, and they felt the anxiety drain out of themselves, if only for the few moments Segis would speak.

"Welcome, Colonials," Segis began, her voice like a balm. "It is I who should thank you for honoring us with your heroic presence after the courageous journey from which you've only so recently disembarked. I want to assure you, as I did your commanders and governing body, that we are all completely safe, and protected by the advanced technology of the Kobollian defense system. It has kept this city and its caretakers safe and undetected for many millennia, and will, we feel sure, continue to provide safe haven for all of you, as well, for as long as you choose to make Kobol your new home, until you are strong enough to take the fight to the Cylons and reclaim the colonies . . . *your* colonies.

"My servants and I are eager to welcome you, and will always be at your faithful service."

The hooded man who had been hiding in the shadows near the stage slipped deeper into the darkness and, without sound or notice, quit the hall for the streets of the underground city.

Apollo was late.

As he and Gar'Tokk rounded the corner of one of the city's narrow corridors, he spotted one of the hooded acolytes approaching him. Somehow, Apollo instinctively knew it was the same man who had warned him about drinking too much ambrosa the night before, even though all of the robed figures seemed identical. Apollo raised a hand to the man to signal him to wait, when the hooded figure's hand reached, snake-quick, into his robes and withdrew something Apollo recognized, even from this distance. His suspicions were borne out a moment later when the figure raised his hand and pointed the laser pistol at the commander. Whatever sect this acolyte belonged to, it was obviously not one that adhered to non-violent principles.

Gar'Tokk threw himself in front of Apollo, but even his animal-like reflexes weren't fast enough to stop the hooded stranger from firing. The Noman grimaced, expecting the searing laserfire to cut through his breastbone and boil his heart in its own blood, but the stranger was not aiming at Apollo or Gar'Tokk, but rather something behind them.

Apollo turned in the direction of the laser blast and saw another of the hooded men, his robes still smoking from the flash of energy, tumble backward to the stone streets with a crash. His hood fell away from his face, and now Apollo could see Segis's acolytes were not human at all, but humanlike *robots*.

Did Segis know this? Apollo wondered, and was sure she must. With this revelation, Apollo was more sure than ever that Baltar must be in league with Segis. He couldn't quite make the link, but it was closer now.

"Apollo!" Gar'Tokk shouted, and Apollo saw more of the mandroids surrounding them, preparing to take out the commander and his bodyguard. The Noman let loose a ululating war cry and his mighty fist pistoned out, burying itself elbow-deep in the nearest acolyte's chest. A spray of sparks and sluggish liquid spurted out of the mortal wound, and Gar'Tokk jerked his arm free with a wrench. He plucked a few splinters of metal from his forearm and tossed them aside.

Apollo grabbed his own sidearm and fired at the figure bearing down on him. The mandroid was hellishly fast, and the shot missed a direct score, instead zinging off the robot's shoulder. The mandroid raised both hands over its head and laced its fingers together, forming a deadly club of steel, which it swung at Apollo. The commander just dodged out of the way as the mandroid's fists descended, slamming into the street and gouging out a huge divot of stone. Before the mandroid could strike again, Apollo placed his laser against the shelf of the robot's jaw and squeezed the trigger.

The automaton's head exploded, its artificial brain spewing everywhere. Apollo knew they weren't really alive, but still, they were near enough to human in their appearance that it was very disquieting to watch one die in such a gruesome manner. The headless corpse collapsed, and its legs kicked stiffly as programmed synaptic reflexes could not complete their circuit. Then the body lay still.

Gar'Tokk was not plagued by such thoughts; he was enjoying himself, finally able to let his berserker side rise to the fore and deal as violently with his opponents as he wanted. One of the robots had grabbed the giant Noman from behind and had his arms pinned. The robots, despite their smaller size, were incredibly powerful, and Apollo could hear Gar'Tokk's ribs shift and groan in protest.

Apollo's bodyguard put everything he had into freeing himself from the pinioning grasp, flexing his mighty arms and raising them over his head. The robot's own arms came loose from its shoulders with a metallic shriek, and fell to the street. Smiling, Gar'Tokk gripped the robot's head between his massive palms and squeezed them together, crushing the metallic skull into a shapeless mass.

And that's what I challenged to a death-duel aboard the Icarus? Apollo thought, randomly. Gar'Tokk caught Apollo staring at him, and he smiled in return. *Next time I'm about to do something stupid, someone stop me!*

The original hooded figure who had fired first and saved Apollo's life fired once more, cutting in half the last two automatons trying to flank Apollo. The entire battle had taken less than two centari, and the streets were deserted, save for the wreckage of the false acolytes and the trio of survivors. No one else had heard a thing. The streets seemed unnaturally quiet now, following the short but furious din of battle.

"Who are you?" Apollo asked his robed savior; the commander did not point his laser directly at the man, but neither did he holster it.

"You couldn't outdraw me on your best day," the robed man boasted, his voice echoing off the walls of the narrow corridor in which they stood.

Apollo squinted; he knew that voice, but he also knew he would never hear that voice again. Whoever the man was, he was treading on very dangerous, hallowed ground now. "Let's hope we don't have to find that out," Apollo said.

"Fine with me," the acolyte said, and slipped his sidearm back into the holster he wore beneath his robes. Apollo thought again that was probably not standard issue. Slowly, the man reached up and drew back his hood, and Apollo's eyes grew wide with disbelief. He shook his head, as if sheer force of will could negate what he was seeing.

"What . . . how did . . . this is not possible . . ." Apollo stammered. A thousand different things begged to be spoken at once, and not more than a few snippets of each could be managed.

Starbuck's eyes twinkled merrily and he nodded with a big grin.

"You mean . . . ?" Apollo managed.

Starbuck nodded again, walking closer.

Apollo laughed, a sound of pure, unfettered joy, a sound he didn't realize he still knew how to make. "I *knew* it! You must be pure Kobollian!"

Starbuck was only a few feet away from Apollo now, near enough for Gar'Tokk to surreptitiously sniff his aroma. It was *changed,* but it was also the same, somehow.

"You know, Apollo, I think somewhere, along the way, someone got it all wrong. We're all Kobollians. Maybe some of us are more pure-blooded than others, more directly descended, but I think they told me we all have the potential to evolve, and . . . what did they call it? Oh, yeah . . . *accelerate.* It's just that you direct descendants of certain houses had more of a head-start on the rest of us," Starbuck explained, and then, had to add, "well, all except me, of course."

"Of course," Apollo agreed, drunk with laughter. He suddenly felt as if he could take whatever it was the gods wanted to throw his way. They had at least restored Apollo's friend to him, and nothing was impossible, now.

Starbuck nodded at the commander's pistol, still half-raised in his direction. Apollo grinned sheepishly and slid the sidearm back into its holster. The two old friends laughed and embraced, then gripped one another's hand in a Warrior's handshake. "You ever notice, everywhere you go, someone wants to kill you?" Starbuck observed.

"I've noticed."

"Who were those guys, anyway?" Starbuck asked, looking down at the robots.

Apollo suddenly recalled he had somewhere very important he needed to be, and nodded in the direction of the hall. "I don't have the time to explain right now," he said. "I have to get to that ceremony. There's someone I'd like to talk to." Starbuck slipped his hood back over his head as the trio hurried along the eerily deserted streets.

"What do you mean, I couldn't outdraw you on my best day?" Apollo asked as they ran.

"You couldn't," Starbuck told him. "Frack, and here I thought *I* was the one who was brain-damaged."

"You *are*."

"Let's not argue," Gar'Tokk interjected, voicing the final word on the matter. "You're *both* brain-damaged."

Events that would affect Apollo continued on with a life of their own, without Apollo's presence. In the hall, President Tigh had searched everywhere for his old friend, had sent a cadre of cadets out to look for him, and Cassiopeia confirmed Apollo had left her compartment almost a centon earlier. Under his breath, Tigh muttered his sincerest apologies to Apollo, wherever he may be, and introduced Commander Cain to the assemblage. The applause was thunderous, almost deafening, and Tigh wondered if it would have made any difference if Apollo had been there to present his side after all.

Cain stood at the rostrum, hands clasped behind his back, drawn up to his full height, looking out over the crowd that called his name, nodding, smiling. His image, bigger than life, repeated every movement Cain made. He knew this, and played to the Tele-Vids, making sure his expressions and gestures were drawn in and toned down, so he was not an exaggeration of himself.

"As you all doubtlessly know," Cain began, and as soon as he spoke, the assembly fell quiet. They all wanted to hear what the great man had to say. "The council have nominated me for the post of supreme commander. My vision and Commander Apollo's differ greatly, making the need for a clear-cut decision necessary. It is not merely a matter of who commands the fleet, but rather, what the fleet does with this rare second chance."

Cain grew more animated, more passionate, but even so, his image, almost as tall as the great hall itself, did not seem a caricature. He seemed . . . right. "Under my leadership, we would make Kobol our home base . . . rebuild our civilization . . . our lives . . . our families . . . our battlestars. While the Cylons look for us near Kirasolia, we will begin laying our plans to launch the campaign that will retake the colonies. We will wrest our worlds out of the Cylons' grasp. We will no longer be on the run, on the defensive, but take the battle *to* them! As our host has pointed out, this has been pre-ordained. We can no longer afford to turn our back on our destiny. We will fight—and, if necessary, we will die—like men!"

The crowd rose to its feet as if it were one great beast with one brain, one mind, one will. And, in one voice, they cried, "Cain! Cain! Cain!"

President Tigh made his way to the rostrum, and he had to shout to be heard over the roar of Cain's name. "Commander Apollo has challenged our decision," he said, although he doubted if anyone really heard him. He could barely hear himself. "Apollo was supposed to address you, himself, but we are unable to find him."

Tigh looked to Athena, but she was unable to meet his gaze. They both know what the vote would be; they both knew it had to be done. But that didn't mean either of them had to like it.

"Without further delay," Tigh began, holding his hands up for silence; this time, it did not come. "Without further delay," he said, again, at the top of his lungs, "we will put the matter of who will lead the fleet to a vote."

The walls of the hall shook, and a roaring, growling, rippling sound reverberated in the perfect acoustics of the room. Everyone felt the bass roar in his or her chest. One of the giant flatscreens groaned as its steel supports twisted and gave way, and the monitor crashed to the ground. The wail of alarm klaxons, like souls in torment, began to sound, at first on the outskirts of the underground city, then, drawing nearer, as more of them sounded.

Cain held up his arms, refusing to allow the surprise he felt to register on his face. He knew he was still being viewed on the other two flatscreens, and did not want to add to the panic by seeming uncertain and indecisive. "Everyone remain calm," Cain commanded them in a sensible and fatherly voice. "Remain seated until we can check out the situation for ourselves—"

One of the returning scouts stood at the edge of the stage, speaking to President Tigh. Cain became aware of the scout's presence and, cursing to himself, grabbed the scout and jerked him around so they stood face to face. "What are you telling him?" he demanded to know.

"Sir," the scout began, "we've spotted them."

"Spotted *who?*"

The man sighed, and he seemed to deflate. "The largest armada of Cylon forces ever seen," he reported; the fear had gone from his voice. But then, the hope had also fled his heart. "They're encircling the planet now . . . and calling for our immediate surrender. The alternative is total annihilation."

14

CYLONS? *HERE*?" Tigh repeated. It made no more sense the third time he said it than it had the first two.

"How is that possible?" Athena demanded to know. "Segis, you assured us the Cylons would be unable to detect us!"

Another blow, more violent than the first, rocked the entire auditorium, and the lights stuttered. For a moment, it felt as if the darkness would fill the room, and then, the lights hummed back on, but they seemed weaker this time. The building continued to shake, as if it were caught in the grip of a tremblor. There were several screams, but they were lost in the wail of the alarm sirens.

Cain stepped to the edge of the stage; these people were his responsibility, and his first order of business was to calm them before they could panic, stampedeand one another in their mad dash for the exits.

"Everyone, just remain seated!" he barked. "We will never surrender to the Cylon threat! If we are going to die, then we are going to die in battle, on our feet, like men, not on our knees, like . . . like weaklings and cowards!" He spat these last words, as if their presence in his mouth was a foul and bitter taste.

But dying like men or dying like cowards, it made no difference to many of the colonials. Most of them were simple civilians, and had seen too much of death, had lost too many family members. Whether they were from Scorpius or Gemon or Caprica, they all loved their families, and they all wanted to live.

There was real concern that Cylon plasma cannons would cause the honeycombed earth to collapse, burying the underground city and all its occupants in an avalance of crushing dirt and rock. Those who didn't die immediately from the falling debris would be trapped within buildings or caverns, to die slowly of suffocation or starvation. To risk leaving the underground city for the surface was merely trading one form of death for a quicker one; the Raiders would cut them down before the civilians got very far on foot, and those the fighters missed, the Centurions would ferret out and slaughter.

Segis, who had been standing nearby all this while, hurried to the rostrum and, in the quiet between attacking volleys, spoke to the assembly: "Please, forgive me," she said, his face pale, his eyes wide and unblinking. "You must believe me, we couldn't have known . . . the Cylons must be using an advanced technology that has found a way to circumvent our protective shields!"

She was not speaking words of comfort, not saying anything the crowd wanted to hear. The panic, far from quieting, only intensified, and threatened to explode at any moment, like a rain-swollen river overflowing its banks.

"It is apparent that the Cylons have arrived in such massive numbers that the only sane and rational course of action is to surrender—"

The crowd was shrieking now, panic rendering their voices useless and inarticulate.

"—at least, that way," Segis continued, almost shouting now, "we might have a chance of surviving, to fight another day."

Cain was furious. He grabbed Segis's shoulder and spun the caretaker around to face him. "*Surrender?*" Cain shouted in her face. "You want me to tell these people to just give up and allow the Cylons to capture them?"

"Do you see another choice, Commander?" Segis asked, pulling out of Cain's grip. "Something that won't result in the death of every man, woman, and child on this planet?"

Baltar, who had been seated at the side of the stage, safely away from the audience and potential assassins, now made his way to the rostrum while Cain was occupied with Segis. "I know how you all feel about me," he told them, "but I agree with Segis." Baltar dabbed at his face; he was perspiring heavily, out of fear. He was clearly shaken and badly frightened, but he felt he had a message to deliver, and he would do so. "The Cylons have no intentions of destroying the human race. I lived among them for many yahren . . . and they obviously did not kill me. I convinced them then, and believe I can convince them once more, that the human race are a peace-loving people. All we want is to be left alone and allowed to follow our own destiny."

Shouts of "*Traitor!*" hopscotched around the audience, growing louder, as more voices joined the chorus. Baltar knew he was risking his life by standing there, but he had an insight into the Cylons these people did not, and he had to make them understand that before it was too late, for all of them.

"The Cylons can be benevolent rulers as long as they are in control," he said. "Perhaps they will listen to me . . . I could negotiate a peace agreement—"

And there it was. Everything had come around, full circle, with Baltar offering to hammer out some manner of peace with the Cylons, and the Cylon armada filling the sky, ready to reduce the planet to dust. They'd been here before, and things had not ended well the first time. The nearest rows of civilians rose and stormed the stage, grabbed Baltar roughly, and began beating him with their fists and kicking him with their feet. The security guards made their way forward, but the other civilians grabbed them, too, tearing at their clothes and flesh, pulling them back.

"Please!" Segis cried, her hands waving helplessly in the air. "Please, this is not the time to be fighting among ourselves! Whatever you think this man has done, is it worth spilling his blood? Is it worth violating this planet's sacred principles and taking his life?" Her appeal fell on deaf ears and hearts of stone, but she pressed on. "Think about what you're doing! Once done, it can never be undone!"

Segis's acolytes stepped forward to try to free Baltar from the mob's hold, but didn't get more than a pace or two before a strident voice rang through the hall, halting their advance.

"The Cylons plan to use us as lab animals!"

Baltar squinted through the blood dripping in his eyes, trying to attach a face to the voice that had just spoken. He saw three figures running down the main aisle of the hall, coming directly for the platform on which he stood.

"Who said that?" he asked. "What are you—?"

Apollo and the hooded Starbuck were leaping up onto the platform, followed by Gar'Tokk. Segis looked momentarily surprised, but recovered so quickly that the look of surprise might not have been there at all. The Noman grabbed Baltar and pulled him from the grips of the surprised civilians with contemptuous ease. Apollo stood at the rostrum to address the confused and terrified assemblage.

"It's true," he said. "The Cylons plan to use our DNA to upgrade and evolve their race." The hooded figure who had entered with Starbuck stayed back, hugging the shadows around himself like a cloak.

Baltar shook his head, angrily. "That's not true!" he cried. "In all my time with the Cylons, I never saw anything that would support such a preposterous—"

"Ask Dr. Salik," Apollo said, turning to face Baltar. Such was the look of pure anger on his face that Baltar fell silent, took two or three steps back. He had never seen Apollo like this before.

Near the front of the audience, Dr. Salik stood and turned to face the back of the hall. "It's true," he shouted. "Doctor Wilker and I discovered the human DNA splices when we examined the corpse of a Cylon we'd kept in storage. They're trying to use our genes to evolve their race."

"That's a lie!" Baltar erupted, blood and spittle flying from his beaten lips in a fine spray. There was a Borellian saying: Don't pray too loud, you might draw the gods' attention. Baltar would have done well to take that advice and apply it to his own situation, because his outburst only drew the commander's focus and ire. Apollo grabbed Baltar by the collar and swung him around, hard, throwing him against the proscenium wall.

"You've played us like puppets all along," Apollo said through gritted teeth. His fingers tightened on Baltar's neck, his thumbs dimpling the soft flesh of the traitor's throat. Apollo was going to squeeze the life from this man with his bare hands. The colonials may well all die here today, but Baltar would not live to see his duplicitous scheme borne out. Baltar's face purpled, and his eyes bulging almost comically, his tongue protruding from his mouth. His hands, gripping Apollo's wrists, twitched and spasmed as the flow of oxygen to his brain dwindled. "How did you do it, Baltar?" Apollo asked. "How did you and Segis plan this? What did she promise you?"

"Commander!" Segis said, gesturing once more for her acolytes to step forward. "You have my assurance this man and I are not in collusion, and please forgive me, but I cannot allow you to make such a terrible mistake."

The acolytes gripped the commander's wrist and squeezed down with near-crippling pressure. He could hear the bones in his wrist grinding together. Apollo could no longer maintain his grip on Baltar and he gasped, despite himself, out of pain and surprise, and when he was sure the acolytes would shatter his wrist, the hooded men pulled Apollo back and held him in their insanely powerful grips. To the audience, nothing looked out of place; nothing wrong here, other than the fact Baltar was still alive and breathing.

Gar'Tokk leapt immediately to Apollo's defense, but the acolyte holding him moved with lightning swiftness, and threw up his palm to catch the Noman's massive fist. The hooded figure squeezed down on Gar'Tokk's hand, but the warrior refused to yield, despite the terrible pain. He brought his foot up, but the caretaker blocked the kick with his other hand, and flung the bewildered Noman through the rostrum and off the edge of the platform, into the first row of the assembly. However powerful the mandroids they had faced in the alley, these hooded figures were more powerful still, enough to take on even Gar'Tokk. The Noman was staggering to his feet, dazed from the force of the impact, but he sensed the approach of his enemies and turned to face them.

Gar'Tokk!" Apollo shouted; the acolyte whose arms were locked around Apollo's chest was tightening his grip, grinding the commander's ribs, squeezing the air from his lungs. It would just be a matter of moments before a rib shattered, or his spine. Apollo tried to reach his sidearm, but the maniacal pressure around his chest increased exponentially.

"Sorry to hear about that short life span of yours," Apollo's hooded companion said as he finally got a clear shot and fired his laser. The acolyte's head vanished in a mist of shrapnel and a gout of flame, and then, the body was falling away from the commander, trailing a plume of smoke as thick as a hangman's noose. Apollo's sidearm was in his hand before his former attacker's body hit the ground, and he blasted the acolyte attacking Gar'Tokk. The cyber-priest threw its arms up, as if some holy revelation had dawned, and then toppled face-forward. The audience gasped in first horror and then surprise as shock continued after shock: Starbuck whipped off his cowl while keeping the remaining caretakers and acolytes at bay with his laser.

"Got your back, buddy," Starbuck told Apollo.

Apollo never had a doubt that he did.

Athena stared in open-mouthed bewilderment at Starbuck, unable to accept the proof of her eyes. "Starbuck?" she said, softly, afraid to speak his name loudly for fear the very force of her breath might cause this apparition to dissolve. He turned to her and smiled, pretending to doff an imaginary hat in mock chivalry. Cassiopeia and Dalton were no better prepared to see Starbuck returned from the dead in full vigor and fighting glory. It was either a desecration of Starbuck's memory, or a full-blown miracle, and although they had all witnessed many strange and wonderful things over the yahren, they had never seen a miracle. Until now.

"Your father has some tall explaining to do," Cassiopeia promised Dalton, as if she were speaking of nothing more than Starbuck having spent the night in the company of another woman. But her voice warbled and climbed high with emotion as she fought back her tears of elation. "And I can't wait to hear what he has to say."

"This game's gone on long enough!" Apollo shouted, standing at the edge of the platform, facing Segis. Starbuck had taken his position on the steps leading to the platform, and both he and Apollo had their lasers drawn and trained on their enigmatic host.

Athena ran forward, placed her hand on Apollo's shoulder. "Apollo, stop!" she said. "What are you doing? She hasn't done anything!"

"Miss me?" Starbuck asked Athena, and flashed his rogue's smile at her. He never let his gun hand waver from its target as he swept her into his free arm, dipped her, and kissed her. She blinked and looked at him, mouth agape.

"Just in case there was any doubt," he told her.

"She's done plenty," Apollo said, and looked again at Segis. The uploading and awakening of his mind in the city beneath them let him see things Athena could not, and as he watched now Segis's features seemed to shift and run, first a woman, now a man, now genderless. Apollo squeezed his eyes shut, and when he opened them, Segis was once more a smiling, charming woman, as fine and kind as any had ever known.

"You were behind it all . . . not Baltar," Apollo said, and he felt the tumblers all click into place. "You masterminded our return to Kobol."

"You are mistaken, Commander Apollo," Segis said reasonably; she was smiling, but that smile never quite reached her eyes. "My people and I have always been subservient to the will of your people. We would never do anything to harm anyone. It would be a gross violation of our most sacred laws."

"Whose laws would that be?" Apollo asked, and squeezed the trigger.

People screamed in horror as the ruby light struck the unarmed caretaker. Cain cursed and drew his own weapon. But Starbuck turned, his laser pointed at the old commander, and warned him with a wave of his weapon not to interfere.

"Trust him? He just gunned down a woman in cold blood!" Cain shouted.

"Really?" Starbuck asked, gesturing with the barrel of his laser. "Look again."

They all looked on as the body of Segis crumpled bonelessly to the floor, as if it were nothing but a sack of flesh . . . but it wasn't really a body, at all, just the robes she had worn. There *was* no body. Standing where Segis had stood, the robes pooled at her feet, was a shadowy creature that not only swallowed the light, but radiated darkness, its body rippling with nightmare images. To look for long upon this monster, this shape cut out of negative space, would be to know true despair, would surely result in gibbering, irretrievable madness. It was the Void, given shape, and it called itself Count Iblis.

"*Welcome home,*" he said with deep, rising laughter.

15

SUPPOSE YOU'RE wondering why I've called you all together?" Iblis laughed with a sound like decay, or the death of love and hope. It was a voice that crawled inside one's brain, in the wee, dark hours of the night, and whispered things, sick things, crazy things. It was the voice of madness; Count Iblis was quite mad in fact, but nonetheless dangerous for all of that.

Many of the colonials had heard the tales of Count Iblis, but to them, he was the Kobollian boogeyman, a tale told to frighten unruly children at bedtime. No one who was not familiar with the Kobollian legends truly believed he existed. But the great hall was now full of believers.

Athena understood in a lightning stroke that Iblis had presented himself in an image they each would trust, and understand; they all saw something different. The women of the fleet had seen a handsome, godlike man, the men, a beautiful, angelic woman. And Athena bet that each of the different races of the fleet saw Iblis as a trusted figure from his or her own lost world.

"What kind of twisted game have you been playing with us now, monster?" Apollo asked. He still clung to his gun, but conventional weapons were useless against this creature of pure, malevolent thought.

"Generations ago, on this very spot, your Kobollian forefathers cast me and my followers out of the House of Kobol," the Count said, his voice seething venom. "We were exiled to the most hostile and uninhabitable planet in the galaxy . . . Cylon. There, we were left to die. Instead, we . . . nurtured . . . the planet's life forms along the evolutionary path—instilling in them an insatiable hatred for humankind. I vowed never again to be at the mercy of humans. Humans are weak, destined for extinction. I've known this for millennia, and on Kobol began my experiments, culminating at last with the Cylons, a perfect race, a species truly worthy of inheriting the universe."

Iblis's red eyes sparked and danced, and he made a sound like a death rattle; Apollo realized with horror the Count was laughing.

"The Cylons are your next-of-kin," Iblis said, raising his hands, palms up, to his sides. "They're here for a family reunion." He turned toward Apollo, his red eyes growing darker until they were the color of spilled blood. "You and your sister, Athena, are the last of the direct descendants of the House of Kobol, and, as such, must die to avenge the deaths of millions of my tribe."

The Count's image did not appear on the flatscreen; instead, static and white noise filled the screen. His likeness, his *true* likeness, not that which he chose to broadcast, could not be captured or contained by simple technology. Iblis was beyond any mortal understanding. Occasional subliminal flashes of the Count would appear on the screen, too quick to register on the naked eye or conscious thought, but those images burrowed down into the brain and soul of any who dared look, and those who looked too long would simply go mad.

Iblis shook his head, as if speaking to children, or particularly thick-witted daggits. "I have been watching and playing with you and the colonials for aeons as you acted out your pitiful little life games, waiting for just the right moment to guide you back to Kobol. It is only here, in the land of my birth, and death, so to speak, that I have the power to reclaim my physical body and soul as I destroy yours.

"I am the nightmare that has been following you and your ancestors all your life, Apollo, the face at the edge of the shadows in your sleep chamber, the voice in your ear corrupting your better judgment," Iblis said. "You and the lovely Athena will now know the full weight of the horror that I have had to endure."

Iblis's eyes glowed brighter, and his body actually seemed to grow blacker; twin beams stabbed out from his eye sockets and struck Apollo. The force of the light staggered Apollo, throwing him back on his heels, but the corona of light that enveloped him began to fade, and the Star of Kobol Apollo wore around his neck flared as it drank the light into itself. Apollo realized at once what had happened, and so did Iblis.

One of the Warriors had taken advantage of Iblis's preoccupation with the commander to sneak up on the Count and draw his sidearm. The Warrior held the weapon scant centimetrons from the back of the Iblis's head, and pulled the trigger. The laser blast entered the Count's body, but did not emerge, as if Iblis had swallowed the light—a black hole in human form.

Iblis's hand snapped out behind and gripped the Warrior's throat, crushing his larynx closed. The man tried to scream, but all that emerged was a high-pitched, reedy, wailing sound. Iblis twisted his wrist, and the Warrior's neck snapped like dry kindling. Iblis threw the body aside as if the mere fact of it offended him.

The people who had been seated or standing nearest Iblis all backed away, fearing they might be next.

"Take off that trinket, Apollo," the Count commanded, gesturing at the Star of Kobol. As he did, whorls of light flashed and flowed slowly, back and forth, somewhere deep within the medallion. "Take it off, and let me banish you and your sister to the oblivion that is my existence, and perhaps I'll be merciful. Perhaps I can still convince the Cylons to spare the lives of some of your people."

Iblis glanced at the gathering contained within the great hall. Many had taken the opportunity of the confusion to leave; many more remained seated. Where was there to go?

The Count smiled, a thin gash of ruby in the blackness of his aura, as if he contained within him all the fires of hell. "The Cylons have a mind of their own, as willfull children often do, but there is a use for your race, so I don't think they'll want to kill you all."

Apollo looked at Athena, who had made her way across the platform to stand near Starbuck. "Don't listen to him," she warned her brother. "You know Iblis is evil incarnate. You can't trust him . . . *it*."

"You hurt me, Athena," Iblis said. "Perhaps I can reply in kind."

With that, the man-shaped abyss turned toward the civilians who still occupied the hall, and raised his hand. A wave of darkness rippled from his outstretched fingers, shimmering across the cavernous room to envelop a Gemon woman whose lifemate had perished in the battle with the Chitain. She shrieked horribly, a scream that seemed to go on forever in the perfect acoustics of the hall, as the darkness settled on her flesh and broke into countless, insectoid-sized particles that burrowed their way under her skin, into her bones, and devoured her from within.

She was nothing more than a paper-thin husk that stood in place for a moment, then collapsed under the weight of itself, then vanished in a puff of dust.

Iblis's eyes blazed and he snapped his head around, directing his deadly eye-beams at a father who was trying to shield his motherless child behind his own body. A nimbus of ruby light danced around the father, and his body darkened as if in eclipse. The light shrank inward, drawing to a central point, erasing the man as it dwindled down to nothingess.

"I can keep this up forever," Iblis warned Apollo. "Every second you delay in giving me what I want, I'll take one more life."

At the back of the hall, the security guards tried to force open the doors, but Iblis had mentally sealed them. The guards drew their lasers and fired at the doors, but their blasts ricocheted back at them, punching ragged, bloody holes through their chests. The men barely had time to register what had happened before they slumped against one another, like weary children after a day's hard play.

"Stop it, you perverted monster!" Apollo shouted, his hands fisted at his sides in helpless rage. "Leave them alone! They've done nothing to you! Your quarrel is with me!"

Iblis shrugged, indicating he was powerless to act otherwise. "Only you can stop the slaughter, Apollo, and you know what you have to do. Otherwise, I'd suggest you get comfortable; this could take a while." He turned away from Apollo, as if he were beneath notice, and let his red, glowing eyes roam over the sea of terrified faces laid out before him.

"All right!" Apollo said, "all right."

"Apollo!" Athena gasped. She knew what he meant to do.

"It's the only way," he told her, and, with great solemnity he removed the Star of Kobol from around his neck. He touched it to his forehead in a gesture of reverence, and placed it on the edge of the platform, then turned to face Iblis, his shoulders squared and his back straight.

Iblis nodded his approval, and motioned for Apollo to come nearer. Apollo looked to his closest friends and cohorts, and his eyes met theirs: Athena, Tigh, Starbuck. They all watched in mute horror as Apollo stepped closer to Iblis, walking willingly to his own death. But then, as he had said, it was the only way to spare the lives of the others.

"Smart boy," Iblis said, and his eyes blazed red as quartz. The light beams scorched the air between them and slammed into Apollo, making him jitter and jump as if he had grabbed a handful of lightning. He made small, glottal noises in the back of his throat and struggled to retain consciousness, for he knew instinctively that if he now were to lose his waking contact with this existence, he would find himself forevermore in the hated oblivion of which Iblis spoke.

"Give in to it, last son of the House of Kobol," the Count advised; "believe me, the pain *will* get worse . . . much worse."

Apollo didn't see how that was possible, but then, Iblis torqued the agony up another notch and Apollo realized, on this much, at least, the Count was telling the truth.

"This is but the merest fraction of the agony of every micron of my existence," Iblis told him. "Imagine what pain like this can do to a man, over the millennia." Iblis chuckled. "But then, you won't have to *imagine* much longer, will you? You'll discover first hand what it can do, as I discovered for myself, thanks to your cursed ancestors."

"Stop it!" Starbuck roared, and fired his laser at Iblis; Cain and a score of other Warriors likewise trained their sidearms on the shadow figure, but the blasts were swallowed by the Count's darkness.

"There's no need to rush," Iblis assured them in a calm, patient voice. "I'll get to all of you after I deal with your friend."

Apollo slumped to his knees, his arms hanging uselessly at his side, twitching and jerking helplessly, his head thrown back, mouth open in a silent rictus of pure agony. Veins stood out in bas relief against his neck and temples, throbbing and pulsing until it seemed they would simply explode. Gods, why didn't Iblis just kill him and get it over with? Even death had to be better than this.

"I have one other, little thing I'd like to show you," Iblis whispered, like a dry wind rattling dead leaves and grasses. And suddenly, Apollo's tortured mind was filled with a series of rapid images, and he saw Count Iblis and Adama's distant ancestor, going back many generations, both in line to replace the retiring elder and the Council Head of the House of Kobol. There was a deep and powerful love between the two men, who were brothers, as deep as the love Apollo felt for Starbuck. But Iblis, a scientific genius, was also deeply jealous of his gifted, older brother. And, although he tried his best to outdo him, time and again, Iblis could never understand why his scientific accomplishments never meant as much to their father as his brother's wisdom, charisma, and strength of character. More images, more poisoned emotions, all told from Iblis's biased and corrupted point of view: Iblis felt as if their parents had always favored his brother, as it seemed all children believed, never affording Iblis the respect his accomplishments deserved.

Faster now, Apollo was forced to relive all of Iblis's pain as his brother continued to best him in every possible way, until the final blow, the last insult, when the brother was awarded the position of council head. Iblis plotted in dark secrecy to have his brother murdered, a crime almost unheard of on Kobol. The new council head discovered the plan, and even then was willing to forgive his brother, but was forced by the council to discipline Iblis. Faster, still, the images of Iblis working to create his master race, until this, too, was discovered, and the Kobollians had no choice at all but to banish his beloved sibling to Cylon. All of these images came to Apollo in less than a microcentari, but they felt to his agonized soul to last yahren.

One by one, the lasers the Warriors were firing at Iblis failed; one moment they had power, and the next, they were dead, the charge dissipated. "Frack," Starbuck muttered, checking his weapon. The power pack indicator read completely drained.

"You're going to beg, Adama-son," Iblis promised Apollo, his eyes glowing brighter still. As they did, Apollo's sufferings increased with an almost exponential progression. "You're going to beg as I did all those long yahren ago; you're going to renounce your heritage, the House of Kobol, even your very father, before I let you slip away from this life."

Apollo thought the joke was going to be on Iblis, because he didn't believe he would live long enough to renounce anything, even if he wanted to. He toppled backward, unable to catch himself, but Gar'Tokk was there to support him. The Borellian Noman knew no attack he could muster against Iblis would accomplish anything, but he could at least perish with his master. "I think we finally found that suicidal situation you were asking about," Gar'Tokk grunted against the pain. "And now we know the answer."

Apollo wanted to tell him not to throw his life away so foolishly, but he couldn't form the words, either with his tongue or inside his own mind.

Athena, unable to watch her brother's suffering, leaped from her place on the platform and gripped his hand tightly. For a moment, new life and strength flowed into him, and he blinked his eyes, focusing on her concerned face.

"Athena?" he managed. But then the circuit of pain expanded, enveloping her as well. Athena's mouth slipped open and her eyes rolled back into her skull.

"We have to form a shield!" Starbuck shouted, running forward into the line of fire. He gripped Athena's hand, lending his strength to her, and she, in turn, lending her strength to Apollo. Now, Boomer and Sheba and Cain and Cassie and Dalton and Troy, more and more Warriors and brave civilians from all the dead worlds ran forward and held hands, and still more came, until they formed a living circle that surrounded Iblis. Each link in the human chain fed his or her strength to the person next to him or her, letting it flow round and round, as fluid as the tides. It was a coming together of mind and spirit, a unification such as the woefully divided fleet had not seen for many yahren.

Apollo's eyes once again grew focused and determined and full of resistance, as he felt himself refilling with life. The web of energy Iblis was spinning circled around the group, accelerating, until a powerful bolt discharged from Apollo, directed back at Iblis. Far from weakening Apollo's resolve, Iblis's tortured tale strengthened Apollo, and made him feel closer to Athena, closer than he had felt in longer than he could recall. The Count screamed in pain as the feedback grew more and more powerful, more lethal.

The men and women forming the shield that surrounded Iblis saw what was happening and concentrated their wills, letting the energy flow along the circuit, hand to hand to hand, back to Apollo. Iblis was a creature of darkness and despair, and could not withstand so much life and hope; it was anathema to him, as sunlight is to a vampire. He threw his head back and shrieked, unable to stand the pain any longer.

His body exploded in a spray of black embers and hellfire, and the scream echoed and re-echoed throughout the great hall. The black particles swarmed and swirled on the air, graying as they did, skirling up and up, to the ceiling, until they finally faded from sight altogether.

"Did we . . . ?" Athena was the first to break the silence and ask the question they all wanted to ask.

Apollo shook his head. "I doubt it. Iblis isn't a physical creature. The most we've done is hurt him. I don't know if he can be destroyed." He retrieved the Star of Kobol from its place upon the platform and returned it, with a silent prayer of thanks, to its rightful place around his neck.

"Apollo," Cain began, his hand resting on the commander's shoulder; he was looking at Apollo in a new light. He had always admired Adama's son; now, he respected him. Adama was still very much alive, in his children. "That was one of the bravest, most selfless acts I've ever been privileged to witn—"

Another explosion, larger and directly overhead, crushed the ceiling of the cavernous hall. Boulders and huge blocks of stone from spilled down into the center of the auditorium, crushing those few who were unfortunate enough to still be standing there. Most of the colonials had made their way to forward, to join in the living circle to defend Apollo against Iblis. But they were still doomed if the Cylons were left to ravage the planet unchecked.

Light from above filtered down through the veins of dirt and dust that hung thickly in the air. Cain looked up, squinting against the grit. "I want everyone in the ships' crews to head for the asteroid," Cain ordered in a loud, clear voice.

"You can't be serious," Apollo said, gripping Cain's arm. "Even if we make it to the asteroid, the Cylons will blast us out of the sky before we can even begin to fight back."

"Those are my orders!" Cain barked. "As supreme commander—"

"The vote was never taken," Apollo reminded him. "I am still in command."

Cain spat his rage and frustration. "Then I'm seizing command from you and ordering you and all the rest of the ships' crews up to that asteroid!"

Another blast, farther away, but still powerful enough to shake loose smaller boulders and dirt, rattled the hall. They could debate who was in charge and what was the best way to proceed until the roof collapsed and made the whole matter academic. Apollo raked his hand through his hair, glanced up, over Cain's shoulder, and saw Talen standing there.

"The dream," he said, their eyes locked, "was it real?"

She said nothing, but she had given him his answer earlier. *Choose wisely,* she had said, as had Adama. To say more than that would remove the article of faith. Apollo hesitated only a moment, then stood up and addressed the hallful of terrified colonials. "Our only chance of surviving this is to head further down into the city," he said, loudly and clearly.

Athena looked at him as if he had begun speaking in some forgotten, incomprehensible language. What he said made no sense. "What are you talking about?" she asked. "What—"

He cut her off. "I believe there's another city beneath this one," he said. "A city that leads deep into the bowels of the planet."

"You *believe?*" Cain repeated.

Apollo looked at him; he would not back down on this one. "Sometimes, faith is all we have," he said. "I don't know how far down the city extends, but it may be our only chance of evading the Cylons until we can formulate a plan of escape or negotiate a surrender."

"No surrender!" Cain thundered.

Apollo turned, his arm held out to encompass the colonials who were huddling in blind fear at the back and sides of the hall. "You tell that to them!" he said, his face almost touching Cain's. "You tell them we'd rather all die than negotiate surrender! Haven't these people lost enough already, without losing their own lives, too?"

"Do you really think the Cylons will let any of us live?" Cain asked, a note of amusement in his voice. "If we surrender, we're doing their dirty work for them."

Apollo shook his head. "They need some of us alive for

research," he reminded the old war-daggit. "We might be able to leverage some kind of deal with them . . . something, *anything,* that keeps us all alive until we can form a plan of escape."

The matter seemed to be at a deadlock, until Starbuck stepped forward to stand beside his oldest friend. "I'm in," he said. As if there were ever any doubt. But it helped decide matters for others, and Boomer and Sheba stepped away from Cain and walked to Apollo's side. More civilians and Warriors joined the commander.

Apollo and Cain stood looking at one another; if Cain had anything to say, he kept it to himself. Apollo turned to Athena, who bit her lip and shook her head. She was not ready yet to trust her inner vision. "We need to do this," Apollo said to Cain. "Now." He nodded.

With Iblis' influence gone, the exits were opened once more, and Cain and Athena and their fellow Warriors made their way out of the hall, heading for the shuttles. Athena paused at the doorway and looked back at Apollo and, forcing a smile, she gave him a thumbs-up, and ran out of the building . . . but not before blowing Starbuck a kiss. He caught it and held it to his heart.

Starbuck thought again that maybe the time had come for a serious relationship, and laughed; how typical of himself to start thinking about such things when death seemed imminent.

"What's so funny?" Apollo asked.

"Just thinking," he answered, "the more things change, the more they remain insane."

"The same," Apollo corrected. "Remain the *same.*"

"You said it," Starbuck said with a wide grin, and gave his friend a Warrior's handshake. "Let's do this."

Apollo and Starbuck, with Gar'Tokk nearby, took point and led their followers out through the rear exits. The damage to the underground city had been more extensive than anyone might have guessed; a huge section of the cavern ceiling had collapsed under the barrage of the plasma cannons and buried or crushed many buildings and dwelling units. It was only by the grace of the

Lords of Light that the great hall and its occupants had been spared the same terrible fate.

Through the rip in the earth, Apollo and his group could see the shuttles as they bulleted away from the planet, past the Cylon Raiders and their hail of turbolaser fire. The shuttles had their own shields and defense systems, and Apollo prayed it would be enough to get them safely to the asteroid.

As he thought that, a Raider targeted one of the shuttles with its lasers, but another shuttle raked a barrage of firepower along the Raider's side, shredding it in half before it could bring its own lasers into play.

"Keep running," Apollo ordered, forcing himself to look away from the aerial pandemonium. Strobes of light, the flare of plasma cannons and turbolasers, washed down through the opening in the earth and painted the buildings in bold strokes of red, but whatever was happening up there, they could not afford to let themselves be distracted. They had to find the underground entrance or risk death or capture.

Baltar had grabbed Siress Kiera and joined Apollo's group of refugees. To his credit, Baltar thought he might still be of some use in negotiating a bloodless surrender to the Cylons, if capture did seem imminent.

Apollo tried to recall the path he had taken in his dreamwalk, and the harder he concentrated, the more indistinct and hazy his memories became. Cold sweat began to dot his forehead and upper lip. Gods, what if it really was just a dream? He was gambling their lives on an ambrosa-fueled hallucination!

He shook his head and pushed that thought away. He couldn't allow himself to doubt. He had listened to his inner vision, as he had told Athena she must, and he had chosen accordingly. The comm-line he wore at his belt chirrupped and he snagged it, opened it. "Apollo, here" he hailed his caller. The little holo-vid projected Athena's flickering, three-dimensional image to him.

"Athena, here," the image crackled back, the transmission sputtering from the massive charges of energy from Cylon weapons filling the air around them. "We're almost there," she reported. "We're going to make it . . . "

Apollo breathed a sigh of relief. "Stay in contact," he told her, and added, "And don't take any foolish risks."

She laughed. "It's been nothing but risks these past twenty yahren," she reminded him. "It's you I'm worried about. At least we'll have battlestars and Vipers; you . . . you just have a dream and a hole in the ground."

"Well, of course it sounds bad, if you put it like that," Starbuck muttered to Apollo, and, despite the situation, they both laughed like naughty children.

Far above Kobol, the shuttles bearing the Warriors back to their battlestars and Vipers reached the asteroid; a command from the shuttle's computer to the asteroid's opened the concealed docking bay, and the shuttles jockeyed into position. As soon as the first shuttle landed, its passengers disembarked and began running for the battlestars.

Cylon Raiders had tracked the shuttles to their destination, and Athena realized with some horror that that had been their plan, all along, to discover where the fleet had been hidden. Well, she thought, grimly, nothing to do for it now but see it through. . . .

The first wave of Raiders fired their turbolasers at the docked shuttles and peeled away; the shuttles jumped as the lasers struck, then exploded in a spray of burning fuel and shrapnel.

Emergency fire controls kicked into life, pumping thick foam from vents in the ceiling and walls and floor to extinguish the blaze. Athena thought that if their luck just held, they were going to get through this. The shuttle in which she and Cain were passengers docked, and they leaped out before the hatch had completely opened and pelted across the foam-slick runway—she for the *Galactica* and he for the *Pegasus.*

Laser fire scorched the air behind Athena's head, and she felt the tremendous heat singeing her back. She looked around, saw a

Raider had followed them into the docking bay and was targeting the Warriors as they ran from the shuttles to the battlestars.

"Oh no you don't," Athena grumbled, and turned from the battlestar and ran for a control panel in the nearby wall. She found the one she was looking for and slammed her fist against it; instantly, a thick spray of the fire-dampening foam gushed from the ceiling and walls, blanketing the Raider's canopy. The fighter, blinded now, veered sharply, scraped against the ceiling, then racketed off the wall and finally slammed into the foam-covered floor, where it slid out of control, slewing wildly, pulsars still firing. The Raider lifted, dropped, lifted once more and plowed straight on into the wall.

It fell again, and this time did not rise.

"What's going on up there?" Apollo's voice sputtered across her comm-line. It had been open all the while, and he had doubtless heard the Raider's none-too-quiet demise.

"Nothing serious, just a little disagreement with one of the neighbors. I think we're going to make it," Athena reported back, running for the *Galactica*. Cain had already boarded the *Pegasus* and was powering up her engines. The other battlestars were ready to launch; she was the last to board. "What's your situation?"

She looked out through the asteroid's open doorway, and realized that whatever Apollo's situation, it had to be better than theirs. Apollo answered, but she couldn't hear him over the runaway thudding of her own heart and the pounding of blood in her ears. Filling the starfield and continuing to grow in size as it closed the distance, was a Cylon Class IV basestar.

"Athena?" Apollo's voice again, breaking up on the ether. The air around the basestar was charged with plasma as the deadly cannons were trained upon the asteroid and powered up. Her inner vision told her they were in a world of sorrow.

She shook herself out of her torpor and boarded the *Galactica*. The ship's crew had already begun firing the engines; all that was left to be done was for her to order the battlestar away. It was still not too late, she told herself as she ran for the bridge. "Prepare to launch!" she shouted into the ship's comm-system, relaying her order to the bridge crew.

More plasma cannons along the weapon-prickled face of the basestar swung about to bear upon the asteroid. The first blast from the cannons struck the asteroid and shook it violently, like dice in a gambler's hand. Emergency klaxons shrieked and power was diverted to the shields. Dozens of fires erupted around the docking bay as equipment shorted and sparked. The force of the cannon fire had actually rocked the asteroid from its orbit above the planet, and it began to lose altitude. Mighty engines buried deep within the ship of rock and steel kicked in, and pulsars fired from secret exhausts, correcting their orbit automatically. Another set of alarms added their strident message to the first, but they weren't saying anything Athena didn't already know: they were royally fracked.

The massive door concealing the battlestars had been damaged in the first blast and would not fully open. The fleet was trapped aboard the asteroid. They would have to train the battlestars's firepower on the door from within and blow their way out.

The basestar's second level of cannons fired, training their planet-rending force on one spot on the asteroid. Explosion after explosion leaped across the surface of the artificial construct, geysers of fire leaping high into the air.

The asteroid began to crumble, and as the unstable Tylium mine reacted to the plasma bursts, the asteroid erupted in a blaze of blinding flame that, to anyone watching from the surface of the planet, looked like a new star being born.

And then, the new star began its long, horrible tumble toward the surface of Kobol, marking its passage in the heavens with a jagged, flaming tail.

16

THE FLAMING asteroid seemed to move in slow motion through its new course in the sky, heading inexorably to the planet's atmosphere. As it fell, the Tylium veins that snaked through the asteroid exploded, sending huge, flaming divots spinning away from the main body, and these, also, exploded into smaller fragments.

Their erratic course sent them tumbling into several Cylon Raiders, crushing them outright, but that was of scant consolation to the survivors who could only watch in mute horror as so many friends and loved ones came to such a terrible end. Human grief meant nothing to the Cylons; the basestar's launch bay windows opened and more Raiders roared forth, while the original armada began to set down on Kobol's battle-pocked surface.

"Keep moving," Apollo heard himself say; he was in a state of shock, but he could not let that interfere with his obligation to his people. They had trusted him with their lives by remaining on the planet with him; he would do his best to justify their faith.

"Your sister just *died,* Apollo," Starbuck said, a tear falling from his eye. His voice was thick with emotion. "My *daughter* and your son just died! It'd be all right to be a little human, you know."

"What do you want me to do?" Apollo snapped. He was hurting

worse than he would allow anyone to see, and Starbuck, of all people, should have known that. But then, as Starbuck had rightly pointed out, his daughter had just perished up there as well. "I don't have the luxury right now of mourning, and neither do you!" he said, and jabbed his finger into Starbuck's chest. He hated talking so bluntly, so coldly, to his dearest friend, but their chance of survival was growing smaller by the micron. It would avail them nothing to give themselves over to grief now.

Starbuck's jaw muscles tightened and tensed, but he said nothing. Apollo was right, of course. But, still. . . .

"All right," he said through gritted teeth. "What do we do?"

Apollo recognized this part of the city, knew the kiosk that led downward to the crystal city was nearby. They might still survive this, if the collapsing cavern roof had not buried the entrance. But, one disaster at a time, he told himself. "You, Sheba, and Boomer take up the rear," he ordered. "Everyone else, follow me."

He began running for the only hope they had now, and he had to force himself not to look heavenward, through the rend in the cavern roof, as if he could possibly catch one last glimpse of the fleet's funeral pyre, the star that was his sister, as it made its final return to Kobol.

It takes a tremendous amount of strength sometimes to just hang on, but it took even more to simply let go.

The first of the Cylon ground troops landed and immediately began unloading mech soldiers and their weapons. They launched their flying attack droid, and it swooped down into the caverns housing the underground city. The attack droid resembled a Raider, with its disquieting curves and arclike, forward-swept wings, and, in lieu of a canopy window, it had the same long, narrow aperture as the Cylons themselves had, from which emitted fine, concentrated beams of ruby light. It soared along the surviving rooftops, thermal imaged a large cluster of heat sources, and streaked toward them, transmitting the images back to the ground troops.

As one, the troops began to march forward.

*   *   *

Apollo had managed to find the building housing the kiosk that led down into the hidden city; it had not been crushed under falling debris from the collapsing cavern, as he had feared. Unfortunately, the attack droid had found them, as well. He stood at the base of the winding staircase, studying the sigils etched into the stone walls. The snippet of song almost came to him . . . like a bit of song that never quite leaves one's head, but refuses to step forward and be finally identified.

The attack droid swirled down the spiral stone staircase, skimming over the heads of the colonials, startling those who reacted quickly enough to catch a glimpse of it before it moved on. At the base of the steps, it targeted Apollo and the others nearest him, but Gar'Tokk's keen senses had been alerted by its shrill, almost imperceptible whine. Certainly, no human ears could have detected it. He spotted the source of the sound at once, but the attack droid had already powered up its deadly turbolaser charge. Gar'Tokk flung himself between Apollo and the blast without thought or hesitation.

Apollo turned, just in time to watch in horror as the laser sliced into Gar'Tokk's massive chest. Apollo's sidearm was in his hand immediately, before Gar'Tokk's twitching, still-smoking body had hit the ground, and he fired at the droid, his first shot splashing off its arclike wing. The droid was shoved back by Apollo's shot, where it whanged against the wall and dropped to the floor, but it was up again at once, its red aperture glowing brighter as if it were angry at the attack. It prepared to defend itself. Apollo fired again, catching the droid straight-on, and this time, when it fell, it did not get up.

Apollo holstered his sidearm and knelt beside Gar'Tokk, wincing at the severity of the wound the Noman had taken for him. Apollo didn't see how it was possible, but Gar'Tokk was still alive, and he opened his eyes and forced a weak smile to his lips. "Looks like I've . . . finally paid my debt to you . . ." Gar'Tokk managed to say.

Apollo nodded, biting his lower lip. "Looks like," he said. But how would he ever repay his debt to Gar'Tokk?

The wound Gar'Tokk suffered was ghastly to behold; the laser had cauterized the nerves and veins even as it punched its fatal hole through his chest, so there was little blood, but the internal damage was great—too great for even Gar'Tokk to walk away from. Organs Apollo couldn't recognize had been exposed by the blast, and they had all suffered trauma of one degree or another.

"I didn't . . . do this . . . for no reason, you know," Gar'Tokk reminded him, managing to point his numb fingers toward the secret entrance to the crystal city beneath their feet.

Apollo nodded; Gar'Tokk was right. There was no time to say good-bye to Athena, or Cain, or the Noman he had come to consider a close friend. He stood and, with great effort, turned his back on Gar'Tokk and concentrated once more on the sigils before him.

Now that Gar'Tokk's debt to Apollo had been paid, the Borellian Nomen once more recognized him as one of their own, and jumped down from their places on the winding stone staircase to hustle to his side, to offer what aid or comfort they could. It wasn't much, but it was better than dying alone and apart.

The line of civilians wound through the narrow back streets of the city, like people waiting for some overly hyped band to take the stage. Bringing up the rear of the line were Starbuck, Boomer, and Sheba, keeping their eyes open for Cylon ground forces; they didn't have to wait long. Starbuck noticed the approaching Centurions first, and alerted Boomer, Sheba, and the Warriors nearest them. Starbuck grabbed his comm-line and shouted down to Apollo, "Hurry up and pay the frackin' toll, will you? We've got some new neighbors up here, and they don't look happy to see us!"

Starbuck drew his sidearm instinctively and fired at the advancing Cylons; the laser pistol fired, and only when it slammed into the first Centurion did Starbuck remember that Iblis had drained its power. Apparently, the Count's powers and ability to affect things extended only so far as those within his immediate range. Boomer and Sheba took their positions inside the doorways of the nearest edifices and began returning fire at the Cylons, who simply marched straight into the laser fire. It didn't matter; their numbers were so plentiful that the Centurions would sacrifice themselves without hesitation, knowing even more would take their place. They were not the greatest battlefield tacticians in the galaxy, but then, they didn't need to be. Numbers and fanaticism were on their side.

"Take cover! Take cover!" Boomer shouted to the civilians, but there was really no place to hide. They had been herded into a narrow, warren-like maze, with few offerings of shelter. The Warriors did their best to form a shield between the Cylons and the civilians, but the invading numbers were too plentiful, their firepower too great.

"We're really going to surrender . . . to *that?*" Sheba wondered aloud.

The Centurions raised their pulse rifles and began firing. The laser pulses struck the sides of the building, sending gouts of stone and dust soaring in every direction, ripping through the bodies of civilians like bullets. The narrow corridors filled with dust, but the gleaming Centurion armor could still be seen as they approached, their red eye slits blazing, searching.

They advanced, they fired, they were shot at, they fell. Another line of Centurions, just behind the previous, would march blindly over the still corpses of their own fallen, their pulse rifles firing as they advanced. Civilians, huddled against the walls of the buildings, were cut down instantly, if they were lucky. Others were crushed by the flying debris of laser-blasted streets or walls. But Starbuck noticed something very disturbing about the Cylons: each succeeding wave of Centurions was somehow more agile, faster, more cunning . . . more . . . *human* in their behavior. The advanced Cylons, the more evolved Centurions, were using the old race as laser fodder. "Oh . . . *frack,"* he muttered under his breath. Just when he thought things couldn't get worse.

There was nowhere to run; the back street they occupied led

only to one destination, to the building in which the kiosk to the secret underground city lay.

Apollo remembered the few, sparse notes of the song, and sang them to the sigils set into the stone wall. For a moment, a very long moment, nothing happened, and Apollo worried he had not remembered the key properly, and that he had led these people here to a gruesome, unavoidable end, but then, the runes began to glow, growing brighter, filling the small underground room with their light.

The wall shimmered, as it had the night before, and dissolved beneath the spreading radiance. The people nearest Apollo all heaved a sigh of relief, and the commander stood at the entrance, ushering everyone safely through, into the cavern of cystal.

Apollo had heard the familiar sounds of pitched battle from above, and slapped his comm-line. "Starbuck! Fall back! Lead everyone into the building! We're through!"

"I wish you wouldn't put it like that," Starbuck's voice answered. A moment later, a huge *Crash!* came across the comm-line. Something big had just collapsed.

"Starbuck?" Apollo shouted into his communicator, still ushering the Civilians past him and through the secret passageway.

"Yeah, we're all right," Starbuck replied. "Boomer and a couple of Warriors blasted one of the buildings . . . it collapsed and blocked the passage, us on this side, them on the other."

"That buys us time," Apollo said to no one in particular. He closed the connection, and concentrated on the matter at hand, of getting his people to safety. The civilians on the stone staircase made their way down, some of them too frightened to wait any longer, and leaped off the sides of the spiraling steps to the ground. Apollo realized it was just a miracle they hadn't panicked worse than this, but then, they had lived with fear for the past twenty yahren. What was one more afternoon?

Baltar hurried past Apollo, with Siress Kiera's hand in his. Baltar's look was ashen, his face puffy and covered with drying blood, but he met Apollo's eyes. Why not? He had done nothing wrong, and wanted to remind the commander of that. "For the record," Baltar paused just long enough to say, "I didn't know that Count Iblis—"

Apollo nodded, placing his palm against the broad of Baltar's back and giving him a nudge to get him going. "Gotcha," he said. "Completely innocent." The commander glanced up toward the head of the stairway far above, and saw Starbuck, Boomer, and Sheba hurrying in. He didn't realize he'd been holding his breath until he felt himself release it in a slow, uncoiling exhalation.

"They're right behind us!" Starbuck shouted down to Apollo. "The flying droids—!"

"Keep moving!" Apollo commanded, drawing his laser and watching the shadow-clotted darkness that filled the levels above his head. The last of the civilians thundered down the staircase and through the passageway into the crystal city. Starbuck and his band were just a few feet away from the bottom of the steps when a laser pulse from above shattered the base of the stairway. The people dropped hard to the ground as the stone steps crumbled out from beneath their feet, but none were seriously hurt.

Flying droids swooped in through the above-ground opening and dived down the shaft in opposing arcs, weaving in and out around each other, their red apertures glowing brighter as they prepared to fire. Apollo sighted the nearest one and fired, letting his hand lead him. He fired automatically, and took down three more of the deadly batlike weapons.

Starbuck rolled out of the way of a laser pulse, and fired his own pistol straight up at the diving droid, tearing it to steel confetti. But now, the ground troops had arrived and were descending the spiral stairway, stopping long enough to fire their pulse rifles, then hurry down another few risers where they paused and fired again.

Sheba and Boomer returned fire, blasting their targeted Centurions off the steps, where they fell with a loud crash to the stone floor, and lay still. The first group of soldiers had descended the steps, and were beginning to advance across the small chamber toward Apollo and his group. The humans backed away from them, toward the opening, firing their lasers as they retreated. A stray shot struck the staircase and cracked the stone; the weight of the descending Centurions caused the ancient rock to give way, and a horde of the armored creatures dropped straight down, plunging in eerie silence to their deaths.

The humans turned and ran, taking advantage of the confusion as more of the weakened stairs collapsed beneath the concentrated weight; the stairs were ancient, and had not been designed to hold this much weight at one time. Apollo knew it was only the will of the Lords of Light that the risers had held the civilians as long as they had.

Starbuck looked around at the soaring crystal buildings, rising as high above them as they descended into the earth. "Oh, good thinking," he said dryly, "let's all go hide in a city of *glass!* They'll *never* find us *here!*"

"Well, sure, of course it sounds bad if you put it like *that*," Apollo said, answering with one of Starbuck's pet phrases. "You've been a real pain in the ass since you died and came back, you know that?"

Apollo's group joined with the civilians and Warriors who were already making their way into the heart of the crystal city, looking for a position from which to defend themselves. Several Warriors had taken up places on the walkways far overhead, using the advantage of high ground to blast the Cylons as they filed into the cavern. The Centurions were forced to enter two abreast through the narrow opening, and they were gunned down by the snipers as soon as they stepped through the breach.

But the flying droids came winging through the opening, heading for the walkways, weaving in and out around the laser fire directed at them. Their red slits glowed, and energy pulses stabbed out, shattering the walkway at either end. The crystal made a chilling, cracking sound, and the men dropped down and down, through the levels of the impossible city, the glass buildings reflecting and magnifying their horrible deaths, disappearing from view at last, their death cries echoing off the smooth, polished crystal walls of the buildings. The broken shards of catwalk tinkled and chattered as they fell, like delicate wind chimes.

The wall containing the entrance shuddered, began to crumble, then collapsed, as the Cylons blasted it with their pulse rifles. They shared a group intelligence: what one had learned, they all had learned, and they knew now it was a waste of resources to enter the chamber two abreast, easy targets for the humans. Instead, with the wall out of their way, the Centurions could swarm in, too many for the humans to strike down before their superior numbers could overwhelm the cornered colonials. It was part of the developing cunning Starbuck had glimpsed. For now, it was still rudimentary, but the gods only knew how long it would be, given the Cylons' rapid ability to assimilate and adapt, before they were on level evolutionary ground with the humans. How long before the Cylons evolved *past* them?

Apollo led his group deeper into the city, down ever deeper, level after level. He was hoping to find a series of caverns in which they could hide long enough to formulate some kind of plan. The prisming crystal walls reflected the pulse flashes of the Cylon rifles and laser blasts of the mech droids. Rainbow-hued lights rippled along the beveled edges of the structures and walkways, seeming to inform every building in the city.

Starbuck fired his pistol at the right angle of the nearest building; the laser light entered, refracted into prisms, and spread out, striking down the advancing Cylons with multiple laser beams.

One of the Centurions leveled his pulse rifle at Sheba and squeezed the trigger before she could bring her sidearm around to bear. She turned her head away out of instinct, waiting for the blast that would slap her off the catwalk and right out of this life, but the blast never came. Instead, seemingly out of nowhere, a pulse identical to the rifle shot fired by the Centurion struck the mech soldier, felling him instantly.

More soldiers washed into the city, firing their pule rifles at the fleeing civilians. For every blast that the Cylons fired, a matching blast, directed with pinpoint accuracy back at the shooter, came from somewhere within the city. The flying mechs suffered the same fate as the Centurions, their turbolaser fire matched by laser fire from the city. Starbuck looked up, around, trying to find the source of the returned fire; he wondered if fleet Warriors had recaptured the high ground, or perhaps this city had its own set of caretakers, like the one of stone directly above them.

He continued to search, but there was no one.

Was it possible. . . ?

Starbuck laughed at that thought; he had come back from the dead! Once you crossed that feat off the list, everything else was a dawdle, just varying degrees of possible and improbable.

"Cease firing!" Starbuck shouted, his voice carrying loud and clear through the city, the buildings resonating with the sound of his words. "That's an order!"

The Warriors and armed civilians looked at one another, puzzled beyond words. "Are we surrendering?" one Warrior muttered aloud.

"A lot more people would have been alive now if we had," the civilian nearest him said.

They lowered their weapons but did not holster them until they could see which way the wind was blowing on this unlikely tactic. They didn't need to wait long, for the Cylons continued to fire their pulse rifles, and identical beams from unseen sources cut them down. Starbuck threw his head back and let fly a wild, unfettered cheer: The city defensively responded to any attack by reflecting the assault back on its aggressor!

Starbuck waved his arms, drawing the Centurions' attention to him. They raised and fired their pulse rifles, mirror laser flashes striking them a micron after they squeezed the trigger. Laughing, Starbuck ran to join Boomer and Sheba, who had suffered a deep gouge in her arm from the rampant laser fire before they'd descended into the crystal underground. Now that she had a moment to relax, the pain caught up to her, and she grimaced, hissing through gritted teeth. She hadn't been aware she was hit, but she knew it now.

Boomer looked at it, peeling back the flexi-weave of her uniform's sleeve; the heat from the pulse rifle had seared the material to her flesh, and she gasped as Boomer pulled it loose. "Missed the bone," he observed. "But you need a bio-plasteen on that as soon as we can get you to safety."

"Safety?" she asked, her face pale from the pain that pounded in her shoulder. "Where would that be, do you suppose?"

Starbuck helped her along, and they ran deeper into the city, after Apollo and his group. They didn't need to look far, for Apollo's group had come to a dead-end at the back of the cavern into which he had led them. And yet, he didn't think it *was* a dead-end, because there were more ancient sigils carved into the crystalline walls.

Far behind them, the Centurions at last realized their own attack was being reflected back upon them, and they all ceased firing at once. They lowered their weapons and began moving forward after the humans who had conveniently penned themselves in a shallow cavern. They would capture the remaining humans; those who resisted would be crushed.

"What do we do now?" Baltar bleated to Apollo while judiciously holding Siress Kiera close to him for protection. "We trusted you!"

The corners of Apollo's mouth turned down as he shot Baltar a look. "Do I really need to remind you we're here because *I* trusted *you?*" he said.

Screams now came from the back of the group, near the mouth of the cavern, and rippled back along the line of trapped humans as the Cylons stalked ever nearer. There was nowhere to run now that would not lead the colonials either deeper into the cavern, or straight into the clutches of the Centurions.

Apollo ran his fingers along the carved figures of the Kobollian text and shook his head. Frustrated, he gripped the Star of Kobol around his neck and prayed, "Lords of Kobol, aid your people!" In seeming response to his heartfelt prayer, Talen was now standing at Apollo's side, although no one had seen her approach. She was just . . . *there.*

"What do I do?" Apollo asked her. "Tell me what to do."

But her only response was to favor him with a peace-giving smile, and to gaze at him intensely, with eyes as bright as the city of glass around them. Her eyes seemed to look into him, beyond him, passing through him like cosmic rays, but she had touched something buried deep in his subconscious and stirred it to wakeful life. He looked again at the symbols, and he remembered Adama telling him, *Your brain had to be rewired.* If everything else that had happened in his dreamwalk was real, then it stood to reason that much had been real, as well.

Apollo looked at Talen, nodded, and turned back to study the carvings. He blinked as they seemed to move like snakes before his eyes, crawling over one another, reforming themselves into words he could understand. Apollo placed his hand on them; they weren't actually moving, but in his brain, they continued to writhe and realign themselves into translated writings. And then, as his mind processed the information suddenly revealed to him, his subconscious transcribed the words into a melodic scale of aeolian cadences.

He stepped back and let the music flow through him and out of his mouth. Those near him could only blink in wonderment and a sure, rising sense the commander had gone quite mad, and at a particularly inconvenient moment, at that. Apollo stared at the wall, but nothing happened. He tugged at his lower lip, his brow furrowed, trying to understand what he was missing. Once again, he voiced the notes he heard in his head, and the wall shimmered oh-so-slightly, then grew solid once more. Apollo looked at Talen, who smiled softly. It was nice, but it wasn't an answer that was going to save them.

Choose wisely, both she and Adama had told him; *trust your inner vision.*

Apollo looked at the civilians gathered near him, and told them to listen carefully as he voiced the few, plaintive notes he felt certain were the key to their salvation. "I want you all to repeat that with me," he shouted, the acoustics of the crystal cavern carrying his voice to the end of the group. "Just do it! If you want to live, trust me!"

He turned, looked at Talen; he thought, just perhaps, she might have nodded, but it was so slight and imperceptible, it might not have been there at all. Apollo raised his hand and led the colonials through the seven notes. The acoustics of the cave amplified the chorus, taking it higher and higher until it reached a perfect resonance that shook the sigil-marked wall. Cracks, as fine as crawlonwebs, formed in the crystal face, spreading ever outward, and then they grew larger, wider, deeper, as the echo of those voices all raised together continued to vibrate the cavern, long after the singers had stopped.

Chips of crystal flaked away, falling like scales, followed by larger blocks, larger and larger, until those nearest the collapsing wall began to shriek in terror, convinced they had somehow managed to sing an avalanche into being. But the massive slabs of crystal fell away from them, collapsing into the cavern on the other side of the crumbling wall. The sound of the song reached almost deafening proportions, echoing and re-echoing off the walls and bouncing back off the sides of the crystalline buildings.

Apollo leaped over the rubble of the fallen quartz blocks strewn about the floor and into the revealed cavern, blinking at what he saw: it was the mirror image of the asteroid's interior, a shipping port built inside a massive cavern. No, not a cavern. The immense scope of the interior space, which curved off to vanish into the far distance, was like a gigantic blown egg within the center of the planet. Kobol was hollow. But that alone was not what stunned Apollo into silence, as incredible as it was. Rather, it was the sight of the entire colonial fleet that this shipping port housed, and the crew of those ships, which Apollo would have sworn he would never see again on this side of a Light Ship.

Cain, Athena, and all the rest were waiting there to greet them all as they made their way to their ships; as soon as one ferry left the platform, another ferry arrived to board more passengers.

Apollo approached Athena and Cain, his mouth hanging open. Athena slipped her arms around him and hugged him and, after only a micron, he returned the embrace. And, throwing decorum to the wind, Athena hugged Starbuck, as well. He did not hesitate to return the hug, and had to check himself before his hand could stray farther down her backside.

"How is this possible?" Apollo managed to ask; finding these words was not that much less a task than translating the ancient Kobollian script that had marked this cavern. "This *isn't* possible."

Athena laughed and squeezed Apollo's hand, hard enough to make him hiss. "Do I feel like a haunt to you?" He shook his head; no, she certainly did not. "An automated mechanism aboard the asteroid transported the fleet down here before the Tylium ignited. The technology here is even more advanced than we first imagined, but then, they did manage to traverse the universe long before the Twelve Colonies ever reached deep space. Kobol has given us a second chance . . . all of us," she said.

Perhaps it was one last application of the QSE technology that they were still only coming to understand, but Apollo wouldn't have been upset if anyone wanted to call it a miracle.

Behind them, the last of the colonials hurried through the cavern opening, and the wall began to shimmer back into solidity. Two Borellian Nomen, who carried the mortally wounded Gar'Tokk between them, passed through the warbling crystalline facade, just before it completely reformed and solidified.

"Get him to the med-unit!" Apollo shouted as Starbuck and the Noman loaded Gar'Tokk onto the shuttle. "We're not losing anyone else on my watch!"

Athena joined the shuttle back to the *Galactica;* Apollo started forward to board with them, and spotted Talen standing at the railing of the platform. She was smiling, but it seemed to be a sad smile, somehow, a smile of bittersweet resignation. Apollo stepped off the ferry, and motioned for them to wait for him. He moved nearer to Talen, feeling the strong reaction between them building ike an electrical charge.

"The fleet's QSE technology has been modified," Talen said.

"You can't just brush me off like that anymore," he told her. "There are too many questions I have to ask you—"

"There is no time, Apollo," she said, and he thought there was something like regret in her voice. "You need to join your fleet, and quickly. Kobol is preparing to self-destruct in a very few microns."

Apollo was incredulous. "What? Why?" But he knew it was only a matter of time before the planet would die anyway, since the hollow asteroid no longer in orbit was destined to impact the surface; it would be a mortal blow to Kobol.

She laughed, gently, a sound of crystalline chimes, and this time, he knew that laugh. It was impossible, and yet, on this planet, he thought it was *just* possible . . . and exactly right.

"You and your people have done very well," Talen said. "The Lords of Kobol are proud of their children." She turned away and began to dissolve through the crystalline wall that had once again sealed the shipping port. Apollo ran after her, and she stood halfway through the wall, facing into the chamber. He placed his hands on either side of her, pressing nearer, until his face was only centimetrons from her's, near enough to kiss.

"Who are you?" he asked.

She smiled again, and this time he knew. "Someone who has loved you for an eternity," she said. Her features flowed for a moment, rearranging themselves into their original form, revealing the one great love of Apollo's life. It was the face he had known in his dreams, even before he had been born, before he had met her, before he had fallen, heart and soul, in love with her. It was the face he would know in any life; know her, and call her by her name. The face that still came to him, night after night, the ghost that still haunted his heart.

"Good-bye, Apollo," Serina said.

17

SERINA!"

He began to weep, and to laugh, and he wasn't sure which he needed to do more.

"I've missed you so much..." Apollo managed. "No one else has ever been able to take your place."

"You won't allow anyone else to try," she told him, and stroked his face. Oh, gods, he remembered that; how he had missed that.

"I love you," he said. "I'll always love you."

"And I, you," Serina told him, and kissed him softly. "But you must find room in your heart for other loves."

She smiled, and he heard these words in his head: *You must let go, and live. I've moved on, and so must you...*

"Wait!" he cried. "Will I see you again? *Serina!*"

But she had already gone, fading back into the quartz wall, and for a moment Apollo was staring at the place where her face had been; but *had* she really been there, or was it just a trick of the light, playing on the facets of crystal? He touched the speckled, glittering surface, traced the contours of quartz that may or may not have been the face he thought he saw.

"Serina," he repeated softly. "I can't lose you again."

Apollo bowed his head, his chin touching his chest, his hands clutching weakly at the crystalline wall. It *was* Serina, he was sure of that, and even though his heart howled after her like a lupus at the full moon, he was oddly at peace. She was gone; this place of miracles was not going to return her to life, but it had returned her, however briefly, to *his* life. Apollo would always love her, and would always miss her, but he felt as if he had achieved . . . closure. The great wheel of life had turned and brought them back together for one last time, and now, he thought he might just be able to move on.

I've moved on . . . and you must, as well . . .

"Are you all right?" Cain asked. He placed his hand on Apollo's shoulder and gave it a fatherly squeeze. Apollo blinked his eyes dry and turned to look at the old legend. "What happened?"

Apollo shrugged. Just another miracle. To speak of it would somehow make it less, and he couldn't do that to Serina. "Everyone boarded?" he asked; he knew they were, but it was something he could speak of safely.

Cain nodded. "Probably neither one of us ever thought I'd say these words, but, *you were right.* I've misjudged you, Apollo," he said. "Maybe I've misjudged you all along. It looks as if you have more of your father in you than I thought."

Apollo managed a crooked smile. "And maybe more than a little of you, too, Commander Cain," he said, and placed his hand on Cain's shoulder, a reflection of the old man's affectionate embrace of Apollo. It was as close to a hug as these two were ever likely to come, but a deep sense of understanding and respect flowed between them at that moment.

Cain laughed a genuine, unguarded, non-political laugh. "Lords of Kobol help you if that's true," he said. Well, since you're still supreme commander, what are your orders?"

Apollo raised an eyebrow in question and surprise; he was shocked and moved at Cain's willingness to set aside his own immense pride and accept Apollo's advice. "We've got just under thirty microns to clear a path through the Cylon fleet and get our ships to clear space where we can jump to light speed before this place blows. We need to get word to the rest of the fleet as soon as we're back on our ships."

Cain's lips compressed in a thin, bloodless line. "The holocube was severely damaged when one of our shuttles was destroyed," he said. "We'll have to determine our destination ourselves, or jump blind."

Behind them, through the thick wall of crystal, they could hear the Centurions trying to blast their way through the barrier; Apollo suspected the force of the assault was hurled back at them, but the Cylons were, if anything, persistant, and it was a matter of time before they made their way through the wall.

"We'll have to cross that bridge when we get to it," Apollo said.

"I'm sure you will," Cain said, without a trace of guile, and added, "I'll lead the way in the *Pegasus,* you follow with the *Galactica,* and the *Daedelus* bringing up the rear."

Apollo chuckled to himself: Cain had changed, but not that much. He was always going to be, or try to be, the alpha daggit.

"You have the honor of leading us out, Commander Cain," Apollo said, and the old man nodded in satisfaction. "Fighters will escort the battlestars and lead us all to the surface."

Cain studied the younger man, and placed his hand gently on Apollo's jaw, a gesture so reminiscent of Adama that Apollo had to fight back sudden tears. "And I will have the honor of following you into this final battle with the Cylon hordes," he said. "Believe me when I tell you I don't say these things lightly: it *is* an honor, Commander."

Athena and Starbuck had been standing nearby but apart, to give the two commanders the chance to resolve any last moment differences, and now they stepped forward to take part in the planning of humankind's final, glorious exodus from Kobol. "There's an opening that leads up to the surface of the planet," Athena reported to Apollo.

He nodded. "Hopefully, we'll have the benefit of surprise, long enough to allow us time to escort our ships through, before we have to contend with the Cylon basestars. They have enough fire-power to blow away a whole fleet of battlestars."

Cain puffed himself up with pride, and reminded the Supreme Commander, "We're not talking about just any battlestars, we're talking about the *Pegasus, Galactica,* and the *Daedelus!*"

They all laughed, the last time they would all laugh together, but deep down, close to the bone, where the truth lies, they all knew the odds were stacked against them. Even Starbuck, inveterate gambler that he was, wouldn't bet on a hand this bad.

"Hey, we've been in tough spots before," Starbuck reminded them. "Let's go get those gull-mongering tin buckets."

"Are you joining me on the bridge?" Athena asked her brother.

Apollo glaned at Starbuck. "Boomer and Sheba report we're critically short on experienced pilots. We really could use you in a Viper's cockpit instead of driving that tanker," Starbuck said.

Apollo was not just being diplomatic when he earlier told Cain there was quite a bit of the old man in him; he had never been able to completely relinquish the need to fly combat missions, preferring to balance time on the bridge between time in a Viper, but this time, his inner vision told Apollo his place was on board the battlestar. "Athena, you're in charge of the *Daedelus,*" he decided. She opened her mouth to say something, but there was really nothing to say. Athena just nodded, pleasantly surprised by her brother's decision.

He understood a great many things now, and chief among them was the need to not just tell Athena he respected her, but to show it, as well.

Did you hear anything I told you in the temple? Apollo's mind touched hers. *I've always thought of you as my equal, and my complement. You aren't going to choose now to prove me wrong, are you?*

In Apollo's mind, he could hear Athena laughing.

"I'll take the bridge of the *Galactica,* with Tigh."

Later, as these things tend to go, Apollo would recall that Cain had been remarkably quiet and compliant, as if he had known, even then, how this would end. Some things, of course, have to happen certain ways.

Apollo looked at their faces, and he couldn't help adding, "Now, let's go kick some shiny metal asses."

In the launch bay of the *Galactica,* pilots were scrambling for their ships; they were about to see some real action, and the cadets, who thought they were indestructible, were revved up and raring to go. They just couldn't believe that, when this day was done, many of them would not be returning home.

Boys and girl, older men and women, climbed into their waiting Vipers and made their orderly way to the launch tracks.

Trays was the most vocal of the lot, but he wasn't saying anything most of the young upstart cadets weren't thinking. He watched with Dalton, Troy, and Bree, as Starbuck, Boomer, Jolly, and Sheba, each prepared to launch. "What a waste of our new Vipers," Trays smirked. Bo jay, who was making a last minute repair to a frizzort in Trays' apex pulsar, heard the comment but said nothing.

"What are you, blind?" Bree asked, and jerked a thumb back over his shoulder. "Apart from Commander Apollo, they're the best pilots this fleet ever has or will ever see."

Trays made a deprecatory noise at that notion, loud enough that Starbuck, the next fighter over, heard it all and knew that it was time to shut down someone's afterburners. He shouted to Bo jay, "Take off your overalls! You're taking Trays' Viper up!"

Bo jay couldn't believe his good fortune; a quick look at Starbuck's face told him this was not a joke, and he let fly a loud whoop and holler and began peeling out of his grimy uniform. Trays couldn't believe what he was hearing, either, and he swung out of the Viper's cockpit and stalked over to Starbuck, waving his arms and filling the air with invectives as he went.

"What the frack do you think you're doing?" he thundered.

"Saving you from yourself," Starbuck said. "But in more

guarded terms, let's just say I'm replacing you with a far superior pilot, the only pilot who's ever outflown me, except for Apollo, and maybe Sheba on one of my bad days, and believe me when I say I don't often tell the truth in these matters."

Trays grew more animated, and Starbuck sat quietly, patiently listening to everything the young pilot had to say, and that was a lot. But when he was finished, Starbuck calmly lit a fumarello and watched the smoke rafter lazily up. "And while you're at it, why don't you see if Bo jay's overalls fit you, because you just got demoted, hotshot."

Everyone laughed, and Trays' face turned a shade of crimson only slightly less scarlet than Starbuck's favorite Viper. Starbuck, sitting on the edge of his cockpit, leaned over and gripped Trays by the shoulder, bearing down on the nerve cluster there, making the boy wince. He leaned in close enough the boy could smell the foul fumarello on his breath, and whispered, with an undercurrent of menace, "And just between us, if you ever lay another hand on my daughter, I'll personally rip your pogees off and fire them into the nearest sun . . . got me?"

Trays nodded, stiffly. Starbuck gave the boy's shoulder an extra tweak, just to show him *this* fossil, at least, still had a lot of fight left in him and that they hadn't even come anywhere near the limits of the pain he could inflict on Trays, if Starbuck felt he had the occasion to.

"Time to eat sky," Starbuck said, and let go of Trays' shoulder.

The Vipers fired up and moved forward, along the tracks toward the launch tubes. Dalton and Troy followed after, in their Viper Duet. The Duet was an odd looking craft, ungainly to look at, resembling nothing so much as two Vipers attached at the side. Strung between the two ships was a long, flat weapons module that could be fired both fore and aft, and the ships shared a single fuel source, which allowed the yoked fighters to travel farther on the same amount of fuel. Navigation and weapons could be passed back and forth instantly, shared or separated.

Dalton didn't like to admit it, but she was glad to be sharing the

Duet with Troy. It was intimate, somehow, and she now found that she liked the idea of shared intimacy with him.

"We've had difficulties in the past . . ." Troy began, and quickly amended, "handling this ship, but maybe, this one time, we can let go of our egos and work together."

The cockpits were side by side, and the pilots could see one another, so Troy noticed the sheepish smile Dalton offered when she answered, "Just as long as you follow my orders."

He smiled, and she felt that somehow, through the barriers, they had touched.

All across the fleet, everyone took a moment to gather himself or herself, realizing the enormity of the stakes, and that some of them, surely, would not be coming back. Those who believed said a silent prayer, for himself, and for the others.

Apollo checked all the flight crews and ships, and found them ready to go. "I want everyone to set their timers for ten microns," he said, cutting to the heart of things. "This is the amount of time we have to clear the planet, or we will all die."

"Nice morale booster," Starbuck quipped over the fighters' comm-line.

Everyone laughed, perhaps a little harder and a little more than the joke deserved, but they were releasing tension. There wasn't going to be much to laugh about in a few more centons.

Aboard the *Pegasus,* Commander Cain took the captain's chair on the bridge, and settled himself into its familiar seat, rested his hands on the arms. How many battles had he led from this seat? Cain closed his eyes, and let the surge of fear and ecstasy that impending battle always brought wash through him. Commander Cain always acknowledged the fear, to himself and to his pilots; any Warrior who didn't feel the fear before impending battle was a fool, and quickly ended up a *dead* fool.

Athena, likewise, felt the tickle of adrenaline flushing through her system; her blood was up, but she was also afraid. She acknowledged the fear, and took her place in the command chair on the *Daedelus*'s bridge. On the flatscreen, Apollo's image towered over her, as it seemed he, himself, had towered over her all their lives.

"By the Lords of Kobol!" Apollo screamed, and raised his fist over his head.

Across the fleet, Warriors, officers and civilians alike raised their own voices in cheer. There are moments on which lives hinge, and they all knew that this was the biggest such moment they had ever faced.

In the launch bay, Starbuck smiled and gave the thumbs-up to his squadron of pilots. Then, one by one, the Vipers boomed down the launch track, through the aperture and out of the bay, and up and up through the long, vast tunnel leading to the surface. But then, it was not just a tunnel to the surface, it was a path that led the ragtag fleet into their most heroic and desperate battle since the destruction of the colonies.

Aboard the Cylon basestar, Raiders continued to blast from the twin sets of launch bays and scream down toward the planet's surface. Lucifer and the Chitain chieftan, Lord Schikik, watched it all from the bridge of the great mother ship, a combination of Cylon and Chitain technology.

Lucifer found the creatures repugnant, but, on the whole, more pleasant to spend time around than humans. The Chitain stood nearly two metrons tall, and their torsos were plated with natural, scaled armor, of a dark gray-green, so dark as to be nearly black. Rather than two arms, the Chitain had four apendages, the upper set of limbs that ended in three scimitar-like digits, and a lower set of limbs that were trunklike, enormous pincers. The lower portions of their bodies were serpentine, which, like their limbs, was the color of spilled blood. Impossibly, the Chitain carried themselves upright, like snakes that had learned a particularly good trick, and advanced in the same slithering, rippling fashion. Not only did they move upright, their great bulk belied their blinding speed. The lower end of their tails narrowed to a wicked, sharp spike, not unlike a scorpion's stinger. Every centimetron of their bodies was designed only for battle; whatever harsh and hellish world they had come from, it was hard to imagine these things had any natural predators.

Chitain warships were fashioned after their own bodies, part starship, part armor, a long cylinder that tapered to a point; their forward propulsion was managed by the engine strands that hung from the front of the ship and curled around to the sides, while their weapons systems was a long tail that originated at the back of the ship. This tail could fire a laser pulse, or whip about and shatter any starfighter that had been foolhardy enough to venture too near. This new class of basestar combined the cold, Cylon mech look with the technorganic Chitain weapons array.

The Chitain were scavengers, leaving nothing to waste, not even the bodies of their own dead; their cities were built from the hollowed shells of their fallen. What they didn't plunder and use as salvage, if it moved, they ate. They were ruthlessly efficient, and had a growing hatred for humans, following their last encounter with, and unlikely defeat at the hands of, the colonials.

Lord Schikik particularly wanted to see Apollo again.

"The humans have trapped themselves in an underground cavern," Lucifer reported the dispatch from the Centurion captain to the Chitain leader. "They also report an underground city made of fused silicate, granite and sandstone."

Lord Schikik might have smiled; it was hard to tell. "A crystalline city," he said, but already he was thinking of the scavengability. "Interesting."

"The city apparently reflects any act of hostility back upon its attacker," Lucifer added, and this time, he was certain Lord Schikik *did* smile. If such a thing were true, Schikik ruminated, what could possibly stand against an armada fashioned of such material?

In the exact center of the basestar, in the center of the room, the Imperious Leader sat high upon the tiered platform, its jagged spikes tearing the light and making diamonds. He wondered, momentarily, why Count Iblis had not contacted them, and decided this was not necessarily a bad thing. Eons ago, Cylon was home to a race of warlike, savage-yet-sentient reptillian creatures. But one day, an outsider, a stranger filled with as much hate as the ancient Cylons themselves possessed, appeared in their midst and introduced them to technology. They were indebted and in fear of him for decades, but he promised to make them the most ruthless, fearsome warriors the universe had ever seen, and he kept that promise by introducing human DNA—*his* DNA—into the Cylon genetic structure, evolving them into bipedal creatures. Cloning followed, making females of the species redundant and unnecessary. Soon, genetic manipulation also bred all emotion out of the reptiallian creatures; all except hatred. They had plenty of that, but then, so did the stranger known as Count Iblis.

He had bred them to hate all humankind, and, predictably, the Cylons had turned upon Iblis, destroyed his human body, leaving his brain under their control, but the Count had proven more resilient and unpredictable than most. Although his brain remained slaved to the Cylons, Iblis's *mind,* his *consciousness,* continued to evolve, until he could project his esoteric body through space and time. He had escaped the remains of his physical embodiment and, as a result, became even more powerful. Freed of the tyranny of flesh, Iblis had been able to meddle in the Cylons' affairs, their evolution and the upward crawl of many other races, as well.

It was time, the Imperious Leader thought, for the Cylons to at last go their own way, free of Iblis's meddlings and interference. They were his children, true, but, as children will, they had grown up and were ready to find their own way, to write their destiny in flame and blood across the stars. Yes, *past* time. But how?

His third brain began to move in abstracts, positing, sifting, analyzing, rejecting. There was nothing the Imperious Leader enjoyed more than a good challenge, and he suspected the answer might be simpler than anyone thought.

Starbuck's Scarlet Viper at last roared out of the long, sloping fissure running from the secret shipping port to Kobol's surface, followed closely by the fighter squadron, and, at last, the entire colonial fleet, led by the three battlestars.

Aboard the *Galactica,* Apollo checked his timepiece, and opened the comm-line to the Vipers' cockpits. "This is where the felgercarb hits the numo," he said.

"You've really gotta work on those pep talks," Starbuck muttered around the butt of the fumarello he held clenched in his teeth. He caught himself whistling a simple tune, then realized it was the string of notes Apollo had led them to sing in the crystal city. Frack! Now that tune was stuck in his mind like a musical splinter! "Thanks, buddy," he groused.

"I want the cadet trainees to remain calm and stay close to the more experienced pilots," Apollo continued. "Starbuck, you just got a field promotion. You're wing commander. Look after our cadets."

Starbuck bit down on his fumarello. Wing commander? Frack, he'd never assumed command of anything before, but then, the idea began to sink in, and he tilted his head proudly. He liked the thought. Maybe he was actually starting to take life more seriously, since he had spent some time away from it. Whatever the reason, he slipped into the role as easily as a hand fits a glove. "Jolly, Bo jay, Boomer," he ordered, "don't let the cadets out of your sight, and remember, all of you, we're going to need to watch each other's ass if we plan on dancing on the tables in the ODOC tonight."

The gradual slope of the underground launch tube worked to the fleet's advantage, bringing them out on the blind side of the concentrated Cylon and Chitain forces. Starbuck immediately spotted the large opening in the enemy's position the colonials could exploit. "Boomer, you and Bo jay begin escorting some of the less-armed civilian ships through," he said.

The Forge and *Scorpius Ascendant* slipped through the Cylon armada, but there were too many Raiders for the fleet's good fortune to hold for long, and one of the Chitain fighters, its propulsion tendrils doubling as sensors like insectoid antennae, detected the sudden appearance of the colonials. The Chitain fighter peeled away from the main attack force, its weapons stinger whipping back and forth, spitting deadly energy beams at the Civilian ships just emerging from the fissure.

"We're spotted!" Starbuck warned his squadron. "Engage the enemy, but protecting the civilians is your first priority!"

The Chitain fighter dodged and darted, its tail stinger flaring brighter as its attack intensified. "I'm on him," Boomer called, and veered away to confront the approaching craft. Energy scored across the Viper's forward shields, sloughing harmlessly away, giving Boomer all the chance he needed to slip in beneath the hostile ship and take his fighter into a climb, thumbing the turbolaser as he ascended. His first salvo tore the stinger away from the Chitain craft's underbelly, and his next shot ripped straight up through the craft, tearing it, and its pilot, in half.

But more laser pulses burned past him, and Boomer saw the first wing of the Cylon and Chitain fighters bearing down on him. "This would be a good time to listen to what Commander Apollo said and start covering the other guy's ass," Boomer reminded the other pilots. He held the firing button down on his navi-hilt and watched his laser fire rip across a starfield full of Raiders. Two went down, spiraling out of control into one another, but the rest thundered overhead, past Boomer and after the civilian ships still rising out of the fissure.

The battlestars formed a blockade between the civilians and the onrushing Cylon fighters, taking the brunt of the enemy laser fire while responding with their own barrage. The shielding on the battlestars was stronger, able to withstand more than the ragtag, unarmed civilian ships, but even so, they couldn't take the pounding they were receiving forever.

Athena, aboard the *Daedelus,* gripped the arms of her command chair as the battlestar rocked and jumped under the beating it was taking. A bridge officer reported to Athena that three Cylon Raiders that had been on the planet's surface were rising now, trying to slip in through the cloud cover their attack on the hidden city had thrown into the air. The battlestar trained its artillery on the three Raiders as they attempted a flyby, strafing the unarmed civilian ships. It was a tricky maneuver, firing at the Raiders through the clutter of civilian ships and weaving Vipers, but the *Daedelus's* gunnery crew scored two direct hits on the Cylon fighters before they had to cease fire or risk hitting the *Cerebus*.

"Frack!" she cried, and banged her fist on the arm of her command chair. She watched the third fighter disappear on the far side of the civilian ship, impossible for the *Daedelus* to target.

But just beyond the civilian ships, a Viper had broken away from the aerial battle and bulleted for the Raider. Bo jay guided his Viper between the *Cerebus* and the Raider and opened fire. A moment later, the flaming wreckage of the Cylon ship went spinning down to the surface of Kobol, leaving a long, black tail of smoke in the air.

Everyone aboard the bridge of the *Daedelus* let out a heartfelt cheer of joy and relief.

On the screen, Bo jay started blasting at a cluster of Chitain Stingers that had chased after his ship. One, two, three, the Stingers exploded in a glittering cloud of particles.

Athena squinted at the fast-moving object on the screen. "Is that Trays' Viper?" she asked. "When did *he* get so good?"

"He didn't," Apollo answered over her open commline. "That's Bo jay. Starbuck benched Trays."

Athena smiled behind her hand. Leave it to Starbuck to change the seating arrangements at the last moment. "You be careful out there," Athena whispered softly, as if by the magic of the heart in love Starbuck would hear her. "You come back to me this time."

"Captain?" the bridge officer interrupted; there was something like fear in his voice.

Athena looked at the new image the officer put up on the screen; the Cylon basestar was approaching from the other side of the planet, where it had been stationed earlier, during the invasion of the underground city. It was hurrying into position now to become part of the attack. Farther away, but also changing position, was the second Cylon mothership.

"How many civilian ships left in the fissure?" she asked.

The bridge officer checked his sensor display, bit his lip. "Still about one-third of the fleet," he reported.

"One-third," she repeated, her heart sinking. They couldn't desert the rest of the fleet; they would simply have to stand fast and guard the fissure from the Cylon basestars as long as they had to. "Tighten the formation," she ordered, and the *Daedelus* slowly swung around to face the onrushing basestars.

Apollo had seen the new additions to the battle, and reassured his sister, "Have faith. We've come through tighter spots than this."

We have? she thought. *Funny, I can't think of a single one.* But she forced herself to remain calm; it was all right to be frightened, which she was. It was *not* all right to panic, and she would not allow herself to do that. Athena realized it was not just the impending battle which frightened her, but the enormous responsibility with which she had been entrusted. Apollo picked the worst damned times to show he had faith in her. Well, it wasn't as if Adama hadn't trained her just as hard, if not harder, than he had Apollo for this moment. She took deep, steadying breaths, let her memory replay Adama's teachings, and waited for the basestars to come within range of the battlestars' weapons. This was shaping up to be a long afternoon.

In his quarters, Baltar sat next to Siress Kiera on his sleep module. He held her, and she held him, trying to talk of anything except the moment, making plans for what they would do later that night, after the fleet had once again escaped destruction and was once again sailing the cold sea of space, but they both knew any plans beyond this battle were not likely to be carried out. Had he really been the one to once declare, "A human is never so confident as when he has his back against the wall"? Well, their backs were against the wall, all right, and the wall was on fire and crumbling, but he certainly didn't feel confident. He felt anything *but*.

For a moment Baltar wondered if he could still contact Count Iblis; the Count had always been able to seemingly read his former minion's thoughts, coming and going like some demon Baltar had conjured up by the force of his mind. And he thought, momentarily, of begging the Count to intervene, save them, save *him*, at least. After all, what did he owe the colonials? For all he had done on their behalf, none of them yet trusted him. They had beaten him, humiliated him, and would have killed him, had Apollo not intervened. Even Apollo had been ready to strangle him, and Baltar's hand unconsciously went to his still-swollen throat, and he winced at the pain.

But he had tried so hard to be a good man once more that the idea of selling what little of his soul he had regained frightened him. If he died here, then at least he would perish in the arms of someone who cared for him, and for whom he cared. There were worse fates than that, he knew all too well.

"Cubit for your thoughts," Kiera said.

"A moment ago, they weren't worth a cubit," he told her.

"And now?" she asked.

He kissed her softly, on the crown of her head. "Now, they're priceless," he said.

The course of love was one that, despite all those who had traveled it before, had never gone smoothly, and it was that much more difficult piloting the Duet. For everything Troy and Dalton had gained the last time they flew the twinner, in battle with the Chitain, it seemed they had lost just as much, if not more, this time.

The Duet moved jerkily through the sky, as they each tried to be in control. "Stop trying to run everything," Dalton told him. "You fly, I'll fight." But even before Troy could answer, Dalton thumbed the turbolaser on her navi-hilt, loosing a barrage from both crafts' weapons system, taking out two Chitain Stingers, fore and aft.

"What was that again?" Troy chided her. "I'll do what, now?"

"You've got the audio turned off on your scanners again, don't you?" she asked. He frowned. As a matter of fact, Troy *had* dialed down the volume; all the noise from the scanners alerting him to the threats at hand was driving him insane, but he tickled the control just enough that his cockpit filled with the din of the scanners. When he flew solo, he could afford to close out the cacophony of battle, but he was flying the Duet now, and her safety depended on his attention, just as his depended on her.

"Sorry," he said.

"Not a problem . . . lover," she replied across their comm-link. He smiled; she had first called him that in the Duet the last time they flew. He remembered, and so did she. And, he thought, it was easier for her to say the word when she wasn't looking at him, when they were separated by two darkened Viper canopies.

He laughed to himself; what kind of romantic future lay ahead of them if she couldn't even say the word in the same room with him?

Troy didn't have the opportunity to consider this particular quirk of Dalton's nature for long, because his cockpit's proximity alarm began to shriek at him like a bat trapped in a closet. The scanners revealed two Cylon Raiders coming up at them, at an alarming speed. They had been damaged in battle, and were determined to take down the nearest colonial ship with them when they went. Troy instinctively reached for the navi-hilt, checked himself. Hadn't he and Dalton just had this discussion?

"Raiders," he informed her.

"I'm on it," she answered, and brought the array of weapons strung between the Duet Vipers to bear on the Raiders. She waited until the last possible second and fired, blasting the first, and Troy dipped the Duet beneath the deadly trajectory of the second ship. Dalton fired the turbolasers just a micron too late to connect, and her shot went wild. She cursed hot and loud.

The Raider, already a massive, out-of-control ball of fire, passed by overhead, the light from its burning hull bright enough to make the screen of Troy's helmet opaque. The Raider plowed into another Chitain Stinger, which had been jockeying into position behind the Duet for a kill shot.

"What was *that?*" Dalton's voice shouted across the comm-link. Troy winced, wished he could adjust the volume on the helm. "You made me miss the second kill!"

"You just relax," he suggested, "and leave the driving to me."

One after the other, Starbuck shot down the four Cylon Raiders. They had surrounded the *Adena* in a loose pinwheel formation, slipping in under the *Galactica*'s artillery by hugging the ground. The Raiders were too close to the rest of the fleet as it emerged from the fissure to risk firing upon with the battlestar's weaponry, making it necessary for Starbuck to break from the battle and police the exodus.

It was a divide and conquer tactic the Cylons knew well; after all, Count Iblis had practiced it internally, within the fleet, turning Cain, Athena, and Apollo against one another, and the council against Apollo. Starbuck wondered just how long the Count had been pulling their strings, and if they'd ever done anything out of free will. That was a sobering thought. Even their return to Kobol had not been truly of their own volition.

By forcing Starbuck to drop out of the clash overhead, the Cylons had successfully caused the group of cadets to lose their guardian angel. The Chitain pilots had watched the little group of Vipers in battle, and the way Starbuck time and again had to rescue them when the attack grew too chaotic, and the Chitain's war-directed minds understood these pilots were inexperienced, and, separated from the flock, easily eradicated.

The Stingers' tails whipped back and forth, filling the sooty sky with dazzling arcs of deadly energy. Starbuck fed his apex pulsar a little extra fuel, trying to get back up to the cadets, but he could only watch in horror and rising fury as his starfield filled with the sight of his squadron, his responsibility, being coldly and ruthlessly slaughtered.

"Bastards!"

Starbuck couldn't prevent the destruction of the cadets, but he could at least avenge them. He was joined by Boomer and Jolly, and they flew into a triangle formation, soaring along the wall of Chitain and Cylon fighters. The Vipers fired their weapons, left, right, up, down, scattering the enemy ranks. Then, the Vipers wheeled away in a tight formation, ahead of the counterattack.

"Just like shooting daggits in the pound,"Jolly quipped.

They were losing too many fighters, too many pilots. Far more, Starbuck was certain, than the enemy was losing. As he thought that, the Chitain Stingers broke off pursuit of the three more experienced pilots and went after an undefended civilian ship as it emerged from the fissure. Their weapons tails glowed and whipped around, splashing off the side of the *Dawntreader*. But then, the Stingers concentrated their deadly assault on the ship's fuel tanks, igniting the unstable Tylium. The *Dawntreader* erupted in a series of explosions, beginning at the aft and travelling in leaps and bounds toward the fore, shredding the ship apart. Hull plates flew off like leaves in a gale-force wind, and the ship, burning too brightly for the naked eye to look at, crashed back down to Kobol, just clearing the edge of the fissure.

Had the *Dawntreader* fallen back down into the cavern, the ships following after would have been destroyed, as well. Things were spinning horribly out of control, too many cracks in the wall for the colonials to adequately plug. They had to get out of here, and soon, or the entire Fleet was going to be destroyed.

"Starbuck!" Sheba's voice buzzed in his ear over his comm-line.

He tipped the wing of his Viper so he could see what had her so agitated; a handful of Chitain Stingers had swarmed down into the mouth of the fissure, where they began blasting at the undefended fleet ships.

"Don't these mugjapes ever *quit?*" Starbuck growled, and put his Viper into a dive, chasing after the Stingers.

They had already entered the fissure, and were firing at the sides of the emerging colonial ships as they passed each other in the great stone runway. Starbuck tried to insinuate his Viper between the civilian ships and the Stingers, but it was a risky gamble, with a very real possibility he would slam into the side of one the fleet as easily as he would a Stinger.

He managed to pull ahead of the nearest Chitain craft, and drop into position directly in front of it. Before the Stinger could bring its tail weapons around to fire at the Viper, Apollo kicked the apex pulsar to full, the backwash of flame instantly slagging the Chitain fighter's viewscreens. Blinded, the fighter rammed the side of the cavern, vanishing in a spray of blazing shrapnel.

Unfortunately, Starbuck's Viper was now accelerating down the long runway, coming up fast behind another Stinger. He thumbed the turbolaser, ripping through the Chitain's defense screens and detonating its fuel tank.

Starbuck grimaced, his Viper passing through the flaming cloud of fuel. Even through the protective shielding, he could feel the enormous heat, and then, he was through, his speed decreasing, his Viper under control once more.

The tunnel suddenly opened into the shipping port, and Starbuck saw the rest of the Chitain intruders ahead, swinging around at the far end of the bay, entering a strafing pattern, headed for the last few fleet ships still waiting for take-off.

His thumb went for the turbolaser button . . . and stopped. He laughed, and shouted, "Go ahead, you bunch of fish-heads!"

The Chitain craft brought · their tail weapons around and fired . . . and the defensive mirroring effect of the crystal cavern instantly threw their own assault back at them, with deadly, pinpoint accuracy. The Stingers exploded, one after the other, like links in a chain. Still laughing, Starbuck brought his Viper around and began the long, sloping ascent along the fissure. He was once again whistling the tune Apollo had taught them.

The battle was not going well for the colonials, as Starbuck saw when his Viper emerged from the fissure. The Cylon basestars had at last maneuvered into place, and their plasma cannons were cycling up to release a salvo of destruction. More civilian ships had been destroyed, and were lying in smoking ruins on the planet's surface, strewn about like bones of dead marine animals on the bottom of a suddenly-dry ocean bed. Beside them lay the ashen remains of the Vipers that had fought, and died, trying to protect them. Around about them lay the wreckage of the enemy craft; death was impartial.

The battlestars had engaged the Cylon basestars, matching them blow for blow, doing their best to ignore the harrying Raiders and Stingers, leaving the lesser threats for the Vipers. The *Pegasus* had already suffered terrible damage, and the basestar's bristling array of weapons swung around to train on Cain's ship.

The battlestars had the advantage of maneuverability; the basestars, while packed with unimaginable power, were not designed for battle within a planet's atmosphere, and were slower moving as a result. Unfortunately, they could withstand more hits. The *Galactica* swung around and fired all of her port artillery, destroying an emplacement of plasma cannons, effectively halving the base star's assault capabilities.

But half of unimaginable was still unimaginable, and the basestar remained a looming threat to the fleet. Its second tier of cannons *did* fire before the battlestar could train its firepower on them, and the *Galactica*'s weapons system suffered the brunt of the attack.

At their posts, weapons officers were thrown back out of their seats as the tremendous feedback of power slammed into them, tossing them against the far wall. Small electrical fires erupted in a spray of sparks up and down the work stations. Those who still had enough presence of mind to do so began putting out the fires and instantly set about repairing the electrical damage. But it was going to take time.

On the bridge, Apollo looked at the time. There wasn't much left before the planet blew itself to atoms, but, even before that could happen, he knew the other Cylon motherships, positioned around the planet, would join these basestars in the battle. If that were allowed to happen, Apollo knew the fleet would not stand a chance.

"Starbuck," Apollo said, "I need you and your squadron to take out that basestar's main weapons before they can get in place to blow us apart."

"On it," Starbuck's voice came back. "And by the way, whatever happened to the magic word, *please*?"

Good old Starbuck, Apollo thought, and had to laugh. "Please," he added.

"That's better," Starbuck answered. "While we're at it, maybe this would be a good time for you to admit you've never been able to outgun me on your best day."

"We'll talk about that one," Apollo said. He knew Starbuck was just blue-skying, talking and joking to keep from thinking too closely about what he was about to do. Everyone dealt with stress in his or her own fashion, and this was Starbuck's. Apollo thought Starbuck would have to make a lot more jokes before this one was over. The end wasn't even in sight.

Boomer's and Sheba's Vipers, badly damaged and barely able to fly, limped back to the *Galactica*'s landing bay. The loss of two fighters was bad; the loss of two experienced pilots was worse. As soon as they docked, they told the techs to prep two more Vipers. They had to get back into the battle as soon as possible.

"If Starbuck can just damage the basestar's forward-facing weapons," Apollo was saying to Cain and Athena, "that should give us long enough to get the rest of the fleet through and make the jump to hyperspace."

Cain nodded, his face grave. "I agree, but the *Pegasus* has been badly damaged by the plasma cannons. I'm not sure we can make it."

Apollo felt his heart drop. Cain was not one to exaggerate; if he said the battlestar might not make it, then that was probably the case. Still, this had been a day for miracles; perhaps Kobol still held one more in reserve for them. "Hold on, Commander Cain," Apollo said, refusing to acknowledge defeat. "We'll do everything we can to protect you."

"The *Daedelus* will cover you, Commander Cain," Athena said.

"Thank you, Apollo, Athena, but that may be a foolish gesture that could end up costing you more than it gains the fleet," Cain said.

"Still trying to make decisions for me, I see," Apollo said, and turned to Athena's image on the monitor.

"Frack, how do you stand this?" Athena asked her brother. "This is driving me insane!"

He smiled. "Well, you know, the first day on the job is always the hardest," he said. "It never goes like you planned."

Athena laughed; it was just the release of tension, but it was a release she had desperately needed. "You're doing a good job, Athena," Apollo added. "I'm proud of you. Father would have been proud."

Is *proud*, he thought. He felt quite sure Adama was watching over them, and guiding them as best he could, even from the other side of the Light.

"Apollo, this is Wing Commander Starbuck," the comm-line crackled. "I hate to tell you this, but we don't have enough experienced pilots left out here to accomplish your assignment. Boomer and Sheba just headed back to the bay for new fighters, but even so, we're short-handed."

Tigh looked over at his old friend. As before, on this same spot but under different circumstances, their silent expressions carried more information and understanding than words could.

Apollo turned back to the monitor, but instead of Cain or Athena, he found himself staring at Count Iblis's countenance, his eyes glowing red. The screen was filled with static and white noise, and only projected the Count's image because Iblis so willed it. "Did you really think you could rid yourself of me so easily, Adama-child?" Iblis purred like some great primordial cat. "How disappointingly naive of you. Your house's moment of reckoning has arrived, at last, and you cannot divert it again."

Apollo's hand unconsciously went to the Star of Kobol around his neck, and drew succor from it. Iblis saw the gesture and smirked. "That piece of costume jewelry can't help you from the threat you face now," Iblis scoffed. "Within a few microns, you and the rest of your fleet will be annihilated, and as you watch everyone around you that you loved and cherished suffer and die, and curse your name, I want you to reflect upon the fact I could have spared them. They could have been saved, if it hadn't been for you."

Apollo knew that Iblis's message was going out to every ship in the fleet, because that was the way he worked: divide and conquer. Corrupt from within. He was like a slow poison, beginning at the extremities and slowly working its way inward, toward the heart.

"You and your bloodline will finally be terminated and I . . . will be reborn," Iblis said, and raised his hands, palms-up before him, in a delicate gesture. "The Lords of Kobol were right, at least, about one thing: time and chance will either curse or bless you, and with all eternity at my disposal, how can I help but be blessed? Farewell, Apollo."

Iblis laughed, but even his laughter was a sad, desolate, despairing sound. And then he was gone. Apollo wasted no time, but opened his comm-line to Starbuck. "Wait for me," he said. "I'm about to send you an experienced pilot."

"You could've saved us all a lot of trouble if you'd have just done that in the first place," Starbuck chided him.

"Where do you think you're going?" Sheba asked.

She had just finished tending to Boomer's wounds, applying a hasty bio-plasteen patch to a nasty gash on the side of his throat, put there by the shrapnel of his exploded canopy. Another centimetron and the shrapnel would have torn through his jugular. Even so, he had lost a frightful amount of blood, and really should have been in a med-unit, receiving proper care, instead of just slapping a patch on the wound and going back out to engage the enemy. Sheba's own injury, sustained in the battle with Cylon ground troops, was quite painful, and her arm had just about gone numb, but what else could she do? They needed everyone out there they could muster, and unless *both* arms went numb, she decided that included her.

"Boomer?" Apollo began, wincing at the amount of blood that stained his old teacher's jumpsuit.

"You should see the other guy," Boomer said, trying to sound more confident than he felt.

"I'm about to," Apollo said, and quickly briefed them on the situation and the plan.

"Vipers," Boomer repeated, "taking on a basestar." He turned his head, stiffly, looked at Sheba. "Can you believe one of my former students would be so foolhardy?"

"I learned from the best," Apollo said, and clapped Boomer on the shoulder. He offered his hand, and helped Boomer, who had been sitting on a tool chest while Sheba patched him, to his feet. "You up for this?"

"Sure," Boomer said. "I haven't done anything stupid in about five centari."

"Then, you're overdue," Apollo told him.

He and Sheba ran for the training Vipers that had been prepped for them, while Apollo made his way to his own fighter. Trays looked up from the Viper he was working on as Apollo approached. The commander stopped, looked at the benched pilot, and said, "Hey, Trays, can that Viper fly?"

Trays brushed away a lock of hair that had fallen in his eyes. "Yeah, I think so."

"You think, or you know?"

Trays studied the commander's face, understood what he was asking, and nodded. "I know it can."

"Then let's go."

Trays let out a cry of joy and jumped to his feet, then bounded onto the wing of the fighter and swung his legs into the cockpit, settling into the seat. Apollo, Boomer, and Sheba were already racing down the track toward the launch aperture and, moments later, Trays was following closely after.

Apollo settled at once into the easy rhythm of his Viper; each fighter had its own feel, its own personality, and he felt as if this one responded best to his pilot's skills, just as Starbuck favored the Scarlet Viper. He needed to be at the navi-hilt of a Viper as much as he needed to be on the bridge of the *Galactica*. He could never be wholly satisfied or fulfilled if he devoted himself to just one or the other.

"Keep in tight formation," Apollo told the trio of pilots flying with him. "Sheba, keep an eye on Trays, and Trays, if you say one word, I'll order you back to the *Galactica* . . . am I clear?"

"Clear," Trays answered succinctly.

Apollo winced at the incessant buzzing in his ear . . . except, it wasn't actually in his ear. It was in his brain, humming like a frizzort. He checked his instrument panels, but it was nothing external. About to fly into pitched battle was not the best place to receive incoming messages, he knew, but Apollo allowed his mind to clear enough that whoever or whatever was trying to contact him could come through without interference.

The moment he took a step back from his consciousness, Apollo heard the musical language once again. Over and over it played, and he understood what it was telling him. He broadcast a top priority scrambled code back to Athena, Tigh, and Cain; if the Cylons intercepted the message, it would be useless to them without the decryption program. "Everyone, be prepared to receive and program coordinates into the QSE devices," Apollo said.

He listened for more, but the musical language had fallen silent. Apollo chewed his lip; he hadn't received a whole set of coordinates. Without them, the QSE was useless. Still, he passed along the incomplete settings he had received, and told them the rest would follow. He had faith they would.

Starbuck's Viper soared up alongside Apollo's and they gave one another the thumbs-up signal.

Bo jay brought his Viper into formation with the rest of the fighters arrowing for the base star. "Hey, Starbuck, if we survive this, could I borrow a couple of your women for the night?" he asked.

"Bo jay," Sheba purred across the comm-line and straight into his ear; "if we survive this, *I'll* sleep with you."

"You're on!" Bo jay shouted, and clapped his hands together. "Now I really have something to fight for!"

The Viper Duet roared up, filling out the formation. "Sorry," Troy said. "We lost communications temporarily, but we were able to fix it."

Apollo and Starbuck both breathed a sigh of relief at the same moment, and both rolled their eyes heavenward in thanks. Far, far above, twinkling brighter than a star, was a light both Apollo and Starbuck knew quite well. "Do you see what I see, Apollo?" Starbuck asked.

Apollo smiled, unable to take his eyes off the light. "Oh, yeah, I see it," he answered. "I guess they didn't want to miss the show."

"Well, let's make it a good one, then," Starbuck suggested, and puffed on his fumarello. "Wouldn't want to disappoint the viewing public. I've already been cancelled once, and that's nothing I want to go through again, any time soon."

The squadron of Vipers, led by Apollo, raced onward.

18

STARBUCK FELT a cold chill slither from the base of his brain to the small of his back as he approached the Cylon basestar. It looked different, with its weapons system trailing out long beneath it like a scorpion's tail. It was too much like the Chitain warship that he had destroyed, the act that had cost him his life. He looked again at the hard, brilliant light far above, and wondered if the ship were there not to view the battle so much as to collect the souls of the brave Warriors who would die here this day.

Was his resurrection nothing more than a reprieve and not a full pardon?

Starbuck gripped his navi-hilt a little tighter between his sweat-slicked hands and told himself it didn't matter. Whether pardon or reprieve, he knew he was brought back for a purpose. Certain events cast certain shadows, and he felt they were in the shadow of some great and portentous event cast long ago. He was beginning to believe the universe was not as random as he had once thought, and that some things happened because they had to.

"All right," he muttered around the fumarello clenched in his teeth, "all right. I get the message: there's no frackin' with fate. Got'cha." But he was still badly frightened. Being dead was nothing he was in a hurry to repeat.

The sky around the basestar was filled with enemy traffic; they did not wait for the little squadron of Vipers to get too near before they began their attack. The first wing of Raiders came at the colonial fighters, and Starbuck was, thankfully, able to push his concerns aside and let instinct take over. He knew, if the Cylon brain ever did evolve to the point it had the same instinctive capabilities as the human one, they would be an even more formidable foe. As it was, they weren't exactly the shiniest cubit in the fountain, but there were enough of them that it didn't make much difference.

Starbuck piloted his Viper perilously close between two Raiders, who fired simultaneously at him. Their lasers destroyed each other in a flash of fire. Nope, not the brightest, at all.

"I like this new breed of Cylon," Bo jay observed. "They do the job for us. A few more like that, we won't even be needed."

But the maneuver had cost Starbuck, as well; as he passed between the Raiders, the aft wing of the nearer ship sliced through his canopy, and he only avoided decapitation by flinging himself forward, just beneath the scythe that ripped through his protection. Plastiglas flew around the small cockpit like angry skreeters, tearing into Starbuck's back and arms and hands. Blood trickled from dozens of lacerations, flowing more freely from deeper gashes.

Starbuck sat upright in his seat, surprised to learn his head was still attached to his neck and shoulders. A spike of twisted steel had punched its way into his arm, tearing out through the other side, and he winced at the sight.

"That's gonna hurt like a son-of-a-daggit in the morning," he observed. Assuming there *was* a morning for any of them.

Trays kept an eye on the info-stream on the inside of his helm. He had been in skirmishes before, of course, but this was pure pandemonium. He forced himself to remain calm, even as red plasma bolts sizzled past just above his canopy, so bright he had to throw an arm up to shield his eyes from their brilliance. Blinded, Trays panicked and fired his turbolasers, narrowly missing the Viper Duet as it swung around to blast the Raider dogging the new cadet.

"Hey!" Dalton's voice thundered across their comm-line. "Haven't you done enough already without trying to shoot us in the back?"

Trays blinked the world back into focus and saw at once what he had almost done.

"You'll be all right, Trays," Troy told him. "Just stay calm and you'll be all right."

"I don't need you to—" Trays began, and caught himself. Whatever differences he and Troy had, they had on the ground. No one could afford to be at odds with anyone else up here, in the middle of all this chaos. "Thanks," he said.

"No problem."

Shrapnel filled the air.

Exploding Vipers, Stingers, and Raiders were all around Apollo, in the heart of the worst of the battle, and he saw a huge piece of Raider tail assembly whickering upward, toward his fighter. He banked hard, avoiding the worst of it, but the trailing wreckage still banged into the bottom plates of the Viper. Plates buckled and crinkled like ancient parchment, and Apollo felt the impact strike his right leg, and the blinding pain that followed. He gasped, felt himself starting to gray out, and held onto consciousness by a supreme effort of will Apollo looked down, afraid he would be minus a limb, and was crazily relieved when he saw he still had both legs. He tried to move his right, and a dazzling pain shot through him. Broken. Well, better than missing in action, he told himself. Beneath his feet a section of hull had been laid open, and he could see the clouds and faraway face of Kobol race past underneath his ship.

He shifted his leg, carefully, using his hands to lift, and placed it so his foot rested on firmer ground. He groaned, and pushed the pain aside as best he could. He didn't think anyone was going to escape this battle unscarred.

*   *   *

Athena watched the *Pegasus* burn, and knew she could do nothing to help them.

The *Daedelus* had moved into position to protect the other, injured battlestar, but Cain still valiantly used his own ship to protect the last of the fleet as it emerged from the fissure and made its way toward open space. The *Pegasus* continued to fire at Cylon and Chitain fighters that slipped past the Vipers and came at the fleet, and continued to take hit after hit from the enemy craft.

The *Daedelus* did her part, its artillery blasting at many of the fighters before they could reach the damaged ship, but there were too many for one battlestar to contain, and the best Athena could do was try to minimize the injuries the *Pegasus* suffered, while Cain, in turn, defended the fleet. It was all she could do, but her best felt woefully inadequate to Athena. Perhaps, she thought, if the attack slowed, ever for a moment, she could get a shuttle over to Cain, begin evacuating the dying ship. She had already ordered a shuttle craft prepared for take-off, and would go over there and drag Cain back herself, kicking and screaming, if that was what it took.

"How are you faring, Athena?" Cain asked her. He looked weary and haggard. A rill of blood ran from a wound on his forehead, and more blood ran from the corner of his mouth. He looked old . . . mortal.

"We're coping," she answered. "The last of the fleet is through. If you can just hold on a few more microns . . . "

Cain nodded. Behind him, gouts of fire leaped and capered about the bridge, and the bodies of wounded and dead crewmen lay scattered about. It was as if someone had opened a window to hell and let Athena look in. "You know I'll do whatever is necessary to safeguard the fleet," he said.

"I know," she said. "I was asking if you can hold on, get the *Pegasus* space-borne."

The old legend smiled, softly. "Of course," he replied. "You and your brother won't be rid of me that easily."

"He respects you," Athena blurted. Something told her to say it now, or risk never saying it at all, and for once, she listened to her intuition, logic be damned.

"And I respect him," Cain admitted. "I respect both of you. I watched you grow up, and love you both as much as if you were my own ch—"

Another blast rocked the *Daedelus,* making the image sputter and swim and finally dissolve. Exterior sensors showed the other battlestar was still there, but the flames were spreading, the hull integrity compromised. The battlestar's weapons were useless slag, reducing the *Pegasus* to little more than just one more civilian ship.

And still the Raiders and Stingers came.

The cogitator known as Lucifer watched with Lord Schikik as the little squadron of Vipers began their first assault on the basestar's weapons array. The plasma cannons primed and fired at the fighters, but the Vipers were fast and had superior maneuverability, while the cannons could only be trained and fired. They were not designed for dealing with such annoying, gnatlike objects, but for greater targets, such as battlestars and civilian ships and hapless civilizations.

From afar, the only battlestar still remaining in the fight continued to fire its long-range artillery, scoring solid blows against the bas star, while the Vipers harried the basestar's weapons system.

"They fight on, despite impossible odds," Schikik observed.

"Let them believe they have hope," Lucifer said. "Their defeat will only be that much more crushing and dispiriting when it occurs."

And if Lucifer could have smiled, he would have.

Sheba stared out her starfield, watched the face of the basestar loom larger and nearer. The rest of the squadron had made its pass, and it remained to her and the Viper Duet to inflict what damage they could.

The plasma cannons were powering up for another barrage, but she knew this time they wouldn't try to destroy the Vipers, but would instead train their deadly beams on the fleet. On her pass, Athena flew directly in front of the cannons, firing her turbolaser as she went, some shots scoring direct hits, traveling directly down the massive bore of the barrel. Deep within the basestar, muffled explosions could be heard, like some giant clearing his throat, even over the chatter of the Viper's sensor system.

And then, she was past the basestar and the Duet was making its pass.

"We've got a tail," Troy warned Dalton.

A Stinger had followed the Viper and was closing the distance between them with alarming speed. Its weapons tail was beginning to angle forward, to blast the fighter.

"Hang on," Troy said, and gripped the navi-hilt. "And trust me . . . please."

He jammed the navi-hilt hard to the left, before Dalton could ask what he had planned, bringing the Viper within a hair's breadth of the outer hull of the basestar. Over his comm-line, Troy could hear Dalton gasp and begin to swear at him. Troy reckoned he hadn't heard anything yet, because it was about to get worse.

The tier of plasma cannons protruded from the imposing face of the basestar like quills set in an orderly line, with the space of perhaps an eighth of a metron between them. Troy threw the Viper at the first barrel, and pulled back on the hilt at the last moment, bringing the fighter up and over the cannon, then dived beneath the next, weaving in and out of the obstacle course like a slalom racer.

The Stinger fired its tail weapons at them and missed, slagging one of the cannons instead. Troy goosed the little Viper to move faster still, forcing the Stinger to increase its speed to keep up.

Troy dipped the Viper at the last moment, narrowly avoiding the weapon's barrel directly ahead of them. The Stinger was not so fortunate, and slammed full-bore into the cannon. The resultant explosion vaporized the cannon and peeled back a section of the basestar's hull, exposing the weapons bay and the weaponeers within. Some of them had been wounded grievously by the explosion. Others hurried to take their place, not stopping to tend to the fallen.

The Duet veered away from the basestar, and Troy was laughing as if he'd been sniffing plant vapors.

"Nice flyin', hotshot," Dalton congratulated him, and added the sound of her laughter to his.

Despite their best efforts and their heroic flying, the Viper squadron was falling short of their goal. The big ships continued to close the distance to the colonial fleet, while the last of the fleet made its way into open space. Trays' Viper had been struck by one of the stray blasts from the Chitain ships, and he was having difficulty maintaining altitude. He looked at the info-scroll on the inside of his helm, saw his gyro-capacitator had been damaged and was on the verge of failing altogether.

Still, he thought he could push the little fighter a bit harder, at least finish his pass, when the ship began to shudder violently, as if it were in the grip of a grande mal seizure. "I'm losing altitude," Trays reported. "I think I'm going to have to drop out."

"Head back to base," Starbuck ordered him. "This party's about to break up anyway."

Trays banked sharply and started back to the landing bay, his Viper shaking harder by the moment. His proximity alarm began to sound, and his monitor showed a Cylon Raider on his tail. Through his canopy, Trays could see the *Galactica,* but she was still many metrons away. A crimson splash of energy scorched his starboard wing, another beam just skipping beneath the port.

He looked out again, hoping for some kind of salvation, spotting only the wreckage of the old city below. With barely a thought, he banked his Viper for the ruins, and the Raider followed.

Trays' Viper handled more easily at a lower altitude, restoring some maneuverability. But the Raider was close and closing fast. Trays took it lower still, and dived through the space between the wreckage of the ancient buildings. The Raider fired at him, missed, fired again, and smacked his apex pulsar.

The Viper banked and turned down a juncture, keeping as low to the debris-choked streets as it could. Trays was playing a game of hide-and-seek with the Raider, counting on the clutter of buildings to hide his Viper from the Raider's monitors and hoping inspiration would strike him before a turbolsaer could.

Trays was hoping he could wind back around behind the Raider and blast it to dust, but he didn't think his Viper was going to last that long. He looked ahead, down the length of the long, narrow avenue through which he pushed his limping fighter, and smiled.

He looked at the info-scroll inside his helm, gauged his speed and the Raider's, and fired his turbolasers at the front of a tall, crumbling edifice on his port side. The lasers blew great chunks of stone out of the building, and, already weakened, the building began to collapse in a shower of stone and smoke. Trays' Viper passed by the avalanche just in time, hearing smaller stones banging off the wings and hull of his fighter. A larger stone struck and starred his canopy, and the young Warrior had to throw it open to see where he was going.

Behind him, the Raider disappeared in the avalanche of falling debris.

"Eat that!" Trays shouted with a maniacal laugh.

Trays brought his fighter in for a rough landing in the middle of the avenue, and sat quietly a few moments, unable to force his fingers to relinquish their grip on the navi-hilt, trying to bring his heart rate and breathing back to normal. When he thought his legs would support him, Trays swung down out of his Viper and looked down the length of the street, his heart thudding in his chest at what he saw. The Cylon had survived the collapsing building, even if his Raider had not, and now stalked after Trays, pulse rifle drawn.

"Ohhh, frack," Trays said. He had not worn his own sidearm because he was called off the bench at the last moment, and now, that was about to cost him.

The Cylon was badly injured, his left leg shattered and dragging behind him, his armor dented in a dozen places, his helmet smashed and part of his brain laid open, more dead than alive, but on and on he came. Trays looked around, trying to find a weapon, someplace to take refuge, but he didn't think he could get far before the pulse rifle burned a hold through his body between his shoulder blades.

Trays jumped out of the way as the first blast came, leaping up onto the ring of his Viper and into the cockpit. There was no weapon but the Viper itself; the turbolasers were facing forward, away from the staggering Cylon, but the pulsars . . . Trays' hand slammed down on the controls, firing the pulsars to life. The thrusters flared out in a long, deadly tail, striking the Cylon, the enormous heat of the thrusters melting his armor, gobbets of it flying backward, carried by the force of the pulsar like silvery rain. A moment later, the Cylon reached its vapor point, and turned into a bipedal stack of ashes, then, scattered on the winds.

Trays had forgotten, in the rush of the moment, that Cylons traveled in pairs, and now its companion Centurion climbed from the wreckage, clearly in better shape than the first mech soldier. This one came charging across the broken terrain, hellishly fast. It didn't have a weapon, but Trays suspected that wasn't going to make much difference.

Its armor, he had time to observe, was sleeker, more streamlined, and the red, pulsing light in its visor burned with a greater intensity. Trays couldn't know it, but the brighter light signified more brain activity in the new and evolved Centurions. Trays looked about the landscape for a weapon, something with which he might at least inflict some damage upon the Cylon, but there was only rubble, too large for him to lift and hurl. He would simply have to make an accounting of himself with his bare hands, and even as he raised his fisted hands, Trays had a ludicrous image of what he must look like, and how sad and futile a gesture it was, trying to bare-knuckle box with an armored killer. As it turned out, he didn't have to worry about it, because the Centurion suddenly, inexplicably staggered forward, its arms thrown in the air, and Trays sidestepped its tumbling body as it fell to the ground. Trays was ready to bash its head in, but the massive scorched and smoking patch on the Cylon's back told him that wasn't going to be necessary.

Someone had shot the Centurion in the back, and Trays looked up to see Bo jay's Viper coming in for a landing near him.

The cockpit popped open. "You the fella that called for a ride?" he asked, gesturing for Trays to hurry up and get in. Trays pelted across the cracked, uneven ground, leaped up onto the wing of Bo jay's fighter and slipped into the cockpit behind him. It was a cramped fit, but better than trying to walk.

"I saw you break away from the group," Bo jay said, letting his Viper taxi down the uneven street. There wasn't much room to get up a good start, so he had to jerk back hard on the navi-hilt and almost climb the face of a shattered structure at the end of his makeshift runway. Trays grimaced, half convinced this madman would do the job the Cylon couldn't, but Bo jay banked and brought the Viper around and angled it toward wide-open spaces. "I saw the Cylon on your butt, but I had some company of my own that refused to leave. Sorry I didn't get here earlier."

"As long as you got here in time," Trays said. "And . . . thanks. For everything."

The *Pegasus* was dying.

Apollo and all the pilots could see the old battlestar burning brighter, faster, out of control, falling toward the planet in a slow, slow, graceful descent.

Cain had managed to get his comm-lines functioning once more, at least for the few moments he would need them. His image appeared on the screens of the other battlestars, the movements herky-jerky, as the digital imager shorted and lost power from centon to centon.

Cassiopeia had come to the bridge of the *Galactica* and watched Cain's final transmission. His face was painted in bold red strokes by the countless fires that raged around him, and he coughed as much from the suffocating smoke in the air as from the massive internal trauma he had suffered from the Cylon's barrage. But he stood upright and proud, and only those who knew him well would know the enormous pain he was in.

"Cassie," he said, his voice like stones grinding together, "I'll always love you. And tell Sheba I have always been proud to be her father."

Athena had patched the transmission through to the Vipers, and Sheba heard her father's words, like a deathbed confessional. She looked back, away from the battle, and saw for the first time just how terrible and overwhelming was the damage the *Pegasus* had suffered. Her heart broke, as if the indignities heaped upon the battlestar had been done to her father, and, in a way, she supposed that was true. He and his old war-star were one.

She broke out of formation and punched her Viper, heading back for the *Pegasus,* screaming at the top of her lungs for her father to hang on just another micron.

Count Iblis could taste victory.

Aboard the big Cylon mothership, he watched it all, and laughed at the futility of the colonials' struggles. He hadn't been lying when he said the Cylons wanted to take some humans alive, but then, their experiments with DNA would work just as well using the genes from the recently dead. It was all the same at the end of the day, and the sun was rapidly setting on the colonials.

Lucifer, whose basestar was the nearer of the two motherships to the battlestars, listened to Iblis's command to prepare to launch everything they had at the fleet. Apollo's desperate assault had damaged a few of the basestar's plasma cannons, but there was still enough firepower to finish the job.

It was a moment Lucifer had long awaited, had imagined, as much as Cylons imagine anything, and he made the mistake of savoring it.

Before he could give the order to fire, Lucifer stopped, aghast at the sight that filled his monitors: the *Pegasus,* burning out of control, long tongues of flame licking the sky behind it, was rising at full-speed, heading straight for the mothership.

Sheba pushed her Viper flat-out, but she knew she was too late the moment Cain made his farewell speech. There was nothing she could do to change his mind, once he had made it up, but still, she had to try. Her Viper managed to get within range of the battlestar's landing bay, but the apertures refused to iris open for her. Wherever Cain was going, he was not going to allow her to join him.

"Father!" she cried, the tears tracking in slow rivulets down her cheeks. "No!"

"Sheba?" Cain's voice came back, weak, breaking up, as if beamed from some faraway land. "Sheba, I—" and the rest of it was lost in a hiss of static.

The *Pegasus* was breaking up; hull plates, twisted by the explosions and warped by the staggering heat of the fires, popped rivets and flew off like projectiles. Parts of the superstructure cried in a voice of tortured steel and ripped away, tumbling back to the surface of the planet, kicking up great spumes of dust where they struck. Sheba had to get away or risk perishing herself, and forcing her hand to turn the the navi-hilt on her Viper and her back on her father was the hardest thing she had ever had to do.

All around him, the bodies of the wounded, the dying, and the dead. Pools of liquid collected on the deck, and fires raged crazily.

There were no lights upon the bridge, only the illumination the flames provided. All power had been diverted to the battlestar's propulsion system. That was really all Cain needed.

He forced himself to stand tall, gripping the back of his command chair to remain upright as the ship climbed at an ever-steeper angle. His eyes were ablaze with a light the reflection of the fire wasn't wholly responsible for; it was the light of faraway places, the humble light of home, the fire of courage and duty that few men ever quite see so clearly. It was the light, quite simply, by which he had always guided his life.

"Take this, you gull-mongering black devil!" Cain cried, and guided the *Pegasus* straight into the heart of the monstrous basestar. He was laughing, and he had never felt more alive than in the moment before impact.

The battlestar's prow pierced the basestar's heart, slamming through the hull, explosions hopping and ripping through the mothership like chain lightning. And still the *Pegasus* drove forward, as if it were some arrow fired from a giant's bow, burying itself deep within its target. It seemed as if the battlestar would continue traveling and erupt from the mothership's other side, but its fiery corpse breached the Tylium fuel cells of the basestar and both ships exploded in a blinding flash. The terrific shockwave that rippled out before the flaming petals slapped and buffeted the Vipers, making the pilots grip the navi-hilt with both hands and struggle wildly to remain airborne.

The *Galactica* and the *Daedelus* also suffered the concussive impact, yawing and pitching, threatening to spin out of control and crash to the ground. Athena gripped the arms of her command chair and braced herself, while the bridge crews tried to stabilize the ship's course.

The fireball that was once the basestar and the *Pegasus* was as bright as any sun that had been torn from the heavens and flung to earth, and only slightly less hot. The light of the explosion lit the landscape of Kobol for many metrons, turning the shadows of falling dusk into high noon. Huge, flaming spikes of twisted steel spun slowly, gracefully, through the night-turned-daylight sky, driving themselves through the sides of buildings in the ancient city like straws shoved through trees by a hurricane. Wreckage whirled and whipped through the air in all directions, like anchor spikes fired from a numon, impaling Cylon pilots in the seats of their Raiders, decapitating Chitain warriors in their Stingers.

"We have to get out of here!" the bridge officer warned Athena.

"We have to stay right where we are," she snapped back. "Those Vipers won't stand a chance in that firestorm unless they have a landing bay to shelter in!"

The officer looked at her as if she were quite mad, but said, "Yes, Sir." Athena smiled. She'd earned that *Sir*.

"Stay ahead of it!" Apollo shouted over his comm.-line to the other Vipers in the squadron. They were surfing on the very periphery of the fiery wave, streaking back to the *Galactica*'s landing bay. If they were caught by the fire, their Vipers would be atomized at once.

The apertures irised open, and the Vipers bulleted into their berths. Tongues of flame followed them through the recovery tubes, and it seemed fiery death would not be cheated, but at last the flames fell back, retreated, and the Vipers sped down the tubes to their docking bays.

Apollo barely waited for his Viper to come to a halt before he popped the canopy and leaped out, hitting the deck running. The pain of his broken leg, numbed and sleeping, woke up with a scream as soon as he put his weight upon it. He hissed through gritted teeth, and hop-skipped as fast as he could for the ascensior to the bridge.

Athena was shouting at him through their telepathic link, asking him for the rest of the coordinates, reminding him they'd accomplished nothing if they couldn't get out of Kobol's vicinity before it self-destructed.

But the musical language he had heard in his head had left him with an unfinished symphony.

* * *

Count Iblis watched the brutally spectacular destruction of the lead mothership and laughed. He knew the cogitator calling himself Lucifer had been planning to usurp Iblis's place in the Cylon empire, and this fortuitous turn of events spared Iblis the bother of ridding himself of a nettlesome situation. Better still, the fleet had lost a battlestar and was doubtless demoralized by the violent death of Commander Cain. He ordered the second basestar, the one in which he stood, to move into position to attack the colonials.

The plasma cannons whined up through the octaves as they charged with deadly power. Iblis was going to enjoy this. He promised himself he'd save the *Galactica* for the last, and deal with Apollo, personally. "Your laughable heroics will win you nothing this time, Adama-son," Iblis said.

Apollo played the incomplete melody over and over in his head, hoping the rest of it would follow as naturally as the next breath, but it was a song that refused to come. He rode the ascensior up to the bridge, leaning against the wall, trying to keep the weight off his bad leg as much as possible, praying for understanding, asking the spirit of Adama for his aid, but the song remained the same.

Apollo, please, the coordinates . . .

I know, Athena, I know.

They were close, he felt that. But he was beginning to think they weren't close enough.

The basestar had moved into position, sailing through the thick, black cloud that still filled the air to mark the tremendous, explosive end the mother ship and the battlestar. Metrons-high columns of flame rose from the tangled, twisted wreckage that dotted the surface of Kobol. To those watching from the fleet, the basestar looked like something rising from the fiery pits of hell, and that might not have been too far wrong, for the creature at the command post of the mothership was surely the personification of evil.

Iblis smiled and trained the plasma cannons on the *Daedelus*. "Your sister dies first, Apollo," he said. "But, don't worry; you won't have to live with the guilt for long."

Apollo! I know the coordinates! I know the rest of the coordinates!
Apollo hit the bridge running, ordering the navigators to stand by to receive coordinates.
Athena, how—?
Speaking with you, telepathically. . . . The information came to me in a musical language . . . Apollo, I understand! Here, let me tell you . . .

And she played for him the musical language she had heard, and trusted her inner vision to understand. Apollo heard her memory of it in his mind, nodded as he received the notes. He knew they fit together with the notes he had received, and also knew he and Athena had both been touched by the hand of Fate.

"That's it!" he shouted, his heart so light he thought it would fly away. "Program the coordinates immediately!"

"On my command," Iblis said, savoring the moment, "*fire!*"
The Centurion's hands danced over the weapons keypad.

Zero.
Apollo looked away, knowing Kobol's time had run out. He just hoped theirs hadn't vanished with it. Far below, the surface of the planet seemed to shudder, and ripple, and begin to jump and spasm. The skin of the planet jerked wildly, and then collapsed inward upon itself, as the incredible network of underground caverns and passageways crumbled.

Kobol was in its death throes and it did not plan on dying easily.

The buildings on the surface screamed and twisted as their

bedrock vanished from beneath them. Huge volcanoes thrust themselves up through the face of Kobol, while tectonic plates screamed the agony of their death throes. A fissure as large as the city itself opened, and swallowed all that remained, like the slavering maw of some ravenous creature. The pyramids flung themselves apart, layer by layer of terraced stone, exposing their ancient secrets for anyone who had an eye to see them. And then, they, too, were swallowed by the greedy planet.

Count Iblis's laugh turned into a long, high, shriek of thwarted rage and fury.

"Damn you, Adama-son!" he thundered, and the air around him seemed to roil and seethe as his shadow form seeped poison into the atmosphere. The Cylons, dreamless, unimaginative drones that they were, could not help but shudder with sick terror at the hideous, primordial race memories Iblis stirred in them. The weaponeer looked dumbly at the Count, the staggeringly frightful images freezing him in his seat. These emotions, fear, especially, were new and overwhelming to him, having known only hatred before this moment, and he was facing a psychic overload. Iblis cursed, threw the paralyzed Cylon out of his seat, and finished the weapons firing sequence on the keypad.

The plasma cannons whined, grew brighter, and spat out their deadly charge.

One moment, Athena was watching death bullet its way across space toward her, and the next she was suddenly staring at the shifting view of hyperspace. When she realized what had happened, that they had cheated death one more time, she laughed. And then, she sat quietly in the command chair, bowed her head, and gave silent thanks to the Lords of Kobol. Apollo watched the destruction of Kobol, and whispered one word: "Serina." Cassiopeia was near enough to hear the sound of his whispered farewell, and thought it was the sound a man might make when he lays down a heavy burden he has carried for far too long. She touched him lightly on his back, but he didn't look up. There were tears in his eyes.

The planet was swallowing itself.

Kobol's surface and its underground miracles had vanished, falling down vast seams and fissures of the planet's crust, being devoured by the molten core. Volcanoes as big as the city itself rose and wept flowing lava before they, too, were swallowed by the rising tide of fire. For a moment, only the beating, magma heart of the world remained, beautiful and terrifying, and then, the heart exploded. A force like a mini-nova spread out in an ever-widening ring, traveling faster, vaporizing the space-borne Cylon and Chitain fighters, slamming like a flaming tsunami into the basestar. The burning wall lapped at the mothership, reducing the forward-facing hull to slag. The basestars were built considerably tougher than the fighters, but that just made the mothership's destruction that much longer and torturous.

The destructive force washed through the ship, nothing slowing its progress. The superstructure collapsed inward upon itself, into the molten wave, and vanished. The ring of fire continued to expand, devouring moons and asteroids, until, at last, the fury of the dying world subsided, the wave disspitated, and the void was calm and still once more.

A ball of burning gas remained in space where once the proud Kobollian world had stood, and from the fiery heart, there rose a luminous Light Ship, like a phoenix, or a butteryfly emerging from its chrysalis. The ship was as beautiful as the destruction of the world was complete and awesome, and, on new wings, the Light Ship soared away from the inferno, joining the other two ships that awaited it, and, together the three of them accelerated into space, and then were gone.

Aboard the *Galactica,* as the fleet was making its leap into hyperspace, the monitors showed the Light Ships rising from the flaming corpse of Kobol. Athena, aboard the *Daedelus,* saw them, too.

It was just a momentary thing, so quick as to be nearly subliminal, but anyone who saw them felt an overwhelming sense of peace, and awe, and wonder.

"What the frack is *that?*" Cassie asked, staring at the monitor long after the Light Ships had gone. At last, she had to look away.

Apollo smiled, knowingly, and steepled his fingers together against his chin. "Our destiny, of course," he answered.

EPILOGUE

Life goes on.

If they had learned nothing else from their return to Kobol, the colonials had learned that necessary lesson. Sometimes the ending of the old life overlapped the beginning of the new, but that was all right; it made the transition easier, and made letting go of the past not quite so hard. Sometimes, it was not until we looked back that we even realize that we have set something down, perhaps only for a moment, and then moved on, without it.

We seldom find again what has been lost, as if it were something that had been swept away down the ever-rolling river of time. But sometimes the river bends, and for a moment, we are faced again with that which we cherished and lost. The problem then becomes, whether to let loose of everything else we've gathered and grab for that which we've lost, and hope this time we do a better job of holding it, or hold tight to all we have, and let the past claim its own.

Apollo sat in his sanctuary, feeling the tug on his heart, like gravity, of the memory of Serina. He had loved her, and she had loved him, but she had moved on and he had not. He still clung to her, the way a man will cling to a slippery handhold in the middle of a raging river or be swept away, but he had begun to realize at what horrible cost he had done so. Life and love had come and gone, come and gone, while he held fast to the past and refused to let go long enough to reach out. He could not bear the thought of Serina fading into the distance. If he forgot her, then she was gone forever.

But that was not so, and he knew it now.

As with Kobol, Apollo knew there were different levels of existence, spiraling like the streets of the cities had done, carrying the traveler ever onward, ever upward, toward places he could only reach in their appointed time. Apollo smiled, running the ball of his thumb over the shallow nicks Adama had worn into the arm of the chair, and Apollo supposed, one day, wherever the fleet ended up, his son or daughter might sit here and also trace the scars that life leaves on one.

"Thank you, Father," he said, softly. "Thank you, Lords of Kobol." Apollo stood, looked at the meditation womb as if seeing it with new eyes, and, still smiling, left the room and went down to the celebration in the ODOC.

The party was in full swing when Apollo arrived, but he thought, this time, he would stay to close it down. He felt like being with these people, among the living once more. Identical parties went on across all the ships of the fleet. Despite their terrible losses, there was still much to celebrate. They had been able to replenish their depleted Tylium reserves, stored away a veritable treasure trove of foodstuffs, and, best of all, they had been judged worthy by the Lords of Light.

They had been sorely tested, by the powers of darkness and the forces of light, and it was hard to say whose test was the more arduous, but they had passed both tests, and had been rewarded by the ancient Kobollians with modified QSE technology. Apollo understood how necessary this technology was; without it, the fleet could travel at the speed of light and still not reach their unimaginably far-off destination, but, with the dimension-warping capabilities of the QSE engines, their journey, although per-

haps twenty-some yahren later, could at last begin. They had had
to go home to wake up, step back to go forward, but now, at last,
they were truly free to move on.

How foolish they had been, how vain, how proud, to think they
could have made the voyage without the help of the Lords of
Kobol. How foolish to believe the Thirteenth Tribe had not used the
same QSE technology millennia ago, when they spread the seed of
humanity throughout the farthest galaxies.

Apollo squeezed in at the table between Tigh and Starbuck,
and, as if by magic, a flagon of ambrosa appeared before him. He
glanced up and saw Cassiopeia standing there, smiling, a matching
mug in her hand. She had to shout to be heard over the music and
the laughter; instead, she bent close enough for Apollo to feel her
breath on his skin, and spoke into his ear, "It was touch and go,
but I think Gar'Tokk is going to make it."

She started to straighten up, but Apollo took her hand in his,
and kissed the back of it, surprising her. "What's that for?" Cassiopeia asked.

"Why ask why?" he answered.

"As long as you're in the mood," she said, and set her mug
down. Standing behind him, she gripped the sides of his face and
bent his head back, so he was looking directly up at her, and
leaned in to kiss him deeply on the mouth. He was no more surprised than she had been, but reached up, placed his hand on the
back of her head, and returned the kiss. She pulled away, blinking
and smiling.

"Okay, who are you . . . really?" Starbuck asked Apollo. "You
look like my best friend, but you sure don't act like him."

Apollo laughed and took a drink of his ambrosa. "I've been
away for a while," he said, "but I'm back now."

He looked around the table, at Starbuck, Tigh, Athena, Sheba,
Boomer, Phaedra, Bo jay, and Cassiopeia. They all looked at him as
if he were Count Iblis in a very cunning but flawed disguise.

"What?" he asked, and sat back in his chair, smiling bemusedly.

Bo jay shrugged, and drained his grog in three quick swallows.

"I know what that's like, Apollo," he said. "It's hell not bein' yourself."

They all laughed at Bo jay's ability to cut to the heart of the matter, and, while everyone was gathered there, Apollo stood up, wincing at the pain in his casted leg, and raised his flagon. "We should take a moment to remember someone who can't be here tonight," he said. "A man who wanted the best for the fleet, and was not afraid to fight—and die—for it. To Commander Cain. The last of our generation's great battle commanders, and the last of the great men."

"To Cain," President Tigh said, and stood, holding his own flagon high. "And his great, selfless sacrifice."

"To Cain," they repeated, and raised their drinks in toast. They drank to his honor and his memory, and then, because it was a celebration of life and not a wake, Dalton grabbed Troy and kissed him fiercely, before he could react. The Warriors laughed, and pounded their approval on the tabletop. Troy, smiling, pulled Dalton down onto his lap, and, cupping her face in his hand, kissed her. Trays, watching from his table with his cadets, sighed, and drank his grog in silence.

Athena?

She looked across the table at her brother, her eyebrow raised in question. *Yes, Apollo? Are we going to "talk" about someone behind their back, or was there something you wanted to say?*

Apollo had to chuckle, but that was all right; no one noticed. Everyone else was having a good time, too. *I wanted to tell you I'm proud of you, and that you did a fine job today. I just didn't want to have to shout it.*

Athena looked down at her ambrosa, but when she looked up again, she was smiling. *Thank you, Apollo.*

Something else I wanted to say . . . or think . . .

She waited, mug of ambrosa at her lips, her dark eyes staring at him over the rim of her flagon.

I learned . . . or accepted . . . today that I'm not going to be happy just commanding the action from the bridge of a battlestar. I need to be a part of it. I also realized we were meant to share command, when you received the second half of the coordinates. Individually, we're halves of the whole; together, we're so much more than the sum of our parts. I think this is what the Lords of Kobol want . . . It's what I want.

Athena considered her brother's request, and decided it made sense: while he was on the bridge, Apollo would be supreme commander, but when he was flying a mission, she would command the *Galactica.*

She mouthed the words, *Thank you,* and raised her mug to him in a salute. He smiled, and raised his own to her.

"What are you drinking to?" Starbuck asked, noticing their salute.

"Beginnings, of course," Apollo answered. "What else?"

Starbuck shrugged, and drank to the future. It was all they had. Athena looked over Starbuck's shoulder at Cassie, who understood that look and nodded. Athena took another drink, and turned to Starbuck and took him by the hand. "As the fleet's new co-commander," she said, "my first order is that you give me a big, sloppy kiss and then take me out on that floor and dance every dance with me."

Starbuck laughed, looked at Apollo. "Sorry, old buddy," he told Apollo. "But orders is orders."

They all laughed, and Starbuck stood and swept Athena into his arms, and kissed her with all the fire and passion she had expected, and more. She blinked, her mouth open wide, as he led her onto the dance floor and pulled her close.

"Any further orders, Commander?" he asked, her head resting on his shoulder.

"Plenty," she said. "And you'd better follow every one of them. Pretty boy like you wouldn't last ten minutes in the brig."

Cassiopeia, standing behind Apollo, her hands resting on his shoulders, felt an odd chill, and hear a voice slithering in her ear, as softly and as horrible as grave beetles: *I will always be with you,* the voice said, oily-slick; *Our child will be a very, very special child.*

Cassie brushed at her ear, as if the source of that rasping voice were there, and turned to see who had spoken to her, but there was no one. No one at all. "Did you say something?" she asked Jolly, who was standing nearby. She thought it might have been one of his jokes. Jolly looked at her and shrugged.

"Everything all right?" Apollo asked her, looking back over his shoulder.

Cassie thought about it, and realized she didn't know. But, she supposed it was. After all, they had left Kobol and its hidden evils far, far behind them. What could harm them here? "Everything's perfect," she said, but she found herself thinking of a hooded man with red, glowing eyes. She wrapped her arms around Apollo's neck, and he placed his hands upon her arms, and for a moment, she could forget the man of darkness.

Sheba, with just enough grog in her, stalked boldly to where Bo jay sat at the table, gripped the collar of his shirt, spun him around to face her, and kissed him. "A promise is a promise," she told the astonished onlookers, and none was more astonished than Bo jay. Sheba took him by the hand and pulled him to his feet, and led him from the party.

"If I'm not back by tomorrow, declare me missing in action!" Bo jay called back over his shoulder, and followed Sheba from the room, chased by the sound of applause and good-humored cheers.

Boomer shook his head, and pushed his mug away from him. "Obviously, I'm altered, because I couldn't have just seen what I just saw," he said. He sat quietly a moment, then pulled the mug back and took a big draught from it. "But, just in case I really *did* see it, I think I'd rather forget it."

Phaedra smiled, and her hand absently strayed to her belly, heavy with child, and her other hand sought the circle of Boomer's. He gripped her hand in his, and they all sat and talked, and laughed, and drank to absent friends, and sometimes wept—because endings overlap beginnings—all that night and far into the next morning.

* * *

Alone, Baltar sat in his quarters, once more the traitor, even though he had honestly tried to do the right thing. Every choice he made seemed to be foredoomed, destined to turn into betrayal. He would never be trusted again, but he could not understand why this was so. In the story of his life, Baltar was the hero; no one ever sees himself as the villain of the piece, and Baltar, greatest traitor the human race had ever known, was no different in that respect.

All that remained was to decide on which path he would travel, but in the darkness of his quarters, as the shadows closed in and took him in their velvety embrace, Baltar was sure he heard a voice he knew well. It was weak and injured, faraway and small; a voice of the past, easily enough ignored.

In the Xeric star system, word reached the Chitain homeworld of the Cylon and Chitain defeat at Kobol. Lord Schikik had apparently been killed in the same fiery armageddon that had claimed Lucifer and the alliance armada. There would be another who would replace Lucifer, just as there would be another to replace Lord Schikik.

But to anyone who replaced Lord Schikik, the course of action the Chitain must follow seemed quite clear: they would continue to lick their deep wounds, all the while accelerating the rebuilding of the fleet and home world. They would plot to avenge their humiliating defeat at the hands of the humans, both here and in the Kobollian system. But the Cylons would also be greatly weakened with the destruction of the armada, and the Chitain would look with great hunger at the map of the Cylon empire.

Fleeing from the Cylon tyranny, the last battlestar, *Galactica*, leads a ragtag, fugitive fleet, on a lonely quest—for a shining planet known as Earth. . . .

An Open Letter to Our Valued Readers

What do Raymond Chandler, Arthur C. Clarke, Isaac Asimov, Irving Wallace, Ben Bova, Stuart Kaminsky and over a dozen other authors have in common? They are all part of an exciting new line of **ibooks** distributed by Simon and Schuster.

ibooks represent the best of the future and the best of the past...a voyage into the future of books that unites traditional printed books with the excitement of the web.

Please join us in developing the first new publishing imprint of the 21st century.

We're planning terrific offers for ibooks readers...virtual reading groups where you can chat online about ibooks authors...message boards where you can communicate with fellow readers...downloadable free chapters of ibooks for your reading pleasure...free readers services such as a directory of where to find electronic books on the web...special discounts on books and other items of interest to readers...

The evolution of the book is www.ibooksinc.com.